Critical acclaim for *Mr Darcy's Daughters*:

'I read [*Mr Darcy's Daughters*] in two gulps and greatly enjoyed it . . . The invented daughters are fun – prissy Letty, witty Camilla, musical Alethea, the unbridled twins – their ups and downs in London society make a lively story'

Joan Aiken, author of *Jane Fairfax*

'Imagine poor Mr Darcy with five marriageable daughters of his own! And in Mr Darcy's daughters, Elizabeth Aston has them all at large in dissolute London . . . Aston takes us on a romp through late Regency society'

Julia Barrett, author of Jane Austen's *Charlotte*

'The book has some memorable dialogue and the author has a good ear for the Regency idiom . . . The author has cleverly distanced herself from Jane Austen's creation and created a new world in which her own characters define the story. The result is a lively romp and is sure to please readers who like Regencies of the sharp-witted variety rather than simply romances in muslin'   Geraldine Perriam, *Historical Novels Review*

'Great characters, great comic moments, great romance'

Chicago Sun-Times

'In the mode of Heyer and Austen, Elizabeth Aston turns her talents to the early 19th century . . . Aston comments on the period with affection, respect and a ready wit'

Good Book Guide

Elizabeth Aston lives in Oxford and Lazio, Italy. She is married with a son and a daughter. Her second Regency novel, *The Exploits and Adventures of Miss Alethea Darcy*, is also available in Orion paperback.

MR DARCY'S DAUGHTERS

Elizabeth Aston

ORION

An Orion paperback

First published in Great Britain in 2003
by Orion
under the title *The Way of the World*
This paperback edition published in 2004
by Orion Books Ltd,
Orion House, 5 Upper St Martin's Lane,
London WC2H 9EA

3 5 7 9 10 8 6 4

A CIP catalogue record for this book is available
from the British Library.

ISBN-13 978-0-7528-5966-8
ISBN-10 0-7528-5966-8

Printed and bound in Great Britain by
Clays Ltd, St Ives plc

The Orion Publishing Group's policy is to use papers that
are natural, renewable and recyclable products and
made from wood grown in sustainable forests. The logging
and manufacturing processes are expected to conform to
the environmental regulations of the country of origin.

www.orionbooks.co.uk

For James Hale
with love and gratitude

ONE

'Town and country are different worlds. No matter how rich and self-possessed they are, country-bred young ladies need to keep their wits well about them when they come to London.'

Camilla wasn't listening to her sister's well-modulated tones. Nor was she paying much attention to the words, her father's words, for Letty had repeated them so often that Camilla knew them by heart. For herself, she found the lively descriptions of her travels that flowed from her mother's pen far more interesting than her father's worldly advice.

Letitia put down her pen with a sigh of irritation. 'The noise,' she said. 'The constant sound of carriages and horses and voices and dogs barking – however can people support living in the midst of such a din?'

Camilla was regretting her decision to join Letty in the morning parlour. It was extraordinary that in their cousin Fitzwilliam's large town house in Aubrey Square, there was nowhere she could be alone. She was delighted to be in London, but she did miss the moments of privacy easily obtained at home in Derbyshire where so many public and private rooms were at her disposal.

Letty had fallen silent. Camilla glanced across the room at her older sister, who was sitting at a small elegant table, a sheet of hot-pressed notepaper lying in front of her, trying to compose a letter to their father. Her peevish tone wasn't reflected in the calm beauty of her face, which, with its wide brow and fine nose, caused her sisters, when in teasing mood, to call her Galatea, declaring she was exactly like a classical statue come to life.

Camilla didn't grudge Letty her perfection of feature; she was quite used to people exclaiming at Letty's beauty and the knowledge that she was no match for her sister in looks never troubled her.

She turned her attention to more interesting matters. She was sitting at the window, delighting in the sights and sounds of the smart London square. A carriage and pair rattled by, driven by a stout young man in a many-caped coat, his well-bred chestnuts picking up their hooves in a brisk trot. The driver sent a lingering glance towards a pretty governess in a blue pelisse, who was walking her charges, two lively little boys, along the pavement. The smaller child was dragging a small wooden horse on wheels, which kept tipping over, his brother darting back to set it right to the accompaniment of squeals of annoyance and mirth.

A fine, tall footman in morning livery was exercising a pair of Cavalier spaniels, their feathery tails waving to and fro as they frisked and jumped about, uttering sharp barks. An oyster seller shouted her wares in a great bellow of a voice, and a knife grinder cried out for business on the other side of the square. A delivery boy sauntered along the railings, whistling, one package under his arm and another swinging round on its length of twine.

'There are those who find the crowing of the cock and the rumble of the farmer's cart and the baaing of sheep insupportably noisy,' she said, without taking her eyes from the busy scene outside.

'Camilla, how can you say so? The tranquillity, the sweet serenity of the countryside, the silent beauty of our woods and river, I do so miss them.'

Camilla listened with only half her attention, as Letty launched into her favourite lament of how unfair it was, how unreasonable of their parents to drag them from the peace and happiness of Derbyshire to a house in London. 'It is so especially hard on Belle and Georgina; how they will hate to be staying here.'

Camilla prudently kept her opinion on that to herself and laughed out loud as the two spaniels wrapped their leashes round the footman's handsome calves and threatened to upturn him.

'Come away from that window, you must not be sitting there for anyone to see.'

'What harm is there in anyone seeing me? I'm not ogling the footman, merely admiring the scene.'

'Ogling the footman indeed! Camilla, don't say such things. I know you mean it for a joke, but others won't understand your sense of fun, and may take you seriously.'

'Only a fool would take it seriously, and why should we care for the opinion of fools? Besides, he is such a handsome footman.'

Letty spoke with real earnestness. 'Your free way of speaking is likely to get you into such trouble! Mr Fitzwilliam would not approve.'

Camilla knew that to be true. Their cousin, Mr Fitzwilliam, a fashionable, amiable man of fifty, had sold out of the army and was now a Member of Parliament. He had a strong feeling for the proprieties, and expected his womenfolk to behave with decorum. There was bound to be another side to him, shown only to his masculine intimates and cronies at the club or at sporting events; a side that would be a good deal coarser and not at all averse to improper behaviour among females of the *demimonde*, but that was an aspect of his life not seen in Aubrey Square.

She also knew that Letty had a great regard for Mr Fitzwilliam's high moral tone – a regard she didn't share. Letty was her cousin's favourite among the sisters, and always had been. Camilla felt no hurt at this, she knew she didn't conform at all to her cousin's ideal of womanhood. She had too much of a sense of humour, too witty a tongue and too clever a mind, apart from inheriting all her father's strength of character. She was perfectly aware that she made her cousin uncomfortable; she could often see him wondering what was going through her mind, and fearing the worst.

Letty was still prosing on. 'Mama would tell you so, as she has often had to, if she were here. Since she isn't – and who knows when we may see her again, if ever? – it is my duty to warn you about how you should behave. This is not a country house, manners are different here.'

'I had noticed,' Camilla said.

Letitia was just twenty-one, and perhaps felt the importance of her position as the oldest of the five Darcy sisters a little too keenly. Their father, Fitzwilliam Darcy, had been sent abroad on a diplomatic mission, and his wife Elizabeth, reluctant to be separated from him for a year or more, had chosen to accompany him to Constantinople. The girls could profitably spend several months in London, while their two young boys were to stay at Pemberley, their house in Derbyshire, under the care of a tutor and their maternal grandfather, Mr Bennet.

There had been some talk of Mr Bennet accompanying his granddaughters to London, but he had been much alarmed at the plan. He had no notion of looking after young ladies of fashion in London, he had found bringing up his own daughters exhausting and troublesome enough and would by no means embark on such duties again, not even for a few months. He would be extremely happy to care for young William and Charles and to keep an eye on the smooth running of Pemberley in his son-in-law's absence, although with his excellent steward and household staff, he imagined the house and estate would manage very well while its master and mistress were off among the Muslims.

Letitia knew, with a conviction amounting to certainty, that Mama and Papa would never return. Even if they survived the drive to Dover – such a dangerous road, the coachmen inclined to go so fast, highwaymen lurking on every heath – then the sea voyage would be bound to end in a watery tragedy; should they somehow safely make it as far as Ostend, then there would be the perilous journey across Europe. There were tracts of such wildness, forests and hostile landscapes, wolves, bears and bandits.

In the unlikely event of their reaching their destination, their fate would be sealed; if the Muslims did not rise in revolution and mow them down with scimitars, then the plague would carry them off. Or smallpox; only imagine Mama all pock-marked and scarred, if she by any chance recovered.

'But Letty, Mama has been inoculated against the smallpox,' Camilla protested.

'Only the English variety. In Turkey, everything will be different, and infinitely more dangerous.'

Fanny Fitzwilliam flew into the room in a babble of talk, as was her way, in time to catch the last of Letitia's predictions of gloom.

'Why, however can you speak so? Here is Mr Tilson back from China, with all his wits and health about him, and Lord Wincanton goes backwards and forwards to America as though he were posting down to Somerset. Travel these days is so safe and comfortable, you need have no concern for your parents' safety.'

'I hope you are right,' said Letty with a sigh. 'I fear, though, that they are sure to meet with some misfortune. I shall be left, at twenty-one, to take on the care of my brothers and sisters, and however shall I manage?'

'Lord, what melancholy thoughts,' said Fanny. A lively woman in her late twenties, Fanny was Mr Fitzwilliam's second wife, a fact which had caused Letitia to utter several grave reflections to Camilla on the frailty of human affections. Fanny thought it the greatest fun to have her cousins to stay, and her eyes sparkled with delight at the prospect of the parties, fashions, gossip and liveliness five young ladies would bring into the house. She would have them all married by the time Darcy and Elizabeth returned, she declared in private to her husband.

'No, no,' cried Fitzwilliam. 'You are not to be match-making; the girls can very well wait for husbands until their parents are come home.'

'Letitia is one-and-twenty, and Camilla nineteen, more than old enough to be thinking of husbands.'

'Take them to parties and balls, rig them out in the first style of fashion and let them enjoy what London has to offer in the way of plays and music, that is quite enough for you to be doing.'

Fanny kept her counsel, exclaimed at Letitia's classically beautiful features, especially since brunettes were all the fashion just now, privately thought that the men would find Camilla's liveliness and laughter more taking, and longed for the rest of the sisters to arrive and complete the party.

Meanwhile, her mind was running on clothes, as she informed the sisters. 'Pray turn your mind to something more agreeable. The dressmaker will be here later this morning, and I long to see how that Indian patterned muslin has made up.'

'How can we need half so many dresses?' Letitia had exclaimed when Fanny, tutting with dismay at their countrified clothes, had summoned her modiste and reeled off a string of absolute necessities: morning dresses, walking costumes, afternoon dresses, ball gowns, carriage dresses, a riding habit—

'Not for me, Cousin Fanny,' Camilla said. 'Letty is a good horsewoman, but I never ride if I can possibly help it. It is a form of exercise I do not enjoy.'

'Even without a riding habit, you cannot possibly want so many clothes!' said her sister now.

'Fanny must be our guide,' Camilla said. She loved fashions and was perfectly happy to spend an hour or more poring over *La Belle Assemblée* or inspecting muslins and silks new in from France and the East.

'This is nothing,' said Fanny. 'Not half of what you must have in due course. However, they need not all be ordered immediately. First we must make you fit to be seen. Those sleeves are quite out of fashion, Letty, you would be laughed at if you wore them out. Then you may look about you at your leisure and choose for yourselves. You may buy anything you want in London, anything you can think of. And hats, too, your bonnets are quite hideous.'

'The expense,' cried Letitia.

'Oh, it is not so very much, and your papa is fortunately so rich that a few dresses and hats will make no difference to him. He would not want his daughters to be dowdy, I assure you. He will expect you to be as elegant as any young ladies in London, and I shall take pains to see that you are. I have no wish to receive one of his cold looks should he return and find a pair of frights.'

'It is lucky that the others are still in the schoolroom,' said Letitia. 'They will not need new clothes.'

'To be sure,' said Fanny, her mind on muslins and trimmings. 'Although I long for Alethea to be out, such striking looks as she has. Are Belle and Georgina pretty? It is more than three years since I saw them. They will mind not going about in society, I dare say, but their turn will come.'

'They must pay attention to their studies and music and drawing and take advantage of London masters while they are here,' said Letitia primly. 'They are country girls at heart, Fanny, and I think will be glad to be spared the rattle and bustle of too much town life.'

An image of Georgina and Belle came into Camilla's mind. Could Letty possibly believe what she was saying? She feared that she did; her sister wasn't given to considering whether others shared her opinions. She always took it for granted that her sisters agreed with her on all important topics, regardless of evidence to the contrary. Since she knew herself to be in the right, any objections were the result of imperfect understanding, and she need not take any account of them.

Camilla had her own ideas about the twins, chief of which was that Belle and Georgina would assuredly scheme themselves out of the schoolroom within a week of their arrival in London.

Fanny was still talking. 'We must find husbands for you two, the twins will be grateful to me if I do so, since they can then come out.'

'Husbands!' Letitia was shocked. 'Thank you, Fanny, but we are not in London to find husbands. Our parents would not wish it, and besides, for my part—' Her pretty mouth quivered, and tears started in her eyes.

'Oh, my dear, how heartless of me. Only, you know, it has been three years, and Tom would not wish you never to form another attachment.'

'It is not in my power to do so. I am the kind of person who loves so truly that there can never be a second attachment. Tom would have been faithful to my memory, had I been cruelly torn from him, and I can do no less. He had no eyes for any other woman but me, and I consider our betrothal a sacred trust.'

Fanny and Camilla exchanged glances. Camilla was perfectly used to her sister's ways, and Fanny, who had a vein of shrewd common sense beneath a frivolous exterior, was beginning to take her cousin's measure. 'So many women lost lovers and husbands at Waterloo, it is all very sad. Yet many of them have found consolation – after a proper time, of course.'

'Tom and I were soul mates. I was his first and only love, and I shall remain true to him for the rest of my life, as he was true to me.'

Camilla couldn't help thinking of the two red-headed youngsters who were growing up and thriving in separate cottages in Hilted, the village nearest to Tom's house. The flaming hair and freckles were unmistakable – even Letty must have been startled by the likeness – and a gossiping friend in Derbyshire had told her of another child of just such a colouring born to one of the chambermaids in a neighbouring house where Tom visited.

Letitia had known Tom Busby from childhood, and the engagement had pleased both families, although Camilla had had her doubts about Tom's enthusiasm for the match. 'I must, I suppose,' he'd said to her one rainy afternoon, as they played cards in the yellow saloon at Pemberley. 'My parents expect it, and I've known Letty for ever, and I always thought we'd probably marry some day or another – I am fond of her, you know, very fond. Only she's such a one for driving a man on. She's barely seventeen, too, it's young to be married. It would have been better to wait for a year or two, perhaps – however, she is set on it.'

Letty's grief at the news of Tom's death at Waterloo had been deep and lasting. Camilla, too had been truly saddened by his death and missed his company, but she felt it was no justification for her sister's adopting a kind of perpetual maiden widowhood. In the Middle Ages, she might have taken her woe and faithfulness into the convent; in 1818, she felt that time should be allowed to heal her sister's sorrows and that reason – not to mention those red-haired children – should remind Letty that Tom was a man and not a saint.

'I hope we may enjoy the company of many new acquaintances, Fanny,' Camilla said, 'but I by no means wish to find a husband, thank you. I have noticed that husbands have a way of restricting a young woman's friendships and flirts, and are prone to carry their wives off to rusticate in the country.'

Fanny shook her head at this and said that Camilla was only funning, but Letitia was so shocked by these remarks that it took her a minute or two to gather her wits for a suitable rebuke, and she was forestalled by the entry to the morning parlour of Alethea, with Miss Griffin in tow.

Alethea, black eyes aglow, her curls in their usual disarray, bade her cousin a civil good morning, cast a knowing eye at Letitia and asked cheerfully what had happened to put her on her high horse now, and, tucking her arm into Camilla's, began a passionate plea to be allowed to have singing lessons with one Signor Silvestrini.

'Camilla, you love music as much as I do. You must see that I have to learn with him. Why, there is no teacher to match him in all London, in Europe!'

Camilla unwound her sister's arm. 'I never heard of this person. He is an Italian master, I suppose?'

'I thought you were to take lessons with Mrs Deane,' said Letitia.

'Who will want me to sing sweet ballads and simper as I do so,' said Alethea impatiently. 'Only you would think of her for a moment, Letty. Now, Signor Silvestrini is a real musician.'

Letitia's eyes gleamed as she saw an opportunity to preach. 'Alethea,' she cried, 'listen to the passion in your voice, that alone is enough to warn us that your music must be watched and the time you devote to it controlled and curtailed.'

Alethea rarely paid any attention to her eldest sister, especially on the subject of music. Camilla saw that her eagerness was going to provoke her into some hot outburst that might alarm Fanny and embroil them all in one of Letty's tedious homilies on behaviour, emotion and the degree of artistic indulgence suitable for a young lady – that is, none at all, Letty's approved accomplishments comprising no more than pale and innocuous watercolours, dull pieces learned painstakingly for performance on the pianoforte and a little exquisite embroidery.

This attitude wasn't shared, Camilla knew perfectly well, by their parents, who were pleased by her own performance on the pianoforte and rejoiced in their youngest daughter's much greater and very real love of music, which was combined with considerable talent and application.

Letty was being tiresome. Their parents had been gone a mere three days, and already she was inflicting her own narrow way of thinking on them. Angry at not being left in charge of Pemberley and the family, she was nonetheless determined to take control of her and her sisters.

Would Fanny stand up to her? She doubted it. Letty was quite as strong-minded as any of the Darcys, which was to say very strong-minded indeed; it was unfortunate that her inclinations tended so strongly to restriction and repression and a numbing belief in propriety and restrained behaviour.

Alethea's governess, Miss Griffin, a tall, gaunt woman with clever eyes, intervened. 'I did mention the matter of Signor Silvestrini to Mr Darcy before his departure,' she said in her deep voice. 'He felt that we should approach him on the matter of lessons, and that, if he would consent to teach Alethea, for he takes few new pupils, then it should be arranged.'

Alethea let out a whoop of delight, Letty frowned, Fanny – who hated dissension and, as an only child, felt uneasy when the sisters argued – brightened. 'That's quite settled then. Only tell me when you would like the carriage, Miss Griffin; I shall leave it all to you.'

Camilla could see the light of battle in Letty's eye and feared that a protesting letter would be off to Vienna by the next post, there to await her parents' arrival.

'I think,' said Fanny, when presently she found herself alone in the room with Camilla, 'that it would be fortunate if we were to find a suitable young man for Letitia. To help her get over Tom's loss, you know, and give her thoughts a new direction. Since he was a military man, I'm inclined to think I should look around among my acquaintance in the regiments; should she be likely to fancy a fine, well set-up hussar, do you suppose?'

TWO

Letitia wasn't at all pleased with her fashionable hat. 'Only look at this wide forward brim! It resembles nothing so much as a coal scuttle.'

Dressed in new walking costumes, which had been inspected and approved by Fanny, Letitia and Camilla were getting ready to show themselves in public – and to pay a morning visit to their Gardiner cousins.

'A very pretty coal scuttle, and trimmed more fine than any coal bucket I ever saw,' said Camilla. 'Be grateful; it will shelter your complexion from these bitter winds.'

'February in London is the most miserable thing imaginable. I cannot think why anyone who has the choice would spend the month in London,' Letitia complained.

The Fitzwilliams were among those who had chosen to remain in London. Mr Fitzwilliam was a younger son and had no country house of his own, and besides, it was better for an ambitious politician not to be away from London when the House was sitting; a thin attendance might let dangerous Radical views slip past.

Camilla had no great opinion of February anywhere, and she could remember many a dull February day at Pemberley, watching the rain driving against the windows and listening to the plop, plink of raindrops falling from the water-laden branches of the trees outside. 'If I could choose where to be, it would be in Constantinople, where I believe it hardly ever rains, and February may be as cheerful a month as any other.' She took the gloves that her maid was holding out to her. 'Thank you, Sackree.'

'It's going to come on to rain, miss. You'd much better go in the carriage.'

'I know the sky is grey, but I think it's content merely to threaten us with a downpour. I hope so; I feel the need of a walk and we aren't to be requesting the carriage for every little outing.'

Camilla wanted to go first to Hookham's circulating library in Bond Street. She loved reading and was happy in the knowledge that all the newest novels would be available in London. Meanwhile, Letty would undoubtedly borrow some worthy volumes of biography or a collection of the most tedious sermons, which might impress other borrowers but would not deceive her sister, who knew quite well that Letty dearly loved a novel.

'Choose a book for me,' Alethea had commanded. 'Any new Minerva novel will do, a wild, romantic read, set in foreign parts with plenty of excitement and mysterious characters. I was recommended *The Demon of Sicily*, should you happen to see it, or I've heard that *The Spectre of the Druid* is particularly thrilling.' She had run upstairs before Letitia had had time to take her to task for her frivolity; Alethea trusted Camilla to pick out the very thing.

They reached Hookham's library without a drop of rain falling on their smart new bonnets. It was busy inside, with men and women exchanging books and gossip. Letitia duly selected a heavy looking *Life*; Camilla found a novel by Peacock, which she had long wanted to read, and took the most preposterous of the romances for Alethea. They waited their turn to have the titles written down, Letitia wishing that she knew anyone in the room, while Camilla flicked through the pages of her sister's heavy tome.

She knew very well what the fate of the books would be. Letty, having struggled through some fifty pages of her dull work, would cast it aside, look into the Peacock, criticise the author for his nonsense and cruel jests, and finally, sighing and saying there was nothing to amuse her, would take up the first volume of Alethea's book – it would barely take a day for Alethea to read it – and settle down with ill-disguised zest to lose herself in its fantastical pages. Thus vexing Miss Griffin, a keen devourer of novels, who would have to possess her soul in patience until Letty, who was not a quick reader, had finished.

Sackree grumbled at the weight of the books she was asked to carry. 'I wonder at you young ladies, I do really, filling your heads with all these words. It's bad enough with you haunting the library at Pemberley without your wanting more books now you are come to London. I should have thought you'd read all the books that had ever been written.'

'That's the trouble, Sackree,' Camilla replied, watching her step on the mucky paving stones and jumping nimbly over a puddle. 'Authors go on writing books, and so we go on reading them. It is a sad state of affairs.'

'And Mrs Darcy just the same, packing up a boxful of books to take with her all the way to that nasty Constantinople. Mind you, if they have books there, which is unlikely, they'll all be written in a heathen tongue, and no use to any Christian born. A box of books! All that way!'

'Mama will need the consolation of books in such a strange and unfamiliar world,' said Letitia.

'If Mama has any sense, she'll be out and about and not have a second to spare for reading. Oh, how I envy her, able to visit palaces and harems and St Sophia and to wander in the markets among the veiled women and camels! All the delights of the Arabian nights laid out before her.'

'I have heard it is a dirty, inconvenient city, with thieves and murderers lurking at every corner,' said Letitia immediately. 'Poor Mama, to be taken into such danger. And Papa, so tall, so English, he will be the object of every crazed assassin in the city.'

Camilla let her sister's pictures of woe flow over her. Her vivid imagination could easily conjure up an entrancing vision of fabled foreign places, and although her sense told her that her notions were likely to be as far from the truth as Letty's ideas, they were still pleasing enough.

'Well, here we are at last,' declared Sackree, 'and not a moment too soon, for it's coming on to rain, just as I said it was going to. Miss Sophie never walks out without she has her maid and a footman with her,' she added as she followed her mistress and Letitia up the wide stone steps to the door and gave several brisk raps on the large brass knocker. 'Very particular, Mrs Gardiner is.'

'Mrs Gardiner takes a very proper care of her,' said Letitia, coming out of her ill humour at the thought of this concern for the proprieties.

And she might need to, Camilla said to herself, for even at fourteen, when they had last seen her, Sophie was a wilful, difficult girl – apart from being a remarkably pretty one. Camilla looked forward with interest to seeing how her cousin had turned out. What a change three years must have wrought; years that had taken Sophie from girlhood to the status of a betrothed young lady and her father, Mr Gardiner, from prosperity to great wealth and from Gracechurch Street to this considerable mansion in the best part of town.

The door was opened by an imposing butler, and they hurried into the Gardiners' house just as the heavens opened and the rain came scudding down.

Mrs Gardiner greeted them with real warmth and affection, exclaiming at their walking all that way. 'You shall have the carriage to take you back, no, I insist upon it.' She bade them come nearer to the fire and get warm. 'Sophie is wild to see you, she will be down directly.'

It was as Camilla had predicted; the three years since they had last seen Sophie had turned her into the most elegant, prettiest creature imaginable, a vision in a pale pink silk dress, her shining light brown hair fashionably dressed, her cheeks tinged with colour, her eyes sparkling with pleasure at seeing her cousins.

It was a pleasure increased for Sophie by the fact that, although she and Camilla were alike in looks, a single glance was enough to reassure her that the last three years had not, as she had feared, turned Camilla into any kind of a rival.

For her part, Camilla was perfectly well aware of what Sophie was thinking, and it made her want to laugh. Nothing could persuade Sophie that she didn't envy her cousin her lovely features and figure, or wish that she had the same exquisite air of fragile femininity. She knew it for no more than an air; she had long ago taken Sophie's measure. Beneath the soft exterior lurked a resolute and tougher being, and woe betide the cousin or anyone else who threatened to steal her thunder.

Compliments and congratulations were made, news given and received, and they were so absorbed in conversation that none of them heard the door open, and a servant announce more visitors. Mrs Gardiner looked vexed for a moment, and then her face cleared. 'Why, it is Mr Wytton, I am so glad to see you. And Mr Layard, how do you do?'

Camilla was surprised by this tall man with a saturnine expression; however she had imagined Sophie's future husband, it wasn't like this man. He looked intelligent and angry – what had he to be angry about? She was amused by the contrast between him and his short, round friend. On closer scrutiny she decided that she liked the look of Mr Layard, and thought he had a merry eye. There was, however, nothing merry about Mr Wytton, who gave her a look of cool appraisal before making his bow as introductions were made.

Mrs Gardiner watched with complacency as Mr Wytton kissed her daughter's hand, and then stood back, his eyes fixed on her with evident warmth and admiration. Sophie blushed and smiled, and accepted his present with little cries of delight. The cameo he had brought for her was exclaimed over and praised by everyone, and Sophie's maid was sent running to find a ribbon for her to tie it round her pretty neck.

'A cornelian, I think, Mr Wytton?' Mrs Gardiner asked. 'Such fine workmanship.'

'It is, ma'am. From Italy. It represents the goddess Venus.'

'Oh, more of your old gods and goddesses,' said Sophie with an arch look.

'Mr Wytton is by way of being an antiquarian,' Mrs Gardiner said in an aside to Camilla. 'He has travelled widely, and published articles upon Greek ruins of various kinds. He is held to be a fine scholar.'

'Is he indeed?'

'You may talk about your travels and discoveries to Miss Camilla, Mr Wytton, for she is interested in such things.'

Camilla had to smile at the expression on Mr Wytton's face;

it was clear that he would no more discuss his journeys and findings with her than he would talk them over with his mother's poodle.

He felt obliged to reply to Mrs Gardiner, however. 'It is a pleasure to find a member of the fair sex who knows a Greek from a Roman. Have you been long in London, Miss Camilla? Have you visited the British Museum? I dare say you may see some things there to catch your interest.'

'I have been to the museum, yes, but not recently. We are only just arrived in London. I shall certainly go again, but we women have to ration our visits, you know, lest the excitement and learning tax our brains and affect our wits.'

He gave her a suspicious look, and she turned away, hiding a smile. Letty, always on the watch for signs of Camilla forgetting herself in company, hastily broke in with a compliment on Sophie's looks and an enquiry about plans for the honeymoon.

'Brighton,' cried Sophie, her eyes shining.

'We go to Rome,' said Wytton.

It was as well for Camilla's composure that she didn't hear the conversation between the two men as they walked away from the house.

'They are fine young ladies, the Miss Darcys,' Layard began. 'Although it must be hard for Miss Camilla, I believe.'

Wytton had been lost in thought, but his head came up at this remark. 'Why?'

'Wytton, what a fellow you are! You had eyes only for your Sophie, I do not think you noticed them at all, Miss Darcy and her sister. They are not blessed with the same degree of looks.'

'Neither of them seemed remarkable to me.'

'The younger one has a satirical eye.'

'I hate a clever woman.'

'You are out of humour, Wytton, you are always out of humour these days. You should ask your physician for a powder.'

'Physic! No, no, I leave that to you hypochondriacs. No one ever needed physicking less than I. I am in the rudest health, as it happens.'

Not, however, in the rudest spirits, Mr Layard thought, but did not say. It was a trying time for the most even-tempered man; an engagement often made men low, he had noticed it before. 'We are to dine with the Gardiners this evening,' he went on. 'I dare say Sophie's cousins will be present. I understand they are worth fifty thousand apiece.'

'They are in London to find themselves husbands, I suppose.'

Mr Layard was sorry to hear the acid tone in his friend's voice. He hooked his arm into his. 'Come, friend, you should be in happier spirits, indeed you should. I never saw Miss Sophie in better looks. You are a lucky man, by God you are. All that and ninety thousand pounds.'

'You are a vulgar fellow, Layard,' said Wytton.

Mrs Gardiner was as good as her word, and sent Camilla and Letitia home in her carriage after inviting them to return later in the day to dine. 'If Fanny can spare you, and I am sure she can, even such a giddy creature as she is can't have fixed engagements for you every evening.'

'She certainly hasn't today,' said Camilla. 'She and Mr Fitzwilliam are dining out this evening, a political gathering.'

Fanny was pleased to hear of their invitation, but bewailed the lack of an evening dress for Camilla. 'Why, here is Letitia's cream silk come home, and very pretty it is too, but not a single one of your evening dresses, Camilla, which is most provoking. I shall lend you one of my gowns.'

Letitia was quick to protest. 'It will not do. Camilla should not wear anything so fine as your dresses. What is suitable for a married woman is quite wrong for a single girl.'

Fanny took no notice. 'Ring for Dawson this instant, Camilla, and we shall see what it is to be done.'

'I can wear one of my own dresses, Fanny, they are not so very dowdy. You are shorter than me, you know, and while a dress may be pinned up, I never heard that it could be made longer.'

'To be sure, and I am plumper across the bosom than you.' At that moment, her maid came into the room. 'Dawson,' she cried, 'here is Miss Camilla asked to dine at Mr Gardiner's house, and none of her evening dresses ready. What is to be done? You must find her maid and look over the clothes she has brought from Derbyshire and see what can be contrived to give one of her dresses a more modish look. Hurry now, there is not a moment to lose.'

Fanny's concern for her appearance was kind. Camilla was too sensible to feel that her whole stay in London would be marred by attending one dinner in a dress not as fashionable as it might be, but she couldn't help feeling a pang of envy when she saw Letitia's dress. 'It is a family occasion, you know, and I am sure my unfashionable gown will pass unnoticed.'

'I am sure it will not,' said Fanny at once. 'The Gardiners are not such fools as to have a mere family dinner when the Miss Darcys are just arrived in town! No, no, Mrs Gardiner will have invited some men of rank and property and wealth, you may depend upon it. She has caught an excellent *parti* in Wytton for her Sophie, and she married her other two daughters very well, very well indeed when you think their portions were not half so big as Sophie will have. She has her hand in, and will have been thinking of likely men for you before ever you left Pemberley.'

Letitia was looking troubled when they went upstairs to dress. 'Fanny means to be kind, but I wish she wouldn't harp so on husbands. I am not looking for any kind of a husband, and Papa and Mama would not at all wish to have you hunting for a husband while you are in London. I am sure they are not in the least concerned that you have not yet met a man you felt you could love, even though you are nineteen. And my case is different, as you know, for I did know such a man, had fallen in love with him when I was no more than sixteen; in my case, it is of no matter how many eligible men I may meet.'

Camilla's thoughts were on more mundane matters as she saw how well Sackree had altered her dress under Dawson's directions. 'I raised the bodice just a little, miss, seeing as how that Dawson says the dress was too low in the waist for present fashion, and apparently no dress can be worn without it has more flounces, so an extra row of lace flounces do you have. There now, I do admit it looks very fine on you.' She tweaked the skirt into place. 'Here are your satin shoes, and it's to be supposed you're taking a carriage tonight and not intending to splash your way there in the mud?'

'Of course we go in the carriage,' said Camilla, turning this way and that to look at her image in the cheval glass. 'Thank you, Sackree, and give my thanks to Dawson also.'

'You'll wear your seed pearls with that dress, miss. You need a necklace with it being cut so low. And Mrs Fitzwilliam wants you to go to her room and choose some bracelets to wear. Dawson tells me that no lady stirs out without she has a veritable jingle-jangle all up and down her arms. Mrs Darcy was right to advise you to choose this shade of green, miss, it suits your complexion very well. Pale yellows and pinks aren't the right style for you.'

Whatever your sister may say, she added to herself, as she marched out of the room.

Mr Gardiner's chef, one M. Halavant, was famous throughout London for the excellence of his cuisine. The Gardiners' friends and enemies alike did not scruple to tempt him away to preside over their kitchens, but Halavant was not to be bought. He had been rescued by Mr Gardiner from the prison in which he had been thrown on suspicion of being a French spy – a case of mistaken identity – and his loyalty to Mr Gardiner thereafter was absolute. Besides, his employer was able to pay him a startlingly high wage, and entertained lavishly enough to allow his chef every opportunity to exercise his culinary genius.

Camilla had to confess herself amazed by her first London dinner party. She was used to dining out at various great houses in the country, but there was a different quality to this gathering. The conversation was quicker and covered a wide range of subjects, and what with the splendour of the dishes and the wine, the glittering silver and crystal of the table settings, the flowers, the army of liveried servants and the magnificence of the women's silks and jewels, she felt almost light-headed.

Her attention had at once been caught by a guest sitting a little way down the table, next to Mrs Gardiner. He was a tall, fine-looking man of about thirty-five with a good air and address, and he had a smooth, mobile mouth that suggested a humorous spirit. She thought he looked to be more interesting company than her neighbour, Mr Wytton, who spoke in monosyllables, gazed a great deal at Sophie, and when Camilla ventured any remark looked at her with chilling indifference.

Although Camilla was unaware of it, the tall man was asking Mrs Gardiner about her. 'She is the second sister, I believe?'

'She is, Sir Sidney. Letitia is the eldest, she is there, talking to Latouche.'

'Very beautiful.' His voice was cool. 'There are five daughters, I think?'

'There are three younger girls as well as these.'

'And all heiresses. Darcy has done well for himself. Derbyshire is a good county for landowners. I heard they have found rich mineral deposits on his land.'

'I believe so.'

He turned amused eyes on her. 'We cannot all be so fortunate as your husband, Mrs Gardiner. We do not all have the Midas touch and must rely on our land to bring us what wealth it can.'

'Midas touch! I hope not. Now, that gentleman there, he truly has the ability to make everything he touches turn to gold.'

Sir Sidney Leigh's gaze drifted over the ruddy-complexioned man sitting across from them, his attention on the lady beside him; from the snatches of conversation that could be heard, they were talking about turtles. 'Pagoda Portal,' he said. 'Yes, indeed, one of the richest men in England. But is he a happy man, Mrs Gardiner, can you tell me that?'

Mrs Gardiner was laughing. 'No, he is not, for he is in love with that strange woman, Mrs Rowan, and she will not have him, however much he is worth.'

'A woman of character, to turn away from such a fortune.'

'She has a fortune of her own, now her husband is dead.'

'Perhaps she cares more for a man's face than his fortune. One could not describe Portal as a handsome man.'

'You wrong him; he has an amiable appearance. Indeed, many women would consider him a well-looking man.'

'That, my dear Mrs Gardiner, is because a man's looks are measured by the depth of his pockets.'

'It is not the case, however, with Mrs Rowan. She only declares she will never submit to the oppressive yoke of marriage again. Her words, not mine, Sir Sidney; I should never describe marriage as oppressive.'

'You would not? I think many men find it so, and women have even more reason to discover that what they hoped would be connubial felicity turns out to be a bed of nails.'

Mrs Gardiner cried out at this. 'Shame on you, Sir Sidney, for such cynicism.'

'Let me sit next to your Miss Darcy when we gather for tea. I am well acquainted with her father, you know, and I dare say she will be glad to talk about him. Grave young ladies are always eager to talk about their fathers. Her sister does not look like a woman who wants to talk about her father. I shall leave her to the younger men. She seems to be getting on capitally well with Mr Layard. I never saw him look so amused.'

'Camilla has a pretty wit.'

'In that case, I'm right to prefer Miss Gravity; the Lord save me from a witty woman.'

'Tell me,' Camilla whispered to Mr Layard, who was sitting on her other side, 'why do they call Mr Portal, Pagoda Portal? It seems such an extraordinary name.'

'Ah,' he said, 'you could not have come to a better person for information. The pagoda, you know, is a gold coin from India. It is so called from its shape, which resembles the leaf of the pagoda tree. Mr Portal has made an immense fortune in India, and so earned himself this nickname. He has bought land and built himself a fine house, called Pagoda Place – he has a sense of humour, as you can tell – and gone into Parliament. What is surprising about him is that he is a Radical! Now, what do you think of that?'

'Is it not unusual for a rich man to have Radical views?'

'Unusual for any man of sense to have Radical views. I

suspect my friend Wytton there of such views; he is always talking about Reform, but he denies Radicalism.'

'I should hope so. Are not the Radicals dangerous? Are they not forever stirring up riots and disturbances?'

'With Mr Portal, it is all theory; I believe he draws the line at actual riots. I shall introduce you after dinner; you will like to talk to him about India. He knows a great deal about that country, he's always prosing on about it, but I dare say you may find it interesting. Ladies are always enchanted by the idea of India.'

The covers were removed and the dessert set on the table. As the servants left the room and the level of conversation rose, she felt she could risk a question without its subject overhearing her. 'Has your friend Mr Wytton been to India?' she asked Mr Layard. 'Mrs Gardiner tells me he has travelled a good deal.'

'Not to India. He loves best to scramble around the dusty landscapes of Greece and Turkey, and since the end of the war he has been twice to Egypt.'

Her face lit up. 'Egypt, how I envy him! But tell me, is he always so terse? Does he not enjoy company?'

'Oh, do not judge him by affairs such as this. It is hard on a man to be engaged, you know; becoming part of a new family, being constantly petted and made much of is enough to try any fellow's patience.'

'I hope it is only the engagement that makes him so cross. I would wish Sophie a good-tempered husband.'

'He is never cross with her; why should he be? She does not contradict him or argue with him and has hardly a thought in her pretty head.'

She could not help laughing. 'And *that* is what he likes? Perhaps he may get a shock or two once he is married.'

'Never tell me he's marrying a termagant!'

'I'm sure Sophie is as good-natured as anyone else, but we women, you know, do not usually let our husbands have it all their own way.'

Mr Wytton, his attention drawn from his other companion by the laughter and liveliness of Camilla and Layard's conversation, turned to look at them. It must be the effect of visiting Egypt, she thought irreverently, that made his expression so greatly resemble the severe gaze of the Great Sphinx.

Camilla was not unpleased to find herself standing next to Sir Sidney later in the evening, as they stood waiting for the tea to be poured. She made some remarks about the company, and he replied with a civil smile and a bow, then made an apology and moved away. A little while later she saw him seated on a sofa, talking to Letty. He must have used some adroitness to be there; Letty's beauty was attracting a good deal of attention.

Perhaps Letty was right; perhaps she should mind her tongue and mend her ways. She was used to the dull and callow men of her acquaintance, who would slide away from her with murmured excuses and a look of panic on their faces, but it wasn't so easy to overlook the fact that a man such as Sir Sidney obviously preferred Letty's company to hers.

However, she wasn't self-centred or given to worrying about the impression she made for more than a minute or two, and here was Mr Portal, full of amiability, perfectly willing to stay by her side and make amusing conversation.

'Come and sit beside me, Miss Camilla, and tell me how you do. Are you liking London?'

'Indeed I am.' Which was the truth, for she was revelling in the sense of freedom that coming to London had given her. She loved her parents, but, oh, it was a joy to be in bustling London, to be meeting so many new people, ordering new and fashionable clothes, hearing Fanny talk of parties and balls, and not to be under Mr and Mrs Darcy's scrutiny.

'Mr Gardiner is your mother's uncle, is that not right?'

'It is, and Mrs Gardiner, who is much of an age with my mother, was always her great friend. She has always been very kind to us, and indeed, we would have stayed here with them if Mrs Gardiner had not been indisposed last year. My parents felt it would not be quite convenient for her to have us to stay just at present, what with the activity and confusion attendant upon Sophie's approaching nuptials.'

Camilla could have added that she had been sorry for this, for she liked the Gardiners, and knew that they liked her. She had more in common with Mr Gardiner than she had with Mr Fitzwilliam, to whom it never occurred that a young woman might have views and concerns beyond clothes, beaux and making a good marriage.

And she was aware that, although the Fitzwilliams were on excellent terms with the Gardiners, and Lady Fanny had a warm affection for Mr Gardiner, Mr Fitzwilliam was very conscious of the fact that Mr Gardiner's great wealth came from trade, a disadvantage somewhat ameliorated by Sophie's forthcoming match with the highly eligible Wytton.

Here was Mr Gardiner; having done his duty as host, he now came to join them. After congratulating him on Sophie's betrothal, Camilla was happy to hear about his recent voyage to Bombay, a city which Pagoda Portal also knew well.

How lucky men were to have such control of their lives, and go off to Bombay or wherever they chose, provided they had the means at their disposal, with never a domestic care to bother them.

Mr Gardiner laughed when she told him so. 'No, no, Camilla, you must not say such things. Why, whatever would we men do if we didn't have our wives and children and comfortable homes waiting for our return? Women need not despise their role. Indeed, we men would achieve nothing without the love and support of our families; we rely on that, I do assure you.'

THREE

A floorboard was slightly loose, and every time Letitia trod on it, it squeaked.

Camilla was not usually affected by the small irritations of daily life. The squeak was not in itself offensive, only she did wish that Letty were less on the fidget. A firm pacing to and fro would have been preferable to these little dashes about the room. However, since Letty was in a fretful mood, it was no doubt inevitable that her body would mirror her agitation. It was a pity, though, that the cause of all this fuss and bother had its existence only in her sister's head.

Georgina and Belle were expected hourly. They were breaking their journey at Oxford, where they were to dine and spend the night with friends. Letty's mind was full of calculations of distances and times. She knew the route by heart and had fixed on all the most likely places for the various disasters certain to overcome her sisters.

'They may be taken ill.'

Camilla looked up from her book, not for the first time. 'Who is ill?'

'No one is ill. Georgina and Belle may be taken ill, however.'

'Neither is prone to being affected by the motion of the carriage.'

'One of them could have the headache, or a fever coming on. I thought Belle had lost some of her bloom before we left Pemberley. It is only to be expected, she will feel leaving her home very acutely. She will not be looking forward to London, her sensibility is too delicate for city life.'

Camilla went back to her book. She had no fears for Belle's

health, nor for Georgina's. They had fallen ill with the usual childhood ailments, had suffered the measles and the chicken pox, had endured heavy colds and passing fevers, and bounced themselves back into perfect health in no time at all; their physician in Derbyshire declared them a wonderful advertisement for his skills. It would take more than a coach ride and the prospect of dizzying delights in Town to affect their well-being.

Letitia took up her embroidery again, but hadn't set more than half a dozen neat stitches before she laid it by. 'Hark, is that a carriage I hear?'

'Letty, a carriage is to be heard in the square several times an hour. The twins cannot possibly be here yet, not unless they left Oxford before dawn, and why should they do such a thing?' Considering how reluctant Belle and Georgina were to rise at any hour of the morning, this hardly needed to be said.

'However, a wheel may come off the coach, have you thought of that?'

Letty's flow of irrational fears was interrupted by a servant coming to tell them that a luncheon had been laid in the morning room, and Camilla was spared the effort of a reply. She made quickly for the door; Letty came after her, shaking her head and sighing in a most depressing way and still murmuring about horses going lame, being bitten by horse-flies and driven wild, abduction, highwaymen and other improbable dangers.

Fanny was already standing by the table, looking ruffled and pink-cheeked from a romp she had been enjoying with her children. 'Little Arthur has another tooth come through, nurse says; such a good boy as he is, it must have hurt and he made no fuss about it at all.'

Camilla was relieved to have a topic of conversation to take Letitia's mind off the terrible hazards of travel, and they talked energetically about the children, how forward and intelligent they were, and what Charlotte had said to her father only yesterday, how it had made him laugh.

'At any moment now your sisters will be here,' Fanny went on. 'How tired they will be after their journey, they will want to rest, I expect. I shall order tea for them, nothing is so refreshing as tea after a long journey.'

'They only come from Oxford today.'

'That is still a way. Forty miles or more, I am sure it is all of that, and maybe more. No, they will want to rest and be quiet. We dine alone tonight, quite alone, *en famille*. To be sure, Mr Grandville from the House is invited, and Mrs Rowan, his sister-in-law – you are sure to like her. We are to be only a small party. Sir Sidney Leigh will be coming, also. He called upon me this morning, while you were walking in the square, you know, and I asked him to dine if he had no prior engagement. He is very rich, and they say he is on the lookout for— Well, no matter.'

'Belle and Georgina had better take their meal upstairs with Alethea,' said Letitia. 'If they are not so shocked and shaken by their journey as to want to retire straightaway.'

Her sisters had never been shocked and shaken by anything, Camilla thought. Their seventeen years had been marked by mirth, frivolity, happiness, wilfulness and an inclination to disregard whatever did not suit their way of thinking. How had Letty, even for a moment, conjured this image of frail females? Let alone summoned up the notion of a pair of young ladies obliging enough to eat upstairs with the governess and Alethea when they might dine in company downstairs.

'Since we are to be such a small party, I thought Alethea might join us,' said Fanny. 'You have been practising at the pianoforte, Camilla. How much I admire your performance, you shall play for us this evening. And Alethea sings so charmingly. I hear her up there, trilling away like a canary bird.'

'I shall certainly play for you if you wish it,' she said. 'Alethea does not always choose to sing in company, but she may be willing to oblige us.'

'What a shame Belle's harp has not yet arrived from Pemberley. With Georgina accompanying her, they would make such a charming picture, one dark and one fair. If they have lost that slight plumpness they had, which is only natural for young girls, I warrant they are grown into very pretty young women.'

'You shall judge for yourself,' Camilla said, catching the sound of a coach drawing up outside. 'Here they are!'

The front door was opening. There was a hubbub in the street in front of the house as a groom came running out to take the horses' heads, the coachman and the manservant exchanged words about the journey and the cursed London streets, passers-by stopped to look at the fine equipage, servants came spilling down the steps to take in bandboxes and unstrap the trunks.

Within, the hall was full of voices raised in excited greetings and exclamations. Alethea hung over the rail on the top landing and added to the noise by calling down in her powerful voice, while Letitia was letting out cries of relief upon discovering that her sisters had reached London with the regular number of legs and arms, quite intact, no blows to the head, no urgent need for the apothecary or physician.

Among the mêlée of girls and servants and bandboxes, Camilla spied a strange young man with a fine head of Byronic curls, who was standing in the hall, holding a cross, vociferous and tiny pug dog in his arms. He seemed bemused by the uproar, but otherwise perfectly self-possessed.

'Georgie, Georgie,' she called. 'Who is this?'

Georgina left off hugging Letty and looked round. 'Lord, Pug, I forgot all about him, didn't I, my little precious?' She flew at the young man and snatched the dog away, ignoring the animal's snarls of protest. 'Isn't he the sweetest thing imaginable? They have a bitch who whelped quite recently, you know, and we begged to bring this dear little dog with us. We thought Cousin Fanny would so like a pug!'

The wriggling, indignant little bundle was thrust into Fanny's arms, where it lay wheezing and panting, giving the tip of her nose the occasional lick.

'Oh, well, to be sure,' Fanny said, dismayed, but word had spread and her two eldest children were beside her, tugging at her skirts and begging to be allowed to hold the pug.

'I'll see to the dog,' said Dawson, her maid, appearing suddenly from nowhere. In a trice the pug, quietened at once, was tucked under her arm. 'You'll be wanting to take the young ladies out of the hall.'

Recalled to her duties, Fanny kissed her cousins, told them they were very welcome, declared that they were grown so pretty she would hardly have known them and glanced questioningly at the young man, who looked as though he would like to make a rapid getaway. 'Georgina, Isabelle, who is this?'

The twins looked around as though expecting to find another pug lurking among the baskets. 'Oh, it is only Mr Roper,' said Isabelle.

Camilla was genuinely pleased to see her sisters, although she always forgot, when they weren't there, what a noise and a stir they made wherever they went. It wasn't that their voices were loud or unpleasant, nor that they were vigorous or clumsy in their movements. Belle tended to languid, flustering gestures that suited her extreme fairness and fragile looks; Georgina, with her shining black hair and dramatic presence, was no more boisterous, yet there was always a feeling of electricity in the air when they were in a room together.

'Those eyes,' Fanny was saying in an aside to Letitia. 'One so angelically fair, one so intensely dark, and both of them with those great violet eyes, Lord, how I envy them their eyes. The gentlemen will be wild when they see them. What an impression they will make.'

'It is kind of you to say so,' said Letitia, alarmed. 'Remember, Fanny, they will be in the schoolroom, there is no question of any gentlemen.'

The two pairs of violet eyes were turned on her, full of reproach. 'Letty, how can you be so unkind?'

'If we do not go about while we are in London now, who knows when we may ever have the chance again?'

'We mean to go to all the plays and dance the nights away.'

'Dance! Indeed, you shall not dance. You are not out. I am not married, and nor is Camilla.'

'Well, I suppose Camilla may manage to find herself a husband if she guards her tongue and doesn't laugh at all the men, but since you swear you mean to die an old maid, there's no hope for us, not if we have to wait for you to marry.'

'It's so unfair.' Georgina turned to Fanny for support. 'Cousin, don't you think it unfair? We're seventeen, we have friends of just our age who have been married these twelve months and more.'

'If you do not behave, I shall write directly to Papa,' said Letitia.

Belle's mouth drooped, and Georgina fixed her eldest sister with a hard stare.

Camilla knew who would win this engagement. Out of reach of their formidable papa, the twins were sure to have their way – Fanny was clearly entranced by them. Meanwhile, Letty would become more and more disagreeable, would scold and criticise them, the twins would sulk, the household would be set all to pieces.

'So here you are, all five of you sisters together once more.' Fanny was spilling words into the frigid silence. 'I know how close you are, you will be so happy with one another's company.'

Had Fanny been in earnest when she had spoken about finding a hussar to console Letty? As things were, it would be a relief for her interests and affections to take a new direction. Although, were a dashing cavalry officer to appear in his red coat, ten to one Belle or Georgina would snatch him away.

Camilla might relish her own freedom from parental supervision, but just now she felt a real sense of regret at her parents' absence, unable to imagine how, without their guidance and control, they were to deal with Georgina and Belle. In only a few days away from their family, as they had felt the lessening of restraint, her sisters had changed in some indefinable way. Her father should not have gone away just now, nor should her mother; that was what came of their being so devoted a couple and of her father having such a strong sense of duty. And they were to be away for so many months!

A year or so ago, and the twins would have been safely in the schoolroom. Two or three years hence, they would be married and beyond their family's responsibility. Now, however, here they were: beautiful, heedless and ripe for every kind of wildness.

Letty, who had not a trace of wildness in her make-up, refused to see it, considering that a firm hand – hers – was all that was needed to keep them within the bounds of acceptable behaviour. Camilla knew that Letty did not appreciate the mischief that Belle and Georgina's high spirits might lead them into, especially when those high spirits were coupled with their glowing good looks and undeniable charm.

Belle was giving her a radiant smile. 'Camilla, why are you so serious? Are you not pleased to see us?' She skipped across the room and put her arm round her waist. 'We are so happy to see you, and to be all together again, aren't we, Georgie? Such fun to be in London. Have you ever been to Oxford, Camilla? It is an astonishing place, for you must know the streets are full of young men. Very young men, for the most part, but we saw some handsome faces, and then, there are so many of them! You can imagine nothing more delightful.'

Camilla could, easily. She returned her sister's hug with affection, but said, 'You will have to behave, you and Georgie, for you don't wish to sound like country bumpkins come to Town. Young ladies in society, you know, are moderate in their praise of men.'

'Oh, what an old maid you sound, and you only nineteen,' exclaimed Georgina.

'Tell me why Mr Roper is here,' Camilla said, lowering her voice.

'Lord, we had forgotten him in all the excitement. He has been in Oxford over some matter connected with his younger brother, who is at Magdalen College or some such place, and we offered to bring him to London. He has such news, and I can tell you haven't heard, for otherwise Letty would not be so calm. Indeed, it is going to shock you all most dreadfully; you had best call for your smelling salts directly.'

'Let him tell them, let Mr Roper tell his news,' cried Belle. 'It is about a man we all know. It is about Tom, Tom Busby, Letty's Tom, for you must know that he and Mr Roper were schoolfellows at Westminster and were well acquainted.'

'Winchester, in fact,' put in Mr Roper diffidently.

'It is all the same,' said Belle. 'Oh, he has such a story to tell, I swear you will none of you believe it. For, not two weeks ago, he was—'

'No, no,' interrupted Georgina. 'Mr Roper must speak, for he has every particular; how we cried out when he told us, and then we laughed, very heartily, for it is all so strange.'

Mr Roper tugged at his neckcloth, lifted his eyebrow and cleared his throat. 'It is like this,' he began.

FOUR

Letty gave a shriek that must have been heard in the next square, and proceeded to throw a fit of the most determined hysterics. Not all the efforts of Camilla, Fanny and Dawson could persuade her to calm herself, and they were little helped by the twins remarking how comical it was, when you considered how Letty despised a jilt, and what fun it would be to tease Tom when next they saw him, how foolish he would look, and he was bound to come to London, was he not?

Dawson's expression was severe, for although her own mistress was a volatile creature, she didn't hold with such conduct as this. How could Miss Darcy allow herself to show her feelings so?

Camilla could see Dawson eyeing the jug of water that held flowers; to be strewn with damp leaves and green water might bring Letty to her senses, but at the cost of much mortification, not to mention a ruined gown, and one she had only put on for the first time that morning. She stepped forward to administer a firm slap to Letty's cheek. The wail dissolved into a hiccup, Letty's drenched eyes lost their tragic look and filled with anger. She raised a trembling hand to her cheek and shot a furious glance at her sister.

'Indeed, I'm sorry to hurt you,' Camilla said, not feeling or sounding in the least contrite, 'only you were working yourself into such a state and alarming poor Fanny so.'

Poor Fanny, now that the din and confusion had ceased, took charge. She dismissed the twins, bidding them summon a maid to take them to their room. Turning to an aghast Mr Roper, who was now perfectly white and edging towards the door, she said he too had better go.

'Certainly, ma'am. I am most dreadfully sorry – I had no idea – I had heard that Tom was – that there was a previous attachment in the case – I never dreamed that Miss Darcy was the one! And her sisters so very amused, and never mentioning a word of it. I never saw such heartless behaviour, I assure you.'

'And pray have the goodness not to mention this scene to your friends,' said Fanny. 'No doubt you like to carry a lively tale, only since there is a lady in the case it would be better for you to hold your tongue.'

Apologising and protesting, he was almost pushed out of the room, promising that he would call to ask how the young lady did, and swearing that not a word of what had occurred would pass his lips.

'Not that it will make the slightest difference,' observed Fanny after Dawson had escorted an exhausted Letty from the room with directions as to smelling salts, tisanes and a brick to her feet following in her wake. 'One way or another, the whole of London will know all about it by this evening, only by then Letty will be said to have died of grief or her brother will have threatened someone or other to a duel, and I dare say your father will be known to be returning posthaste from his mission, horsewhip in hand.'

Camilla knew that what Fanny said was all too true. 'At least it will be a while before the news reaches my parents. Should I write to tell them what has happened?'

Fanny was relieved. She had much rather not be the one to send the news to Mr and Mrs Darcy. 'At once, if you will. It will be best if they learn the unvarnished truth before some strange distorted tale is carried to Turkey to alarm and worry them.'

'Mr Fitzwilliam will no doubt advise how I may most quickly send a letter.'

'I'm sure he will, and you will know just what to say; I do not wish to rouse your father's ire.'

Mr Roper's revelation was so extraordinary; it would be difficult to explain the situation to her parents.

'Can it be possible that a young man has not the wits to know who he is and yet the sense and self-possession to marry? And not some violent fling with a landlord's daughter or a wench of the town, but a lady of quality and standing. It is all very remarkable.'

'Dawson is sending for Dr Molloy, the physician, and after he has seen Letty and prescribed some soothing draught, we may ask him his opinion of such behaviour. For myself, I am not surprised to find that a man's head may be all to pieces without his other parts being in the least affected – it is always the way with men. And so this Count de Broise's daughter is a pretty little woman, according to Mr Roper at least, and he strikes me as being a young man with an eye for beauty.'

Fanny rang the bell to give directions for when Dr Molloy arrived and to order a glass of wine for herself and Camilla. 'To soothe our shattered nerves, my dear; a little wine will do you good.'

While Fanny settled herself on the sofa to flick absentmind-edly through the pages of the *Morning Post*, Camilla sat down to her task at the writing table. The sooner the letter were written and despatched, the better. She tested the pens laid out for use, drew a sheet of paper in front of her, dipped her nib in the inkstand and began to write.

'My dearest Papa and Mama.'

That was easy enough, as were enquiries about their journey, how long the stages had taken, where had they stopped, what sights they had seen. She wrote about how they had settled in at Aubrey Square, the kindness of the Fitzwilliams, the pleasures of new clothes and well-stocked libraries and every day making new acquaintances. The Gardiners were all in sound health, she added for good measure, although much taken up with the preparations for Sophie's nuptials.

She bit the end of the quill as she came to the heart of the letter, looked out of the window for inspiration, found none, and returned to her writing.

Belle and Georgina arrived in London this very day, in excellent spirits and escorted by an amiable young man called Mr Roper, who had also been staying with the Downings in Oxford – he is a connection of theirs, I believe. He brought the strangest news, which has cast Letty into some considerable depression of spirits, as you will understand when I tell you that Tom Busby – our neighbour, Tom Busby, of Derbyshire – is not dead at all, but alive and in Belgium, where he has married the elder daughter of a Count de Broise. You will say that it is no more than a malicious rumour, but indeed it is not. Mr Roper was formerly at school with Tom and knows him well. He – Mr Roper – was in Brussels not a fortnight ago, and was strolling across the Grande Place when he saw Tom, as large as life, walking with a pretty young woman on his arm. He immediately addressed him, as you may imagine, calling out his name, and exclaiming with wonder. Tom did not recognise him at all at first, but on Mr Roper repeating his name and reminding him of school and other times spent together, he seemed to come to some recollection of the friendship.

This was the point when Letty had let out her first faint scream – 'With a woman on his arm?' – and collapsed on to the nearest sofa.

The three of them then repaired to a nearby coffee house, with Tom, Mr Roper said, in a state of some agitation, and the lady also appearing to be startled by the encounter with Mr Roper. Tom remembered nothing of his life in England or in the army, although he did have some vague notion of hearing gunshot. He had come to his senses to find himself alone, in a wood with a dreadful wound to his head and with no recollection of who he was and why he should be there and dressed in little more than his shirt. He wandered about for some considerable time and in the end came to a house, that of the Count, where they assumed he had been attacked by thieves and left for dead. He fell ill of a fever and spent many weeks hovering between this world and the next, during which time, of course, the battle of Waterloo had been fought and won, and his name posted among those slain in the conflict.

The Count knew him for a gentleman, from his manner of speaking and the quality of his few clothes and his dimly recalled life at school and at home. However, he remembered neither his name, nor the place of his birth or his family's residence.

Camilla had heard of blows to the head depriving a man of his memory. Falls caused by hunting could have such an effect, with someone brought home on a hurdle, and coming to with no recollection of anything that had occurred since breakfast. But in such a case, the sufferer generally knew perfectly well who he was, and even after a severe concussion, memory gradually returned. Three years was such a time! Could Tom so thoroughly forget family and friends and home? Have no memory of childhood or time in the army? Have no idea in the world that he was betrothed? Why, he might even have been married already; if he could be unaware of an engagement, then why should he not have forgotten a wedding? A wife, children – surely this must have occurred to the Count's family. A cause for inquiry, at the very least.

She heard a voice outside, and the butler announced Dr Molloy. He was a slight man with grey hair and a most penetrating eye. Miss Darcy, he informed them, was now resting and should soon recover her equanimity. Perhaps they could give him some information about what had caused the nervous attack? He understood it was disagreeable news of some kind, but his patient was disinclined to speak of it.

Fanny gave him a lively account of what had happened; he pursed his lips and looked grave. Would she say that Miss Darcy was of a highly strung temperament? Ah, this young lady was her sister, who better to give him information on this point?

Camilla hesitated. Letty was certainly given to frets and fancies, but she wouldn't describe her as being highly strung. She listened to Dr Molloy's adroit questions with growing respect as he drew out from her a good portrait of her sister's habit of mind.

'It is as I thought. She must be watched, for a shock of this kind can have its effect on the body, the mind and body are, as you must know, inextricably linked, especially where young ladies are concerned. And in this case, if I might say so, her *amour propre* is touched, she would benefit from being encouraged not to dwell on the misfortune, but to have her attention turned in other directions.' He had bled her a little, administered a powder, and in due course a glass of red wine would prove restorative. On the morrow, gentle exercise, a walk in the park with her sister, would refresh her spirits.

Camilla thanked him. Letty was, in her opinion – one she kept to herself – suffering from temper as much as anything. She hated to be thwarted or deflected from her chosen path. It was a remarkable story, she said; Dr Molloy must have considerable experiences of such cases – was such a long-lasting loss of memory really possible?

Dr Molloy, Fanny's physician, has visited, and assures us that Letty will soon recover. I asked him about Tom's case, and he replied that such a sequence of events is indeed possible, and the effects of a blow to the head may remain with a man for the rest of his days. In this case, it is to be hoped that being reunited with his family and returning to formerly familiar places will restore Tom's memory; Dr Molloy says that it is often so.

To continue with my account of Tom's life in Belgium: he stayed with the family for many months, and they developed a great regard for him. Mr Roper told us that Tom and the lady who was the Count's daughter were reticent on the subject of their affection for one another, and he said that he was of the opinion that the Count, although he liked Tom well enough, was far from willing for his daughter to marry a man without a name, a past or a family. However, married they were.

She paused again, not wanting to mention the howl of dismay with which Letty had greeted the news of the marriage.

'Married? No, no it is impossible! You wicked man, you are making up a vile tale to torment me, you have been set to it by my sisters, it is not true, no, not a word of it.'

Belle and Georgina had hotly refuted this suggestion, their voices and Letty's rising to a crescendo of accusation and counter accusation, ending only when Letty buried her face in a handkerchief and collapsed into loud, shuddering sobs.

Letty was much affected by this news, as you may imagine. We exclaimed at the improbability of it ourselves; it seems hardly possible that three years should pass without Tom being recognised, but he

seldom came to Brussels, he said, and indeed, out of uniform and
dressed in the Belgian fashion, he would no doubt pass for a native of
the country. Although to be sure, there is the red hair, so striking; it
was that which caught Mr Roper's eye.

I know you will find this an amazing tale, but we have every
reason to believe it true, and one has to consider the great happiness
that the almost miraculous restoration of their son will have upon
Tom's parents and indeed all his family.

'What a prodigious long letter you are writing,' said Fanny, looking up from her newspaper.

Camilla sat back in her chair, considering the sheets in front of her. 'I want to tell them enough to counteract whatever extravagant rumours may reach them, but I think they would not like to hear of the violence of Letty's reaction upon hearing of Tom's resurrection and marriage.'

'For heaven's sake, do not mention it! I am quite sure it is better that they should not, for what, in Vienna, or Constantinople or wherever they may be, can they do about it? And for my part, I dread hearing that her name is being bandied about the clubs and coffee houses, for Tom Busby has made a fool of her, there is no denying that, even though there was no intention on his part to do so. One must heartily wish that she had not made such a parade of her loss and her grief. To present a picture of such devotion and then to have the object of it reappear, and with another woman as his wife, must make her look ridiculous and set tongues a-wagging.'

'You take a gloomy view. Why, how many people in London know about the strength of her attachment to Tom's memory? We are strangers in London, who will be interested?'

Fanny shook her head. 'No, that will not do,' she said in a decided voice. 'You come from a distinguished family, your father and mother move in the highest circles. Letty is the granddaughter and niece of an earl, and an heiress besides. There will be plenty of tittle-tattles from your part of the country who will remember the engagement and know how ostentatiously Letty has remained true to his memory. It is a mistake to show such sensibility. A young lady, a young unmarried lady, should always be careful to control her feelings. I pity her from the bottom of my heart, however, I know how enjoyable it is to indulge oneself in such a way.'

'Other people will allow that she has reason for being so upset,' Camilla said, although she knew quite well that Fanny, with her worldly sense, was in the right of it.

'Most will find it a source of amusement at the very least, and I can assure you there will be no end of spiteful gossip on the subject. Lord, how am I going to get you vouchers for Almack's with accounts of this affair flying about the town?'

'Oh, never mind Almack's,' Camilla said snappishly. 'Heavens, what does that matter?'

'It matters a great deal; this is London, and reputation is all.'

FIVE

The lamplighter was making his steady way down St James's, setting each gas lamp into glowing life against the gathering dusk. Gentlemen walked in to spend a while at their clubs before embarking on the evening round of social and amorous engagements.

Snipe Woodhead came briskly up the steps of Pink's club, a spruce man, who greeted friends and bowed to acquaintances, eager for news.

Sitting deep in a leather chair in the corner of the lobby, Wytton was hidden behind the sheets of his newspaper. Listening, rather than reading; Snipe's gossip was likely to be a great deal more interesting than an account of a woman taken up for highway robbery, and Wytton idly wondered what the fellow might have to talk about today. There were no great scandals running at this time, no rumours of crim. cons between this duke and that countess, no runs on the bank or alarms at the stock exchange, no riots near country seats to cause members to shake their heads and look solemn.

So the story of Tom Busby's miraculous reappearance in the land of the living caused a considerable stir among the members.

Had he ever met Busby? Wytton thought not, but surely there was some connection there with Sophie's cousins, those Darcy girls.

Men seized eagerly on the news.

'Busby? Tom Busby? Is he a member?'

'There's a Sir Robert Busby belongs to Brooks. A country member, one of your squires.'

'Sir Robert is this man's father. A Derbyshire family, Busby

Hall is somewhere in Derbyshire, I believe.' Snipe Woodhead had all the old families at his fingertips. 'A respectable enough estate, of three or four thousand a year. Only the one son.'

'And he was killed at Waterloo,' said a stocky young man with a cheerful, round face and startled eyebrows.

'That's the very point, Rampton,' Snipe said. 'He wasn't killed, after all. Young Roper saw him in Brussels, large as life. And married, married to some foreigner's daughter!'

'I don't believe it,' cried Rampton.

A thin man, a member Wytton knew only by sight, gave a crack of laughter. 'That is what they are saying, Rampton, and it won't please his father, you may be sure of it. But wasn't Busby betrothed? I am sure I saw the announcement in the *Gazette* at the time. To a Darcy, one of Fitzwilliam Darcy's girls; an excellent match that would have been. Those girls have forty or fifty thousand pounds apiece!'

So there was a connection, his memory hadn't played him false.

There was a moment's silence as those present contemplated the annual sum such a fortune would bring if invested in the five per cents.

'Whatever you may say, I shouldn't care to have Darcy for a father-in-law,' said Snipe Woodhead. 'He's a tremendous stickler, my word, one would have to mind one's Ps and Qs, no cosy armfuls on the side, you may be sure.'

An older member was quick to contradict him. 'Indeed, he can be haughty, but I remember when he was first in town, just down from Cambridge, he was not averse to a trifle of riot and rumpus.'

'That was when he was young and single,' said a new voice.

Wytton rustled the pages to allow himself a clearer view. Not that he needed to be discreet, no one was paying him the least attention. Yes, he thought he recognised that voice. It was Aloysius Harvey. When had he got back to England?

'A single man of one-and-twenty is a very different fellow from a married man with daughters; it is amazing what daughters can do to a man's sense of morality.'

A typical Harvey observation, with three troublesome daughters of his own.

A short, dark, military member – Colonel Pusey, wasn't it? – had been listening attentively to this conversation. 'How many daughters does Darcy have?'

'Four or five,' said Harvey. 'All grown up, I believe; he has boys as well, but they are younger. The Miss Darcys are all in London even now. They stay with Fitzwilliam's family while their father and mother are abroad. Constantinople, you know.'

'Are they pretty?' Pusey enquired.

'I'm not acquainted with them. You may ask Wytton if he comes in this evening; he is engaged to a cousin of theirs.'

'What, is his heiress a Darcy?' said Pusey. 'Surely not, I thought she was a merchant's daughter.'

His heiress, indeed! Wytton was stung. Merchant's daughter? He found he didn't relish having Sophie described in quite that way. They saw her as an object, a *res*. He saw her as all person, alive and so very charming. Charming in a way that many women were not. Give him an enchanting face, and a slender body and an innocent coquetry any day. You could keep your bewitching dazzler with the face of an angel and the soul of a harlot; he was done with fascinating women.

'I never thought Wytton would escape the clutches of Mrs B.'

'Did he escape, or did she?' said Harvey. 'I heard she found solace in George Warren's arms. She has a pretty foot.'

This raised a laugh, and Wytton shifted in his chair. Curse Harvey for his damnable gossiping remarks.

'Wytton marries Miss Sophie Gardiner,' Snipe said. 'The Gardiners are relations of Mrs Darcy.'

'Forty or fifty thousand, you say the Darcy girls are worth? And is the eldest wearing the willow for young Busby, do you suppose, Harvey?'

Harvey laughed. 'That won't wash now he's back from the dead.'

'I dare say Lady Fanny will take them about in society,' said Lord Rampton, a hopeful note in his voice.

Trust Rampton, a notorious gambler, to show an interest. He

was a man well known to his friends to be on the lookout for a likely heiress.

'I believe Grandville dines with the Fitzwilliams today,' said Snipe Woodhead. 'We can ask him about the young ladies if he is in the club tomorrow.'

'He'll be no use,' said Rampton. 'Tight as a button, that man, comes of all those years in the army. You will get nothing from him. I think I shall call on Lady F, a morning call would be quite in order. Then I can get a glimpse of the young ladies. Four or five of them, you say? It's too much to hope that they are beauties, but with portions like that, it don't much matter.'

'My sister saw them in Hookham's library,' said Harvey. 'Miss Darcy is uncommon fine-looking, she said. The next sister is nothing to her, perfectly amiable in appearance, though.'

Harvey's sister was an ethereal blonde, Wytton recalled; no, she wouldn't have a word of praise for a fair woman. Not that the second Darcy sister was so fair. Her looks had made no great impression on him, she was quite outshone by his Sophie, but she did have much the same colouring. Of course, Sophie's eyes were a softer grey and full of warmth; they held none of the unfeminine mirth he had noticed in her cousin's expressive eyes.

Unaware of the interest in her and her sisters, Camilla was endeavouring to bring Letty to see reason.

'You are a stranger to the tenderer emotions,' Letty said into her damp handkerchief. 'You do not know what it is to love, or to be betrayed.'

Camilla's patience was at snapping point. 'For heaven's sake, Letty, you haven't set eyes on Tom for three years. It is not as though he jilted you yesterday – or indeed, jilted you at all, in any real sense,' she added hastily, seeing her sister's lip begin to tremble again.

Fanny came rustling into the room. 'My dear Letty, let us be done with this. It is all very affecting, and distressing, too, but he is no more lost to you than he already was. Now, Sackree will be here directly to dress you and do your hair. You must change, you know, and make yourself ready for company.'

Letitia would have none of it. She wanted to spend the evening sighing and sobbing and giving way to her feelings. She didn't care what the world might say, she minded none of them, she had no intention of staying in London but would return – with her sisters – to Pemberley as soon as ever it could be arranged, where she would be away from curious eyes and could indulge her sorrow to her heart's content.

'You may run away to the country if you wish, but I shan't accompany you,' Camilla said roundly. 'And nothing short of main force would remove Georgina and Belle from town, no, nor Alethea either.' Her sympathy for the shock Letty had suffered had given way to irritation, and some degree of alarm. Fanny's worldly words had had no influence on Letty, yet somehow her sister must be brought to pull herself together and show, if not a happy countenance, at least a calm one.

She and Fanny exchanged despairing looks over Letty's bowed head. She shrugged, then sank down beside her sister. 'Listen to me, Letty. If you do not come down to dinner, it will be remarked upon, I assure you it will. The tale will be all round London; people will be agog to know how you have taken the news, you may count upon it.'

'Then they should have something better to think about. They do not know me. Why should I care for the opinion or gossip of a parcel of strangers? Fanny may say I am indisposed, that I have the headache.'

'Exactly what they wish to hear,' cried Fanny. 'Nothing could be more calculated to set people talking. No, no, you must come down and dine, and do the civil. If but a hint of your distress gets out, a whisper of how *desolée* you are made by this news, why, you will never live it down; society will judge you harshly, and you will feel the effects of it, indeed you will.'

Camilla saw that her sister, determined to abjure society, was unmoved. 'How they will laugh at you! Imagine how cross Papa will be when the news reaches him that his daughter is the laughing-stock of London.'

Letty bounced up from her chair, her wet handkerchief abandoned, her eyes flashing, her bosom heaving. 'Laugh! Laugh at me? They shall not do so.'

Fanny was quick to take her cue. She shook her head sadly. 'Camilla is right, indeed she is. I should not care to be the butt of such ridicule myself, although I am the most easy-going of creatures, but that, I admit, would upset me greatly. To be considered a joke – It is not to be thought of.'

Thank goodness, their words were finally reaching the mark. Laughter, ridicule, a joke? Letty took herself far too seriously to be able to dismiss the prospect of being an object of derision – a possibility that had never occurred to her, lost as she was in the image of herself as a wronged figure of enduring love.

Letty collapsed with some grace on to the nearest sofa. 'Send Sackree to me,' she said in weak tones. 'I shall try to endure this ordeal, although God knows, it will be hard.'

Camilla took Letty's hand. 'Fanny will be so grateful to you,' she whispered into her ear. 'Only think how she would blame herself if you were to become the talk of the town, and how bad you would feel for ruining the first party she has given for us. Papa would not be pleased at all, you know.'

With these final words, she led Fanny quickly from the room.

'Do not you think we should stay with her?' Fanny asked.

'No, for she would feel obliged to keep her face as long as can be; she needs to compose herself into some semblance of normality.'

And, she might have added, if sisterly loyalty hadn't pre-vented her, that Letty needed to work herself into the new role of distress valiantly hidden for the sake of others.

Fanny's dinners were usually successful, thanks to an excellent cook and her talent for choosing guests who were well-matched. However, tonight's was not one that she would recall with any satisfaction.

She had worried about Letitia all through her own toilette. Would she break down? Would she disgrace herself and her sisters through a display of emotion in front of others? Would she play her proper role?

Camilla had wondered this, too, but Miss Griffin, summoned to help her dress since Sackree was attending to her sister, had no doubts. Letty knew very well what was expected of her, and the difference between private and public behaviour. She had, after all, been bred up from childhood to company manners, had all the Darcy self-control within her power; in the end, the governess declared, pride would carry her through.

'And it is her pride rather than her heart that has been most affected, I may tell you,' said Miss Griffin, as she fastened the tiny hooks at the back of Camilla's bodice. 'For all her tears and protestations of undying love.'

'Do you not believe in undying love, Griffy?'

'Not outside the pages of a novel. Now hold still, or you will never be ready in time.'

'Will Alethea come downstairs to sing?'

'She says she would rather not.'

'It would annoy Letty if she were to join the company, even at Fanny's invitation.'

Miss Griffin thought about this as she set a jewel in Camilla's hair. 'Better angry than sad, is that it? I shall just mention that to Alethea. Only there's no persuading her to do what she does not want to, as you very well know. Not when it comes to music.'

At first, it seemed that all would go well. Letitia came down looking even more beautiful than usual, her eyes lustrous from all the tears, but without a trace of the puffiness or redness about her eyelids that might have been expected. She held herself straight with her head high; she was grave, but not sullen; she even smiled at a sally from Sir Sidney Leigh who stood talking to her before dinner was served, and she went through the round of introductions with composure and ease.

Which allowed Camilla to relax and survey the assembled company. Her heart had lifted when Sir Sidney came in. He was just as good-looking as she had remembered, his excellent figure set off by the well-cut black coat he was wearing. He looked to be in a good mood, saying something to Mr Fitz-william that made his host laugh and brought a smile and most flirtatious look from Fanny in response.

Well, so Fanny found Sir Sidney attractive, what was surprising about that? Or about Sir Sidney leaning down towards his hostess with an amused expression in his eyes and making what must be some outrageous remark, to judge by her sudden laughter?

Camilla's slight feeling of chagrin vanished as Pagoda Portal surged into the room, his twinkling amorous eyes resting with evident enthusiasm on Letty's bosom and then fastening themselves with a connoisseur's approval on the twins. Belle and Georgina sat beside one another on a small sofa, all smiles and inviting glances; even Mr Fitzwilliam had a softened look on his rather stern countenance as his gaze fell on his young cousins.

True to her word, Fanny had produced one Captain Allington, a dashing officer with a proud moustachio, who smiled and nodded when anyone looked in his direction, and was otherwise apparently quite content to stand as though on duty, looking handsome.

'He is a dolt, of course,' Fanny whispered to Camilla. 'Only so handsome, all the girls are in love with him. Do you think Letty demands sense in a man? Was – is, I mean – her Tom a man of sense?'

'That is a question indeed, ma'am, especially in the light of what we have learned about him today.'

'I do not mean her to fall in love with Captain Allington precisely, that would never do, but he might serve to give her thoughts a new direction.'

Camilla was watching Sir Sidney, deep in conversation with Letty, who looked almost cheerful. 'I believe Sir Sidney is doing his best as far as that is concerned,' Camilla said. 'Has he never married?'

Fanny frowned. 'No, although there was an attachment, an engagement, in fact, only the lady in question broke it off, a little before her wedding day. The day before, in fact. She was a Miss Harper, I believe. I do not know why she thought they would not suit. An excellent catch, I assure you, and with such an air, so much the man of fashion. He is the best of company, and all the hostesses compete for his presence. I was delighted he accepted for this evening.'

Lord and Lady Warren had been announced hard on Allington's heels. Camilla took an instant dislike to Lord

Warren, a burly, heavy-browed man with grizzled hair, who merely touched her fingertips when he was introduced to her, and then sauntered away to get a better look at the twins. Lady Warren was a thin, stylishly dressed woman, and she gave the twins a shrewish look before turning a sharp eye on Letitia and running her eyes over her face, figure and gown. Lady Warren was, Camilla knew, a connection through marriage on her mother's side, although neither she nor her sisters had previously met her.

'A distant connection,' her ladyship said in condescending tones when Letitia mentioned it.

Not so distant, Camilla said to herself: Lady Warren's brother, Mr Bingley, was married to their Aunt Jane. Lady Warren had spoken as though Letty were some encroaching upstart; well, if she did not care to make anything of the relationship, so much the better. Camilla did not, she decided, care for Lady Warren any more than for her husband, an opinion reinforced a few minutes afterwards when Lady Warren came over to ask barbed questions about her parents.

'Of course, I have seen so little of them this past few years, buried in the country as they all are. Quite rustic, I always say. So Mr Darcy is gone abroad? And your mother with him? I dare say she does not care to let him out of her sight. We know how gentlemen behave when they are on their own in other countries. They are such sad creatures.'

The bustle of another arrival gave Camilla a moment to think better of the retort she had been about to make, and a balding, middle-aged man of medium height walked into the room, a younger woman, who must be his daughter, on his arm.

'Grandville,' cried Fitzwilliam, crossing the room with quick strides to greet him. 'Here you are. And Mrs Rowan, your servant, ma'am.'

Camilla looked at Mrs Rowan, and then looked again, sure that her face was familiar. Mrs Rowan smiled, and moved to her side. 'I believe we know one another. We were both boarders at Mrs Charlton's school, only you were a mere girl, and I was a parlour boarder while my father was abroad.'

'Why, of course,' Camilla cried, pleased.

She had spent a year at this fashionable seminary in London, and although she hadn't been exactly unhappy, she had been homesick, and had made few friends among the other young ladies. Henrietta Rowan, as she now was, had been an exception. Her intelligence, vivacity and sense of fun had greatly appealed to her.

Mrs Rowan was also a woman of fashion, but it was her own fashion. She was by no means small, either in height or personality, and she was adorned with a trailing oriental scarf, a vivid silk sash and several bracelets. She had numerous ornaments dotted about her person, and wore more pearls round her neck than Camilla would have thought possible. She had large pearls in her ears and more in the silk turban on her head. The effect could have been ridiculous, but on her, it was most striking.

'You are thinking how oddly I am dressed, and indeed it is so, for I dress to please myself. When I was married, for I am a widow, you know, I used to wear such correct clothes, so dull, so proper. After my husband's death, I made up my mind to wear all the garments and ornaments I like best. I am no kind of a beauty, you see, and so it does me no harm to have a style of my own.'

Her almond eyes narrowed with laughter at the sight of Camilla's face. 'Are you shocked to hear me speaking with such lightness of my late husband?'

Camilla was too honest to deny it.

'He died only a year after we were married, of a fever he contracted while abroad and I never really got to know him. He was much older than I, and although affectionate, he was not a memorable person. Why did I marry him? That is not a story for this company. Now, tell me all about yourself. Have you been in London long? Why are you come here at this dismal time of year? That is your sister Letitia, is it not? Was she not at Mrs Charlton's with you? Who are the two dazzlers on the sofa? I am sure I have never seen them before. One would most certainly remember them.'

'My younger sisters. They are twins, you know.'

'Good gracious, and so different in colouring, although one cannot help noticing those remarkable eyes. Are you all out?'

'Letty and I are; the twins are supposed still to be in the schoolroom.'

Henrietta Rowan looked surprised. 'The schoolroom? You amaze me. Not for much longer, perhaps.'

'I fear not. I suspect they will lead us all a merry dance now we are in town and without my mother and father to keep them in check.'

'Your parents are abroad. I read of your father's appointment in the *Gazette*. So you are left in Lady Fanny's care, are you? She knows how to go on well enough and will keep a close eye on your sisters, you may be sure, if one is needed.'

No one mentioned the name of Busby at dinner, although Camilla felt sure it was on the tip of more than one tongue, and Fanny could hardly eat a mouthful for fear that something would occur to overset Letitia's admirable poise; surely she was too serene, too well-behaved, such a contrast to the scenes upstairs.

For Camilla's part, she had no worries about Letty while she was in company. Her sister had a slightly tragic look about her, the air of one acquainted with suffering, but only when she was not being addressed, and she felt quite sure that her party manners would carry her through the evening – at least, they would if everyone behaved as well as they had so far. For she was sure they all knew the story, and that they were all, overtly or covertly, eyeing Letty to see how she was bearing up.

Camilla gave Fanny a reassuring smile, and turned her attention back to Mr Portal, who was being most entertaining about elephants. Dinner drew to a close, the covers were drawn, and finally the ladies left the men to their port and withdrew to the drawing-room on the first floor of the house.

Fanny headed off Lady Warren, who had made a beeline for Letitia upon their entering the room. Mrs Rowan took in the situation at a glance, and moved over to join Letitia on the sofa. The twins headed for the pianoforte at the far end of the room and began to play duets in a careless way, quite uninterested in impressing such an exclusively female gathering.

With another sharp glance in Letitia's direction, Lady Warren came across to Camilla, whose heart sank as her disagreeable companion resumed her interrupted interrogation. She felt that it would be almost impossible to stem the tide of impertinent questions and assertions from this clever, determined woman, with her pushing and forceful ways; impossible, that was, without replying to her in such a way as must horrify Fanny. Lady Warren was, after all, a guest in this house.

'Your father, of course, was quite one of my beaux in the old days. Your mother is related to the Gardiners, is she not?' She didn't wait for an answer. 'One may meet the Gardiners everywhere these days, or almost everywhere, I do not believe their daughter has vouchers for Almack's, although I may be mistaken. I do not recall ever having seen her there. She is engaged to Mr Wytton, a good catch for her, I must say, an old and distinguished family, and there is the abbey, of course.'

For a moment, Camilla lost the thread of what Lady Warren was saying. Abbey? Gothic visions of hooded monks crowded into her mind, and then she pulled herself together. Was Mr Wytton rich enough to buy an abbey as the saying was, or did he possess one? She didn't like to ask, but Lady Warren soon enlightened her. 'In the family since the time of the Dissolution, of course, I wonder how Miss Sophie will go on in such a place, it is hardly what she has been used to.'

Vulgar woman, she thought, answering with no more than a polite smile.

Lady Warren didn't care to see her arrows go astray. 'They say Wytton's mother is not happy with the match, not happy at all. There is no more to it than the money, so they say.'

'I believe Mr Wytton to be sincerely attached to my cousin,' she said coldly.

'Ninety thousand pounds is a consideration indeed. He is a rich man on his own account, but they say he neglects his estate to go on these jaunts abroad, and he mounts expeditions, you know. To out of the way places, and underground, too.'

'Underground, ma'am?'

Lady Warren's eyes were icy, her laugh tinkling. 'I mean, he sets men to digging up old pots and relics. It is costly, digging up such things.'

'But rewarding from the point of view of scholarship.'

'Oh, scholarship! Well, if you are to talk of scholarship – I know nothing of such matters. It is hardly a suitable subject for a woman.'

There was a long pause, and one of those coincidental silences fell over the room, as the twins left off playing to search for another piece of music, and Fanny's conversation with Henrietta Rowan and Letitia reached a lull. Lady Warren's voice held the stage.

'Are not you and your sisters particularly acquainted with Mr Busby? It is so remarkable, this news of his return to the living, and of his marriage. It is all over town. They say he was engaged to an English young lady, that he preferred oblivion to such a marriage and that this talk of his losing his memory is all a ruse. People say he has all his wits, and knew quite well what he was about.'

Despite herself, Camilla turned to look at Letty, while Belle gave a whoop of laughter and Georgina exclaimed, 'Oh, you must not say that, it is all quite untrue, for Tom Busby had no idea what he was about.'

Fanny had gone quite pale, and the colour had drained from Letty's face, leaving only a flash of brightness on her cheeks. She had stiffened, but was still controlling herself admirably. Thank God, Camilla said inwardly; she could hear footsteps, masculine voices, laughter. Here were the men come to join them at last.

They entered the room, bringing energetic conversation and a waft of port with them. Mr Fitzwilliam was deep in conversation with Mr Grandville, while Mr Portal's shrewd eyes flickered to the sofa and the rigid figure of Letitia. Lord Warren exchanged knowing glances with his wife, and Captain Allington looked imposingly vacant.

Sir Sidney, with a quick look at Lady Warren and a mocking glance in the direction of the giggling twins, made his way to Letitia's side, begged leave to sit beside her, and began to talk about the weather in Derbyshire.

This had only been an opening skirmish for Lady Warren, who was by no means done with the subject of Tom Busby.

'The young man we were just now speaking of came from

your part of the world, I believe, Miss Camilla? Is he not from Derbyshire?'

'The Busbys are near neighbours of ours.'

'Why then,' cried Lady Warren with an affected laugh, 'you are the very person to tell us more. My love,' she said, addressing herself to her husband, who was leaning on the pianoforte, and ogling the twins, 'we may now hear all about the Busbys. How I feel for Mrs Busby! How distracted she must be, how delighted to have her son restored to her.'

'Devil of a shock,' said Lord Warren. 'Especially when he comes tripping up to the door with a foreign wife on his arm. Nobody seems to know who this count is, or what the girl's fortune may be. If she has any fortune at all, which is doubtful, not after old Boney's rampages across the continent. Many an old family has suffered irretrievable losses.' He looked pleased at this notion. 'Yes, there are many over there who do not hold their heads quite so high these days. Not that they ever did, not according to our way of things. A foreign title is not to be compared with an English one.'

'There's no knowing what kind of a family this girl is from,' said Lady Warren with a flick of her eyes to where Letitia was still resolutely discussing how often the frost prevented hunting in her native county. 'She may be anyone, a merchant's daughter, some jumped-up cit who took a title during the Bonapartist confusion.'

Mr Fitzwilliam had caught the sense of unease in the room. 'Count de Broise's title is an ancient one, Lady Warren, going back to the days of the Holy Roman Empire. No, no, the Busbys need not blush for such a match.'

Lady Warren would not contradict her host. 'I most sincerely pity the young lady he left behind, however. So lowering to lose your future husband in the war and then have him return with a wife to his name!'

'Oh, as to that,' cried Fanny, 'it was all long ago, quite three years and more. Nothing more tedious than old stories, don't you agree? Pray, have you seen these new shawls in from Paris? I declare, I shall be positively mopish if my dear Fitzwilliam does not let me have one, although they are a shocking price.

54

Camilla, my dear, ring the bell and ask Fell if Alethea and Miss Griffin are coming down.'

'Why, here they are, Fanny,' said her husband, as Miss Griffin stalked into the room behind Alethea, a picture of maidenly virtue in frothy white muslin and a pink sash. 'My nieces, you must know, are notable musicians, and since we are only family and friends here tonight, Alethea has ventured out of the schoolroom to join us.'

'So have Belle and Georgina, sir,' Alethea pointed out as she sat on the chair Mr Portal had courteously put forward for her. 'Are they going to play?'

Georgina gave her younger sister a scornful look and announced that she and Belle were happy to play. They charmed their way through two or three duets; both of them musical, they played well, and looked enchanting. The men watched with great complaisance, and Camilla could breathe again, as good manners prevented even Lady Warren from carrying on with her spiteful conversation during their performance.

Letitia declined to sing, declaring that she had had a slight sore throat, it was always so in Town on foggy days. This was true enough, although Camilla knew quite well that her spring sore throats were an annual source of considerable misery in Derbyshire, far from the dirt and bad air of the capital.

Lady Warren was ready with remarks about how depression of the spirits could make a girl ill, how affairs of the heart rendered young women peculiarly susceptible to infections of the lungs and throat, how—

Alethea gave her a look of contempt and brushed past her chair on the way to take her place at the pianoforte. 'Camilla, will you play for me?'

The company put on an approving face. Modestly-dressed, pretty-behaved young ladies who were soon to emerge from the schoolroom showing off their expensively acquired accomplishments gave a sense of order and decorum in an alarming world. The youngest Miss Darcy would sing two or three sweet airs, they would applaud and congratulate, tea would be drunk, the familiar rituals of society would once again have been observed.

Camilla looked at the music Alethea had placed on the stand and shot Miss Griffin a swift look of enquiry. Miss Griffin gave a tiny shrug of her bony shoulders, as if to say, it is nothing to do with me, and fixed her gaze on the fireplace. Well, if Alethea wanted to sing Mozart, so be it.

The effect of her singing was electric.

Lady Warren gave an exaggerated jolt of surprise and then fixed her features into a look of prim disapproval. Lord Warren cleared his throat and looked uneasy. He was unfamiliar with the works of Mozart and was not at all sure that he liked what he was hearing.

'By Jove,' whispered Captain Allington, who had an ear. 'Ain't that the thing?'

Pagoda Portal sat back in frank enjoyment, his foot moving and his fingers waving in time to the music.

The twins had moved across to the window. They twitched the heavy drapes aside and surveyed the street. Alethea's music held no novelty for them, and a handsome buck might be passing in the street below, a more pleasing object of their interest.

Letitia sat with her eyes closed for a moment, affected against her will by the power of the music. She considered Mozart wholly unsuitable for Alethea to sing; indeed, unsuitable for performance anywhere.

Camilla, looking up from the instrument, saw Sir Sidney's attention fixed on Alethea. There was nothing of the satyr in his regard, he rather had the air of a connoisseur, of a collector who had found some new and exquisite item. His eyes met Camilla's, and he smiled, shook his head slightly and was lost once more in the music.

'Well,' said Fanny as the last of her guests' carriages rumbled away into the night. 'I declare, I never want to go through such an evening again. Letty, my love, I have nothing but praise for you. That odious woman! Mr Fitzwilliam, whatever possessed you to invite the Warrens? I beg you will not do so again in a hurry, for he is a fool and she is the greatest scandalmonger in Town!'

'He is not so very bad, and his family has some influence in Lincolnshire where there is soon to be an election; we hope the result may be favourable for us, and every vote counts, as you know.'

'Oh, politics. Politics are the ruin of any woman's dinners. Alethea, how well you sang, such an astonishing and beautiful voice as you have. Sir Sidney and Allington were entranced by the music, and Mr Portal, whose good opinion is worth having, let me tell you young ladies, for he is so rich and influential, said he had never been so well-entertained at a private party. I hope he was referring to the music,' she added, with a doubtful look at her husband.

'It would not be suitable for a more formal gathering, however,' said Mr Fitzwilliam. 'Perhaps, Alethea, if you are to sing for us again, as I hope you will, for young ladies must learn to perform in company without appearing self-conscious or nervous, there are some English songs you could learn. I'm sure Miss Griffin—'

'I will mention it to her teachers, sir,' said Miss Griffin. 'Alethea's singing has long been the concern of visiting masters, as she is beyond a governess's skills.'

'Yes, quite, I do see. For myself I like a ballad or some such song. That kind of music must always be acceptable.'

Alethea smiled sardonically at her sisters and bid the company a civil good night, with a pitying look for Fitzwilliam as she left the room.

SIX

February, said Mrs Gardiner, seemed to be lasting for ever, with its chilly, blustery winds and violent rainstorms. London was still thin of company; it would be a little while before the rich, the giddy and the gay came flocking for the season proper, but this and the bad weather led to a certain cosy intimacy among those who were, for whatever reason, fixed in Town.

Bankers and rich merchants such as Mr Gardiner were at their places of business, of course, mostly regarding with a benevolent contempt those of their more genteel acquaintance who went to be idle in the country. Some longed for the day when they could purchase a country estate and set up for a gentleman; for many, the pleasures of making money and deals were far greater than any delights offered by the round of country-house visiting and the Englishman's outdoor pursuits of killing anything that moved.

Mr Gardiner was not among those hankering for admittance to the ranks of the landed gentry. He was pleased that one of his daughters had married a gentleman of position and fortune with a snug property in Kent, but he secretly preferred the company of his other son-in-law, a busy, active lawyer who was rising fast in his profession. He was happy with the match that had been made between his youngest girl and Alexander Wytton; he liked the man for himself, and had a high regard for his brains and learning.

'You had better apply yourself to some study before you are caught up in a whirl of parties,' he told Sophie. 'A frivolous girl such as you is no wife for a sensible man.'

'He likes me just as I am,' said Sophie. 'He doesn't want a

blue-stocking. for a wife. Like my cousin Camilla,' she added cattily. 'She frightens all her beaux away. That's what comes of having your nose in a book half the day and walking round London looking at a lot of ugly old buildings and statues and such like. No one will ever want to marry her if she don't change her ways.'

Mrs Gardiner exclaimed at her daughter's vulgarity. 'Camilla is very like her mother, and look what a splendid marriage she made.'

'Aunt Elizabeth is full of fun, and loves clothes and balls, even now,' said Sophie. 'She doesn't care at all for a lot of old Greeks and Egyptians, or if she does, she didn't when she was.on the lookout for a husband.'

'Camilla loves a party,' said her father, rising from the table. 'And I thought she looked as pretty as anything the other night at that little dance Lady Rampton put on for you young people.'

Sophie made a moue at her father's departing back, but not an unpleasant one, for she was very fond of him, despite what she considered his old-fashioned ways. 'Jamie Rampton is hanging out for a rich wife,' she said. 'That's why his mother is come back to town, all in a rush when she got wind of five heiresses. I suppose she thinks that one of my cousins might be persuaded to take to her precious son.'

Mrs Gardiner wondered, yet again, why the exclusive girls' seminary that Sophie had attended for three years, not to mention the attentions of a series of the most highly trained and ladylike governesses before she went to school, had left Sophie's mind so little improved. Her behaviour in company was un-exceptionable, but within doors, among the immediate members of her family, her views and speech left much to be desired.

'I do not think Camilla is on the lookout for a husband just at present, although a young woman must always be mindful that it is her duty to marry, and, if she is of good family and has a large fortune, to marry well. Nor does Letty appear to be in want of a husband; indeed, I fear that she is quite opposed to the married state at this moment.'

Mrs Gardiner reached for another piece of toast and then,

with a sigh, withdrew her hand; she must take care of what she ate, or none of her new dresses ordered for the season would fit her. She had a tendency to plumpness, and no wish to look like a parcel in the high-waisted dresses that were still the fashion. It would be a mercy when waists and stays came back into fashion, as was sure to happen. 'It is a pity so many people know of Letty's disappointment.'

'It's hardly a secret that could be kept, when her engagement had been announced in the *Gazette*.'

'True, but that was a while ago, and memories are short. If she had formed another attachment, no one would have had anything to say about it.'

Sophie tightened a curl round her finger. 'If she didn't go round looking such a misery, people would talk less. I think it ill-bred of her to sulk, for that is what she's doing.'

Mrs Gardiner couldn't but agree. Letty was doing herself no good in the eyes of the fashionable world, always eager for a fresh scandal. Men were laying bets in the clubs, she had heard, as to whether Letty would faint clean away when she came face to face with Tom Busby.

'Men are so horrid,' said Sophie, who was on her third slice of toast, having a good appetite and no fears for her figure.

'It isn't as if she had been thrown over in any direct way. Mr Busby could hardly help losing his memory.'

'People are saying that it was no such thing, that when he had been wounded, he saw it as a way out of an engagement he regretted.'

'Indeed, the circumstances are such— It is impossible, of course, for a man to end an engagement, quite out of the question. However, it would almost have done Letty less harm if she herself had broken the engagement.'

'That would have made her a jilt, and there is nothing worse than a jilt,' said Sophie with scorn. 'You know how the old tabbies go on when a girl ends a formal engagement. Would you not be angry with me if I said that I didn't want to marry Mr Wytton after all?'

Sophie's eyes were on her plate as she spoke, and she stabbed at a crumb with her finger.

'Oh, my love, don't be ridiculous, it is not at all the same, Letty was never in your happy situation. Her engagement was a mistake, and I said so at the time. It was folly to rush into it simply because Tom Busby had been recalled to his regiment and was going to Belgium. All very well in the pages of a novel, but I cannot think why her parents gave their consent.'

In fact, she knew perfectly well why Mr and Mrs Darcy had agreed to it; there was no dealing with Letitia in one of her obstinate moods, and the young couple had seemed to be much attached. 'I hear from Fanny Fitzwilliam that Captain Allington is showing Letty a good deal of attention, so perhaps one soldier will drive out another.'

'Captain Allington!' cried Sophie, her last piece of toast suspended in mid-air. 'You must be wrong, you are quite mistaken. He has no fortune, he cannot be considered a suitable match for a Miss Darcy.'

'Oh, I dare say there is nothing serious to it. I believe they share a great love of riding; Letty is a notable horsewoman, and Camilla does not ride, so she will be glad of the Captain's company.'

Sophie put down her toast, uneaten, and rose from the table. 'You would never let me ride in the park with Captain Allington.'

'The cases are quite different, my love. Your cousin is a woman of one-and-twenty, not a girl of seventeen.'

'You even objected to my dancing with the Captain more than twice in one evening,' said Sophie, pausing in the doorway.

'My dear, that is all behind you now you are engaged.'

Sophie's mind was on another track. 'I suppose my cousins will receive vouchers for Almack's.'

This was a sore subject, and Mrs Gardiner sighed. Not all Mr Gardiner's wealth nor his wide circle of influential friends had enabled Mrs Gardiner to persuade the patronesses of Almack's to give her the vouchers that would have allowed Sophie to attend the weekly subscription balls. Heiress she might be, but her fortune came from trade.

'When you consider that Lady Jersey's fortune was a banking

one, and what is banking if not trade, it is unreasonable. But do not dwell on it, I beg you. Mr Wytton seldom attends Almack's, he has told us more than once that he considers such affairs a dreadful bore.'

Sophie went to her room, and Mrs Gardiner told the servants to take away the toast before she succumbed to temptation. She sat at the table with the coffeepot, consoling herself for Sophie's exclusion from the balls by the knowledge that although the older Miss Darcys might have the entrée to Almack's, they were neither of them able to hold a candle to Sophie as far as prettiness went.

Had Mrs Gardiner but known it, Fanny Fitzwilliam was exercised in her mind on the subject of Almack's. She was likewise at the breakfast table, sitting alone with her husband. The girls had breakfasted earlier.

'They must go,' she said to her husband, who was deep in his morning newspaper.

'Eh? Who must go? Are you turning off a servant? That is entirely your affair, my dear. Do not be bothering me with such things.'

'I am talking about Almack's; Letty and Camilla and Almack's.'

'Do you go to Almack's? But it is not Wednesday today – and, indeed, the balls do not begin before March.'

'You are quite right, but when they do begin, the girls will need vouchers.' She looked pensive, and sighed as she pushed her cup away.

'Is there a problem? Are you not on good terms with the patronesses? Surely you have not crossed Lady Jersey, or Countess Lieven?'

'No, no, I know my duty as far as they are concerned, I am on perfectly good terms with them all – or at least, not on bad terms. Only, you know how it is. If the patronesses, dreadful hypocrites that they are, take it into their heads that there is any breath of scandal hanging over Letty, then she – and Camilla – will be refused vouchers of admission. Which would lead to a great deal more talk and gossip. Mrs Burrell – horrid woman, always such a cold fish – passed a chilly comment only yesterday about Letty and the Busby affair.'

Mr Fitzwilliam frowned, folded up his paper and laid it on the table. 'Letty behaved very well the other evening, in the circumstances. She seems a little down, to be sure, but what can she have done to set the world talking?'

'Her spirits are depressed, and it shows. Especially when she is with Camilla, who is so full of life and laughter. Sir Sidney commented on it when we were at the Ramptons. I had quite thought he was a little *épris* in that direction, he did seem to admire Letty, only she has become quite dull, you see.'

'Sir Sidney? I suppose he may be looking out for a wife. At least he is no fortune hunter. He has a considerable income and is not one of your gamesters; he manages his affairs very well. Does Letty have a liking for him?'

'Letty,' said Fanny tartly, 'has no interest in the male sex whatsoever. She wants nothing to do with London, or society; she says she only wishes to be allowed to return to Pemberley.'

'Let her rusticate in Derbyshire for a while, then, if it will help her. I should have thought it would have the opposite effect; young Busby hails from those parts, does he not? The whole neighbourhood is bound to be abuzz with the story.'

'Exactly, besides the unhappiness of being where all the scenes of her courtship will come flooding into her memory. No, she shan't go home. It would cause no end of talk, to be off just at the start of the season. Everyone would know why it was. And she declares that not only she, but all her sisters must go back to Derbyshire. Imagine how impossible it would be to explain to Mr Darcy why all his girls had decamped from London even before the season had got under way.'

Her cousins must be aware how important an appearance at Almack's was, but they didn't seem at all concerned when Fanny mentioned that there might be a problem with vouchers.

'For my own part, Fanny, I do not mind so much,' said Camilla, who was getting ready to go out for a walk. 'I love a ball, indeed I do, but there are plenty of dances we may go to, are there not, apart from Almack's? And indeed, there can be no question of Belle and Georgina going this year, and they will object violently if Letty and I go and they are excluded.'

Fanny smiled as she thought of the twins. 'It is a shame they may not go, but I take your word for it that your parents would not wish it.'

Privately, she agreed with this view. Belle and Georgina, each a very pretty girl, made such a ravishing pair, that there was a danger of even Letty's beauty being eclipsed, and Camilla's own modest good looks would be quite overshadowed. Although Camilla did have her own charms of liveliness and a playful wit, these were not necessarily ones that showed to advantage in the stuffy and somewhat subdued atmosphere of an Almack's ball.

If she could find a husband for Letty, and for Camilla, too, then the twins— Only the older girls were far from desperate for husbands, what with Letty cherishing her broken heart and prating about Pemberley and the hatefulness of Town, and Camilla casting an all too cynical eye over all the eligible young men. Perhaps Sir Sidney would win her favour – she had thought the other evening that he seemed to be paying her some attention – although the matrons and dowagers these days tended to consider him a confirmed bachelor. No one had ever got to the bottom of that unfortunate business with Miss Harper, to be sure, but what had that to do with his marrying now? He must be in need of an heir.

He was an attractive man, she felt his attraction herself. Handsome, with an assured air and a good deal of cleverness about him, he might be the very man to catch Camilla's fancy. He was older than she was, which was all to the good, since she found so much in younger men to make her laugh. He was cultured, well-travelled – hadn't he spent a year abroad after the Peace of Amiens, in the year two? He had gone to Italy, and had travelled in France as well, she remembered hearing, and had been lucky not to have been stranded there like so many of his fellow countrymen and women when Bonaparte marked the resumption of hostilities by ordering the arrest of any English person on French soil.

Sir Sidney was a connoisseur and altogether an urbane man;

yes, he was just such a one as might do for Camilla. He was not rumoured to be of an ardent temperament, gossip had never linked his name with any of the flightier high-born ladies in his circle, but then no doubt he looked for his amorous encounters in the world of the *demi-monde*, like so many other men.

She was not sure what Camilla's feelings might be, for beneath the laughter and liveliness lay a good deal of reserve. She was like her father, who had never been one to show his innermost feelings. His contemporaries might laugh and cry and be as emotional as they liked; she had never seen him other than in control of himself.

It was a pity that Letty did not take after Darcy in that. She was all too willing to indulge her emotions. As for Belle and Georgina – well, they were young and overflowing with good humour. Belle's languid airs had an appeal quite lacking in Letty's worries and glooms, and Georgina was as full of spirit as you could wish.

'That reminds me,' Fanny said to Camilla, 'Dawson tells me that Belle and Georgina have hardly a dress fit to wear, she says they must have grown since the gowns they have were made.'

Camilla nodded. 'They have grown, I noticed it as soon as they arrived. How tiresome of them, for now they are in London, they will want more fashionable gowns. It will be impossible to keep them in schoolroom clothes.'

'No, indeed not, and it would be unsuitable, for they are quite grown up, you know, however much you and Letty want them to keep upstairs.'

Miss Griffin had her own views on this subject, and she had expressed them to Camilla in her outspoken way. 'It won't do. I cannot have them up here, buzzing around like flies in a bottle, discontented, their minds full of nothing but parties and beaux, as they will call the young men, full of resentment at being kept away from all the pleasures of town. I confess I have failed with them. Nothing I have done has given their minds a proper turn; they are bent on frivolity and enjoyment, and I wash my hands of them.'

Miss Griffin was seated at a small writing table in one of the top-floor rooms, a pile of paper beside her. She was engaged upon a literary work; much given to reading novels and to telling the girls exciting and improbable stories while they were gathered round the schoolroom fire, she had yielded to their persuasion and set about taking up her pen to record the more lurid of her heroine's doings.

'How is it coming on?' Camilla asked hanging over the back of her chair, trying to sneak a quick read; she longed to know what Miss Griffin's story was about.

Miss Griffin waved a deprecatory hand towards the quarto pages, neatly covering up any visible words with another sheet of paper. The sound of scales came from next door, where Alethea was practising. 'That is another thing; it is hard to keep Alethea's attention on her books, when all she can think of is music. Next week she goes to sing to Signor Silvestrini, and if he chooses to take her as a pupil, I dare say she will be even worse. I cannot feel I am fulfilling the terms of my engagement with your family, Camilla, indeed I am not.'

'Oh, such stuff,' Camilla said at once. 'Why, you know how pleased Papa and Mama have always been with you, and Papa often says he is delighted to have two educated daughters. He knows as well as I do that there is nothing to be done about Belle and Georgina, indeed, you have done more than any-one else could have, you must believe me. They have some accomplishments, they can speak French and keep accounts. They have empty heads otherwise, but that is their nature, and no one could change that.'

She paused and patted Miss Griffin's shoulder. 'My Aunt Georgiana says that they take after my Aunt Lydia, who was very wild when she was young. She married a man Papa would not have in the house. You will remember her coming to stay on her own.'

'I remember Mrs Wickham, as she was then, very well. She lost her husband in the Peninsula, is that not so? And has married again.'

'I believe so, to some man of fashion. She lives in London, but I know that Papa does not wish us to see her more than politeness dictates. I fancy she moves in quite different circles to those of the Fitzwilliams.'

Miss Griffin was not to be deflected from the subject of Belle and Georgina. 'If they are not to be in the schoolroom with Alethea, then they must go about in society. Lady Fanny seems willing enough to take on such a responsibility, although I fear they will eat up her time; it will leave you and Letty to your own devices.'

'Oh, do not worry about us. Letty is determined to mope for the present, and as long as Fanny will escort me to the kind of evening parties where I cannot go alone, I shall be perfectly content.'

'Miss Griffin is of your mind,' Camilla told Fanny, knowing that this would please her cousin. 'She is no longer prepared – that is, she does not think the twins belong in the schoolroom any more. Only, she says that if they are to go about in society, they must have a maid. It will be too much for Sackree to look after and dress all four of us.'

Fanny's face brightened. 'Does she say so indeed? Well, in that case, there can be no objection, for I would not for the world cause your governess to go off in a miff. You know how it is with these family retainers; I dare say your parents would never forgive me if she left.'

'There is no question of that. Letty and I would never agree to her going, especially not on account of Belle and Georgina, and how would Alethea go on without her? It would not be so easy to find a new governess for her, I can tell you.'

Fanny stood somewhat in awe of Alethea's character and talents, even though she told herself it was absurd to take any notice of a chit of a sixteen-year-old girl, and she had not the slightest wish to see Miss Griffin depart – besides, for the twins to come downstairs and go about in society was exactly what she wished for.

'I will summon my dressmaker immediately,' she said. 'And I shall talk to Dawson about a maid, she will know what is best.'

It was not a day for walking in the park. There was a bitterness in the wind, and a greyness in the sky that took away any pleasure in being out, even for Camilla, who usually delighted in the exercise. The smells of London were caught in the damp air: horses, smoke, the scent of the river carried on the wind. Sackree had been grumbling from the moment they had turned the corner out of Aubrey Square and had been struck by a particularly icy gust of wind. A quarter of an hour of this was enough to make Camilla abandon her walk and decide instead to call on Mrs Rowan in nearby Bruton Street.

Mrs Rowan's house was one of those up-and-down houses built at the beginning of the previous century with a flat façade, prim windows and neat red brickwork. The hall was not large, and the staircase plain, so the first-floor apartment into which she was shown by a little black page was therefore even more of a surprise. It was a fine, large room with three sash windows overlooking a small square, bare of greenery at this time of year.

Outside, all was grey and forlorn. Within, the room was a blaze of colour; reds and dark pinks with splashes of purple and gold. There were Turkey carpets on the floor, and others hanging on the wall between a spread of pictures: portraits, landscapes, miniatures, watercolours and a number of unusual drawings of be-sworded men in strange robes, with red tasselled hats upon their heads. Chairs and sofas were set in little groups, some near to a merrily crackling fire, others placed round tables, or in an intimate huddle in a corner of the room.

The coverings were silk brocade, in shades of pink that she had never seen before, and everywhere more glowing colour was provided by the silks and damasks of the cushions to be found on every seat and heaped on the floor – delightful, plump, soft cushions redolent of comfort and ease.

There were a number of people in the room. Mrs Rowan detached herself from a small group gathered near the fireplace and came forward at once to greet her, both hands outstretched.

'How glad I am that you are come.' She laughed at the expression on Camilla's face. 'You are looking round with an air of astonishment at finding yourself in such strange surroundings! It is often so with people on their first visit. My father lived in Turkey when I was a child and I stayed there with him for several years after my mother died. I developed a taste for the furnishings and indeed for some of the customs of the Ottomans. Now, let me see, whom do you know?'

Pagoda Portal was there, together with a surprising number of other morning callers, although after a few minutes Camilla found herself wondering only that Mrs Rowan's friends and acquaintances should choose ever to call on anyone else.

She was pleased to find that Sir Sidney Leigh was there, and gratified when he smiled at her and came over.

'Come, here is a sofa we may sit upon. Let us take possession of it instantly, for I hear footsteps on the stairs, and Mrs Rowan's guests are often so numerous that one is obliged to stand, or to loll upon her cushions.'

'The cushions look very comfortable,' she said.

'Indeed, they may be, but I do not choose to loll. One may be comfortable when down, but then one cuts such an undistinguished figure while striving to be up again. Let the young cubs have the cushions. One may grant the young suppleness of limb, if one cannot say as much for their minds.'

'I see no young cubs,' she said, looking around the room. She saw Mr Wytton, caught his eye, received a cool nod. Mr Layard was beside him, and he gave her a lively wave of greeting, accompanied by the friendliest smile.

'They will come later. I tell Mrs Rowan not to admit them. What have we to do with these callow young fellows, some of them not even down from the university?'

'And what does Mrs Rowan reply to that?'

'Oh, she says they must learn to be civilised, and if they do not begin at that age, they will be insupportable by the time they are six- or seven-and-twenty.'

'Mrs Rowan is quite right, in my opinion. Young men must learn how to behave in society.'

'Young men may learn their manners elsewhere. There is no excuse for them now, they may travel abroad at their leisure, and get polish and address that way. Let the French and Italians give them their lessons and spare us the trouble.'

She laughed. 'I believe you have travelled abroad a good deal, sir.'

'Yes, with interruptions for war; I consider it not the least of that Frenchman's sins that he treated travellers so cavalierly.'

'Do not speak of the war, I beg you,' called Mrs Rowan from the other side of the room. 'It is a banned subject in my house; we are to be concerned only with the present.'

'Why, surely not, ma'am,' protested Mr Wytton. 'For here am I telling Pagoda all about the antiquities that have lately been shipped to this country and transported to the abbey – they are certainly not of the present, so must I not mention them?'

'Oh, classical subjects are all very well, and so fashionable that you may hear them talked of wherever you go. I will permit talk of antiquities, but not if you start upon Thucydides and how like a certain campaign in Spain was to how some Athenian general took on the Spartans or the Persians.'

'Antiquities?' said Sir Sidney, turning his attention to Mr Wytton. 'What does your shipment consist of?'

'Statues, for the most part. I bought them in Paris, where all the plunder in the world is to be found on sale. They are from Italy: some Roman busts and a fine Greek nymph. She formerly belonged in the Vatican, and was stolen by that man whose name is not to be mentioned.' He gave a slight bow in Mrs Rowan's direction. 'It was for some reason not among the items returned to Rome at the expense of the Prince Regent. A loss for Pope Pius, but I am the gainer for it.'

'At the expense of the Prince Regent?' Camilla asked, curious to know more. 'What had he to do with the Vatican's statues?'

'After the war, the cost of conveying so many stolen treasures back to Italy was too great to be undertaken by the Pope,' Sir Sidney said. 'They were offered for sale to the Prince, who is a notable collector, as you are no doubt aware, but with a rare burst of magnanimity, he said that such treasures belonged to Rome, and he paid for them to be transported back to Italy.'

'Did he do that indeed?' she said. 'I honour him for it.'

'So must we all, although pray do not let your enthusiasm run away with you, Miss Camilla,' said Sir Sidney dryly. 'When you have been in London a little while, you will find any admiration for the Regent is misplaced.'

'Shall I? I doubt if I shall have any occasion to form an opinion one way or the other, I am hardly likely to move in those circles.'

'Is not your aunt married to one of the Carlton House set?' asked Mr Layard, coming across to the sofa and seating himself on a convenient low stool beside it. 'I believe Mrs Pollexfen is your aunt.'

'Mrs Pollexfen your aunt!' cried Mrs Rowan. 'Dear me, Camilla, you will find yourself flying high if you take up with that company.'

'I have seldom seen her,' she said, 'and not at all since her remarriage.'

'She was formerly a Mrs Wickham, was she not?' said Mr Portal.

'Yes,' she said. 'Mr Wickham was killed in the Peninsula, at the battle of Salamanca. Oh, I am sorry, ma'am,' she added, sending Mrs Rowan a repentant look. 'There is the war again. However, that has nothing to do with her present husband. All I know is that they live in London, I know nothing of any Carlton House set.'

'They live in considerable style,' said Mr Portal. 'You will see for yourself; you will be calling on her, I dare say.'

'I do not think – that is, when my parents return from Constantinople, perhaps we may—'

A rather pretty woman sitting next to Mr Wytton whispered in his ear that Mrs Pollexfen had always been considered fast. Her first marriage had some breath of scandal about it, some elopement or disgrace, covered up by her family. That was all in the past, of course, and of no consequence, but the lady had not improved her reputation by marrying Francis Pollexfen, for although wealthy and well-connected, he was not at all the thing. Mr Wytton must have met him.

Mr Wytton, bored, bowed his head and said nothing, although he briefly wondered why Sophie, who must be a cousin of Mrs Pollexfen, had never mentioned her name. Sophie loved to talk about her grander relations, even though he was not at all interested, having plenty of dull, grand connections of his own and preferring the company of men that Sophie stigmatised as prosy nonentities: poets, scribblers and the like. She was happy enough for him to know Lord Byron, so wicked and so fashionable, but all these learned fellows he went about with were, in her opinion, the most tedious kind of people.

What a frivolous creature she was, just what a girl of seventeen ought to be. For himself, he hated any affectation of learning in a woman. Miss Camilla Darcy, for instance; there was a young lady who was full of opinions, and not afraid to express them. Sophie would stigmatise her cousin's conversation as a great bore, and he was glad of it.

Mrs Rowan was bidding goodbye to a whimsical looking man in a grubby coat.

'That was Mr Algernon Watson, the historian,' she said, coming back to join Camilla. 'He is shy, but once you have met him some half dozen times, he may speak a few words to you. After that, you will wish you never were introduced, for he talks more than any man I have ever met, and although wonderfully clever, he has no sense of humour, none at all. He is engaged upon writing a history of the Ottoman Turks, and he comes to argue with me about Turkish ways and customs.'

'He must be glad of your knowledge on the subject,' said Camilla.

'Oh, no, none of it is the least use to Mr Watson, for he believes that no woman can ever be right. All that I experienced and observed during my years in that country count for nothing; he, who has never been there at all, must have a better idea of it than I do.'

'How prejudiced! His history will hardly be worth the reading.'

'It will be a great success, and admired by any number of learned men. Only I will laugh at it, and perhaps your mother when she returns, for I am sure she will have her eyes and wits about her, and learn a good deal about the Turks while she is in Constantinople.'

'Indeed, I hope she does, and my father too.'

'No, no, he will spend his time talking to other Europeans and attending only formal gatherings. It is left for us women to get under the skin of a foreign land, you know, for we have less dignity and more curiosity and so, despite the many restrictions placed upon our freedom, see far more than the men.'

Wytton raised a quizzical eyebrow at her. 'You are hard upon my sex, Mrs Rowan, and claim much for your own.'

'And with good reason.'

'You look thoughtful, Miss Camilla,' said Mr Portal. 'Do not tell me that you disagree with Mrs Rowan.'

'I am not in a position to do so, for I know no country except England, and little enough of that. Oh, how I long to travel, to see all these places that others talk of.'

'I advise you to put aside such revolutionary thoughts,' said Mrs Rowan. 'A young lady in your situation is destined to marry a respectable man and settle down in the country to have children. You may be allowed, if you are lucky in your choice of husband, to spend a few weeks in London for the season.'

'Destined! Indeed, I hope not. Your fate was different, after all.'

'I was widowed young, which many would consider a misfortune. However, it is only as a widow that a woman may lead an independent life, you know, and it suits me very well. I have not the joy some women find in their children, but I have other compensations.'

Camilla caught the swift, intimate smile that Mrs Rowan gave Pagoda Portal as she spoke and wondered if the gossip about her new friend might not be true.

'I would not be a married woman again for anything,' Mrs Rowan went on. 'It is amazing how pleasant it is to have control of one's own fortune!'

While her sister had been visiting in Bruton Street, Letitia had been out riding with Captain Allington. On the back of a horse, she became a different woman; her fears vanished, her oppressed spirits lifted, her pale cheeks filled with colour. She was an excellent horsewoman, and had had a rare disagreement with Mr Fitzwilliam over her choice of a horse; when he saw the big, raw-boned bay she had brought with her from the country, he expressed his disapproval in no uncertain words.

'You cannot ride that great brute of a horse; he is far too strong for you. I never saw a more unsuitable horse for a lady. What can your father be thinking of? Let me mount you from my stables. Fanny's mare is just the ride for you, a lovely creature, the safest ride imaginable; she will carry you quite safely.'

Amused, Camilla noticed the tightening of Letty's jaw and the effort it took her sister to reply with the necessary politeness.

'You are too kind, sir, but believe me, I am accustomed to Sir Lancelot here; we have been companions these three years, and go on very well together. He is big, to be sure, but that makes for a comfortable ride, you know, and he is well-schooled. He has never bolted nor thrown me.'

'In the country, it is different. He will be alarmed by the traffic in town, he will shy and you will be unable to hold him.'

Camilla thought it time to come to her sister's aid. 'Indeed, sir, he was given to Letty for her own use by my father, and he is of my father's breeding. He is a lively ride, but there is no vice in him at all, and he never misbehaves when my sister is in the saddle.'

Mr Fitzwilliam had to give way, there was nothing else for him to do, although he rounded on the Darcy groom, abusing him for allowing his mistress to bring such a horse to London.

'Begging pardon, your honour, but it ain't nothing to do with me. Mr Darcy tells me to bring this here horse up to London for Miss Darcy to ride, and so I did. Mrs Darcy bid me look after the horse myself; she don't ride no more than Miss Camilla does, but she's fond of Sir Lancelot and says she never worries when Miss Darcy is out on his back, for she knows he is a clever horse which will carry her over anything.'

So Letitia had taken Sir Lancelot out, accompanied by her groom. Captain Allington had met them in the park and lost no time in inviting her to join him in further rides. They had now ridden out three times together.

Camilla couldn't decide whether Mr Fitzwilliam's continuing disapproval of Letty's rides was only on account of the size and appearance of her horse, or because of the transformation her sister underwent once on Sir Lancelot's back. Today, Letty's return, complexion glowing from the vigorous exercise, was greeted with pleasure by Fanny, glad to see her cousin in better spirits even if only for a while, and with chilly reserve by her husband.

Captain Allington had no doubts. 'My word, she is a capital horsewoman indeed,' he cried. 'Lord, we had a splendid ride.' And, turning to Letitia, 'I hope you will come one day to Richmond or Bushey, where we may stretch the horses' legs in a proper gallop.'

Fanny, distracted by her small daughter, merely smiled and said she was sure Letty would like to ride out again. Mr Fitzwilliam frowned, and seemed about to speak, but fortunately Captain Allington was already bowing himself out of the room.

Fanny was made to feel less sanguine about such an outing later that evening, when her husband came to her room as she was changing for dinner. He liked to see her in her undergarments and with her hair down; it aroused the strongest feelings in him, and he watched with amorous eyes as she sat at her dressing-table in a silk wrap while her maid brushed and put up her hair. She dismissed her maid, and turned round to him with a smile, putting out a hand to hold him away. 'No, no, sir, my hair is done, you will have to wait until later.'

He took it in good part, used to her particularity with regards to her clothes and hair when she was dressing for a formal occasion. On her side, there was cunning in her tactics; her mother, a worldly woman, had given her several excellent tips on ensuring that a man was with his wife at those hours of the day when temptation was greatest. 'Even the most affectionate of husbands will be ready to find their way to the various bagnios frequented by men of our sort,' she had told Fanny. 'Make him want to spend that time with you. It is not a matter of morals, all men shed their morals with their breeches, it is a matter of accustoming him to other ways. A little flirting with other men does no harm, either; it will increase his ardour for you.'

Her husband, who would have been incapable of imagining that such a conversation could ever take place between mother and daughter, put aside his present ardour to bring up the matter of Letitia and her horse.

'I was not at all pleased to see Letty when she returned from her ride today. I do not care to see her dashing about on such an animal, nor is it a welcome sign that she finds the exercise so exhilarating. I own, I am disappointed in her, and surprised, for in all other ways she is a good, obliging girl.'

Fanny fiddled with the lid of a jar of cream. 'Why, as to that, you must remember that she has been raised in the country; you know how it is with country people, they are restless and must be active. Only think how Camilla likes to take some exercise on foot every day. Letty needs to shake off her fidgets, for she is still low in her spirits and worries constantly about her sisters and her parents.'

She put down the jar and, taking up several bracelets, began to thread them on to her slim arm.

'Why, only yesterday Belle and Georgina went to Bond Street and were a little late returning, they had met some acquaintance and lost track of the time, you know, and Letty was in such a fret, imagining every conceivable disaster: they had been run down by a carriage, or abducted, or had fallen from the kerb and broken a limb!'

Fitzwilliam could appreciate this kind of feminine weakness, although perhaps Letty took it to extremes, and, he demanded, if she were so worried about accidents, why did she choose to ride such a horse?

'Oh, it is only what may happen to others that worries her, she has no fears for her own safety or well-being,' said Fanny.

'And how much time is she spending with the Captain? I know you wish to take her mind off that wretched Busby fellow – I am heartily sick of hearing his name all over town, I may tell you – but Captain Allington can never be considered a suitable connection for her. He is a younger son and has no income apart from his army pay, and no prospects; he may look very fine and all the young ladies may dote on his whiskers, will not do, Fanny.'

'Letty has no romantic interest in Captain Allington, nor he in her.'

Mr Fitzwilliam had to accept this. He had rarely known his Fanny to be wrong in affairs of the heart.

'And he will not be at Almack's this evening, few soldiers are, and so she will have to talk and dance with other men.'

'Two young women, worth a hundred thousand pounds between them; you shall have to take care of them, Fanny, very good care.'

SEVEN

'Although why it is called full dress, when one's bosom and shoulders are quite bare, while undress means being ruffed up to the chin, I shall never understand,' said Camilla, twisting and turning to get a better look at herself in the glass.

Fanny had obtained the precious vouchers for Almack's, resisted the wails and entreaties of Belle and Georgina to be included in the party – 'You cannot, for there are no vouchers for you' – and had personally inspected every item of the evening dress laid out for Camilla and Letty to wear for the first subscription ball of the season.

Their ball gowns were the crack of fashion, with satin slips beneath gauze overdresses. The hem of each dress was deep, set with flounces and showed their ankles, encased for the evening in silk stockings. Camilla loved the feel of the silk, and the rustle and movement of her dress, although she had been startled at first to see how low it was cut across the bosom, and how much the tight, high waist and small, puffed, off-the-shoulder sleeves emphasised her and Letty's breasts.

Letty, meanwhile, was engaged in a tugging match with Sackree, as she tried to cover up more of her bosom, talked of quickly adding some lace. Fanny, coming in to see how they were doing, would have none of it.

'Nothing more deplorable than a prude, indeed you will see many women this evening in far more revealing gowns, take my word for it. These are modest enough. Letty, you may hang that pearl and ruby ornament in the centre there, just so. Camilla, here is a corsage sent by Sir Sidney, and you should attach it like this.'

'From Sir Sidney?' Camilla tried not to show how pleased she was. 'Is there a card?'

'Compliments and so forth. He has sent a posy for Letty also, it is downstairs as she will want to carry hers. Necklaces, now, and bracelets; Letty, the merest touch of rouge – no, do not draw away, you look too pale, it is of the first importance that you have a bloom on you tonight.'

Sackree and Fanny pinned and fastened and twitched and pulled at Camilla's hair and face and gown. Camilla felt like a horse being groomed for some important occasion. Or even a heifer in classical times, about to be led, beribboned and adorned, to the sacrificial altar. She was going to say this to Fanny, but thought better of it.

Letty looked superb, but decidedly stormy. Which, in Camilla's opinion, only increased her sister's looks, for she could sometimes lack animation, and a still beauty was never so fetching as a lively one. Letty would have to smile though, if she wasn't to lack for partners, for as she was just now, she would terrify any young man and probably most older ones as well. Camilla hoped that the delights of a ballroom would work their familiar magic, and that her sister would forget her sense of affront and allow herself some enjoyment.

They went downstairs, where Mr Fitzwilliam was waiting in the most correct evening dress of silk stockings and black coat with brass buttons. His eyes lingered on the girls' exposed bosoms, until Fanny, resplendent in blue satin and the fine diamonds she had inherited from her mother, tapped him on the shoulder with her fan and said that they were ready to leave.

The carriage was announced and Fanny was handed in, followed by Camilla and Letty. Fitzwilliam gave his orders to the coachman, and they drew away from the house at a spanking pace.

It was not a speed that could be kept up, however, as the approach to King Street, where Almack's was situated, was thronged with carriages depositing their fashionable burdens at the torchlit steps to the club.

Camilla, not wishing to look or feel gauche, like a country girl, couldn't help but marvel at the number of people and conveyances. The carriage lanterns gleamed and glimmered in the dimly-lit street, and there was a buzz of conversation as new arrivals greeted those ahead of them and turned to salute others as they drew up.

'We shall know no one,' exclaimed Letitia. 'Oh, I wish we had not come.'

'Nonsense,' said Fanny. 'A ballroom is the very place to meet people, that is the whole purpose of Almack's. I know everyone, I assure you, or their parents. Every young lady of rank who is out will be here, and all the eligible men, too.'

'I see it isn't called the marriage mart for nothing,' said Camilla.

This earned her a disapproving look from Fitzwilliam and a quick gesture of denial from Fanny. 'You must not say that, it would be vulgar to appear to be on the lookout for a husband.'

'Well, we aren't,' said Letitia, 'so there's no danger of that. That is why we should not have come, for when we are seen here, the whole world will think we are husband hunting.'

'And if you do not come, at your age, and known to be spending the season in London, it will be considered odd, and give rise to even more talk – the last thing you or any of us would wish.'

Letitia sank back into the squabs and her sulks. Camilla leaned forward to see where they had got to in the line just as the carriage stopped, and the footman was at the door to let down the steps and hand the ladies out.

They went up the wide stone staircase that led to the ballroom, their tickets of entry were scrutinised, an eye cast over Mr Fitzwilliam's attire, lest a forbidden pair of pantaloons be admitted to the holy of holies – knee breeches were still *de rigueur* within these portals – and they were in.

Her first impression was of a sea of glittering glass. The huge mirrors along the walls multiplied the throng into an army of fashionables, and the ornate crystal lustres twinkled and sparkled, illuminated by flickering gas lights. The gilded classical columns supported a gallery where the musicians played, the air was hot, the atmosphere stuffy, and apart from the mirrors and gilding, the rooms were in fact quite bare of decoration.

Mrs Rowan had warned her what she might expect: tedious company, only ratafia and lemonade to drink, bread and butter to eat, commonplace conversation, no politics or serious subjects to be spoken of. 'You will find it dull.'

And she might have done, had she not so loved to dance. She wished she were on the floor, waltzing – it was exhilarating just to watch the dancers.

Someone was attempting to hand her a card showing the patterns of the quadrille; she refused it with a smile. All her family could dance the quadrille; all her sisters adored dancing, and many a rainy afternoon at Pemberley had been saved from tedium by learning their steps under the tutelage of a local dancing master, with Griffy at the pianoforte and her mother, who had never lost her own love of dancing, watching with real pleasure and marking the time with her hand.

It was a crush. Bodies pressed against one another, men and women, with some moving forward into the room, some pausing to greet friends, others wanting to look around and watch the dancers.

She caught sight of Sir Sidney, who was standing at the other end of the ballroom, talking to an elegant woman with an extraordinary array of feathers in her hair. How well he looked, so extremely handsome in his beautifully fitting evening coat, his height and figure showing to great advantage in a gathering with so many rather young men – a few golden youths, but rather more inclined to spots and unformed features.

He had seen her, was bowing himself away from the feathered headdress, was coming towards her.

He took her hand and raised it to his lips. 'That was Mrs Beecham I was talking to, do you know her?'

Camilla shook her head. 'She is very lovely.'

'She is a formidable talker, knows everyone's affairs and has no sense of discretion. She is therefore the most feared and fêted woman in London. She was telling me about your sister and Tom Busby, an affair in which I have not the slightest interest. Such childish amours are best forgotten.'

He was rewarded with a glowing smile from Camilla, who was extraordinarily pleased to find herself in the company of someone who felt able to mention Tom's name outright, without the sidelong glances and knowing looks and sudden hushes that had pursued the Darcy sisters for the last few days. It was as she would have expected; Sir Sidney was not one of your London muckrakers and scandalmongers, eager to destroy a reputation or cause mischief among his friends.

'Do you see that fellow over there?' Sir Sidney said, lifting his quizzing-glass and gazing through it. 'I never saw such an ill-fitting coat.'

'That is Mr Valpy. He is a clergyman.'

'A clergyman? Is he indeed? What has he to do with a ball? He had better stay and mind his parishioners and pulpits, and not come amongst us here in that apology for a coat. I hate a dancing clergyman, do not you agree? And he has a disapproving air to him. I wonder at his being admitted here.'

'He is a fashionable clergymen, the *ton* flock to hear his sermons.'

'The *ton* flock to an execution, or to see a dog with two heads. It hardly implies that murderers or freaks should dance at Almack's.'

'You are hard on him,' Camilla said, laughing.

'He is a walking offence.'

He claimed her hand for the next dance, and as they made their way on to the floor, Camilla had the satisfaction of seeing Letty being led into a set by Lord Rampton, a notable dancer, even if high on her cousin's list of ineligible men.

'Who is that dancing with Sir Sidney?' asked Lady Jarvie, a woman in her forties who wore a brilliant purple silk gown topped with a feather and pearl headdress.

Her companion, Lady Warren, let her eyes drift across the floor. 'Why, that is one of the Miss Darcys. I heard that Sir Sidney was *épris* in that direction. She will do well to land him, for one knows he is not naturally inclined to matrimony.'

The two women laughed heartily. 'It is not Miss Darcy he dances with, however, is it?'

'No, that is Miss Camilla Darcy, the second sister.'

'So many sisters,' murmured Lady Jarvie, smoothing her purple skirts. 'They go on for ever, one hears.'

'Oh, five or six, or seven,' said Mrs Naburn, joining them with a flutter of her gaudy fan. 'A nurseryful at home, for all I know. Each with their fifty thousand pounds. Mr Darcy must certainly pay for fathering so many daughters.'

Lady Warren had been infuriated to hear, year by year, of Mr Darcy's steadily increasing fortune 'Very pretty fortunes. I am only surprised they are not larger.'

'They are all beauties, besides, so one hears,' Mrs Naburn went on.

'If you admire those kind of looks,' said Lady Warren, who didn't.

Lady Naburn's mind was running on money. 'Is the Pemberley estate worth so much?'

'My husband was talking of it only yesterday,' said Lady Jarvie. 'There is coal, you know, and some other minerals, I am not sure what kind, but in great demand and fetching a high price. Then they say that Mr Darcy invested heavily when the market was so low, sold out high on rumours of peace, bought once more when the news was at its darkest, and sold after Waterloo having made another fortune.'

'Is he not related to Lady Catherine de Burgh, who is so rich?' Mrs Naburn asked. She nodded and smiled at an acquaintance in pink, adding in an aside, 'What an unfortunate colour for dear Eliza to be wearing, pink with that flaming hair!'

Lady Jarvie frowned as she thought about family trees. 'Lady Catherine must be Darcy's aunt, his mother's sister. Her only child, a daughter, died some years ago, I believe.'

'They say she will leave everything to Mr Fitzwilliam, and I dare say he will be happy with such an inheritance,' said Lady Warren. 'A younger son, you know, even if his father is an earl. He has no estate, and a growing family to provide for.'

'That is the price you pay for marrying a young wife, and Lady Fanny is turning out to be a prolific breeder. Is she not increasing again?'

They all turned to stare at Fanny, whose slim figure seemed to give the lie to their supposition.

'With these high-waisted fashions, it is hard to tell,' said Mrs Naburn after a long scrutiny. 'She takes great pleasure in her children, I am told, as does her husband. He is an uxorious man, not one of your rakes.'

'I should hate to have such a husband,' cried Lady Jarvie. 'For he would be always at home, boring one dreadfully, instead of being off in company.'

'Muslin company?' said Mrs Naburn archly.

'I don't enquire.'

Lady Warren was watching the dancers. 'That is Miss Darcy, there, the one going down the dance with Lord Rampton. He would do very well for her, I dare say they would consider him a good catch.' Yes, it would gratify her to see Miss Darcy married to a wastrel, although a wastrel without even a title to his name would be better.

'Fifty thousand will not be enough to save him from ruin, from all one hears,' Lady Jarvie said, lowering her voice a fraction.

'Perhaps Miss Darcy's papa may be persuaded to do more for the young couple,' said Mrs Naburn. 'He has only to ask advice of Mr Gardiner, who is a relation of his wife's you know, and I am sure he can make thousands in a week.'

'These girls are related to the Gardiners?' said Lady Jarvie. 'I am surprised they are let in here.'

Lady Warren was swift in her reply; after all, she was known to be a relation of the Darcys. 'It is a distant connection, and of course the Darcys are cousins to half the nobility. There can be no question of their being excluded, not even Sally Jersey could do that. Not on grounds of their birth.'

'Who is their mother?'

'A nobody, the daughter of a gentleman of modest estate, one of your two-thousand-a-year country squires. She had no fortune, none at all, and she did well to catch Darcy. There was a great deal of talk at the time.' The minute the words were spoken, Lady Warren regretted them; her companions might at any moment remember that her own brother had married another of the country squire's daughters. She spread her own exquisite fan and fluttered it before her face. 'How hot it is, how close. I declare, it is worse every year.'

Mrs Naburn, the tiresome woman, was not to be deflected from the subject of the Darcys. 'And has she produced nothing but daughters? How he must regret the marriage; neither fortune nor sons is a hard lot for any man.'

'There are two sons, rather younger than the girls,' Lady Warren said. 'Five sisters, and then two boys.'

'Unless their brothers are sickly children, the girls had best marry as well as they can, then,' said Mrs Naburn, pursing her lips. 'The Miss Darcys would be advised not to be hanging out after the likes of Lord Rampton, however much they may fancy a title.'

'Sir Sidney is a man of wealth.'

'If he is serious about Miss Camilla Darcy, it is to be hoped he will get her to the altar; he has not had much luck with his previous attachments. Twice jilted, is that not so?' Lady Warren remembered every piece of gossip that redounded ill on anyone in society. 'Maria Harper ran away from home the very day before the wedding in order not to be married to him. She had a hard time of it afterwards with her father, and in the end did no better for herself than some clergyman in the Midlands.'

Lady Jarvie shook her head, making the feathers tremble. 'While we are talking of jilting, is not Miss Darcy the girl who was to have married Tom Busby, the one who has appeared with a foreign wife? They say she is wearing her heart on her sleeve for her lost love – for all to see.'

'After more than three years? I never heard of such a thing,' cried Mrs Naburn. 'There is not a man in the world who cannot be forgot in three months; nay, three weeks or three days, let alone three years.'

This was a subject Lady Warren was happy to talk about. 'She has done herself no good to become the talk of the town so soon after arriving for her first season. And I hear that the next sister, that one smiling up at Sir Sidney there, has been keeping strange company for a young female. She will turn out to be a blue-stocking, and then no one will want to marry her.'

'The two younger sisters are twins and extravagantly beautiful. I saw them in Bond Street,' said Lady Jarvie. 'One fair, one dark, thus pleasing all tastes.'

'I know who their mother is!' exclaimed Mrs Naburn suddenly. 'It has just come to me. She is Lydia Pollexfen's sister.'

Lady Jarvie's eyebrows rose. 'Is she indeed? I never heard Lydia speak of any nieces.'

'There was some estrangement there. The family did not approve of Lydia Pollexfen's first marriage, there was some scandal connected with the man. He died, however, so it is all forgotten.' Lady Warren spoke with finality; why could they not drop the subject of the Darcys?

'The Darcy girls will be moving in a fast set if they take up with Mrs Pollexfen,' said Mrs Naburn. 'They will find themselves in company with Prinny, and I can't think that Mr Darcy would approve of that.'

'Oh, Lady Fanny is no friend of those people, she will keep her charges away from such pollution.' With relief, Lady Warren sighted a distraction. 'Gracious heavens, do but look, there is Emily Cantor with her hair dressed in the most extraordinary mode, what a fright she does look to be sure. Emily, my dearest,' kissing her friend's cheeks, 'how well you look, how elegantly your hair is done tonight!'

Camilla was in high spirits, delighted to be dancing, especially with Sir Sidney, whom she had to admit she was finding more and more attractive. He was an excellent and witty partner, who knew everyone and kept her much amused by his revelations and anecdotes concerning those around them. And her happiness was increased by seeing that Letty had succumbed to enjoyment of the dance, and had lost, at least for the moment, her look of introspection.

The dance came to an end. Sir Sidney led her from the floor and went away to fetch her a glass of lemonade. She stood by a pillar, her colour high from the exercise, her eyes sparkling, and several men walking by looked at her with admiration. Two young ladies went past, spangled scarves draped nonchalantly over their arms; they gave her a backward glance, which carried more of spite and disapproval than of admiration, and she heard their laughter as they passed some comment to each other.

She did not mind; she was in buoyant mood, and it would take more than the unpleasantness of strangers to cast her down. Then Sir Sidney was back at her side, and she took the offered lemonade gratefully.

'I hope you will favour me with another dance later,' said Sir Sidney. 'I should like to ask you again now, but you know it is not at all the thing and people would look oddly at us.'

She knew perfectly well that to stand up with the same man for more than two dances in an evening would be considered quite improper, but, for herself, she would have been happy to dance every dance with Sir Sidney. It was not to be thought of, however; to do any such thing would distress Fanny and excite comment among those present, many of them eagle-eyed mothers, jealous enough for their own daughters to be keen to find fault with the new heiresses.

Besides, Fanny had no intention of allowing her to spend the evening in one man's company. She came up to them and bore Camilla away. 'You will not mind it, my love, but I wish you to meet other people. You cannot know too many people in society, I assure you.'

Camilla was too elated to mind anything. She smiled, and dutifully said the right things, danced with a young man with dashing looks and no conversation, stood up for the country dances with a supercilious slightly older man who eyed himself in the long glasses with great complaisancy, and then had all the felicity of a waltz with Sir Sidney.

She had danced often enough at country parties and balls, and had attended various assemblies, but she had not before danced in the arms of a man for whom she had any particular warmth of feeling. At first she was slightly confused by the heightened enjoyment she felt in being encircled by Sir Sidney's strong arm, and at the closeness of their bodies and faces as they twirled around the room. Then she grew used to the sensation, and found herself revelling in it and giving herself up to the sense of pleasure. It was heady business, more than sufficient to bring radiant colour to her cheeks and a glow to her eyes.

'How I love to dance,' she cried, as the end of the dance brought her up beside Fanny once more. 'It is intoxicating!'

Mr Fitzwilliam frowned. 'Where is Letty?' was all he said. 'It is time for us to leave, the carriage will be waiting.'

Letty was talking to a man of twenty-six or seven, of medium height, who had a distinguished air and a humorous eye. Camilla liked the look of him, and as they waited at the foot of the stairs for their carriage to be announced, she asked her sister who he was.

'Lord Rampton introduced him, they are old friends and come from the same county. He is Mr Barcombe, a Mr Barleigh Barcombe.'

'Do you like him?'

Letty shrugged, earning herself a cluck of disapproval from Fanny. She apologised, and added that he seemed civil enough. 'Lord Rampton says he is droll, that he makes everybody laugh.'

'But not you,' she said.

'I am not in the mood for laughter,' said Letitia, drawing her cloak around her. 'How cold it is. I hope you may not catch a chill after dancing with such liveliness, Camilla. You should have taken care not to get hot.'

'Catch a cold from dancing? Never in the world. See, I am as snug as anything in my cloak, and here is the carriage.'

Fell had tea for them in the drawing-room when they got back. Fanny was yawning and protesting that she was exhausted, while Mr Fitzwilliam eyed her approvingly and restored his strength with a glass of brandy.

Letty was looking cross. 'Well, Camilla, you were attracting a good deal of attention, dancing in that way with Sir Sidney.'

Fanny stifled another yawn. 'What nonsense you do speak. I remarked to Fitzwilliam – did I not, my dear? – how happy I was to see you dancing, and in particular to see you, Letty, looking cheerful and in great beauty with some colour in your cheeks. I need not be ashamed for your dancing, I find, you both dance so easily and well, with no cause to mind your steps or falter in conversation; it was all natural and graceful, just as it ought to be.'

'Sir Sidney is a notable dancer, and any girl would be glad to be partnered by him,' Camilla said, nettled by her sister's words.

'I think Mama would have been shocked by your waltzing in such a way. I never saw anything so abandoned.'

'To bed with you,' Fanny interposed. 'Or you will be fit for nothing in the morning.'

Camilla was glad to find a fire in her room when she went upstairs. It had been carefully tended by the waiting Sackree, who had her nightdress airing beside it.

'And I shan't wake you in the morning,' Sackree said as she unhooked Camilla's dress, 'for you will need your sleep.'

'Do you think me such a poor creature as to be tired out by a single ball? Shame on you. And besides, I cannot sleep late, for I have promised to take Alethea to her singing lesson tomorrow morning. Griffy has caught one of her head colds and should not go out.'

'Head cold, indeed.' Sackree sniffed as she swept up the discarded ball gown. 'She'll be up there in the schoolroom, scribbling away, while Miss Alethea is off in your charge; see if she isn't.'

'She is writing a novel, Sackree, as you very well know, and must snatch every moment she can to work on it.'

'As if there weren't enough novels filling all your heads full of nonsense without her adding to them. I heard her reading some of that stuff of hers to Miss Alethea, fair made my hair stand on end; such goings on, I don't know what your mother would say.'

'She would laugh,' Camilla said, subduing a great yawn.

'Into bed with you now, and I'll blow out your candle directly.'

The bed was warm from the pan of hot coals that had been lying in it, and with a sigh, Camilla sank back against the pillows, drifting into sleep almost at once, her last conscious thought being of how agreeable a man Sir Sidney was.

EIGHT

Camilla came downstairs in her new walking dress. It was a round dress of jaconet muslin with a tightly fitting, saffron-coloured spencer top, and she was delighted with it. Her pleasant recollections of the ball and this new costume put her in a happy mood, and she swung her French bonnet by its ribbons as she went into the drawing-room to find Alethea, whom she could hear at the pianoforte.

She was surprised to find Mr Fitzwilliam standing in the centre of the room, with a face like a thundercloud. He was holding up a small, leather-bound book – a book she recognised at once.

Fanny was protesting vehemently that there must be some mistake, or that, even if it was as he said, there could be no harm in it.

'No harm, ma'am?' said her husband in icy tones. 'No harm in a young lady, living under our roof, in your care, having in her possession a book such as this? No more unsuitable book can possibly be imagined. No woman should be reading this, and for an unmarried girl – it is not to be thought of.'

Letty entered the room, agog with curiosity as to what the raised voices might signify. Her eyes flickered over the book in Fitzwilliam's hand and took in his enraged countenance. 'What volume is that, sir?' she asked.

'I hardly dare mention its name, Letitia. If it is yours, you have done very wrong, let me tell you, very wrong indeed, miss, both to have such a book in your possession and to bring it into Fanny's sitting-room.'

Oh, Lord, now Letitia was bound to start her moralising.

What a pity that she and Alethea had not already left for the singing lesson – although that would merely have postponed the storm that was clearly about to break about her head. It was with relief that she heard Fell's steady tread, and his announcement of visitors below.

'It is Mrs Gardiner and Sophie,' Fanny said thankfully. 'They have come for Belle and Georgina, to go shopping. Call your sisters, Alethea, they must not keep Mrs Gardiner waiting.'

When Mrs Gardiner and Sophie came into the room, they were accompanied by Mr Wytton and Mr Layard.

'They have offered to go with us this morning,' said Mrs Gardiner, as she kissed Fanny. 'Is it not noble of them? For in general, you know, men dislike shopping. Mr Layard assures us that he has a fine eye for rosettes and ribbons, having often advised his sisters. He has four sisters, you know.' Her voice tailed away as she sensed the tension in the room, and she looked from one to the other of them as though for enlightenment.

Mr Fitzwilliam hesitated, unwilling to continue with a diatribe in front of visitors.

Camilla felt it was worth risking a sortie. 'You have my book, Mr Fitzwilliam,' she said, and held out her hand for it. 'I wondered where I had left it.'

This was too much for Fitzwilliam. 'Yours! Yours, forsooth! And may I know where you acquired such a book?'

'I borrowed it from Mrs Rowan.'

'Shame on her for having such a book. Shame on her for lending it to you.'

'But what is it?' cried Letitia.

'It is the *Decameron*, by Boccaccio,' Camilla said, her colour rising. She saw a look of surprise come over Wytton's face, and Mr Layard's mouth dropped open in a round O of astonishment.

'In the Italian,' she went on. 'I have not read it in Italian before.'

Fanny gave a squeak of horror, but it was too late.

'Do you mean to stand before me and tell me that you have read it in English? Are you not aware of how improper a work this is? It is indeed a highly immoral work, to call it warm would not describe it adequately. How came you to read such stuff, or to admit it without a blush?'

'Why, how can you say such things about Boccaccio?'

'Indeed, sir, Miss Camilla has the right of it. The *Decameron* is one of the glories of European literature.'

It was Mr Wytton who had spoken. She wished he had held his tongue, as Fitzwilliam turned on him.

'That is entirely beside the point, sir. The point is that young ladies should have nothing to do with European anything, let alone immoral tales.'

'Camilla, how could you?' said Letitia in a low, shocked voice. She turned to Mr Fitzwilliam, shaking her head. 'I am ashamed to say, cousin, that it is all too true. My sister has had the run of the library at home and access to all kinds of books she should never even have opened.'

'Oh, what nonsense.' Camilla could feel her temper rising, but at all cost she must control her irritation and anger. 'There can be no harm in books.'

Fitzwilliam rounded on her. 'No harm? I think you must allow others to be the judge of that. There is every harm in books, and books of this kind have no place on a gentleman's shelves except under lock and key – at least in any household where he is unwise enough to let his womenfolk into his library. I never heard of such a thing. I could not have believed it, even of Darcy.'

Letitia was nodding her head in agreement, the priggish creature! Mrs Gardiner was looking embarrassed, as well she might, and Sophie was clearly enjoying the sight of her cousin being dressed down in this way. Camilla lifted her chin. She would not back down, nor stand by while her father was abused – even if her sister saw nothing wrong in that.

'My father has a great deal too much sense to put books under lock and key. Indeed, he has this very book in his library, in translation, and he himself recommended me to read it not twelve months since.'

This brought a smile to Wytton's lips, quickly suppressed as Mrs Gardiner gave him a quelling look.

'Your father?' said Mr Layard, in a vain attempt to restore a conversational tone to the proceedings. 'Did he, by Jove?'

No one paid the least attention to him.

'It is very likely so,' said Letitia, a picture of prim disapproval. 'Indeed, she has read *Tom Jones* and Chaucer and the works of all kinds of writers who form no part of the reading suitable for a modest female mind.'

Modest female mind, indeed. Letitia was growing more and more tiresome and prudish. Where did she get her fustian notions from? Certainly not from either of their parents, who considered wide-ranging reading not only a pleasure but a duty for all their family. True, the twins never opened a book other than the most melodramatic Minerva novel, except under protest, but Letty had benefited as much as she had from the freedom of the well-stocked Pemberley library. To listen to her now, you would think she had never read more than the *Elegant Extracts*.

'Even that most dreadful book, *The Monk*,' Letty was saying in sepulchral tones.

'What a hypocrite you are, Letty,' cried Alethea, jumping in to add coal to the fire. 'I saw you reading *The Monk* yourself, and I have read it, too. Miss Griffin said it was a most interesting book, and I enjoyed every word of it.'

Sophie rarely read a book, but the mention of Monk Lewis's gothic masterpiece rang a bell in her head. 'That is a monstrous horrid book. I swear I did not sleep a wink the night I finished it.'

Wytton took himself off to the window to have his laugh out. Camilla glared at his shaking back. He might find this amusing; it was making her, and what was worse, Fanny, acutely uncomfortable.

Mr Fitzwilliam was nonplussed by Sophie's artless remarks, and Camilla thought it time to soothe his ruffled feelings. 'I am truly sorry to have upset you, cousin, and I will make sure that I do not leave my books lying around in future.'

'While you are in my house, you will refrain from having any such books in your possession at all.'

She opened her mouth to make an indignant rejoinder, saw

Fanny's expression, thought better of it, and swallowed her words. 'I will do as you wish, Mr Fitzwilliam, while I am your guest.'

'And I suggest that you take time to think about your conduct, examine your conscience in this matter, admit you are at fault and give up any idea of reading such books. It will not do, you must believe me, it will not do. No husband will be as indulgent as your father appears to have been, although I am sure he cannot have been aware of half of what you were reading.'

Mr Fitzwilliam might have finished, but Letty was by no means satisfied. She went on berating Camilla, despite Fanny's valiant efforts to deflect her, accusing her sister of indelicacy of mind, of rudeness to her elders, and to her host. She would write to Papa directly, to let him know where his carelessness had led to.

'Do that,' Camilla cried, suddenly furious. 'See how he likes being told what he should and should not do by his daughter. *I* should not care to be in your shoes when he replies to your letter.'

'Oh, please,' said Fanny, putting her hand to her brow. 'Please do not quarrel. I cannot bear to have people falling out with one another, it makes me feel quite ill.'

'I am sorry to cause you such distress,' Camilla said, with genuine contrition. 'Come, Alethea, let us go, or you will be late for your lesson.'

'I still cannot feel easy in my mind about these lessons,' said Letitia, happy to find another opportunity to point out her sisters' folly and wrong-headedness.

'I must agree with Letty,' said Fanny. 'Bloomsbury, you know, is a most ungenteel area, quite beyond the bounds of fashionable London, I do not like to think of you and Alethea venturing there. Why can the singing master not come to Aubrey Square, as other teachers do?'

Ignoring Letty, Camilla set about allaying Fanny's fears. Signor Silvestrini was not like other teachers. He could pick and choose whom he would teach; very likely he would simply give Alethea some advice and perhaps the name of another teacher. One who would no doubt come to the house.

'Pray think no more about Bloomsbury and Italian singing masters,' she said with determined cheerfulness as she drew on her gloves. 'Alethea and I will be safe enough in the carriage, and Figgins is to go with us.'

'Oh, very well, if you take a maid with you,' said Fanny doubtfully.

Mrs Gardiner, who had been engaged in bright conversation with Sophie and an obliging Mr Layard, now came forward. 'We had best be off, Fanny, I hear the twins outside. Mr Wytton, are you ready?'

The whole party moved out of the room and down the stairs into the hall. In all the bustle of taking up shawls and drawing on gloves, Camilla found herself beside Wytton.

He pressed a small volume into her hand, and spoke in a low voice. 'Here you are, Miss Camilla, I think you had better have it back. Do hide it, though, for Lady Fanny's sake, if not for your own.'

It was the Boccaccio. She stared down at it for a second, before tucking it swiftly out of sight in her reticule. 'How came you by it?'

'Mr Fitzwilliam laid it down, and I took it up.' And, in a louder voice, 'Yes, Mrs Gardiner, here I am, quite at your disposal. Come, Sophie, take my arm.'

Figgins was the new schoolroom maid, her predecessor in that role having been promoted to the position of ladies' maid to the twins. Miss Griffin, who was not so absorbed in her charge and her novel as not to use her eyes, had noticed the ebullient Figgins with Fanny's children, and although there was no unkindness in her, it was clear that she far preferred the few chances she had to help with the young ladies' clothes and toilettes to tending the infants. Miss Griffin, at no time an enthusiast for small children, could share her sentiments.

Figgins was a thin, lively girl, the daughter of the Fitzwilliam coachman. Fanny was happy to give her the position and to be able to please an old and valued servant by her choice. 'She will do well, and she is a Londoner, you know, by upbringing. It does no harm for a young lady to have a maid who knows her way about.'

No local knowledge was asked of Figgins today, however, as

she climbed into the carriage after Camilla and Alethea. Alethea was in tearing high spirits, tra-la-ing as they rattled over the cobbles to warm up her voice, oblivious to the effect the vigorous sounds might have on pedestrians and the occupants of other carriages.

Letitia would have been horrified, would have remonstrated, chided, laid down the law. Camilla, still annoyed with Letty and mortified by Fitzwilliam's treatment of her, took little notice. Alethea was doing no one any harm, and she had no wish to cross her. Like Fanny, she felt she had had enough of stormy scenes for one day.

The carriage turned into a large, respectable-looking square, and stopped outside number nineteen. Figgins commented on how clean it was, as to windows, doorstep and brasswork, although she was taken aback to find the door opened by a foreigner. Not that he wasn't handsome enough, she reported back to her particular friends in Aubrey Square, with his dark hair and black eyes – if that was to your taste. Only he spoke foreign, and even his English, well, you could hardly understand a word of it.

Signor Silvestrini had rooms on the first floor, including a fine front apartment, which was fitted up as a studio. Camilla and Alethea paused at the threshold, their eyes taking in the pianoforte, the harp, the music stand, the neat stacks of music, the metronome, the anatomical drawing of the muscles of the throat given pride of place on the wall, and the surrounding prints of various opera houses from across the continent.

The maestro himself was a stocky man with thick, wavy black hair tied back in a club and bow. He wore a neat, dark coat and pantaloons, and would have passed without notice anywhere in the street; there was nothing *outré* about him, nothing of the mountebank or the showman.

His manner was brisk and professional. He introduced himself to the sisters, enquired which was the singer, ushered Camilla to a small, hard sofa and took Alethea over to the light.

'Sixteen? It is too young.'

To Camilla's surprise, Alethea didn't argue or look cross, but simply stood there, looking back at him in her fearless way.

'Still, since you are here, let us hear what you can do. You have had lessons, from a country master, one Mr Thompson, who recommended me to you. Which is very kind of this Mr Thompson, of whom I have never heard; it would be better for him to keep his elegant young pupils to himself, or to pass them on to other Mr Thompsons in Town. We have many, many singing masters in London, that is quite certain.'

'Only one Silvestrini,' remarked Alethea.

Signor Silvestrini's face creased into a smile. 'That is so, that is so. Come, let us begin.'

Alethea sang scales, la-ed and me-ma-ed up and down and in and out of chords, and finally sang a simple ballad in Italian.

Camilla listened, musing on the nature of musical talent. Most young ladies of her acquaintance learnt to play an instrument and to sing. These were necessary accomplishments. They indicated to a censorious world that a girl was properly brought up, and were of benefit in providing music to entertain a private party.

Yet there were those to whom music was not simply part of a limited education. What hope was there for those like Alethea for whom music was a passion and a necessity? She doubted if many men could appreciate or tolerate that in a wife. Alethea's musical fate would rest entirely in the hands of her future husband, whoever he might be; she hoped from the bottom of her heart that her sister would find and marry a man who had a real love of music. It sent a cold chill through her to think of Alethea deprived of music.

She could glean nothing from the singing master's countenance. He was animated in explaining what he wanted, thoughtful while he listened, active while he corrected and demonstrated some point. Yet she had no notion what opinion he had formed of Alethea's voice. Even when she had finished, and stood there, in the centre of the room while he prowled round and round her, caressing his chin between thumb and forefinger, it was impossible to judge what he was thinking.

Finally he broke the silence, breathing out with a long sound as though he had been holding his breath. 'So,' he said. 'Remarkable. You are English?'

Alethea nodded.

'I should have not have believed it possible.' He swung round to Camilla. 'You are her sister? Where are her parents? Who arranges her lessons?'

'My parents are abroad at present, sir. My older sister and I are charged by them to see to Alethea's musical education.'

Alethea addressed Signor Silvestrini directly. 'Will you teach me?'

He looked at her with intense surprise. 'But naturally! It is only a matter of the arrangements.'

The arrangements made Camilla stare; she could not have believed that a singing master could command such a price for his services.

'And because she is so young, and it is not a matter of entering the profession at such an age, I reduce my charges, I bankrupt myself to teach her!'

That was coming it a little strong, but Camilla couldn't help smiling, liking his high opinion of himself and of Alethea, his good humour and his vigorous personality. Entering the profession? She should think not, indeed, not at sixteen or any age, he must realise that, but since there was no question of it, there was no need for any discussion about the matter.

Alethea danced down the stairs, in raptures over the Signor and her lessons. As she bounced off the bottom step, the front door opened, and a tall, fair, very beautiful and fashionably dressed woman came in, a small, pink-cheeked girl at her heels. Seeing strangers, the child seized her mother's skirts. The Signor, coming down the stairs with great rapidity, swung the child into the air, whereupon she shrieked and let out a cascade of Italian.

'The Signora Silvestrini,' he announced to the sisters, catching the woman round the waist despite her laughing protests. She spoke to him in Italian, her voice low and with a rich quality to it that made Alethea look hard at her. Then she greeted Camilla and Alethea in pretty, broken English.

Camilla was surprised to find her an Italian, with those looks, and Signor Silvestrini's sharp eyes noticed the surprise; another crinkling smile came over his face. 'You expect her to be dark, like me and the bambina, and every other Italian. But no, she is from Lombardy, and the Lombards are blonde and big. She is a singer, a famous singer, from Milan, but now my wife and mother of my cherub.'

Camilla summoned Figgins and they went out into the grey, foggy day, feeling they had come away from a brighter, warmer world. On an impulse, she directed the coachman to drive them to Gunters. 'You may eat some pastries and have a dish of hot chocolate,' she said to Alethea, who was always hungry.

Once arrived at Gunters, Camilla dismissed the carriage; they would walk home, she said, it was no distance. They went inside, assailed by the wonderful aromas of chocolate and coffee and baking, and sat at a little table near the window.

Alethea made a careful choice from the splendid display of the pastry-cook's art, and sipped with great contentment at her big bowl of chocolate. They had insisted that Figgins come in with them and have some chocolate too, and she sat in a state of bliss at a stool towards the back of the shop, in the company of several other servants, gossiping every bit as busily as their mistresses.

The place was a hubbub of conversation and activity as people went in and out and servants went through to the back to collect the long orders of desserts for grand dinner parties, since few Londoners kept their own pastry chefs.

As Camilla drank her own chocolate, she looked about her at the people talking at nearby tables, greeting friends, waiting for their orders or making their choices and found herself wondering, with an interest she had never felt before, which of the couples she was watching were man and wife, which lovers, which no more than friends.

She noticed the warmth of a look passing between a man and a woman, indicative of an understanding or rapport that she herself had no experience of. Then there were smiles, little attentions, a clear desire to be closer to a companion. Others were not so sure of their situation and so sent different messages with an arch tilt of the head, a flirtatious glance followed by immediate lowering of eyes on the woman's part; the tipping of a hat, twitch of a stock, slapping of gloves on a masculine thigh from the man.

The door opened once more, and in walked their cousin Sophie, accompanied by Mrs Gardiner. Greetings, exclamations of surprise and pleasure, explanations. The twins had gone on to a lunch engagement with friends – with which friends? Camilla wondered – and the men had gone off somewhere on their own pursuits.

'Although I dare say Mr Wytton at least will call round this afternoon, he had little enough time with Sophie this morning, and she was attending more to buying shoe roses than she was to him. We have called in here to collect some sweetmeats, and then we are going home.'

Sophie was eyeing Alethea, who was tucking into yet another pastry. 'La, cousin, how can you eat all that? You will get monstrous fat.'

'Not I,' said Alethea. 'I never put on weight.'

Mrs Gardiner was urging them to come home with her to Albemarle Street. 'Fanny can spare you. We have not had the pleasure of Alethea's company this visit. I wanted to say this morning, only I could see it was not quite convenient, how much she is grown; she is quite the young lady!'

This earned her a glowering look from Alethea, which she wisely chose not to see. 'And the twins are become great beauties. Everyone talks of them, but I had not seen for myself how lovely they are.'

'I hope everyone does not talk of them.'

'They do,' said Sophie, with a shrug. 'They call them Day and Night, one being so fair and the other dark. The gentlemen are all mad for them.'

'That can hardly be true,' Camilla said, 'since they have scarcely put their noses out of doors except to do some shopping. They have been to no parties, and Fanny does not think it right for them to go to balls.'

'Lady Fanny was talking to Madame Lapierre about ball gowns for them, however,' said Sophie, her angelic countenance taking on a slightly shrewish expression. 'I heard her.'

'A private dance, perhaps,' Camilla said, with a sinking heart. 'They may be allowed to go to a private dance or two.'

Sophie looked unconvinced, and did not seem pleased when Alethea announced that she would like to go back to the Gardiners' house. Could not Figgins be sent home with a message for Fanny? They would not be wanted at home, especially if the twins were out.

'Cousin Fanny can have a peaceful time without the four of us. And as for Letty, she was planning to tidy her writing desk, the travelling one she takes everywhere. It is stuffed full of letters, you know, and I dare say there may be one or two there from Tom; Lord, only think what a state she will work herself into if there are any letters of his. Not that there can be anything so very much, though, when one thinks about it, since he was always a poor hand with a pen.'

Camilla had to agree, although she did not say so. Tom, delightful though he was in so many ways, had passed unscathed through his education, and were he not a gentleman, must count as an illiterate. A scrawl regarding a gun or a dog was his limit; there was nothing unusual in that, however, most men were poor correspondents. Even a scrawl, though, might be enough to set Letty off again.

The Gardiners did seem a better prospect, and she must just hope that Letty would burn any scribbles from Tom that she should find. More likely she would indulge in an orgy of might-have-beens; if so, she would bore herself into a rational frame of mind more quickly if left on her own.

'Mind, Figgins, when you have passed our message to Lady Fanny, you are to reassure Miss Darcy that we are well and have had no mishap on our outing. Tell her we are quite safe in the care of Mrs Gardiner, she need have no concern for us.'

'Say also that I shall send Miss Camilla and Miss Alethea home in my carriage,' added Mrs Gardiner. 'Come along, girls. Sophie, you may carry the box of sweetmeats.'

At Albemarle Street, Camilla had another opportunity to ponder on marriage and courtship. Mr and Mrs Gardiner were a contented couple, easy together and grown in some ways very alike. She was struck by this, for her parents, she considered, were equally affectionate, but they had retained their own very different personalities. Would Sophie Gardiner and Mr Wytton grow to be like the Gardiners after many years of married life together, or be more like Mr and Mrs Darcy?

These reflections came as a result of the promised afternoon call from Mr Wytton, accompanied once more by Mr Layard, whose face brightened as he saw her. He came over to sit beside her, and she asked him his opinion on this matter.

'Why, Wytton will never grow like anyone else, so if they are to become alike, then Miss Sophie will have to become a connoisseur and an antiquarian.'

He had spoken in a low voice, but not so low that Mrs Gardiner did not hear. 'Such an idea, Mr Layard, how can you say such things? No woman can be a connoisseur, nor yet an antiquarian. The notion is absurd!'

Camilla was surprised by the vehemence of these words. Mrs Gardiner turned away to speak to Mr Wytton, and, giving Mr Layard a speaking look, she said, 'I fear we have upset Mrs Gardiner.'

Mr Layard dropped his voice until it was the merest whisper. 'The word connoisseur carries a dangerous meaning to that generation.'

She would have liked to know more, she had never thought of connoisseur as an especially incendiary word, but good manners forbade her to persist, or to continue to hold a whispered conversation with Mr Layard, so she smiled and changed the subject, asking him if *Frankenstein* had yet come his way. It was the strangest book, only just out.

'Lord, there you go again, Camilla, talking of books again,' cried Sophie. 'You will be called bookish, they will say you are a blue-stocking if you do not take care. And how can you speak of that abominable book? It is altogether nonsense, no one reads it, and those that have cry out against it. I am sure I don't want to read it. And I heard that it was written by a young woman; she should know better, indeed she should.'

'They say Mary Shelley is the author,' said Mr Wytton laconically.

'I do not believe it,' said Layard. 'No woman could write such a book – or would want to.'

Wytton agreed with him. 'I do not myself believe it is within a woman's scope to write so powerful a narrative.'

'You are harsh in your judgements.' Camilla had no wish to be drawn into an argument, but she could not let such a remark go past unchallenged. 'Maria Edgeworth is a novelist with considerable powers of expression.'

'That is different, one expects women to write that kind of thing. *Frankenstein* is quite another matter. I dare say Shelley wrote it himself.'

'You mean the poet, Shelley,' said Sophie, with a pout. 'I do not care for poets.'

'Not even for Lord Byron?' asked Mr Layard, quizzing her.

'Oh, he himself is so dashing, so romantic, but his poetry is such stuff! There is no doing with it. Everyone goes on about *The Corsair* and quotes all those lines, but it is not to my taste, I tried it once, and how it made me yawn.'

Her contempt for the works of Europe's most famous poet brought extra colour to her face, and she gave a little shake of her shoulders.

Mr Wytton was looking at her with a kind of hunger in his eyes that made Camilla go quite cold. It was a look that combined affection with a predatoriness that was almost shocking. She had seen ardour in men's faces, had noticed it with the disinterest of an untouched heart, but this look of Mr Wytton hit her with particular force, and she was at a loss to know why.

He had moved closer to Sophie, and stood now behind her chair. His hand fell carelessly on her shoulder, touched a loose curl that had strayed down her neck, and she looked up at him with a smile and moved her face slightly so that his hand brushed her cheek.

She averted her eyes, felt her face burning, was amazed at how this was affecting her. Did she long for such a touch? She supposed she might, with a particular man—

'Daydreaming, Miss Camilla?' Mr Layard's words broke into

her thoughts. 'I was speaking of Dr Frankenstein's monster and the chase across the ice, and you do not attend to a word I have been saying.'

She apologised, thankfully pulling her attention back to the novel, and wondering what her cousin Fitzwilliam would think of that book. He and Fanny were another devoted couple and perhaps it was the disparity in age, the awkwardness of a second marriage that made him so inclined to lay down the law on subjects that her own father would never have worried about. She must buy another copy of *Frankenstein*, as soon as one was to be had, and send it to Constantinople.

'My mother will enjoy it greatly, I feel sure, and my father, too, for it is all about the Pandora's box that is modern science, is it not? Papa takes a great interest in natural philosophy.'

When the gentlemen had left, Camilla and Alethea waited for the carriage to come and take them the short journey home, Mrs Gardiner having made so much fuss about their walking as made it impossible to refuse her kind offer. Mrs Gardiner had hurried out of the room to see to it, and to look for a pattern she had promised Fanny. In her absence, Sophie saw no reason to hold her tongue.

'So you have set up a flirt, cousin,' she said to Camilla.

Camilla said nothing; she had no intention of crossing swords with Sophie.

'They say Sir Sidney Leigh is dangling after you. Some people hold it was Letty he liked, but that now you are the object of his attentions. How do you like to have such a beau? He is quite old, but then—'

Her cousin's pert look amused her; it so clearly implied how great was the difference between the bloom of seventeen and her own withered, spinster state at the age of not yet twenty.

'Letty must feel it, with all the unhappiness she had about Tom Busby, and now that all turns out to be a hum, and she is left on the shelf. Not to be married at one-and-twenty! It must upset her dreadfully every time she thinks about it.'

'Since Letty has too much sense to think any such thing, it does not distress her at all,' she said, wishing Mrs Gardiner would come back into the room and put an end to Sophie's ill-natured comments.

'Of course, there is no abbey in the case with Sir Sidney. He does not have an abbey. Only a country house, I believe, something quite modest. Do you know what his income is? Wytton has thirty thousand a year, and it could be more, Papa says, if he would but attend to his estates instead of gallivanting off abroad.'

Alethea had been listening to her cousin with undisguised contempt. 'How vulgar you are become, Sophie,' she said. 'All this talk of flirts and money. Have you nothing better to fill your mind? Perhaps a few hours every day reading and applying yourself to your music would do you good. How is your playing? Have you made much progress since last we heard you?'

Sophie flushed; she was no musician. 'Oh, we know how superior your performance is.'

'Thank you,' said Alethea, with exaggerated gratitude.

'It is wrong to tease Sophie so,' Camilla said when they were tucked up in the Gardiners' carriage.

'How saucy and bold she has become; you didn't tell me what she was like. Goodness, the way that Mr Wytton looks at her, as though at any minute he would gobble her up! She won't be able to play off her tricks with him once they're married, you may be sure. She's like a gazelle who has caught hold of a tiger's tail and thinks it's a toy.'

'Do you see Sophie as a gazelle?' said Camilla, rather startled by her younger sister's perception.

'Well,' considering, 'to look at, yes.'

'And Mr Wytton a tiger?'

'Just like a caged beast,' said Alethea with a peal of laughter. 'Like a caricature of some animal dressed up in coat and stock.'

'Like an animal? Oh, no, Sophie, he seems to me to be a very civilised man.'

'He is, do not mistake me, but the rooms and minds of London society are too constricting for him. I expect he is more at ease among his male companions, people of his own kind. Sophie will see little of him when they are married. She will not mind. She marries him for his abbey and his thirty thousand a year, not for the virtues of his intellect and character.'

'Alethea!'

'Don't be priggish, Camilla, it don't suit you. You know I'm right.'

NINE

The next Sunday, the girls went to divine service in different places. Fanny was privately relieved; the five striking-looking girls had on previous Sundays attracted a good deal of attention at the Belgrave Chapel where she and her husband worshipped on most Sundays. Fitzwilliam had not liked it, and it had quite destroyed the peaceful pleasure she usually took in going to church, listening to a sensible sermon, meeting friends and walking home afterwards on her husband's arm.

Belle and Georgina at first said they would not go to church at all. It was a bright, windy day, 'It is exceedingly tiresome, this breeze does make the feathers in my hat blow about so,' Belle complained.

'And it whips up such colour in one's cheeks, I look like a milkmaid wandered in from the fields,' said Georgina.

'We can read over the service at home,' Belle offered.

Mr Fitzwilliam, however, would have none of it. He was strict in such matters, and to church they must go.

Alethea had expressed a desire to go to St Paul's. She wished to hear the choir. She looked daggers at Fanny when it was suggested that the twins should go with her, but they declined; nobody of fashion went to St Paul's they said, only dowdy, dreary people would attend the service there.

'I shall be dowdy and dreary, then,' said Camilla. 'I intend to go with Alethea. She should not go there on her own.'

Letitia didn't want to go to St Paul's either. Instead, to every-one's surprise, she announced her intention of going to St Botolph's. Captain Allington had told them what a fine preacher Mr Valpy was, did they not remember him talking of it?

Camilla remembered the conversation perfectly well. Captain Allington had remarked that he sometimes accompanied his Aunt Roland to church – 'Expectations, you know; I have hopes in that direction. My aunt is rich and has no children.'

How odd that Letitia should want to go, for the Captain had described Mr Valpy as the type of clergyman who shook your conscience about and warned that you were teetering on the brink of damnation. 'He's devilish hot against Sunday travel and all that kind of thing, too. He preaches the sort of sermon that makes you glad when it's all over.' Camilla could sympathise with that; she all too often felt glad when a sermon was over, but not necessarily because she had smelt fire and brimstone coming from the pulpit. Letty must be in an unusually bleak frame of mind to choose such a service – which was surprising, because she had recently seemed in better spirits.

That left Belle and Georgina quarrelling over where to take themselves. They finally decided on the Chapel Royal. Mr Fitzwilliam didn't like that idea at all, but was reassured by Miss Griffin's promising to go with them and make sure they behaved properly in such a fashionable and august congregation – for one or two of the royal family often attended service there.

Camilla had not been to St Paul's before, and she was overwhelmed by the immensity of the nave and dome. They had arrived early, so as to be able to view the building, and she wandered about, happy to find the memorial to John Donne, whose sermons she was familiar with and whose poetry, both sacred and profane, she greatly admired, preferring it indeed to that of the nature poets so admired by most of her contemporaries. Then they were approached by a black-robed verger, who informed them they would have time to visit the crypt and see Nelson's tomb before they needed to take their places for divine service. So they descended into the crypt under his guidance, and she stood, much moved, by the newly finished tomb of the great hero; while Alethea, who cared nothing for battles and naval officers of whatever distinction, prowled about among the dusty relics.

Camilla enjoyed the singing at St Paul's, although her sister was more critical. Alethea sang the hymns with unselfconscious enjoyment, turning heads up and down the line as her voice rang out. As they filed out after the service, a man in a clerical collar came up to her and complimented her on her sister's singing. 'Forgive me intruding upon you; you are surprised to be accosted by a stranger, but I have the pleasure of being acquainted with Miss Darcy, and I noticed you at Almack's, although we were not introduced. She spoke of a younger sister with a fine voice, and so I thought, this must be that sister.'

She was somewhat surprised to be addressed by a man she did not recognise – did Letty know any clergymen in London? Then she had it: this was the man her sister had danced with at Almack's, the friend of Lord Rampton. She searched in her mind for his name, surely Letty had mentioned it. 'Mr Barcombe, is it not?'

He bowed. 'At your service. May I present you to my sister, Mrs Seton? Louisa, this is Miss Camilla Darcy.'

The woman beside him smiled and held out her hand. She was very like him, not tall, but with elegant features and a sense of style about her.

'This is my youngest sister, Alethea,' she said.

Alethea gazed disapprovingly at Mr Barcombe's clerical garb, she was apt to be suspicious of clergymen. The little group stood to one side to let some other worshippers pass, and then moved into the space under the dome.

'You have two other younger sisters,' said Mr Barcombe, a trifle awkwardly. 'I met them, I believe, in the park. Twins, are they not, but not so alike? One dark and one fair.'

Alethea favoured him with one of her perceptive glances. 'Belle is the fair one and Georgina is dark. They have the same colour eyes, otherwise they aren't much alike. Except they're both very silly,' she added under her breath.

Camilla gave her a warning look, but Mrs Seton had over-heard the remark and seemed amused by it. 'How charmingly you sing,' she said to Alethea. The two of them walked on ahead, talking music as they went.

'My sister is a keen musician,' said Mr Barcombe. 'She holds musical soirées in her house in Park Street. I am sure she would be delighted if you and your sisters— I am sure all your sisters are musical.'

She liked him, for all that he seemed to have been bowled over by the twins; she wondered which of the two had captivated him. 'Georgina and Belle play the pianoforte and harp together,' she said, helping him out.

'The harp? How enchanting. Then I feel sure . . . and perhaps Miss Alethea?'

'Alethea is still in the schoolroom, so although she loves to listen to music, she cannot go out to parties.'

'Oh, but a private party is different. My eldest sister's children are often there, a girl of fifteen and a boy of sixteen, when he is home from Harrow, that is. They are both musical.'

She smiled and said what was proper, deciding it was better not to go into the question of whether the twins should go to such parties, never mind Alethea, and they made their way out through the great doors and down the steps to where the carriages were waiting.

'May I do myself the honour of waiting upon you and your sisters?' Mr Barcombe enquired, as he handed them into their carriage. 'If Mrs Fitzwilliam has no objection.'

'He's nutty on Belle,' said Alethea confidently, as the carriage started forward. 'What larks, only he seems quite nice. Belle will chew him up and spit him out, just like she does everyone.'

'Alethea!'

'Don't Alethea me. I don't know what's come over you since we arrived in London, you've gone all prosy.'

'Have I? Oh, dear, I do not mean to be.'

'I thought if I mentioned it, you might do something about it,' said Alethea in a kindly way. 'Letty's quite enough, without you going on at one as well.'

Letitia had been delighted by her hellfire sermon, and was wanting to tell them all about it when she returned to Aubrey Square. The Reverend Valpy, she said, was an excellent preacher. And Captain Allington had been there, waiting upon his aunt. 'Who,' she said, with a spurt of humour, 'appeared to be wearing a dead pheasant in her hat!'

Fanny laughed at this, saying that feathers were fashionable, which they knew, but that too many could give an odd appearance, as she had warned them.

Belle and Georgina were full of the excitement of their visit to the Chapel Royal. They had seen a saturnine royal duke, and as for feathers, the hats that the Miss Berrys were wearing made them stare. 'Not only feathers, but fruit. Imagine!'

'Now, my loves, you must not say a word against the Miss Berrys,' said Fanny. 'Their salon is the very smartest place to go. They have entertained everyone who is anyone this past age, and it does not do to get on the wrong side of them.'

'Oh, stuffy people, I dare say,' said Belle. 'Only listen, after the service, this woman in a ravishing green silk dress and a velvet pelisse came up to us, and said she was our aunt. Our Aunt Lydia, who had not seen us since we were in the nursery! Now, what do you think of that? Are you not amazed? For I am sure I do not remember her at all, nor Papa and Mama ever speaking of her.'

No, thought Camilla, for although her mother retained an affection for her younger sister, her father had little time for her. She had an idea that Papa had much disliked her aunt's husband, Mr Wickham, that there had been some major disagreement between them, which lingered even after the unfortunate man had been killed in Spain.

Georgina took up the story. 'She is not at all plump, not in the least bit like Aunt Kitty; she is very slender and lively. She had a vastly smart bonnet on, and was with a dark man, quite short, a good deal older. He is her husband, for he said he was our uncle, which of course he must be if he is married to her. He was very struck with Belle, looked her up and down in that just-so way men have, and bowed over her hand. Aunt Lydia laughed at him, and said she would have to watch him with such pretty nieces about. Then she asked if we were all come to town. She did not know of Papa's going abroad; however, she didn't seem to mind his not being with us.'

'I have her card,' said Belle, producing it with a flourish. 'She wants us to call, and indeed, may we, Cousin Fanny? For she is our aunt, and she promises to take us to all kinds of exciting places.'

Fanny exchanged anguished glances with her husband, who frowned, said it would be proper for all the girls to pay a morning call on their aunt, under the chaperonage of Fanny, but that no further acquaintance than that would be necessary or indeed suitable.

Letitia and Camilla, seeing Belle and Georgina about to embark on arguments, pleadings, protestations and all the other weapons of persuasion in their considerable armoury, quickly turned the conversation into other channels, speaking of sermons, music, the people attending the services and the clothes they had seen, and quelling their sisters with fierce and uncompromising looks every time they threatened to open their mouths.

Alethea, who could no longer contain herself and was overcome by laughter, was escorted from the room by Miss Griffin, and she went uncomplainingly, promising to play to her governess all the music she had heard that morning, and asking in a loud voice if she did she not agree that the twins were the most odious girls in the world.

That night, Fitzwilliam came early to his wife's chamber, his lips prim and his brow furrowed. 'I do not like this connection at all, my love,' he told her, sitting himself down before her fire and stretching out his hands to the flames. 'That was an unfortunate meeting of the twins with Lydia Pollexfen. They were bound to meet sooner or late, but even so, I cannot be altogether happy about the acquaintance. Francis Pollexfen is all very well, and an intimate of the Prince of Wales, he moves in the highest court circles, to be sure, but he is a roué, a man of very doubtful reputation. And does not his wife gamble, and keep company with Lady Aldernay and her set? I shudder to think what Darcy would have to say if he were to discover his daughters mixing with such people as these.'

Fanny was applying cream to her soft cheeks. 'You are quite right. It would be a most unsuitable set for the girls to get in to. I have no worries about Letty and Camilla. I believe they know something of their Aunt Lydia's history, and they will take care not to be drawn into her circle. But the twins! They are so young, they are attracted by everything that is lively and fun, and who can blame them? Do not worry, I shall take good care of them, and they will only attend such parties and outings as I say they may. They will obey me, you know, for if they do not, they will find themselves back in the schoolroom.'

'I had no idea it would cause so many difficulties to have the girls to stay,' grumbled her husband, taking off his robe and climbing into bed beside her. 'I am sure I hope our little girls will not grow up to be so hard at hand.'

'Darcy's daughters are not hard at hand, they are the best-natured girls in all the world, I do assure you. Young ladies are like that at this age; you will find ours just the same.'

He blew out the candle and slid closer to Fanny. 'My dear, I hope not.'

Camilla, in her solitary bed, had not extinguished her candle, but was reading the forbidden volume of Boccaccio. Then her eyes grew tired, and she put the book down on the table beside the bed. She lay there, her mind soothed by the candlelight and the flames from the fire, which sent shadows dancing around the room. The coal hissed and crackled as it burned, and the windowpanes rattled behind the shutters in what had turned from a breeze into a strong wind, an equinoctial gale. Did the equinoctial winds blow in Constantinople? Would Mama and Papa be lying in some richly adorned chamber, with strangely fashioned windows, and the wind howling outside, perhaps in some extreme oriental fashion?

Letty would be fretting over the wind, as she always did. She had gone to bed, shaking her head, full of doubt that they would all come safely through the night. Windowpanes could shatter, tiles be torn off, letting in rain, bringing ceilings down from the force of water. And outside! Chimneypots might come tumbling down into the street, to the peril of those walking below. True, there was not the danger from falling trees and flying branches that were to be expected in the country, but then shop signs in town swung about so violently, and had been known to come hurtling off their fastenings, positively decapitating any unfortunate who stood in their way.

She heard the creak of her sister's bed, and the sound of footsteps crossing the room. She quickly blew out her candle; she really did not feel inclined to hear all Letty's fears, nor to be an object of her concern, with invitations to share her room that they might be a comfort to each other, suggestions that they should make sure their sisters were safe, worries that the servants might have neglected to fasten the doors properly, thus allowing burglars, the weather and Lord knew what else to come visiting in the small dark hours.

She lay still, not answering the gentle knock on the door, and presently she heard Letty return to her own room. Her mind drifted back to the sunlit tales in the *Decameron*, the nature of love between men and women, the possibility of her seeing Sir Sidney upon the morrow, and, more alarmingly, on her Aunt Lydia's two marriages and the likelihood of the twins falling under her influence. Fanny might be sanguine, but she had seen the gleam in Belle and Georgina's eyes; she knew that they had been delighted by their aunt and would not easily be persuaded to keep the acquaintance to a formal visit or two. No matter, she would mention it to Fanny; her cousin must by now be realising just how strong-willed her younger sisters could be. All three of them; what a mercy it was that Alethea was still under Griffy's care.

On the top floor Miss Griffin, a warm shawl wrapped round her head, her nose red and streaming, wrote by the light of a single candle, covering page after page of cream paper in a flowing, beautifully formed hand. In the room on the other side of the passage, Alethea sat in front of the fire as Figgins carefully took a pair of scissors to her curly hair, while she made plans for her time in London; such plans as would have sent her eldest sisters starting from their comfortable beds if they could but have heard her vibrant voice outlining them to Figgins in the warm and private chamber above.

TEN

Mrs Pollexfen came to call on Fanny and her nieces the very next day, before any plans about visiting her or attempts to subdue the twins' expectations could be made. The timing was unlucky, for although Lady Fanny was at home and receiving visitors, her thoughts were all taken up with concern for Charlotte, who had developed a severe sore throat and, overnight had started a rash, thus increasing her mother's alarm that she might be going down with a serious illness.

Letitia at once added to Fanny's maternal fears. She shook her head, looked grave and recommended that a physician be called for without delay.

'I have already sent for Dr Molloy,' said Fanny.

'You cannot be too careful,' Letitia said. 'So many dangerous illnesses start in such a way.'

'And so many cases of a sore throat and rash turn out to be just that,' said Camilla quickly. 'A child is fretful for a day or two, and then he or she is restored to perfect health and forgets all about it. Pray do not worry, Fanny. I assure you, I and all my sisters, to say nothing of my little brothers were forever throwing out rashes of one sort or another, and we are all perfectly healthy.'

'That was in the country,' Letitia felt obliged to point out. 'In London it is different, and the opportunities for catching serious infections are so much greater.'

'Oh, fiddlesticks.' Why did Letty not notice the effect her words were having on their cousin, and hold her tongue? Certainly the little girl did not look well, but there was no need for such a long face, nor of expressing certainty of there being some serious complaint. 'Dr Molloy will be here directly, Fanny, and I am sure he will be able to set your mind at rest.'

'Indeed, I hope so.' Fanny's face brightened as she heard the knocker sound. 'Perhaps that is the doctor now.' She hurried to the door, but only to hear Fell announce Mrs Pollexfen.

'The physician is not yet come, my lady,' he said, as Aunt Lydia came through the door talking and fluttering her hands and uttering little laughs. She stopped, held up her hands in an extravagant gesture of delight and glided forward to clasp Letitia in a scented embrace.

'How lovely you are grown, Letty, so like my sister Jane; a little taller perhaps, but even prettier, I swear.'

Her greeting to Camilla was not quite so warm. 'And you, so like your dear mother, although your hair is a trifle darker, is it not? And you have her satirical eye. I am quite prepared to be afraid of you, for you must know that my sister can be quite provoking at times.'

Camilla greeted her aunt, who then moved away to bestow soft, cooing kisses on the twins, who were clearly much more to her liking. 'I thought, when I set eyes on you, who are those divinely pretty creatures? Having no idea, you may be sure, that you were my own nieces. For when I last saw you, you were two little dumplings in the nursery. Who could imagine you would grow into such beauties? For in our family, you know, there was but the one beauty, and that was my sister Jane. Your mother was well enough, although too sharp-eyed to be called a real beauty. I was pretty, you know, much the prettiest, but Jane was truly beautiful.'

Camilla could believe that her Aunt Lydia had been pretty, for she had kept the faded remnants of her youthful looks. But whereas Aunt Jane was still a beauty – this, in her case, being a matter of bones and feature as much as it had ever been due to youth and bloom – Aunt Lydia's charms were rather those of manner and style. Her smiles, elegance, gestures, the play of her eyes, and her fashionable but individual dressing were the basis of her attractiveness.

And she was attractive. She commanded attention, and if Camilla suspected that the smiling mouth might look waspish in repose, and the darting glances of her eyes give way to a shrewder, colder gaze, none of that was evident at this moment.

'I can see you eyeing my gown,' cried her aunt. 'You are wondering where I had it from, who my dressmaker is, for it is not quite in the English fashion, is it? Well, my dears, I can tell you that I have all my gowns from Paris, and this is the latest stare in France, and will presently be all the rage in London, I assure you. I am not a beauty, as I said, and not so very young, although younger than your mother of course, and all my other sisters, for I was the baby of the family. Therefore I must dress in the first style of elegance, and I have my hair cut and attended to by a Frenchman also. I shall give you his name, he will not see to just anyone, but if you mention you are my nieces, there will not be the least problem in the world. Let me tell you, my dear girls, how important it is to be elegant as you grow older. For now you all have such pretty roses in your cheeks – well, I thank God I have retained my complexion, I regard that as a great blessing – but as the years pass, the bloom fades, and then elegance is your support. And for true elegance, let me tell you, you need to spend a great deal of money on yourself, so be mindful of that, and make sure you all find yourselves rich husbands.'

Did she ever draw breath? Camilla wondered.

There was a diversion, in the shape of Alethea, who had been summoned from the schoolroom to come down to the drawing-room and meet her aunt.

'Oh!' said Mrs Pollexfen, her eyebrows shooting up, and her smile vanishing. 'Good gracious me, who is this?'

'This is Alethea,' Camilla said, pushing her forward to make her curtsy.

'Heavens, how like your father you are, you give me quite a shock.'

'How do you do, ma'am?' Alethea said politely. 'I do take after my father, I believe.'

'Well, I dare say out of the five of you, it was to be expected – however, you others do not have the Darcy look at all, no, nor do any of you resemble his sister Georgiana. Now, she was never considered to be pretty, although she married so well, and in her first season.'

117

Letitia wasn't too happy about these remarks. 'I am not unlike my father, in colouring at least.'

'Oh, do not mistake me,' said Mrs Pollexfen. 'I mean no slight, I assure you, for Darcy was always held to be the handsomest of men, even if I could never see it; he was nothing in comparison to my dear Wickham, you know, who was as agreeable as he was handsome. Alethea here just has that direct look of your father's, you know, it quite takes me back. And in a female, I am not so sure – although you are still young, are you not, Alethea?'

'I am sixteen.'

'There you are, there is time yet for your looks to soften, and you will become as pretty as your sisters, I dare say. Of course, I was married at fifteen, I am a great believer in early marriages. I was amazed that your mother kept you in the country so long. I wrote and told her so: send the young ladies to London, I said, and I shall take care of them. Let them enjoy the delights of town and beaux, and they will find husbands in no time at all. For you all have excellent fortunes, I know. It is all over town that the rich Miss Darcys are here for the season, and I warrant the fortune hunters are already after you, is that not so?'

She turned to Fanny. 'You must take the greatest care of them, and make sure they go everywhere where they may meet men of fashion and wealth. Oh, I shall devise several schemes for them of my own, don't doubt it; we shall have such fun! What a shame that Alethea will not be able to share in these delights.'

Camilla caught sight of Alethea's face, and hoped that she would refrain from expressing her opinion of any such delights as their aunt might offer. Not that anything would come of them; Fanny was already opening her mouth to make such civil apologies as she might for refusing to allow her charges to spend much time with their aunt.

Mrs Pollexfen, however, did not listen to a word Fanny was saying; Camilla felt that she was probably in the habit of not hearing what she did not wish to. She was addressing the twins with great animation on the subject of routs, visits to pleasure gardens, pic-nics, breakfasts and other festivities guaranteed to appeal to their frivolous hearts.

Fanny was called away by the arrival of Dr Molloy, and the minute she was out of the room, Mrs Pollexfen sat down upon a sofa, bade the twins join her, and started to make plans.

Alethea rolled her eyes upwards, shrugged, and asked Camilla if she might be excused, as she had been in the middle of a lesson with Miss Griffin. She made her adieux to her aunt, who gave her a chilly smile, dismissing her with, 'Yes, indeed, you may run along back to your books, my dear, that is the best place for you.'

Camilla had to smile at the face that Alethea pulled over her shoulder at her aunt and the twins before she disappeared. Her sister's feet banged on the stairs as she ran up them; the very sound was expressive of her indignation and contempt. She was incorrigible, and it was lucky that Mrs Pollexfen hadn't noticed the face; on the other hand, Camilla couldn't blame Alethea for her behaviour.

Letitia was listening to her aunt's conversation with a prim look on her face. She drew closer and said in a low voice, 'I do not think Papa and Mama would approve of our seeing very much of our aunt.'

'I am sure they would not. Do not be concerned, and do not berate the twins, for heaven's sake, or you will set their backs up and make them more resolute in wanting what you have disapproved of. Leave it to Fanny, she will put a stop to it soon enough.'

Their aunt was addressing them, patting Belle's arm as she spoke. 'Here we have been discussing an evening party in my house. It is of all things what I enjoy, and so does my dear Francis: he loves to have pretty females in his drawing-room. He is susceptible to beauty, I often tease him about it. We shall summon all the most eligible young men, and one or two older ones, as well; what will you say, Camilla, if I mention the name of one Sir Sidney?'

She gave a trill of laughter, as, despite herself, Camilla flushed.

'I am right, you see, but you need not blush, for all the world knows about it, there is no secret in the case; wherever I go, I hear your names coupled together. It will be a good match for you, for he is a man of substance, with a good intelligence, and since I know your dear parents consider you clever, and I dare say you are, you will need to choose a man of that kind. It is not every man who wants a clever wife, so you have been fortunate to catch his eye. And even if he is— but we shall not talk of that, it don't signify in the least. You are a rational creature, and it is better to marry with one's head than with one's heart. I know I would not have said so when I was a girl, and indeed I am the greatest romantic; however, marriage is more than a matter of yearnings and sighings, and every young girl looking out for a husband should realise that. You are sensible, and have as much prospect of happiness as any young woman I know who is on the verge of matrimony.'

Camilla was thoroughly alarmed by this speech. 'I beg of you, do not say such things! There is nothing in the nature of an attachment between myself and any man, and I have no thoughts of matrimony at present.'

'It is right and proper that you should say so, and you may trust me to say not a word, for it is different here, where we are all family together, and may speak openly and say what we like, is that not so?'

It seemed that the world had chosen that day to beat a path to the Fitzwilliams' door. No sooner had Mrs Pollexfen, exclaiming at the length of her visit and the lateness of the hour and protesting that she would at once set about making arrangements for her various schemes, been shown out, than the knocker sounded again. Masculine steps on the stair, this time, and a thin, sleek clergymen with a supercilious expression was shown into the room.

'The Reverend Mr Valpy,' announced the footman, and withdrew.

Camilla looked at the newcomer with astonishment. She had never been introduced to this man, and nor, judging by their surprised faces, had Belle and Georgina. He advanced into the room with the air of bestowing a favour upon it, and addressed Letty, who had hurried forward on his entrance.

'Ah, my dear Miss Darcy. I see you recognise me, and I beg

your pardon for calling upon you unannounced. I do not apologise for my lack of ceremony in dispensing with any introduction, for I am aware, as you must be, that it is the duty of a clergyman to visit the members of his congregation, and I was told that we numbered you among our worshippers on Sunday last.'

Letitia was flustered. 'Oh. Yes, that is so, I was in the company of— that is to say, I attended the service with Lady Innis and her nephew Captain Allington.'

'Aha, the Captain and I are well acquainted, and so I felt I should call and welcome you to our little circle.'

Letitia had recovered herself by that time. 'I am flattered by the attention, sir, for indeed your congregation is by no means small; I saw that the church was full on Sunday morning. You must have many claims upon your time, I know how onerous are the duties of a busy clergyman. You will have parish duties, and the sick to visit.'

'I visit the sick on Thursdays, unless the matter is urgent,' said Mr Valpy complacently. He turned his attention to Camilla, didn't seem to like what he saw, and then looked at the twins. 'Your sisters, I comprehend, Miss Darcy? Are they not also churchgoers?'

Letitia hastened to explain that they often attended service at different places of worship.

He pursed his lips in clerical disapproval. 'Families should worship together. Sabbath observance begins and ends with the family, you know. I would strongly advise your esteemed father to bring you all to our service next Sunday. Perhaps if he is at home—?'

Camilla had to suppress a laugh at the thought of how her father would react to this absurd man. How could Letty be so civil? The twins had less restraint, and were whispering together on the sofa.

'My parents are presently abroad,' said Letitia.

'But they will have left you in the care of some respectable and watchful relation, surely?' said Mr Valpy.

Camilla frowned at Letty, who was explaining about the Fitzwilliams; what business was it of the Reverend Valpy's whose care they were in – or where and how they went to church?

'My cousins, the Fitzwilliams,' Letitia concluded, 'generally attend divine service at the Belgrave Chapel.'

He looked deeply disappointed, and shook his head. 'Far be it from me to criticise my fellow professionals at any place of worship; however, when one's conscience is at stake, one cannot be too careful.'

He waited expectantly, and Letitia offered him a chair, which he took with the air of a man prepared to sit out his half-hour.

How awkward it was. Camilla wished that Fanny would return; she would be more than a match for a presumptuous clergyman. Really, though, what could even Fanny do, with Letitia encouraging Mr Valpy to stay? There she was, engaging him in earnest conversation, while Belle and Georgina were reduced to staring at him with petulant disbelief.

Another knock, more footsteps, and the footman, himself wearing a faint look of surprise on his well-trained countenance, ushered in the Reverend Barcombe.

One was bad enough, two were impossible. 'Is there a plague of parsons come upon us?' cried Belle.

Mr Barcombe, who had exchanged chilly bows with Mr Valpy amid the general introductions, let his mouth twitch, while Letitia shushed her sisters, who were in fits of laughter, and apologised for their unseemly levity.

Why was Fanny taking so long with Dr Molloy? Camilla hoped there was nothing seriously amiss with Charlotte; indeed, she had looked feverish and somewhat sickly, but not exceptionally so; she seemed more cross than ill, in fact.

Mr Barcombe was making his peace with the twins, rallying them on their prejudice towards men of the cloth, and turning their laughter to pleased smiles as they listened to his extravagant compliments and sallies.

Who next? Their morning callers so far had been an odd and not altogether welcome collection. Why did not Sir Sidney come? There had been mention made of a drive in the park, but he had not called, nor had any servant come round with a note.

How different a knocker sounded when it made your heart

beat in expectation of it being that one person of all others you wished to see. As the door knocker below sounded yet again, she strained to hear the voice that had such particular ability to interest and enliven her feelings. But it was a gravelly voice speaking outside on the landing, not the one she had hoped to hear.

It was Pagoda Portal who followed Fanny and the doctor into the room, expressing his regret at the news of Charlotte's indisposition, and offering to send for fruit from his succession houses at his country estate, if Dr Molloy would sanction such an addition to her diet.

Dr Molloy, quite at his ease, looked approvingly with his cold eyes at the bevy of young ladies and accepted a glass of wine.

Mr Valpy was not happy to find himself in company with a doctor. 'Surely, the tradesmen's entrance and the backstairs rather than in the drawing-room with gentlemen,' he said in a low voice to Letitia.

Dr Molloy, who apparently had excellent hearing, gave Valpy a sardonic look.

Mr Portal, standing beside Letitia and holding up an eyeglass, the better to examine an oval miniature hanging on the wall, gave a guffaw. 'You are quite out there, sir. Dr Molloy is a physician who attends upon the highest in the land. You cannot deny a man who has his place in the royal drawing-rooms a seat in Aubrey Square, now can you?'

'Indeed?' said Valpy frostily. 'I was not aware.'

'Dr Molloy and I are old friends,' said Mr Barcombe. 'I hope you are not here on a professional visit, Molloy?'

Fanny smiled at him. 'He is, for my little girl is far from well, but he insists she is in no danger. She has the measles, but very mildly, it is only a mild case.'

'The measles!' cried Letitia, greatly alarmed. 'Fanny, that must be taken seriously. Charlotte should be removed from London, she will do better in the country. Why do you not take her to Pemberley? We can come with you; you know how good fresh country air is in cases of sickness.'

'Country air and a long journey would do Charlotte no good

at all,' said Dr Molloy firmly. 'I have no great opinion of fresh air in March; cold and damp do nothing for a child's health, you may take my word for it.'

Letty looked disappointed, but Camilla was thankful for the physician's firm words. Letty might want to ruralise, but with every day that passed, she and her other sisters had more reasons to stay in town.

'I wished to ask the young ladies if they have all had the measles,' said Dr Molloy.

'Why, yes,' Camilla said.

'I was very ill,' said Letitia.

'There, you see,' put in Georgina. 'You had the measles at Pemberley, and the country air didn't help you.'

'Had I been stricken with the measles in London, it might have proved fatal, for it often is.'

'Letty,' Camilla said, 'listen to what Dr Molloy has to say and do not always be looking out for disaster.'

Dr Molloy smiled a thin smile. 'There speaks a young lady with sound sense,' he said. 'My young patient is in no danger, Miss Darcy, so do not, I beg of you, go frightening Lady Fanny with vain fears.'

Mr Valpy wrinkled his nose and resumed his conversation with Letitia. 'Pray tell me about Pemberley. It is your home, is that so? In which county is it situated? I cannot but agree with you as to the benefits of country air. I am a great believer in country living.'

'Or livings,' said Pagoda Portal in Camilla's ear. 'Who is this tiresome fellow?'

'He is the incumbent at St Botolph's.'

'Oh, is he indeed? Now I can place him; people who should know better flock to hear him upbraid them and scare them from their wits – no very hard task, I may say – with his promises of hellfire and damnation. He is a great Evangelical, you know, and I am surprised to find him sitting in the same room with Barleigh Barcombe there, who is as staunch a member of the low branch of the Church of England as you may find.'

'I am not used to clergymen of so many different persuasions as you have here in London. We have only dear old Canon Meyrick, who has been our vicar for ever, and times his sermons with a sand-glass; never more than a quarter of an hour.'

'Admirable man!'

'I think Mr Valpy might put up with a great many inconveniences in pursuit of his own advantage.'

She glanced across the room to where Letty was engaged in such close conversation with the man, and felt a twinge of apprehension. Serious-minded to a fault, and still feeling sore about Tom's 'betrayal', her sister might well prove ripe for mischief-making of another kind. Heaven forbid that Papa and Mama should return from their travels and find their eldest daughter turned Evangelical.

ELEVEN

Sir Sidney Leigh stood at one of the tall windows in his elegant drawing-room and looked out at the thin April rain. The month was living up to its reputation, with patches of brilliant sunlight interspersed with sudden, frequent and often heavy showers.

He felt a certain calmness, a fixity of purpose, for he had made up his mind to marry. At the age of thirty-five, with only an estranged younger brother to inherit baronetcy, estate and fortune, it was, as the gossipy matrons had predicted, time for him to find a wife and get an heir.

He had taken his decision before the season began. He would look over the annual crop of debutantes and pick a young woman of beauty – he couldn't bear the prospect of looking at a fright over the breakfast table day after day. Not that he had any intention of sharing his breakfast table or indeed much else of his life with any woman. No, her duties and place would lie in the domestic sphere of household and children, with female friends in a similar situation providing her with any necessary companionship.

He had no intention, either, of being an oppressive or restrictive husband. He was too experienced a man to imagine he could impose conditions on his wife that he would not endure himself. Once the heir and a brother or two were provided, she might amuse herself as she pleased. It was an arrangement that a woman of sense would gladly accede to.

On first acquaintance, he had thought Letitia Darcy might do very well. He admired her beauty and air of calm propriety; she was well-born, rich, and had, or believed she had, that tragedy of the heart behind her, which would possibly spare him the risk of an over-strong attachment on her part. On closer acquaintance, however, he realised that she bored him. She was too solemn, too serious-minded, too likely to involve herself in good works and Church affairs and, heaven forbid, certain to moralise over a husband who strayed even slightly from the path of rectitude. Moreover, she wasn't quite as calm and serene as she seemed, and the last thing he wanted in his house was temperament and passion.

Besides, it had to be admitted that her next sister, Camilla, was much more conversable. She was more intelligent, had a keen sense of wit, was more able to hold her own among clever people than her older sister. He might even be a little proud of such a wife. True, she was not as lovely as Letitia, but she was well enough, and with good dressing and grooming could be turned out very commendably. She had her wits about her, she would understand how her marriage was to be conducted. And, not least among his considerations, her fortune was every bit as handsome as her sister's.

Her father was abroad, but for how long? There must be some male relative whom he might approach, Mr Gardiner, possibly. Better, perhaps, for there not to be a papa asking all those irritating paternal questions that afflicted fathers of unmarried daughters. Yes, it would be much better to deal with a less close relative, and to discuss settlements and money matters with the family man of business. He would be a laughing-stock if he were to be left at the altar again, his reputation would never survive that. They might go to Paris for the honeymoon. He would enjoy showing Paris to Camilla. For himself, he never tired of the place: it was a city of delights.

Meanwhile, he must make himself agreeable. The lady was not indifferent to him, he knew. He gave a tiny shudder. Still, he was used to it; women did find him attractive, they always had done so. And it was necessary if she were to be brought to the point. Even a young lady of her intelligence and rationality would have to be persuaded that a suitor felt some of the tenderer emotions, and that she shared them. In his father's day, marriages had been arranged as a matter of convenience and money, but that was not the case with the modern generation. Today, feeling was all, an ardency of spirit a prerequisite for any attachment. To display a purely practical approach to matrimony would call down accusations of heartlessness and a mercenary nature.

'That man looks at me as though I were a painting hanging on the wall,' said Alethea when she returned to sit beside Camilla, after favouring the company with several songs.

'Which man?'

'Why, Sir Sidney Leigh, standing at the fireplace over there and looking down his long nose.'

They were at Mrs Seton's house, attending one of the musical evenings promised by her brother, Barleigh Barcombe. She had sent a most prettily worded invitation, to include all five sisters.

There was a reason for their presence in the well-appointed salon, beyond the sisters' love of music. While Charlotte Fitzwilliam's measles were not, as Dr Molloy had predicted, of a dangerous sort, they had made her fretful and peevish, and she wanted her mother to be constantly at her side, to comfort her and read to her and amuse her. Fanny was an affectionate mother, who felt it no hardship to sit with a sickly daughter when the nurse took some hours of needful rest. Even Mr Fitzwilliam, who liked to have Fanny visitable in her own chamber, let his fatherly feelings prevail, and urged his wife not to mind her neglect of him, but to attend on Charlotte as much as she felt she ought.

'It is not only you that I am neglecting,' she protested.

'Do not frown, my dear,' he said, taking her face between his hands. 'I hate to see you frown.'

'We have guests, have you forgotten our guests? Who is to chaperon the girls, to escort them to parties, to watch over them to see that they do not get into scrapes?'

'Into scrapes?' – in tones of strong disapproval – 'I trust that no girl staying under my roof is going to get into any scrapes, as you put it.'

'You mistake me. I mean nothing serious. They would not do anything wicked, you know they would not, but they are still new to town and are not always aware of how they should go on.'

'There is no problem. They may do without parties for the present, it will do them no harm, they seem to have been living very giddy lives these past weeks.'

Fanny exclaimed at this. The season was so short, and she wanted every day of their visit to be a pleasure to them.

'I never heard such nonsense. Pray, by what special right must their days be counted lost if not passed in frivolous pursuits and pleasures? They are sensible creatures, I am sure; no child of Darcy's will have grown up not knowing how to behave. They had much better spend their time helping you with Charlotte, and not be thinking of parties just now, with illness in the house.'

'Indeed, Letty and Camilla have both offered to stay up with Charlotte, and they spend a lot of time with her during the day; however it is not right for them to sit with her at night. Alethea, too, has been with Charlotte, but it is not a success. She tires poor Charlotte with her energy and liveliness. She is writing some music for her, a song, and says she will teach it to her when she is better. Charlotte is very taken with the notion; it is kind of Alethea to think of such a thing.'

'And the twins?'

'The twins both have great sensibility, and it distresses them to see the child so poorly. They are truly sympathetic, but they have no place in the sickroom.'

Her husband was not immune to the twins' melting charms. 'Very likely so. They have more of the true feminine nature, of the need to be nurtured and protected, than do their sisters.'

Fanny stared at him, wondering for a moment how his idea of feminine nature would square with the inevitable demands of childbirth and motherhood, but a call from her daughter distracted her and she went away to attend to her.

Letitia and Camilla were eager to set Fanny's mind at rest, protesting that they had no intention of going out in company while Charlotte was ill and her mother so much engaged with her.

'And besides, Fanny, we need not sit at home all the time. Here is our cousin Gardiner asking us to dine with her, if we can be spared, and Letty plans to attend the meeting of one of her societies. Sackree will go with her, it is all most respectable.'

'For remember, I am one-and-twenty,' said Letitia. 'If I have my maid with me, there can be no objection. Mr Valpy asked me to interest myself in the affairs of the society, as you know, and I should not like to seem remiss.'

'Mrs Seton's invitation, too, is quite unexceptionable,' said Fanny, wrinkling her brow at a handful of cards inviting her and the sisters to any number of parties and outings. 'Alethea may go as well. It is a family party and she will enjoy it, for Mrs Seton is famous for inviting good musicians to her house.'

So Letitia had tripped away to a meeting of the Society for the Unfortunate Poor – or was it the Society for the Suppression of Vice she was attending? She had urged her sister to accompany her, but Camilla had refused with a grimace.

'No, Letty, I leave these good works to you.'

It was beyond her understanding how Letty could choose to spend her time with a group of people that she, on the one occasion when she had gone with her sister, had judged to be sanctimonious and far too overtly pious to be truly convincing. Camilla was not impressed by enthusiasm of this kind, and perhaps she was harsh in her judgement of them, but she did not trust Mr Valpy, nor any of his schemes. She strongly suspected that such of Mr Valpy's charity as came from the heart began and ended at home.

Meanwhile the twins had begged permission to go shopping in Bond Street, with their maid in attendance.

'After all, what possible mischief can they get up to in Bond Street?' Camilla said to Letitia, dreading a scene.

'It is encouraging them to think about nothing but frivolous matters, they fritter away their money on trifles and needless finery, and their heads stay as empty as ever they were.'

'Do you suppose, if they are not let go, that they will sit at home with an improving book?'

'It would do them a great deal more good.'

It had been an unreasonably long trip to Bond Street, and

they had seemed unusually elated on their return. Camilla's suspicions were aroused, but she had just received a note from Sir Sidney asking her to make one of a party for the theatre two days hence, and this caused such a surge of happiness to rise in her that she had not the heart to take Belle and Georgina to task for the length of time they had been away. Nor did it occur to her to question their maid, as Letitia would instantly have done, so her sisters merely exchanged secret, relieved glances and went off to change.

Whatever had been the cause of their high spirits, their good humour carried through into the evening, and they saw Belle's harp loaded into the second carriage without any grumbles about tedious evening parties – any party that Alethea was allowed to attend would normally have been stigmatised as the epitome of dullness. Belle and Georgina had played their pieces with style and taste, and were congratulated upon their performance.

'Sir Sidney looks at them as though they were pieces of porcelain in a case,' Alethea said ungraciously to Camilla.

Camilla laughed. 'Pictures, china, what is this? He has a connoisseur's eye.'

'He has a flat mouth, which I do not like. I don't know why you fancy him so, Camilla. I can't take to him at all.'

'Alethea!'

'Oh, don't start one of your lectures. I may feel differently about people from you, may I not? I hope you do not intend to marry him, that's all.'

'Alethea! How can you say such a thing?'

'He looks at you as though you were a filly he is planning to buy. That's not being a connoisseur, nor a lover. I call it bad manners.'

Camilla felt so angry with Alethea that she was obliged to get up and move away to the other side of the room. There she was joined by Mr Barcombe, rhapsodising about the twins. He was loud in his praise of Belle: how exquisitely she played, how enchanting she looked while seated at the instrument! Were they not to have the pleasure of hearing Miss Camilla play?

They were not. She left him to his ecstasies, and went

towards one of the long windows; it was unaccountably hot and stuffy in the room, there might be a breath of air if the shutters had not been closed.

Two women in their forties were sitting on a sofa just in front of her, their elegantly turbaned heads close together as they talked. They had whispered through the twins' and Alethea's music and laughed and gossiped while a trio played a Clementi sonata. What were they speaking of now? She couldn't help listening, for she had caught Sir Sidney's name. She should move away, she was not by nature an eavesdropper. Yet she was rooted to the spot as her eyes were drawn across the room to where the man himself, elegantly attired as always, sat on a chair with one long, silk-clad leg thrust forward. He was wearing breeches and silk stockings rather than pantaloons. Was he going on to a ball?

He had smiled at her when she came into the room, and asked her how she did, but then his hostess had come up to claim his attention, and they had not spoken two words together since. If he was going on elsewhere, he would take his leave of the company soon, without any chance of their talking. Did he not want to talk with her? He seemed to find his present companion agreeable; they were in a flow of conversation, her bright blue eyes fixed to his face, little peals of laughter falling from her pretty mouth.

'Mrs de Witt looks to be enjoying her company,' one of the turbaned women was saying. 'Of course, she was desperately in love with Sir Sidney before she married that fool of a husband.'

'She seems still to have a *tendre* for him. De Witt is away from London a good deal, is he not?'

'Oh, he is always dashing about here and there.'

'I saw her and Sir Sidney in the park, rising in his vis-à-vis, only the day before yesterday. Very much at their ease together.'

'She was wild to marry him, so they say, but her father forbade the match. She shut herself in her room for three days, sobbing and crying out that she would have him.'

'I heard that she wept all through the wedding service when she married Mr de Witt.'

'He is such a fool, I dare say he never noticed.'

'He has a mistress. Snipe told me about her, for she is a pretty little redhead that he had his own eye on; he was much put out when he was trumped by de Witt in that quarter.'

'Mrs de Witt is evidently finding consolations of her own. But Sir Sidney needs a wife, indeed he does. Flirtations and engagements are all very well, but they do not fill a nursery.'

Wretched women, with their evil clacking tongues. It was her own fault for staying and listening, she should have known she would hear nothing but what must hurt her.

How could Sir Sidney be enamoured of Mrs de Witt? A frowsty blonde like that, dressed very fine, to be sure, but with no real beauty or elegance about her.

Why was the room so insufferably hot? Why did not those musicians tune their instruments properly, instead of screeching away in that terrible fashion? Why did Mr Barcombe sit there with that foolish expression on his face? Did he not know how ridiculous he looked? And that young couple by the door, heads close together, fingers slyly touching when they thought they were unobserved, what a way to behave in public.

Then she saw the look the young man in question cast down at the girl standing beside him, a look so full of tenderness that it brought a lump to her throat.

Sir Sidney had never sat at his ease and laughed and smiled and flirted with her as he now did with Mrs de Witt.

A pang of jealousy shot through her. How had this come about? How and when had the unknown, nameless man of her girlish daydreams taken form as Sir Sidney Leigh? And was there any sign that he cared for her any more than he did for his horse, his dog, or any casual acquaintance of his London world?

She bit her lip, pinned a smile on her mouth, strove to keep her face calm and her feelings hidden. That, now, was all she had left to her: the dignity of preserving from the company the knowledge of her sentiments towards the man, which she had hitherto more or less successfully hidden not only from the world but also from herself.

She had allowed him to be agreeable company, and a handsome, attractive man. She had not allowed to herself that she was, in fact, falling in love with him.

And he with her? There had been no sign of anything particular on his side. He had paid her some attention, had danced with her and showed that he took pleasure at her skill in the dance. He enjoyed her company, she was sure. Apart from his delightfully sharp and astute comments on his fellow men and their follies, they had conversed upon various topics. He had talked of her father's mission to Constantinople, of his once meeting her mother at a rout, of Pemberley, of his delight in Italian art when he travelled on the continent.

He had never once attempted to make love to her.

Little enough foundation for her to build a passion upon, and yet that was what she had done. Were her affections returned to the slightest degree? Watching him now with Mrs de Witt, she doubted it, she doubted it very much.

Good-natured or malicious gossip might have coupled her name with his, indeed they had spent some considerable time in each other's company – considerable time for London, that was – but there had been no passages, no murmured words, not the slightest pressure on a hand or involuntary touch on an arm to give her any grounds for hope, or hint of liking that went beyond the everyday.

The planned trip to the theatre, which had so pleased her, now held no joy. Mrs de Witt might be of his party, would almost certainly be there, would demonstrate her superior knowledge of how to attract and keep a man's interest.

She was surely the unhappiest creature in the world. For the first time, she understood how intense Letty's feelings had been when she had lost Tom – and twice over! Once to a soldier's grave and then to a Belgian girl whom nobody knew. Perhaps she, too, should turn to reading tracts and giving her time to furthering the aims of worthy and necessary societies.

She saw her future laid out before her: a spinster in drab gowns, hurrying to and fro; here a meeting of the Society of Satan (one trusted that its members opposed, rather than supported, the works of its namesake), there attending the Society of Virtue (which must, on the contrary, be for rather than against its subject).

She had to smile, if not laugh out loud, at the absurdity of her ideas. There was, after all, consolation to be found in listening to the beautiful tone of the first violin, not at all a harsh sound, how could she have thought it? In a few minutes, she was able to accept a cup of tea with something like cheerfulness.

Alethea was in the habit of telling Miss Griffin all she knew about her sisters. She did not consider herself an informer, for she knew quite well that the substance of these discussions with Griffy never went beyond their four walls.

She shared her concern about Camilla with the governess on her return that evening. 'I do hope that she does not mean to marry that horrid Sir Sidney. He does not like her above much, I would swear it, although he is always paying her attention, and people are beginning to talk about them.'

'Does she care for him?'

'Oh, she is in the saddest way, she is a case; I do wish she would have more sense.'

'Sense is apt to fly out of the window when a girl falls in love.'

'Yes, only it had better fly back in very smartly, before she is in real trouble.'

'Sir Sidney does not sound like a seducer.'

'I did not mean that, no, his behaviour is perfectly correct, and so is hers; she does not follow him round the room with her eyes or anything like that.'

'Indeed, I am glad to hear it. I should not like to think that any girl brought up by me would wear her heart on her sleeve.'

Alethea stopped her pacing, kicked a log on the fire – earning herself a sharp rebuke from her governess – and commented that it was all very well, but look how Letty had behaved when she and Tom were engaged.

'An engagement is different.'

'I don't see why. It is all so exasperating. I do wish Papa and Mama were here, they would see off the baronet soon enough. And they would control the twins.'

'Pray do not tell me what they have been doing.'

'I had better not, for you would be sadly shocked, and you

would blame yourself for their behaviour, although you should not.'

'I expect they have visited your aunt, Mrs Pollexfen.'

'Now, that is just what they have done,' cried Alethea. 'How did you guess?'

Miss Griffin sprinkled sand on the page she had been copying out, and then tapped it off. 'It was inevitable.'

'Fanny is hopeless, she is quite taken in by Belle and Georgina. And so is Mr Fitzwilliam, he has no idea what they are really like, none in the world.'

'I dare say they will come to no great harm at their aunt's. She would not let them, for she is afraid of your father, you know.'

Alethea flung herself down in front of the fire and turned on to her stomach, propping herself on her elbows. 'I hope you are right, that is all. Now, let us forget about love and marriage and turn to romance. I want to hear what has happened to Adelysia – does she escape from the clutches of the wicked Count? Of course she does, I know that, or there would be no more story, but do read it to me, I want to hear it all.'

TWELVE

Camilla's fears were groundless: Mrs de Witt was not among those invited to the theatre by Sir Sidney Leigh. Instead, she was delighted to find Pagoda Portal and Mrs Rowan already seated in the box, together with Sir Sidney's sister, a Mrs Delamere, who lived in Kent. She was a few years her brother's junior, a Roman matron of a young woman, with a haughty nose and a well-bred air. However, she was perfectly civil and professed herself charmed to meet her.

They were joined shortly after by young Mr Roper, rather to Camilla's surprise. Mrs Delamere was about to present him to her when she said, with a smile, that they had already met.

It was clear that Mr Roper recalled the occasion of their former meeting all too clearly. He was seated beside her, and after clearing his throat and looking nervously about him as though inspiration might fly through the air via the candelabra suspended from the roof of the theatre or slip between the plush folds of the curtains, he embarked on a kind of strangled apology. 'I called at Aubrey Square, but Lady Fanny was denied. Both times. I fear I have offended her, and your sisters. Your sister, I mean.'

'I dare say it was merely that you called when my cousin was not at home.'

'Not at home to me, no; I perfectly understand that the embarrassment I caused on my first visit, the news I brought and imparted, inadvertently, in such a thoughtless fashion, must have given her a disgust of me. The more I have thought about it, the more horrified I am to have been the cause of— In short, I believe your sister was greatly distressed. I would not have wished her to have learned about Mr Busby in so abrupt and unfeeling a way.'

He paused, his forehead prickled with beads of sweat, his eyes dark and anxious.

'There is no way she could have learned about Mr Busby without feeling some natural emotion,' she said in a kindly voice, wanting to reassure him. 'It was not your fault that you were the bearer of such unwelcome news, you were not to know the situation.'

'I feel truly sorry for her. But I fear that Lady Fanny – that all of you may think that I was a rumour-monger, that I went from your cousin's house to spread the story about. Indeed, that was not so. I went to my aunt's house, where I am staying, and then on to the club, for I am a member of Pink's, you must know,' this said with the pride of a young man finding his feet in the world of his elders, 'and by the time I went through the doors, everyone was speaking of it.'

'I am sure that was so. Such riveting news as a young man back from the grave, a loss of memory, an unannounced marriage and a former attachment will not long be kept secret anywhere, least of all in London. It has all the appeal of a melodramatic novel with the added delight of being true.'

'I suppose so.' Roper did not seem entirely convinced. 'I am glad to have met you here, however, so that at least one member of your family may know that it was none of my doing that the tale spread so far and so fast.'

Mrs Delamere, who had been talking with some animation to Mrs Rowan, broke in on their conversation. 'What tale is this? Of what do you speak, Mr Roper?'

He hesitated, and Camilla took pity on him. 'On the strange return of one Mr Busby to life, ma'am. He was presumed dead after Waterloo, but it turns out that it was no such thing.'

'Oh, that tale! I am a little acquainted with the Comte de Broise, whose daughter he married. He is a distant connection of my husband, and I believe his daughter is a delightful girl, with a good portion; Busby could do much worse. They come to London soon, so I heard.'

Camilla's heart sank. Heaven only knew how Letty would

behave when she was told. And told she must be; only imagine if she were to encounter Tom unexpectedly at some rout or ball or in the park!

Kean was to act in *Julius Caesar* that evening, and the rest of the party began to talk about the play and whether Kean could ever match Kemble in the role of Brutus. She had never seen Kemble act, nor ever attended a performance of any Shakespeare play, so she turned her attention to her surroundings.

Drury Lane seemed vast to her. It could accommodate some three thousand souls, she had been informed, and indeed, she was staggered by the size and opulence of the theatre and the ornate blaze of red velvet and gilded surfaces, which made her want to blink. They were seated in a box on the third tier to the left of the stage, and she could look down on the throng in the pit – surely there must be at least a thousand people there alone, so tightly pressed and crammed in as they were.

Her eyes travelled over the more genteel seats, where men and women in evening dress were taking their seats, greeting friends, waving to acquaintances in other parts of the house, fluttering their fans and generally giving the scene an air of great brilliance and liveliness. Some of the women were dazzlers, diamonds of the first water, and, recognising several of their male companions, Camilla suspected that these gallants had left their plainer spouses at home to entertain themselves with members of the frail sisterhood.

In the galleries that ran round behind the upper tiers and the boxes, she knew that less-favoured prostitutes were plying their trade, for they had seen them on their way in, quite ready to give any man a saucy eye, whether he was with another woman or among his male friends.

There was something more of a bustle, the lights in the house were extinguished, and the eerier lighting along the edge of the theatre cast its dramatic glow upon the stage as the curtain went up and Flavius and Marullus made their entrance.

She had expected to spend the evening in the state to which she had formerly been a stranger, but to which she was now becoming accustomed: that of pleasure in a man's company and nearness, mingled with doubts about her own sentiments, questions in her mind about his affections, and the necessity of forcing herself to play the normal social role that manners and the occasion demanded.

Instead, she found herself transported, forgetting where she was or who she was with, so lost in the passions and poetry of the drama unfolding on the stage that when the interval came, she started, and looked around her as though she were awaking from a dream to find herself in some unfamiliar place. She was concerned only with Brutus and Cassius, not with Sir Sidney, and she spent the time before the play resumed in something of a daze, saying little, responding to queries and conversational gambits with no more than a smile. She could not find the inconsequential words demanded of her, so she remained silent.

How could the others sit so calmly, appear to be quite unaffected by the performance? Mr Roper did ask her if she did not think it a first-rate play, and Kean a very fine fellow, but she could only nod and smile in response. Then, blessed relief, it was time for the play again, and she could lose herself in those lines, often read, but never, she felt, understood before. Kean was a genius; more than that, he was Brutus, the very essence of the man. She hardly breathed during the great scene where Brutus and Cassius quarrelled, but sat rapt and perfectly still, feeling that if she lived to the age of a hundred, she would never forget Kean's delivery of those noble lines.

She knew Brutus as though he were part of herself, shared with him his virtuous indignation, trembled at the force and nerve of his words. And she felt tears prickle her eyes as she heard Cassius declaim: '*I, that denied thee gold, will give my heart.*'

She felt that no love scene could have moved her half so much; here she was face to face with greatness of heart and spirit, and it touched her to the centre of her being. She, who prided herself on her rationality and her dislike of any display of strong emotion, now found herself helpless in the spell of Shakespeare's verse. How little she knew herself, how trivial were her insights into other people, how small the concerns of the daily round in comparison to this baring of a soul who loved so greatly, yet had to destroy the man he loved to preserve the freedom he loved even more!

The theatre was far from quiet, people spoke and laughed and jostled all through the play, yet such was Kean's power that the other three thousand or so people were quite forgotten. As the curtain swept down, and she became aware of the tears on her cheeks and the rising volume of sound around her, Mr Roper brought her firmly down to earth by whispering in her ear that he couldn't imagine how a writer as good as Shakespeare was generally held to be could kill off the hero of the piece so early on.

'The hero?' she said, blinking and trying to collect her scattered wits.

'Well, the play is about Julius Caesar, ain't it? I mean, he's the great man, and the piece is named for him, after all.'

'Oh, you mistake the matter,' she cried, distressed to think that what she had just experienced could have passed him by. 'Brutus is the hero; that is why Kean takes the part. Were you not deeply affected by Brutus?'

'My God, I believe you may be right,' said Mr Roper, much impressed. 'Do you know, that never occurred to me? That does make some sense, after all, although I still don't know why Shakespeare didn't make Caesar the central character of the play. But it is as you say. Kean was very affecting, although I swear I don't know how he does it, for there's no ranting you notice, no big gestures or fine dramatics, he seems almost not to be acting. Yet you cannot help but watch him, and he certainly knows how to pitch his voice. The merest whisper in places, and yet you could hear him at the top and back of the theatre, I dare say, clear as a bell, even though there was all that hubbub going on.'

The evening was but half over, with the harlequinade still to come, which, as Mr Roper confided to her, was rather more in his line. She, however, despite her inclination to remain in Sir Sidney's company, begged to be excused the farce, feeling that she could not bear it while Shakespeare's lines still rang in her head.

Sir Sidney was all obliging attention, and it turned out that his sister did not care to stay for the farce either, nor Mrs Rowan.

So they left Mr Portal and Mr Roper to enjoy the more raucous delights of the harlequinade farce, and accepted Mrs Rowan's invitation to return to her house for a glass of wine and some supper.

Gradually, Camilla became herself again, as they trotted through the foggy London streets, the chill air filling her lungs and the noisy bustle of the town at night demanding her attention.

'I hear that some carriages were stoned the other night,' Mrs Delamere said to her brother. 'Radicals and revolutionaries and reformers, no doubt; I hope they were caught and will be severely punished. I trust we may meet with no such violence on our way back. I declare, I was in half a mind not to make my trip to London, and Mr Delamere was most anxious about me. However, I did not like to let you down, brother, when you were so insistent about my paying you a visit, so we must make the best of it, and not allow ourselves to be alarmed.'

'The incident was blown up in the newspapers, as is generally the case,' said her brother. 'A few drunken guttersnipes hurled abuse and one or two missiles at carriages drawn up outside Almack's, that is all. I believe we may travel the streets of London with no undue concern, and we have two stout footmen as well as the coachman for protection. I doubt if anyone would venture to attack us.'

They reached their destination unmolested and unscathed. A servant with a flare stood ready to open Mrs Rowan's door; within was light, warmth, attentive servants, a sense of ease. Mrs Delamere clearly had not been a visitor before, and she looked taken aback as Mrs Rowan led the way upstairs and into her pink and crimson apartment.

'Very oriental, upon my word,' Mrs Delamere said under her breath, so that only Camilla caught what she was saying. 'Decidedly eccentric, this is what happens when rich widows are left on the loose in London. I wonder her family allow it.' Her expression was bland, in contrast to her murmured words, although Camilla thought from an amused look on Mrs Rowan's face that her hostess knew quite well what Mrs Delamere was thinking.

The fire was made up, wine brought in and offered. Supper was laid in an adjoining chamber, and while they ate, the talk was of the theatre, of Kean, of other favourite performances, of amateur theatricals at the Delameres' house in Kent over Christmas, of fashions, about which Sir Sidney seemed to know almost as much as the ladies.

'You have a most valuable brother,' Mrs Rowan said to Mrs Delamere. 'What he tells us of shawls and silks and ornaments bespeaks a close attention to female fashions such as is rarely found in a man. For the most part, they care nothing for it beyond to grumble at the size of the dressmaker's account, to abuse their wives for wearing such an ugly bonnet when they are dressed in the latest mode and to protest at the inconvenience and expense of having jewels cleaned or reset.'

'Sidney has a connoisseur's eye in this as so much else,' was Mrs Delamere's cool reply. 'I trust no one more for an opinion for a silk or a gown or a hat. I often send commissions for him to undertake, and he never fails me. I rarely come to town, but I do not feel I am a country dowd on that account, I assure you.'

Talk turned to Kent, and that part of the county where Mrs Delamere resided. It seemed that she lived on the neighbouring estate to her brother, having married their closest neighbour.

Camilla listened with curiosity to this conversation, wanting to know more about Sir Sidney's house and family. She had never been to Kent, although she was sure it was the loveliest of the English counties, the garden of England, people said. She had a great wish, she discovered, to see Kent, and was eager to hear Mrs Delamere say in what good heart her brother's land was, how fine his crops had been in the summer, how promising the winter sowing was thought to be.

Mrs Delamere took a considerable interest in Sir Sidney's property, her own family home, since, she informed them with a knowledgeable air, her brother was so seldom there, and even the best of stewards could not be relied on for every little detail of the estate, but must come to some person in authority for advice on this or that matter.

'If ever my brother marries, then we hope he will choose to spend more time in Kent, and my duties there may lessen,' she said, her eyes flickering for an instant in Camilla's direction. 'A wife and children may do more than we can to bring him regularly into the country. Do you care for the country, Miss Camilla? Your father's property in Derbyshire is famous, of course, for its beauty and for the grandeur of its setting. Have you often been in Town? Do you plan to fix in London?'

'This is my first visit, if you except the time I spent in a seminary. I like Town life, I confess, or what I have seen of it so far. It is easy to fall into the mopes in the country, and when the weather is bad and visits impossible, one cannot help but be dull. In London, there is always something to do, such a bustle and business about the place, such liveliness.'

'I should rather say it is a crowded and noisy city, always in a tumult. And now, with Mr Nash's works under construction, one might as well live on a building site. I prefer the tranquillity and peace of the countryside.'

'That is because you prefer the domestic life,' observed her brother, as they went from the supper room to take tea before the fire in the main apartment. 'For men, London is the only place, except when sport is the purpose of one's day.'

'Are you not a sportsman, Sir Sidney?' Camilla asked.

Mrs Rowan handed her tea in an exquisite porcelain cup of red and gold. Camilla took it and turned back to Sir Sidney. 'I apologise, it was an impertinent question, do not feel obliged to answer.'

'I am sure you meant no impertinence, and my answer is that I am not much of a sportsman,' he said, accepting a cup of his own. 'I prefer to exist amid the beautiful, and there is not much of that on the hunting field or when one is out with a gun, shooting down birds that are lovely on the wing and poor, desolate objects when brought to earth.'

'I warrant you find loveliness in them once more when your chef serves them up to you in a dish,' said Mrs Rowan, a twinkle in her eye.

He laughed at this, and agreed that food, too, was one of the joys of life. 'Anything that pleases the senses must meet with my approval.'

Camilla smiled, liking a man who could laugh at himself as

Sir Sidney could, and feeling a particular warmth towards him for being ready to admit that painting and music and books were of more importance to him than fox hunting or shooting.

'I am no dandy, mind you,' continued Sir Sidney. 'I have a mind beyond neckcloths and the cut of a coat. I enjoy a prize-fight, if I may speak of such things in female company, and am considered to have a good eye for a horse. And I am not one of your namby-pamby Townees, out of sorts if out of town. I delight in a stay – a short stay – in the country as much as any man.'

'Provided there is good company and handsome furnishings and fine paintings and a comfortable chamber for you to sleep in,' Camilla finished for him.

'Ah, you have quite fathomed my character,' he said, smiling into her eyes in a way that made her heart beat fast. 'And you do not condemn me? You do not believe that a man is a contemptible fellow if he is not riding with hounds five days a week and coming home splashed with mud to drink and doze in an exhausted state before a roaring fire?'

'I certainly do not. I like a man to talk, and I have frequently noticed that hunting men talk of nothing but foxes and points and runs, and how their horse went better than anyone else's, all so tedious and tiresome that it makes my head ache to listen to it.'

'My dear, guard your tongue,' said Mrs Rowan, amused. 'Nine out of ten Englishmen are sporting mad; you will earn yourself an ill name among them if you show you despise the chase and the race and the fight. The only thing most of them like better than sport is thumping the French, and of course that particular activity is denied them now.'

For a man who professed to despise sport, Sir Sidney had a firm and muscular figure, Camilla found herself thinking. A well-fitting coat, tight breeches and silk stockings was a costume all too apt to show up any deficiencies of form. Sir Sidney had none that she could discern; she could not but approve his lean and elegant appearance with its underlying strength.

She wrenched herself away from admiration of Sir Sidney's well-set shoulders and handsome legs, to find Mrs Rowan's ironic gaze upon her, just as though she had been able to read her thoughts.

It was lucky that she, in her turn, had not been able to read Mrs Rowan's thoughts, for they would have angered her exceedingly. The ironic gaze hid a sense of alarm, of realisation of her new friend's feelings for Sir Sidney and the inward, silent knowledge that it would not do, it would not do at all. How would a young woman – even one of character, such as Camilla Darcy – who was very much in love, probably for the first time, cope with the fix in which she would inevitably find herself?

Camilla awoke the next morning filled with happiness. She felt at one with all the world, overflowing with goodwill and desire that everyone might be as happy as she. Poor Letty, had her sister been as much in love with Tom as she now was with Sir Sidney? If so, no wonder she had felt his loss so acutely, no wonder she still missed him after all this time, and what anguish must she not be experiencing knowing that her lover was, after all, still on this earth, but denied to her?

Even this new understanding of her sister's heart and the sympathy it aroused in her was not enough to dampen her sense of well-being. The world outside responded by presenting a brilliant spring day, a sparkling day, with a warm and generous sun, a freshness to the air, even in the centre of town, a promise of greenness about the trees and a liveliness to the chirruping and songs of the birds. Swiftly up, and swiftly out of the house, charged with a restlessness that urged her to be active, she walked across the square, Sackree hurrying to match her eager steps.

'Lawks, miss, wherever are you going at such a pace? I can't keep up with you. Look at you, flying along like you'd got wings.'

'Today, Sackree, I do believe I have wings.'

'Some man, that's what it is,' Sackree muttered to herself. 'There's nothing else would account for such a flow of spirits, and if it's that identical fine gentleman as has been sniffing round like a fussy pet dog toying with its supper, then we're in for squalls and no mistake. For he won't do, and that's a fact, and I don't care how much Mr Fitzwilliam and Lady Fanny smile upon him. He may be good for them, but he's no good for her. Lordie, I do wish Mr and Mrs Darcy weren't so far away, they've a deal too much sense not to know what's going on.'

For naturally, Sackree had all the gossip of the servants' hall at her fingertips, and they knew rather more about the situation and the nature and temperament of the principals involved than either the Darcys or the Fitzwilliams would have believed possible.

'He's a good catch, I give you that,' Fell had pronounced. 'Inasmuch as fortune and estate make a man what's wanted. But there's more to that in a happy marriage, and Miss Camilla is the sort who won't put up with any nonsense from a man. He'd have to take a whip to her, before she'd agree to what kind of life he's got in mind, and the gentry don't go in for whipping. Or if they do, it's for pleasure, not for chastisement and keeping a woman in order.'

'Whipping, indeed! No one is going to set about a Miss Darcy with a whip,' said Sackree, outraged at the very suggestion.

'I don't know as how Miss Camilla's gentleman is any worse than that slippery parson fellow set on fixing his interest with Miss Darcy,' said Dawson. 'There's a man with a phizz I don't trust.'

'I'd never trust a parson of any kind,' said a footman darkly. 'He's none too free with his shillings, that one, neither, though he expects answers to his nosy questions: "When is Miss Darcy walking in the park? Is the carriage ordered for this afternoon? What callers came to the house this morning?" '

'And never a civil word when he comes and goes. Mr Portal's always there with a smile and a pleasant enquiry as to how you do,' said the butler. 'And liberal with his blunt, too.'

'They say he's as rich as Christmas.'

'Why should he be as rich as Christmas?'

'I don't know, it's what folk say, isn't it?'

'It's that man in olden times, only it ain't Christmas. Something like, but not Christmas.'

'Made a fortune in India, did Mr Portal. Two fortunes. Chests and chests of gold sitting in the bank, they say. And caskets of rubies and emeralds and I don't know what.'

'He's the sort of man to make a woman a good husband.'

'Only he's after that widow woman, Mrs Rowan, and she won't have him.'

They shook their heads over such wilfulness.

'Where are you going, miss?' cried a panting Sackree. 'At least tell me that.'

'Why, I don't know.'

'Then let's go back, for I've plenty to do if you haven't.'

Camilla agreed, perfectly willing to fall in with anyone's wishes, and they returned to the house. Only for her to be told that Sir Sidney had called in her absence. Her face fell, clouds gathered across the beauty of the day.

'He was wishful to wait upon Mr Fitzwilliam, and he did so, was with him upwards of half an hour, left without enquiring after the ladies.'

Her disappointment was acute. Why should he come, to this house, without at least spending even five minutes in her company? He must have his reasons, a matter of business, some parliamentary matter, no doubt, but even so— Surely he must want to see her, his manner last night had been so marked, so attentive. Inexperienced she might be, but she could not be mistaken in this.

'Camilla, come in here a moment, if you please.'

It was her cousin, standing at the entrance to the library, looking remarkably pleased with himself.

'May I just step upstairs to take off my pelisse and hat, sir?'

'No, no, you do very well as you are, I have to be off out in a minute or two.'

He held the door for her as she went through, and then closed it behind her before crossing to the fireplace and taking up a stance with his arm on the mantel and his foot on the fender.

This room was called the library, and it was indeed lined with leather-bound books. However, it was really far too small to be graced with such a name and was fitted up more as a study for her cousin. There was a handsome desk, a comfortable leather chair set beside the fire, a globe set on an elegant stand, a half-clock made by Tompion, and a variety of military prints in the spaces on the walls between the shelves of books.

It was a masculine room, and Camilla mused for a moment on how much of the house was used by Fanny: for herself, her children and her guests, how much of it was therefore a female domain. This library – study, whatever you might call it – was the master's only clearly defined area in the house, and, she told herself, it was quite adequate for him. He needed no more, since, for him, the outside and larger world was where his territory and stalking grounds lay. His clubs and Parliament and bachelor friends' houses or lodgings were all his to visit as he wished, as were coffee houses, taverns and inns, boxing parlours, the fencing salle and Tattersall's, that most masculine of venues, where men looked over and bought and sold horses and exchanged news and gossip about the turf and horses, riders and owners.

So here in the house, he had merely this room to himself, but out of doors he had no boundaries. Why had this never oc-curred to her before? How constrained were Fanny, and her sisters and herself, with their tiny, enclosed, domestic world, set around by doors and windows within, and by the rectangle of genteel London without.

'Pray attend to what I have to say, Camilla,' said her cousin, frowning. 'It is of the greatest importance. You may be aware that Sir Sidney did me the honour of waiting upon me, here, this morning.' He didn't pause for a reply but went straight on. 'It gives me the greatest satisfaction to tell you the purpose of his visit – or perhaps you can tell me, for young ladies are always beforehand with this kind of news.'

She was startled, and somewhat puzzled. Sir Sidney had said nothing to her about any business he might have with Mr Fitzwilliam, and she would not have expected it. 'Indeed, sir, I have no notion why he called here today.'

'He came to ask me, as your closest male relative and one under whose protection you presently reside, for permission to pay his addresses to you.'

'Pay his addresses?'

'You are to be congratulated, for he intends to ask for your hand in marriage.'

THIRTEEN

Nothing had prepared Camilla for this, and she was utterly astonished. She could say nothing, but simply stared at Fitzwilliam.

How could this be? Sir Sidney had said nothing to her; certainly she felt a powerful attraction to him, was actually in love with him, she must admit it to herself, if to no one else, but she was still unsure of his sentiments. Why approach her cousin in this formal way? How correct, but how old-fashioned, how lacking in romance or feeling! Not to speak to her first – it was wrong of him, very wrong.

Her cousin was looking at her expectantly. 'Well, have you nothing to say? In these cases, the lady usually has some foreknowledge of what is to be said. You cannot have been ignorant of his desire to fix his interest with you. Have you no expressions of gratitude, of pleasure in your conquest – and in having made such a notable conquest? A title – only a baronetcy, to be sure, but none of your new creations, his title is an old and honourable one. A handsome fortune, a house in the best part of town, a pretty little estate in Kent. Cousin, I congratulate you, I do indeed!'

There was a long silence before she could find her voice. Then she could only bring herself to say, 'It is so strange!'

'Strange?' His voice was sharp. 'What is strange about it? A man comes to a time of life when he wants to be looking around for a wife, to get him an heir, there is a younger brother in the case, I understand, and entails and so forth. It is a proper thing for him to be doing, and you are a fortunate woman to be the one his fancy has lit upon. You will be excellently established, your friends will all envy you such a match, and your family will say you have done well for yourself.'

Her mind was in a whirl. To speak to her cousin without saying a word to her, what casual presumption of her willingness it showed. Had her affections been so transparent? No, for matters between them had not reached a stage where such a proposal was possible – although she had been ready to feel, after last night, that Mrs de Witt meant nothing to him, and that she herself might in time come to mean a great deal. The point was that he had never made love to her, never by word or gesture given a hint that he was planning for this greatest of all intimacies.

'It is a connection to please everyone,' her cousin was saying. 'It will bring him closer to our particular group in the House, and since there are some issues on which we need every vote we can get, it will make a difference to know that we may rely on his support. A family alliance is the best assurance of loyalty, you know, for it can't change from day to day. I wish you joy, Camilla, I do so with all my heart. It is a capital thing for you. Letty will not be best pleased,' here he gave a hearty chuckle, 'no elder sister likes to have a younger one married first; her nose will be quite out of joint.'

'But sir, my father – nothing can be agreed or done before my father returns. He must be told, consulted—'

'No, no, a daughter's marriage is not of the same importance as a son's, you know. Sir Sidney is a rich man, a man of sense and breeding, of good reputation and a thorough-going Tory. What more could he ask? What more could any man ask for his daughter, eh? No, no it will do very well, at least as far as a betrothal, we may venture upon a betrothal, and so I told Sir Sidney. We are to dine with him tonight. I took it upon myself to accept his invitation. Fanny has refused all engagements while Charlotte is ill, but the child is better today, and I shall ask her to accompany us. Sir Sidney's sister – you have met her, I think?'

She nodded, speechless once more.

'She acts as hostess, so it is perfectly proper for us to dine at his house. He asked her up from the country for this purpose, a man needs family at such a time. There now, do not look so fraught. Are not you pleased? I would not have given him my consent to address you had I not been sure – aye, and Fanny, too, she will agree with me – that you had a decided *tendre* for Sir Sidney.'

'I hope – I would not in any way have wished for my feelings to be evident. To you, or to anyone. It is a private matter.'

'Well, so you may think, but it is not so. Marriage is not between two people alone, there are many, many other considerations besides. Sir Sidney's man of business will call on me presently, for it is a business arrangement when there is such a fortune involved. Now, I must be off. You will find Fanny in her room, I believe. Tell her the good news, and pass the message about dinner on my behalf, with my love and compliments, if you please. I shall be late if I do not leave this instant.'

The Gardiners had also been invited to dine with Sir Sidney, which was only proper, said Mr Fitzwilliam, as he entered the fine drawing-room with Fanny, Letitia and Camilla. The twins had been left at home, oddly unresisting at not being included. Suspiciously so, Camilla had thought for a moment, as she and her sister climbed into the carriage, but she had too occupied a mind and too excited a heart to think any more about it.

'It is, after all, a family occasion,' Mr Fitzwilliam said, bowing to Mr Wytton, who had accompanied the Gardiners. 'An occasion for present and future members of the family to be together.'

Even in her own confused state, Camilla couldn't help noticing the way Wytton was unable to take his eyes off Sophie. Sophie, however, was happy to let her attention roam, taking in the details of elegant furniture, splendid hangings and magnificent paintings before looking her cousins' toilettes up and down and deciding that her own white muslin was much prettier than their gowns.

It was indeed the house of a connoisseur; Camilla had never seen so many exquisite objects in one place before, nor a single person's possessions arranged with such nicety as to their position on a table, a wall, in a niche. Sir Sidney had a small gallery, designed for his father by Adam, where he kept his collection of Italian statuary, artfully displayed. He would be most happy to show it to them after dinner.

He had greeted her with a smiling countenance, and had made a most elegant leg before taking her hand and brushing it with his lips. An indifferent kind of a kiss for a lover, she thought for an uneasy moment, but then, they were in company, all eyes were upon them, so well-mannered and correct a gentleman as Sir Sidney would hardly attempt to embrace her before them, acknowledged suitor or not. Even so, when she had looked into his eyes she had seen, for a moment, not warmth or passion, but a coldness, a deadly coldness, that for a second sent a stab of apprehension through her. Then it vanished, and nothing was left but apparent admiration.

'You are in great beauty tonight,' he said, before attending to his other guests.

Such perfection! she said inwardly as she gazed around the room. Even the servants were striking to look at. Generally, menservants who waited on guests were chosen for their upright physiques – with the hope of characters equally upright – and servants were most definitely expected to blend into the background. Sir Sidney's servants did not blend; they did not seem intended to blend. One young man in particular caught her eye as he moved swiftly and gracefully about the room, an olive-skinned young man with huge black eyes, his dark skin set off by the powdered footman's wig and the pale blue silk livery he wore.

'Well, Camilla, I hope you know what you are about,' Letty whispered to her. 'I know nothing can be decided finally until Papa has sent word, there can be no formal announcement, but the news will fly around, you know how the polite world loves to gossip, and then, should you wish to withdraw, it will be difficult for you.'

'I shan't wish to withdraw,' Camilla said. 'Can't you be happy for me, Letty?'

Letitia's face was closed. 'I would wish you all the happiness in the world. It is only that—'

'That what?'

'Nothing. Sir Sidney is a handsome man, and you must know what you are doing in accepting him.'

'Could you have cared for him?'

Letitia was startled by the question. 'I? Oh, no, never.'

'Is it still Tom?'

'It is not. It has nothing to do with Tom, it is simply that Sir Sidney is not the kind of man I could have a fancy for. That is all.'

Dinner was served in the French style, which took a good deal of time, but the food was excellent. Camilla could scarcely swallow a morsel of it. The men did not linger long over their wine, and Mr Wytton came out of the dining-room ahead of his companions, eager to sit beside Sophie and make himself agreeable to her. She tossed her head, and flirted with him, pleased to be the object of someone's attention. Etiquette dictated that she must yield the centre stage to her cousin for the evening, but that she didn't care to do so was quite obvious to Letitia and Camilla, and to her mother, who more than once found occasion to quell her with a lifted brow or a slight frown.

'It will be a relief to me when she is married,' Mrs Gardiner confided to Camilla, as they sat together on a sofa, waiting for the rest of the gentlemen to join the company. 'Being engaged does not seem to suit her; she is restless and out of sorts. It is only natural, I dare say.'

'It is wonderful to see Mr Wytton so much in love with her,' Camilla said, remembering the way Wytton's hand had brushed Sophie's, the way his eyes never left her face, the way his mouth softened when she turned and smiled at him.

'He has an ardent temperament,' Mrs Gardiner said, an odd remark to make, even though she was right: Wytton was an ardent man; Sophie was lucky to inspire so strong an attachment.

Then she pulled herself up. She would now be to Sir Sidney what Sophie was to Wytton. The thought sent a frisson shivering up and down her spine. She longed for him to come into the room, and then when he did, at once making his way towards her, she wished she were anywhere but there. Mrs Gardiner rose tactfully, and Sir Sidney begged to be allowed to sit beside Camilla. Welcomed by the glow in her eyes, he moved slightly further away from her, and said how happy she had made him by accepting the offer of his hand.

She could not remember actually accepting him. Had she said as much to Mr Fitzwilliam? Was paying your addresses the same as making an offer? There had, in fact, been no proposal. Sir Sidney must have taken Mr Fitzwilliam's permission as an implied acceptance; did she wish it otherwise? Of course not. She gave herself a little shake, she must not indulge in these absurd fancies.

There was an unreality to the evening, something of the dreamlike about it – perhaps something to do with not eating all day, or was it the almost suffocating correctness of her surroundings, the sense of nothing being so much as a fraction out of place and a sudden, terrible panic as to where, amid all this, would she fit? Would she not be a jarring note amid all this perfection?

Idle fancies, she told herself, her heart stirring as Sir Sidney shifted slightly, calling out something to Wytton, some jesting comment, and she was made suddenly, intensely aware of his physical presence and proximity. Of course she would be at home here. She would belong where he belonged; most young women on the brink of matrimony must wonder about their future lives, how it would be to be married, to be mistress of a strange house? They would travel, surely they would travel together to the places abroad she longed to visit. He would not be wanting a wife to sit at home, a domestic goddess, he did not seem at all that kind of a man.

What kind of a man was he then, this creature she had fallen in love with? Did she know him at all?

Good heavens, why must she have all these provoking thoughts at a time when she should be entirely happy?

She came out of her reverie to see Mrs Delamere standing beside her, an offer of tea on her lips.

'Thank you.'

'We are so pleased,' said Mrs Delamere with her thin smile, her face at once so like her brother's. 'We look forward to welcoming you in Kent.'

This woman would be her sister, Kent her second home. 'Too kind,' she murmured.

'Let it not be too long,' advised Mrs Delamere. 'Long engagements do no good, take my word for it.'

By the time the party was over, and they were safely back in Aubrey Square, the ecstatic spirits with which she had greeted the day had faded. The happiness was there in a muted form, but now a mere background to her more immediate feelings, which were, to her surprise, those of a certain resentment – at the day's events, at the stiffness of the evening party, of the passion Wytton showed for Sophie, although why that should bother her, she did not care to think. She did not altogether like the businesslike way in which Mr Fitzwilliam had received Sir Sidney's proposals for her hand, and wished with all her heart that Constantinople were not so far away, or, alternatively, that she herself were in Constantinople. Or Prague, or Cairo, or indeed anywhere that was not London.

Then she scolded herself for her folly, and sipped at the hot milk sweetened with honey that Sackree considered the fitting end to an evening's festivities, smart young London lady or no. It revived her, but did not chase away her thoughts and fears and questions, and she sat long by the fire, for once not chided into bed by Sackree, who came to the door and stole a look at her mistress more than once, and then tiptoed away.

The letter to her mother and father was hard to write. Camilla had nibbled away the end of her pen, and had crumpled up several sheets of Fanny's elegant note paper before she had a result that satisfied her.

'Finished, my love?' enquired Fanny, putting her head round the door. 'It may go with Mr Fitzwilliam's letter.'

'No,' she said. 'Not yet. My head is heavy, I am not thinking clearly. I should like to read it over again before it is sealed and sent.' She yawned, and stretched her arms.

'You slept ill last night,' said Fanny, observing the dark rings beneath her eyes, and the paleness of her complexion. 'It is an unsettling time for any girl.'

Camilla wondered if Sir Sidney had lost a second's sleep over her, wished he had, thought he probably had not, and then laughed at herself for being so silly.

'I am taking Belle and Georgina for an airing in the carriage,' said Fanny. 'Do you care to come with us?'

'No, I thank you,' she said, jumping to her feet. 'I need a brisk walk. I shall call on Mrs Rowan.'

In Bruton Street, she could look forward to good company and conversation, a distraction from the thoughts still rattling round inside her head, a chance to think and talk about matters that had nothing to do with Sir Sidney, love, matrimony or Kent. Accordingly, she set off at a stirring pace, the keen wind whipping colour into her cheeks, and arrived in a short while at Mrs Rowan's door, pausing on the step to catch her breath.

Within was a buzz of talk, laughter, animated expressions, intelligent faces, a roaring fire and the coffeepot doing its duty on a side-table. She sat down, her cares slipping from her, as Pagoda Portal, deep in conversation with Mr Layard, took a minute to give her a wink and a nod of his head.

Mr Roper came over to greet her. He was pleased to see her, he said, hadn't expected to see her today, since now she would have other calls on her time.

'What do you mean?' she cried.

'Well,' and he gave her a sly look, 'it is all over town that you are to marry Leigh. I was told it by at least three persons, in the strictest secrecy, for of course there can be no formal announcement until your father is come home. But is it not true?'

The room seemed to have gone quite silent, and she looked about her in some consternation.

'I would rather not speak of it, if you will forgive me.'

And the assembled company, taking note of the sudden whitening of her face, and the slight tremble to her voice, behaved with kindness, hiding any curiosity they might feel and returning to their chat.

All except Pagoda Portal, who frowned, looked grave, raised his eyebrows in an interrogatory way at Mrs Rowan, and then made his rather ponderous way across the room. 'Miss Camilla, let me sit myself down here, near you. You will not mind, Mr

Roper, if I am private with Miss Camilla for the merest moment or two?'

He rose at once. 'If you are to talk secrets, then I am best away. This is just the place, sitting here in this alcove you may say what you like, for no one will hear you.'

He moved away, and she smiled at Mr Portal. 'Is there something particular you have to say to me, sir? I am at your disposal.'

He heaved his chair a little closer, one of the legs giving a protesting groan as he did so; Pagoda Portal was no lightweight.

'You will forgive my directness; it is the only way, and you are a sensible, rational creature. You will know that I speak entirely without malice.'

In the mouths of most people, such a disclaimer would at once make her suspect the opposite intent, but with Pagoda Portal, his honesty was so evident, and his goodwill so pronounced, that she felt he spoke no more than the truth.

'I learn that you are to become engaged to Sir Sidney Leigh, that you are going to marry him.'

She coloured, paled, and regained her self-control. 'It seems that secrets are out before they have time to be passed even between the principals,' she said, with an effort at lightness.

'You must think again. You must refuse him. My dear Miss Camilla, you have no notion of what you are at. You swim in deep waters here, deep and murky waters.'

'Murky waters? Good heavens, what are you speaking of?'

'I have known Sir Sidney Leigh these many years. I count him a friend, and he is a good fellow, as good a man as ever lived. But he won't do for you, and I think it wrong of him to even think of venturing upon matrimony – and to you, of all people!'

'Sir, what is this? You terrify me with these mysterious warnings. Tell me plainly, what is the matter with him? Or with me?' An awful thought had struck her, gothic visions floated through her mind. 'He is not married already? He does not have a wife?' A mad wife? Locked in some attic, kept in some lonely house, far from London? 'Oh, for God's sake, Mr Portal, do not keep me in suspense.'

'No, no,' he cried, 'no, no, there is no wife in the question, no, nor should be, that is exactly my point.'

Controlling her temper and fear with a supreme effort, she took a deep breath, unwound her fingers, and said, slowly, 'Please tell me, in a direct manner, what is the problem with Sir Sidney.'

'Very well, then. You will have heard – I dare say, that even young ladies brought up in the countryside must know – I suppose you to be a well-read young woman, with some knowledge of what goes on. Even, as I say, in Derbyshire.'

Camilla stared at him in astonishment. What could he have to say that was causing him to hem and haw in this uncharacteristic way?

'You are aware, I am sure you must be aware that there are men who prefer the company of their own sex to that of women. I speak not of clubs and sporting gatherings, but of—' He paused, seeming to search for a word. 'Of, shall I say, friendship; friendship of a closer kind than is natural.'

FOURTEEN

Sodomite.

The word came unbidden into her head, and unaware that she was doing so, Camilla, aghast, whispered it aloud.

Pagoda Portal let out a little sigh. 'Well, there you are. It is not a word I would choose to use in the presence of any young lady, because apart from the deeply unpleasant implications, the word might have no meaning for you.'

The word did have a meaning for her. She read the newspapers, she had seen an item about a man taken up for a sodomy in Winchester, just as she had read a report of an Isle of Wight man hanged for bestiality. Yet it was one thing to know the meaning of a word, and another to find herself using the word in a drawing-room, to a man, even such a man as Mr Portal, and in such a context. It took her breath away; Mr Portal must be deranged, or how could he ever suggest such a thing? He didn't seem out of his wits, it was true, and he was looking at her with such a concerned, intent expression on his rubicund face.

'I know what a s—' She could not bring herself to repeat the word. 'I know what that is,' she said finally. 'How can you say such a thing? You should not speak of this to me, it is most wrong of you, and there can be no reason to do so, none at all!'

Mr Portal was looking hot and ill at ease, and he flapped a hand before his face. 'Never was there such a fix. I never thought to have had to discuss such a thing. It is like this. Your father is abroad, Fitzwilliam is so taken up with his Parliamentary arithmetic that he prefers not to see what is as plain as the nose beneath his eyes, and he is not the sort of man to have any idea of one of his acquaintance being given over to such practices. Mr Gardiner does not concern himself with such things. I do believe he has no idea of it, he is not the kind of man who – well, in short, you have not had your interests protected as you deserve. However that may be, you must accept the fact that Sir Sidney, the man you are planning to marry, is—'

This time, she didn't allow him to finish his sentence. Pale with agitation and rage, she rose and turned on him. 'Not another word. You spoke of having no malice; what is this, if not malicious?'

'My dear, it is not malice, it is the truth.' He paused, sighed, passed a handkerchief over his perspiring brow. 'I begged Mrs Rowan to broach the subject with you. She is older than you, experienced in the ways of the world, she has been married, it would have come better from her. But she would not do so. She suspected it, has suspected it for a long time, but she would not raise such a matter with you on a suspicion. Mrs Rowan insisted upon my telling you, for I know just how things are with Sir Sidney. I will not tell you how the certainty of his inclinations came to me; it is not necessary, and it would betray a confidence. Suffice it to say that it is so, it is unfortunately in the nature of some men, that is all. You may talk to Mrs Rowan about it – distasteful as the subject is, she can set you right on it, and after all, it does a girl no good to go out into the world in complete ignorance of the many vices and foibles of mankind. It is better that you know than to be hoodwinked as you have been here.'

She had begun to calm down. 'I would be stupid to deny that there are many vices and,' she winced, trying to find the right words, 'unnatural practices among people in all ranks of society. However, I can assure you that I have no reason to believe for a single moment that Sir Sidney indulges in any such behaviour. Why, sir,' she went on in a passionate whisper, 'how would it be possible for me to fall in love with such a man? Or for him to want a wife? What you say goes against all sense.'

'A man's reason may dictate that he marry, while his inclinations lie elsewhere. Have you not found him cold towards you, where you would have expected warmth, ardency, even a touch of the satyr, for Lord's sake, as would be normal between a man and woman in love, physically attracted by one another as they must be?'

Cold! Her heart stood still, and her own flesh seemed to take on a chill. Hadn't she wondered at his lack of ardour, compared his behaviour with that of Wytton towards Sophie, or the young couple at Mrs Seton's soirée – the ardour she had seen displayed over and over, even in the most correct gatherings? Love and a cold cannot be hid, as the saying went; did Sir Sidney have no trouble in hiding his emotions for the simple reason that he felt none towards her?

'He has a footman,' Mr Portal said. 'A fine-looking lad, dark, with great eyes and a smooth skin. Did you observe him last night?'

She nodded, unable to say a word.

'He is a particular favourite.'

That footman. Oh, dear God, it could not be true. This was a nightmare she was living through. Presently she would wake up in her own bed, disturbed by such a vivid dream, but content that the day brought a happier reality.

There was no awakening from this nightmare, however. She groped for her handkerchief. 'I must go home,' she said. 'Say I am taken unwell, say anything you please.'

'It is perfectly true,' Wytton heard Snipe Woodhead say. Snipe was seated in his favourite spot in Pink's famous bow window overlooking St James's Street. From there, Snipe could see which of his friends and enemies were out and about, but this morning he had other fish to fry and was holding court looking inward to the club room rather than out on to the street. He had not noticed Wytton, sitting some distance away in a corner of the big room.

'I had it from Layard, and he must have had it from Wytton, who was present. They are thick as thieves, those two. It was a family party, for Miss Camilla Darcy and Sir Sidney Leigh were to be betrothed, privately betrothed, only Mr Darcy's consent waited for before it was to go into the *Gazette*. Sir Sidney's sister was up from the country – she married Delamere, do you remember him? A Whig, of course, but a nice enough fellow.

Formal party, the Gardiners present, although no one else from Darcy's family, I wonder if that was deliberate. Fifty thousand pounds in Leigh's pocket and she to become Lady Leigh, which she probably thinks sounds well enough, although with such a fortune— However, it all came to nothing, for the next day, the very next day, in the evening, a note was sent round from Aubrey Square: she could not enter into an engagement, wished never to see him again.'

'Obviously those Darcy girls make a habit of nearly but not quite getting to the altar,' said a red-faced member. 'Wasn't it one of the Darcy sisters got dished by young Busby?'

'The eldest sister,' said a man in the naval uniform of a post captain, hot from an uncomfortable session at the Admiralty by the look of him. 'She's a religious woman, one of your Evangelicals, fine if you want to share your bed with a heap of tracts. Waiter! A tankard of ale, and be quick about it.'

There was a momentary silence as the group of men in the long, handsome room considered the dangers of Evangelicalism. 'It's bound to come,' said the red-faced man, glumly. 'Straws in the wind, sign of the times and all that. Our children will grow up to be mealy-mouthed prudes, the whole pack of them. You mark my words.'

There was sympathy for his remarks, especially among those who knew that he had had a thoroughly disagreeable time with his son over some gambling debts and the entail.

'There's a pair of Darcy twins, uncommon beautiful girls,' said the captain. 'Saw them at Mrs Pollexfen's last night, although I wasn't introduced. There was no getting near them for the crush. Day and Night they call them; wonder who they'll jilt?'

'Or who will jilt them. It seems to work both ways with those girls,' said red face.

There was general laughter.

'It's a pity a man can't marry the pair of them,' said Lord Rampton, joining the group. 'Those twins, I mean, Miss Belle and Miss Georgina. Double the money, you know, and then you'd have one for when you were in a cheery mood and t'other for melancholy days.'

'Oh, one wife is more than enough for any man,' said Snipe Woodhead with his braying laugh. 'And so you'll find when you net your heiress, Rampton.'

'It had better be soon,' said Rampton gloomily. 'Otherwise it'll be Calais for me, alongside of the Dowager Dandy and all the other exiles with the bailiffs on their tails.'

'Is George Brummell still in Calais? I thought he'd moved on,' said Snipe Woodhead.

'Mend your ways, reform your life and propose to Miss Darcy,' recommended the captain, clapping Lord Rampton on the shoulder. He drained his tankard, made a small noise of satisfaction and walked off with the slightly rolling gait of his profession to order a substantial dinner.

Damn the lot of them, Wytton said inwardly. So Miss Camilla had given Leigh his *congé*; well, thank God for it. It had upset him surprisingly to learn that she was to marry Leigh. He'd said as much to Sophie, only of course he couldn't explain why such a marriage would be doomed to disaster. For the first time, he had found Sophie's artlessness tiresome. She had laughed affectedly and said that Sir Sidney was a good match for poor Camilla, who might otherwise languish on the shelf until she dwindled into a confirmed spinsterhood.

'I think not,' he had said, with some asperity. 'What, at nineteen, and with her looks?'

'Looks? Letitia is the beauty of that family, and the twins are generally held to be pretty, but Camilla is almost plain.'

He had held his tongue with difficulty, merely saying that Camilla had her fair share of the family's good looks. Sophie took this as a compliment to herself, and was all smiles and sweetness once more. He couldn't help remembering the remark Layard had made when he became engaged to Sophie, that kittens were all very well in their way, were it not that they had an unfortunate tendency to grow into cats.

While the club gossips were making free with her name, Camilla was facing her cousin's wrath. Summoned to his library by a servant, she had entered the room to find him glowering by the fireplace. She shut the door and stood in front of it, pale, gathering all the courage and resolution she knew she would need if she were not to be browbeaten into submission or into admitting that she had done anything wrong.

'Fanny has informed me that you have written to Sir Sidney saying that everything is finished between you. Is this true? Can it possibly be true?'

She swallowed, found her voice. 'It is true. I have written to him.'

'And what reason, what justification do you give for this extraordinary, rash behaviour? I never heard of such a thing: for a young lady to accept a suitor's proposals, with her family's approval, although naturally subject to your father's final agreement – not that there would be any doubt about that, I venture to say – and then, calmly, to announce that it is all off! No engagement, no marriage.'

Mr Fitzwilliam's voice was not, at that moment, the voice he customarily used in society. This was a tone that belonged to his days of military command, the manner in which he would have torn a strip off some young subaltern, wet behind the ears, who had failed in his duty.

Were she not still in such an upheaval of spirits from the revelations of the day and their aftermath, she might have found herself amused by this realisation. As it was, she simply wished he would not speak so loud – bellow was more the word for it – and that he would pay her the compliment of supposing her to have some rational basis to her actions.

'I am perfectly in command of my wits, sir. I cannot marry Sir Sidney Leigh. What I have learned about him precludes any possibility of my marrying him. No woman could marry him in the circumstances.'

'And yet you refuse to say what these circumstances are or what is this special knowledge that means you must throw the house into an uproar, cause your name to be the subject of all kinds of scandalous gossip and supposition, and leave me in an extremely difficult situation?'

'As to that, the blame lies with me for my actions. You can hardly be held responsible.'

'Blame! I am not speaking of blame, I am speaking of votes.

Do you understand what it means to antagonise a man such as Sir Sidney Leigh? For since this is bound to cause considerable ill feelings towards you and all your connections, how can I imagine he will support us in the House? There is a matter of some enclosures coming up shortly, and I have promised Mr Hilbertson, whose land—' He recollected himself. 'Never mind that, it cannot be expected that you would comprehend such issues.'

'I think I can comprehend the counting of votes,' said Camilla, her temper beginning to get the better of her. 'However, you will comprehend that I consider my future happiness of more importance than a vote in the House.' She did not add, as she well might, that she had in any case severe doubts about enclosure of common land, having seen for herself the distress it caused to country folk in her own part of the world, where many of their neighbours had been all too eager to toss tenants off their land and into destitution.

'Happiness! We were not put upon this earth to consider our own happiness, I believe. Duty, miss, comes before happiness.'

'I do not consider it to be my duty to marry Sir Sidney Leigh.'

'It is your duty to be guided by those who know better than you what is and is not acceptable behaviour. Very well, if you will not tell me what objections there are to Sir Sidney – and objections, moreover, that were not apparent before now – then there is no more to be said on the matter.'

Thank goodness for that, although she feared that the whole business would continue to irk her cousin for a good while yet. This would sink her even further in his esteem. Well, it was a pity, but there was nothing to be done about it.

'Charlotte's persistent cough is causing her mother some concern,' Fitzwilliam was saying in a cold, hard voice. 'This may have escaped your notice, being wrapped up as you are in your own affairs. I have therefore decided that Fanny should take Charlotte and the baby to Southend; Dr Molloy believes they would benefit from sea air. While they are away, you will not go about in society, as you will have no chaperon.'

'That is no hardship to me, sir,' she said. And indeed, she

would be thankful to be spared the whispers behind her back, the glances, the barbed comments that would be bound to come her way. The fashionable world loathed a jilt, and despite the fact that there had been no formal announcement of her engagement, society would dub her a jilt and take its polite revenge, as it did on any creature who had the temerity or unwisdom to flout its unwritten rules.

Fitzwilliam was still talking, prating away about Letitia and her sense of duty and service. 'Letty,' he said pointedly, 'will find plenty to occupy her during this time, taken up as she is with her good causes.' Camilla would do well to take a leaf from her book and perhaps gain in humility by so doing.

'I need no lessons in humility from Mr Valpy,' she flashed back. 'All I might learn from him is humbug.'

Mr Fitzwilliam went over to his desk and sat down, his face flushed and frowning. 'It is not your place to criticise a man of the cloth.'

'When a man is a hypocrite, I believe I must be aware of it, whether he is in orders or no.'

He stared at her with dislike. 'Mr Valpy will always be a welcome visitor to my house. You may receive no other callers; it would not be seemly.'

She made her curtsy and fled before her tongue betrayed her. As she shut the door behind her, she felt profoundly relieved – that the interview was over and that Fanny's going away would give her some days' grace before she need face the rigours of a disapproving world. It might be his idea of punishment, but she welcomed it.

Heavens, though, what a fuss the twins would make when they discovered they were to stay at home, receive no callers, be deprived of all their frivolous pleasures. What did her cousin think they would do? Sit and work at their embroidery, practise their instruments and study with Miss Griffin? Letty would be no help, she would no doubt suggest they improve their minds by reading some of her dreary tracts.

Mr Fitzwilliam left the house in an uncomfortable mood. He felt that somehow Camilla had got the better of him, and he did not like the feeling at all. Drat the girl, who would have thought she could be so obstinate? What could have happened to give her such a distaste for Sir Sidney? The more he thought about it, the more he persuaded himself that perhaps there was no more to it than a lover's tiff. Sir Sidney had been too forward, or not forward enough, had offended the young lady, and she, full of the Darcy spirit, had responded in a manner out of all proportion to the supposed offence.

He would call on Sir Sidney, he decided, on his way to the club. Not an easy call to make, but one that he owed the man, considering the abruptness of Camilla's volte-face – which had been made, he suspected, with barely any attempt at politeness. Fanny had told him that when Camilla had sat down to write the note to Sir Sidney, tears flowing down her face, she had jabbed so hard with the pen that she had driven the nib through the paper in more than one place.

'And when she had finished, she could scarcely manage to attach the wafer, her hand was trembling so much, and she gave the bell-pull such a tug I thought it must come away in her hand. When Fell came in answer to the bell, she thrust the letter in his hand, bidding him in so agitated a way to take it to Sackville Street at once, not to lose a moment about it, that it quite overthrew me. What can have upset her so?'

'Pride and an ungoverned temper,' Mr Fitzwilliam had replied, and it still seemed to him to be the only answer. There could be no substance to her insistence that there were good reasons why the relationship must be ended. Could there?

The memory of that unpleasant business with Miss Harper flitted into his mind. That had been worse. It had happened on the very eve of the wedding; at least he had been spared that. The bride-to-be had actually run away from home the day before her wedding, and her family had been extremely tight-lipped about it afterwards. They had retreated to their country estate, hadn't visited London again for a considerable while, not until long after the gossip had died down. The girl had married some neighbouring cleric in the end, he seemed to remember. A man with not a quarter of Sir Sidney's wealth or consequence, you could be sure.

What folly. Yet what was it about the man? It was pointless to dwell on it. His duty was to see if fences could be repaired, bridges mended, breaches repaired. He walked on in a muddle of metaphors, stepping automatically across the road, even forgetting the crossing sweeper until the underfed boy began to berate him in a high, complaining voice. He tossed him a coin and stalked round the corner into Sackville Street.

Camilla's attitude and outspokenness still rankled. Mr Fitzwilliam, at the age of fifty, had nothing of the romantic in him. He was eighteenth-century in his outlook, and he had no idea of this modern business of marrying for love, instead of matrimony being entered into for the practical reasons of money, advancement and mutual benefit to the two families concerned.

This was not to say he was a man lacking in heart. He was truly devoted to Fanny, had fallen in love with her the very first time he met her, and felt about her in a way that he never had with his first wife, a correct, distant woman of respectable fortune, who had married him to please her family and because he was the son of an earl – a younger son, naturally; neither her person nor her portion were handsome enough to merit an earl's eldest son. There was little affection in their marriage, and no children to bind them together, and his mourning for her, when she was carried away by consumption, had been no more than what was obligatory.

How different had been his meeting and wooing of Lady Fanny Erskine, twenty-three years his junior, a vital, warm creature. He was a fortunate man indeed to have Fanny as his wife. How he would miss her. She was not to be away above ten days, but, even so, it was too long. He could post down to Southend, or ride there for a visit. It was scarcely more than thirty miles. Well, there was nothing of Fanny's pretty ways and loving nature in his cousin Camilla.

The twins showed signs of affectionate hearts, beneath their flirtatious ways. Charming girls, as good as gold, likely to make delightful wives for whichever lucky men their fancy alighted on. Letitia, too, he could not but approve of Letty, with her womanly sweetness and concern for others. That Busby business had been shocking; however, it had all blown over, and she had shown herself to be a sensible young woman. He hoped she would find an amiable husband; she would make some worthy fellow an excellent wife.

Unlike Camilla, a shrew if ever he knew one. If she persisted in her folly, she might well rue the day she spurned Sir Sidney. There weren't so many men of property and standing who would be willing to put up with her quick tongue and propensity to argue. Darcy had done her no good, allowing her to grow up into such an opinionated and disagreeable miss. She wasn't as handsome as her sisters, either; she would find herself left on the shelf if she didn't take care and mend her ways.

This curiously satisfying reflection brought him to Sir Sidney's front door, and he was about to mount the stone steps and attack the knocker, when the door opened and Pagoda Portal emerged.

Mr Fitzwilliam was never quite at his ease with Portal, although he liked him well enough. He knew him for a nabob among nabobs, and if his wealth had been the alpha and omega of his position in society, he would have felt better about him. Portal, though, was a man of family, with great connections, who had been sent out to India to remove him from the temptations of London. His had been a wild youth, and he had got into so many tight spots that his family had lost patience with him and packed him off in the care of the Honourable Company to sink or swim as fate dictated.

Portal's own abilities and character had done the rest, and he had returned to an unassailable position in a world that he seemed to care very little for – perhaps it was that most of all that grated on Mr Fitzwilliam. Damn it, the man was hardly better than a Radical, with his outspoken and unTory views and his approval of Reform in all its wicked and evil shapes.

Mr Fitzwilliam tipped his hat to him and was about to go into the house, when Portal put out a restraining hand.

'You won't find Leigh in.'

'No? Then I shall just leave my card.'

'No point in that, neither. He's gone.'

'Gone?' Mr Fitzwilliam stared at Portal. 'Gone where? Down to Kent, I suppose.'

'A good deal further than that. Italy, in fact.'

'Italy! Why should he have gone to Italy?'

'Town too hot to hold him. All kinds of rumours flying about.'

That was just what he'd feared. 'And everyone bandying my cousin Miss Camilla Darcy's name about, I dare say!'

'No longer, for it is set to be a bigger scandal than any jilting, I do assure you.' Seeing that the butler was still standing impassively in the doorway, he took a step back and pressed a coin into the man's cupped hand. 'Now, close that door,' he said, and drew Fitzwilliam further along the pavement. 'See here, he's taken his footman with him. That pretty boy, the olive-skinned one.'

'Why should he not take any servants he likes with him?'

'He ain't going as a servant, that's why. One of the other footmen, jealous, I reckon, has laid charges against Sir Sidney, and there'll be the devil to pay if he ever sets foot in the country again.'

Light began to dawn on Mr Fitzwilliam. His eyes started from his head, and he looked at Portal, aghast. 'Italy! Footman! Pretty boy! You don't mean to tell me—'

'I do, I do indeed. The man's a sodomite. Your cousin has had a lucky escape, Fitzwilliam, a very lucky escape. He might have married her, and what a wretched business that would have been, and it would all have come out, sooner or later, bound to have done, the way the fellow's been carrying on. Only think of the scandal then!'

Mr Fitzwilliam thought, and went pale. 'Good gracious. I can scarcely believe it. Are you telling me, seriously telling me that Leigh is— that he—? I would never have credited it, never. Why, he's one of us! If it's true, sir, then he should be hanged, that's what, hanged. If he were in the army, he'd be shot for it, and good riddance.'

'Oh, I don't think one should make a hanging matter of a man's inclinations,' said Portal annoyingly. 'Only if you're that way, you do need to be discreet. Society don't like it, the ladies don't like it, and the law don't like it.'

'The ladies!' cried Mr Fitzwilliam. 'You see, Portal, you must be mistaken. The ladies have always had an eye to Sir Sidney. Why, Camilla herself was quite in love with the man. So Lady Fanny tells me, and she always knows.'

'It isn't unknown.' Portal's tone was dry. 'Many a sodomite is a married man with a family.'

'Disgraceful. I never heard of such a thing.' A thought occurred to him. 'My God, he's a member of Pink's. He'll be drummed out of the club, of course, we can't have that kind of creature as a member.'

Portal looked at him with commendable gravity, although his mouth twitched. 'No, that would never do.'

'So that's why Camilla— but how did she find out? No innocent girl knows about such things, who would have told her?'

'Who indeed?'

FIFTEEN

Fanny and her entourage bowled away from the house on a misty spring morning; herself, Charlotte, the baby and nurse in the chaise, with Dawson and a nursery maid following behind in a second carriage amid any number of boxes and trunks. A manservant accompanied each carriage; Mr Fitzwilliam was not one to risk his wife being attacked or insulted anywhere along the road. Fanny had protested that little danger was likely on the way from London to Southend, but he had taken no notice.

'It is small enough protection; my mother, you must know, never travelled without she had at least two footmen and a manservant in attendance, besides her own maid.'

Fanny was glad rather than otherwise that the late countess had been laid to rest in the immense and hideous family mausoleum some years before she had met and married Mr Fitzwilliam. She was inclined to think that she would have found her ladyship's ways oppressive. Herself the daughter of an earl, she was familiar with the fads and fancies of the grander end of the aristocracy – not that her own mama, a delightfully eccentric and intrepid woman who loved to travel abroad in the most unpropitious of circumstances, having not an atom of womanly fears about her, was in any way like her dear Mr Fitzwilliam's mother – but she was happier to arrange things in her own, more rational way.

She had some sense of guilt at leaving the five Darcy sisters on their own, but Charlotte's welfare must come first, and they could come to no harm. Like Camilla, she was aware that a few days out of the world – and for a good reason, and one generally known to have the virtue of truth – would be of great benefit both to Camilla's peace of mind and to her reputation. Except that some malicious souls would always be ready to mock her cousin for being so gullible as to fall in love with such a man. And knowledge of her attachment to Sir Sidney would deter other, more eligible men from pressing their suits. It might well be that Camilla and her sisters would, after all, have to end their first London season as single women, despite her best efforts. Then their parents would be back; she shuddered at the thought of attempting to explain to Darcy exactly what had happened between his favourite daughter and such a sad creature as Sir Sidney Leigh had turned out to be.

Still, that was well in the future, and Fanny, blessed with the happy temperament of one not inclined to seek out misfortune, banished the uneasiness from her mind, and settled down to attend to Charlotte's fretful coughing.

The Darcy sisters waved Fanny and the children away with mixed feelings. Letitia approved of Fanny's maternal fears, only warning the others, in a lugubrious undertone, that she did not hope to see Charlotte much improved on her return, that the cough was of a worrying kind that must give rise to the greatest concern for the child's health. Besides delighting in the thoughts of serious illness, she was pleased to find herself in charge, as she saw it, of her younger sisters. She was the eldest, she alone of them was of age, it was natural that the charge of them should fall on her capable shoulders.

And they would not find her wanting in her duties. Already she had schemes for reading and study of languages set out for the twins. Alethea might safely be left to Miss Griffin's care, and indeed, although she would never have admitted it, she was too intimidated by her youngest sister's forceful personality to assert herself in that direction.

As for Camilla, she would need to recover from the shock she had suffered. Of course, she did not have much sensibility, she would not have to endure the torments of a more sensitive woman; Letitia knew that Camilla had never fully entered into her feelings about Tom Busby's demise – or the blow of his reappearance. Perhaps now she would begin to understand a little of what she, Letitia, had been through. 'You will want to rest, Camilla,' she said. 'A period of calmness, of reflection will be beneficial, essential, even, before you venture out to take your place in the world once more. And I think that when you have had time to think the whole matter through, you will agree with me that we should all be better off at Pemberley, away from the false delights of society.'

'Speak for yourself,' said Georgina pertly. 'Nothing will get me back to Pemberley before the summer. And as for Camilla keeping indoors, in a darkened room if you had anything to do with it, it would be a dreadful shame. Let her go about and enjoy herself. There are plenty of eligible men to be met with and a new love is the best way to drive out the old. As you would have found out if you spent more time with Captain Allington and less with that dismal clergyman.'

Letitia rounded on her sister, eyes narrowed, a lecture on the tip of her tongue.

'Save your breath,' said Belle. 'For neither of us will listen to a word you have to say. See if you can keep us under your thumb!'

'Well!' said Letitia. 'Let us find out what Mr Fitzwilliam has to say about this.'

'He has gone out, to his club or Parliament or wherever he goes. We shan't see much of him while Fanny is away, I warrant you. He won't trust himself in our company, so many females will alarm him. He is always uneasy about us, darting glances at our bosoms and then feasting his eyes on Fanny. He is a moral man, he will keep his distance and preserve his reputation.'

'And he'll be off down to Southend to share Fanny's bed-chamber before two or three days are passed,' added Georgina with a peal of laughter.

Now Letitia was truly scandalised. That her younger sisters, innocents of seventeen, should speak like this. Think like this, even; it was beyond anything. Such indelicacy of mind and speech. Such impropriety.

She found herself addressing an empty room. Belle and Georgina had gone laughing up the stairs, and Camilla, taking advantage of Letitia's discomfiture, had made good her own escape, running past the twins and up the next flight of stairs to the nursery where she might be safe from her sister's preaching. Miss Griffin had never had any time for Letty's moralising, and the governess was one of the few people Letty went in awe of.

True to his word, Mr Fitzwilliam had left firm instructions with the butler that the Miss Darcys were not at home during Fanny's absence. With certain exceptions, which was why Camilla, sitting at the pianoforte and absorbed in a new piece, saw to her astonishment – and displeasure – that Mr Valpy was being shown into the drawing-room. A consoling smile spread over his face the instant he realised that the room was not, as he had at first supposed, empty. Advancing on her, he addressed her in a low tone, which might have been suitable for some grieving widow, but which made her want to laugh.

'My dear Miss Camilla, how glad I am of this opportunity to offer you some few words of comfort.'

The fewer the better, she thought, determined to stay seated at the instrument rather than rising to greet him.

'We receive no callers at present,' she said civilly but without any encouragement in her tone. 'My sister is occupied upstairs.'

'Ah, indeed, at a time like this, you do not wish the world to intrude upon you. I understand, I do understand,' he exclaimed, drawing closer to her than she quite liked. 'I would not disturb Miss Darcy in her tasks, but you must not think of me as any mere caller, for a clergyman is bound by his professional duty to succour those sore at heart.'

Her eyebrows rose. 'I do not believe my sister is sore at heart.'

'You misunderstand me. I refer to your own predicament, the sad business of that man whose name should never again be mentioned among righteous people.'

'You mean Sir Sidney Leigh? I thank you, but I am in no need of consolation.' She slid off the stool on the other side to where he stood, and edged round the pianoforte. In a second she had reached the bell and pulled it, and when the servant answered it, she desired him to tell Miss Darcy that she had a visitor. Following the man to the door, she turned, gave the slightest of curtsies, and said, 'You will excuse me, I know, for I too have duties. My sister will be down shortly.' She escaped from the room, closing the door firmly behind her.

The footman was summoning a maid to carry the message to Letitia's bedchamber. 'Be quick, for heaven's sake,' Camilla added. 'Mr Valpy may become restless and start to roam; he is quite capable of visiting the kitchens and preaching to the chef.'

The footman looked horrified. He was well aware what a temperamental man the chef was, him being a Frenchie and a Roman Catholic, apart from having strong opinions against anyone who came traipsing into his domain. Sally was despatched upstairs with an injunction to look lively, and he turned back apologetically to Camilla. 'Fell told him you was none of you at home, miss, but he wouldn't take no for an answer, said that the master had desired him to call, that he was a man of the cloth, not come on a social call.'

'It's not your fault,' she said warmly. 'Goodness, I can hear him coming to the drawing-room door. Tell him Letitia will be down directly, and that I am gone out.'

'And are you, miss?' the footman called down the stairs after her flying figure.

'Yes,' she replied.

'And, miss, there's a note just come for you. I didn't like to bring it up while you were with Mr Valpy. It is on the table in the hall.'

'Thank you,' she said. 'That was quite right.'

Notes held no excitement for her now, no lift of the heart at the expectation of it being from anyone who might have any interest for her. She did not at once recognise the handwriting, which was a firm but feminine script. She broke the wafer and unfolded the paper.

It was from Mrs Rowan. She sighed. She had received a courteous note from Mr Portal, apologising for causing her such distress, but had not felt any desire to answer it. It was not his fault, she knew she could in no way blame him, in fact she owed him a debt of gratitude, and yet she had no wish to see him or to return to Mrs Rowan's elegant rooms where formerly she had passed such pleasant mornings and afternoons.

They would all know her predicament, would laugh at her behind their hands (bad) or sympathise with her (worse).

She ran her eyes down the even lines. Mrs Rowan's letter was overflowing with kindness and goodwill, and it brought a tightness to her throat.

Do not kill the messenger, I beg of you. Mr Portal asked me to explain the situation to you myself, and I refused, which was wrong of me. It might have been easier for you to have received the news from me rather than from him, as I now realise – but I did it from the best of motives, my knowledge of how things stood coming entirely from hearsay. As it turns out, I need not have had any such scruples, and I assure you, my dear friend, that I wish I had been less nice about the matter. Do forgive me, and also Mr Portal, who blames himself for imparting what he knew in such a forthright manner. I do not know how else he could have said what had to be told, and I know you too well to believe that you would hold this against him.

I have heard that Lady Fanny is gone away to the seaside; I hope you have good news of her daughter; I am sure that sea air will quickly restore the child to health. Meanwhile, do not sit at home moping – although I am sure you never mope – but visit us here, where you will find agreeable and intelligent company enough to please anyone. It would gratify me exceedingly to see you, and Mr Portal joins me in wishing very much to meet you again.

It was a kind note, and Camilla was moved by its warmth; she had not experienced much kindness of late. It would be heartless to refuse, and besides, where else was there for her to go? To the library, or to the shops in Bond Street, where she would be bound to run into all the people she least wanted to see at present? No. A walk in the park, at this unfashionable hour? There would be little pleasure in that. She had no desire to roam amid the painful beauty of the spring flowers and budding leaves.

She made up her mind: she would walk round to Bruton Street. She was about to summon Sackree, then hesitated. She would go alone. Fanny would be horrified if she knew, but Fanny was in Southend. She might meet Fitzwilliam – unfortunate if it were so, but unlikely. So she buttoned herself into her pelisse, it being a chilly day for all the signs of spring, and nodded to the alarmed-looking maid who came into the hall as soon as she heard the front door open, and stood hovering by the entrance.

'Are you going out alone, Miss Camilla? Should I not call Sackree to you?'

'There is no need. I am not going far,' she said, and whisked herself out of the house before the maid could call upon any higher authority.

As she walked briskly along, relishing the freedom and invigoration to her spirits that the movement brought her, clergymen crept unbidden into her thoughts. How could Letitia support Valpy's company? How could she listen so eagerly to his slippery, sententious views on religion, society or anything else? How could Mr Fitzwilliam, a man of experience, be so deceived in him?

And then there was the problem of Barleigh Barcombe, a man cut from a very different clerical cloth, who in his way was just as misguided as any Valpy. Whatever had possessed a man of Barcombe's intelligence and sense and position to develop a passion for so unsuitable a creature as Belle?

Belle was as pretty as she was wilful, and her wistful and fragile air had deceived other men than Barcombe into misjudging her, convinced that she needed protection from the cruel winds of the world and that he alone was the man to offer that protection. Absurd; Belle no more needed protection than did a cat. Throw her how you might, she would land on her feet; look for her where you expected to find her and she would be gone; affront her and she would turn on you; give her the opportunity and she would tear a man's heart to shreds – kitty playing with a mouse.

No, Belle was not at all a suitable person for poor Mr Barcombe to lose his heart to, and how Belle mocked and scorned him. She did it, too, with casual indifference. There was no trace of affection in her wholehearted dismissal of him and his attentions, no cruel words concealing a hidden liking.

Georgina was more polite to him than her sister. Since he took no more than a civil interest in her, she returned the compliment, merely laughing heartily at his folly and teasing Belle about her unwanted suitor.

Whom did Belle and Georgina have any feelings for? There must be someone, for ever since they were thirteen or fourteen, some man or other had been the object of their affections. They were not essentially wicked or corrupt or cold-hearted, merely young and thoughtless and given over to their own pleasures; spreading their wings and testing their powers.

Camilla had a shrewd idea that in a year or so, Belle would have lost much of her pert wildness and desire to tease anyone who tried to impose any authority over her. She had a warm heart hidden deep beneath her frivolous ways, a much warmer heart, Camilla believed, than Georgina. Georgina was single-minded, and Camilla did not care to think what might be the consequence of Georgina setting her heart and mind on an idea – or a person.

There could not have been a worse time or way for the twins to be let loose in London. Heavens knew what they might not get up to in the next week or so, and despite Letitia's smug assumption of authority, neither she nor Fitzwilliam would be capable of restraining them. They would run wild, it was inevitable. Perhaps she should speak to Aunt Lydia; indulgent she might be, but surely she was worldly enough to prevent two such young ladies stepping over the invisible boundary of what might and might not be tolerated in the unforgiving milieu of the polite world.

Her mind ran on; she wanted to think about anything and anybody except Sir Sidney Leigh and the blow he had administered to her heart.

Alethea, what was making her so happy and good-humoured? She was growing up, of course, that was part of it, leaving behind the awkward age. Her singing lessons were an obvious source of joy and inspiration, and yet there was more, an imp of mischief in her eye, as though she knew something her sisters did not. It was no good questioning Griffy, she would not discuss Alethea, the last and best-loved of her pupils, with anyone. General assurances and remarks on her charge's untidiness were all you could expect from Griffy on that subject.

Camilla found herself at Mrs Rowan's door, and all thoughts of her sisters, their clerical followers and Alethea's secrets vanished as she remembered how short a time it was since she had paid her last visit to this house, how happy she had then been, and how different her situation now was.

She should not have come. It was a mistake, it was too soon to return to the scene where her hopes, her very future had been tumbled to the ground by a few brutal words. Here were many of the same people who had observed her discomfiture, and who would know – all London must know – what lay behind her hasty and distressed departure.

Too late to turn and run, impossible to blurt out an apology and leave. Her own stupidity had brought her to Mrs Rowan's house, what foolishness to be so affected by a trivial act of kindness and to march into this lion's den. Here was Pagoda Portal, coming forward with a cheerful smile on his face, as though nothing had happened; how could he look like that? Mrs Rowan was full of eager greetings; how good a friend in truth was she? Had Camilla built too much trust on the slender foundation of a slight former acquaintance? She had felt an immediate liking for Mrs Rowan upon meeting her again – but she had felt a pretty immediate liking for Sir Sidney, too. What did that say about her judgement?

Mr Layard was there, beaming at her. He was treating her like a child who has fallen over and is being picked up and consoled, she decided, unreasonably. At least Mr Wytton preserved a cold countenance, and favoured her with no more than a distant smile and a polite bow.

A lifetime of training came to her aid. The manners, decorum and pride instilled in her since she could toddle – and much resented and resisted through the years of her tomboyish girlhood and hoydenish adolescence – now proved their worth. No one seeing her in that room, old friend or new acquaintance, could have known how unsettled and disturbed her mind was. She smiled, chatted, listened, ate, drank, all with unaffected poise. She surprised herself by the ease with which she behaved like this, and was amazed to find how it was possible to detach herself, to be as much an onlooker to the performance as anyone else in the room. Her social being triumphed; her inner being was momentarily stilled.

Despite the misery tugging at her heart, she felt a sense of achievement. It was an astonishing discovery, that her pretence could be so convincing. This must be how women managed to hold their heads high in the face of all odds, smiling through faithlessness and betrayal, defying the world to prove that a marriage was a failure, children a disappointment, money a concern.

To her surprise, Mr Wytton came over and addressed her. 'I was just at the Gardiners,' he said abruptly. 'Mrs Gardiner and Sophie were going out, I believe, to pay a visit to Aubrey Square.' He paused, looked at her intently. 'She has heard something of your recent trouble, although not from you, I think.'

She was flustered. 'No. That is, I was planning to write— Thank you for informing me of this, sir. I shall go home at once, I hope I may be there before them.'

His rather severe face softened into a reluctant smile. 'No fear of that, Miss Camilla. For they plan to call at one or two shops on the way. There are some ribbons from France newly come into the haberdashers, and Sophie can spend half an afternoon choosing ribbons.'

She smiled back at him, thinking how much better he looked when his face lost its moody expression.

Mr Layard joined them. 'I heard Wytton being hard upon Miss Sophie,' he said, winking at her. 'How does he expect her to look so pretty and elegant if she isn't to be allowed time to pick out the nicest fripperies to wear? I dare say you take your time over the choice of a ribbon, and you have a mind that goes beyond female adornment.'

'Not quite half an afternoon,' she said, laughing. 'However, one should have one's mind quite on what one is doing, and therefore, when ribbons are the matter in hand, it is perfectly right to give them their proper attention.'

Wytton gave her a sardonic look and yielded his seat to his friend, who sat himself down at once and proceeded to amuse her very much indeed with an absurd account of his attempts to match a green ribbon for his great-aunt.

'And the end of it was, when I had gone to all that trouble, and was feeling I had acquitted myself excellently, just as a man with an eye to a will ought, she turns up her nose – a nose like a parrot, my great-aunt has – and announces that she has gone off the colour green, has decided it don't become her in the least, and she wished she had desired me to find her a blue ribbon.'

'The moral of which is, Mr Layard, that women are best left to themselves when ribbons are in question.'

'Not at all, not at all. I have a keen eye for colour and excellent taste, I am your man if ever you need an eye cast over ribbon or a length of silk.'

The smile faded from her eyes, and her face clouded. It came back to her with shocking clarity, the scene in Sir Sidney's house on the night of that dinner party, with Lady Delamere declaring how good a judge of a silk or a damask her brother was.

Layard stared at her in surprise. 'Why, whatever have I said to make you look like that?' he demanded. 'I was only funning, you know.'

She shook her head. 'Of course. It was just that you reminded me of someone, for a moment. It is nothing.'

Wytton, although he had moved away, had obviously been listening to their conversation. He drew closer, seemed about to speak, hesitated, looked intently at her and then, in a jesting tone, told Layard he had best hold his tongue, for a man with worse taste was not to be found in London, and Miss Camilla had much better look out for her ribbons and satins herself. Then he took his friend by the elbow, gave her a quick, conspiratorial smile, and led him away.

She was left with the distinct impression that Wytton had known at once and precisely why the reference to choosing silks had bothered her, and that, without pitying her in the least, he regretted her unease and had therefore deflected his friend's questions – all without seeming to take any particular notice of what was being said.

Had she misjudged the man? Perhaps there was more to him than at first appeared. Then a thought occurred to her and brought an involuntary smile to her lips: it would go hard with Sophie if she had to keep pace with a husband who was not only her intellectual superior, but was also capable of such quick-witted insight into the feelings and reactions of others.

SIXTEEN

Lady Warren was in her boudoir, a rose-coloured room of great elegance in its hangings and furnishings, and comfort in the plump plush of the button-backed chair and chaise longue. She kept fashionable hours, and had been at the opera until one in the morning before going on to a series of late parties, where they were still dancing at past three o'clock. Accordingly, she had risen late, and now sat in a cascade of lace and ribbons, her feet set on a little embroidered stool, as she planned the day ahead.

She took no notice of the distant rap of the knocker. If it were a message or a note, it would be brought to her; if a caller, the ignorant fool would be sent off in short order by her admirably trained servants, as politely rude in their own way as she herself was to those she despised or who stepped outside the uncodified but inflexible rules of her fashionable world.

So she was surprised to hear a loud 'rat-tat' on her own door. It opened at once and the personification of the world of fashion walked in without any further ceremony. Lady Warren gave a shriek of delight, kicked away the stool and held out her arms. 'George! My dearest boy! I had no idea you were back in England, not expected before next week at the earliest, how well you look!'

'Yes, I dare say, but don't come too close, it took the devil of a time to get my neckcloth right this morning. Nyers was seasick for almost the whole of the crossing, and it's made him tetchy and evil-fingered. Valets aren't supposed to suffer from seasickness – did you ever hear of such a thing? I was obliged to speak sharply to him.'

Lady Warren paid little attention to this speech, and indeed, George Warren's immaculate, dandified appearance gave the lie to any suggestion of shortcomings in his gentleman's gentleman. She had given the bell-pull a vigorous tug and was now issuing instructions for coffee – Had he breakfasted? No? – and for a breakfast of a size and quality befitting the appetite and importance of Lord Warren's only son.

They gazed upon each other with great mutual satisfaction. George was of middling height, with a distinctly handsome face, a good figure and an air of bored superiority. He for his part approved of Lady Warren's foaming cream and pink peignoir and her still pleasing countenance; he couldn't abide a woman who let herself go.

Despite the evident affection between them, they were not related by any ties of blood. Lady Warren was his stepmother, his own mother having died shortly after he was born. As Caroline Bingley, of no particular family and with a good but not exceptional fortune of twenty thousand pounds, she had married plain Mr Warren, who was at that time several steps removed from the title, then held by his great-uncle. It was considered by her friends and family to be a good if not a brilliant match. She had been a fine-looking girl, as she was now a well-looking woman, but there had always been a coldness in her manner that tended to put men off; she had been glad to catch Mr Warren.

Her marriage had been a success in its chilly way, with a good deal of well-bred indifference on either side. Her husband's unexpected accession to the title – after war, influenza and one toss too many in the hunting field had carried off the more immediate heirs – had delighted them both, and gave them plenty of scope for leading the selfish, indulgent lives that suited them best.

The union had brought her no children, but since one of Mr Warren's intentions on marrying again had been to provide his son with a mother, she had never felt the lack of progeny. Little George, then eight years old, had charmed her at sight, and a strong attachment remained between them, despite all the usual stages in a young man's upbringing designed to sever him from close family ties: Harrow; a spell in the army, although never anywhere that he might see any dangerous action, he was far too canny for that; and, since the peace, European travel.

Now he was just returned from Italy, and his first visit in his native city was this one, to his stepmother. No one better than Lady Warren to bring him up to date on all the latest news, scandal and gossip; no one less inclined than George to set forth into the social whirl without having its state, fashion and current mood at his fingertips.

Overt and, more interestingly, covert, connections and liaisons were discussed: this one's rise in wealth and status, that one's discredit and decline were laid out on the tablecloth alongside the cold beef and ham, and the misfortunes of many of their friends, family and acquaintance were brought forth to be relished and laughed at.

'And so your brother stays mewed up in the country, Caro, with that beautiful wife of his, so absurd with her good nature and refusal to believe ill of anyone; just as well she don't come to London, they'd eat her alive. And I can see Bingley in a pair of gaiters, attending to his land and tenants. Do you suppose he goes out in a smock?'

'It is all Jane's fault, it is all the fault of his marrying so ill,' cried Lady Warren. 'She has such a great deal of influence over him, she has quite turned him to her provincial ways. With his fortune and address he could have lived in London like any fashionable gentleman, and married a woman of consequence and fortune. Instead of which, what did he do but choose Jane Bennet and now see what has become of him, settled down to a life of rustication. I have no patience with it, none at all. I never see them nowadays, you know, since they seldom come to London, and it is so dull at their house. And Derbyshire, you know, is quite the most disagreeable of all counties. No one would go to Derbyshire unless it were to visit Chatsworth, and it's vastly dull even there, so everyone says.'

This was an old grudge, and it put Lady Warren in mind of an especially juicy titbit of gossip she had neglected to mention. 'By the bye, did you hear that Mr Darcy is gone to Turkey, and his tiresome wife with him – can you believe such a thing? His daughters are all come to London for the season. They stay with Lady Fanny Fitzwilliam – they are cousins, of course.'

'All the Darcy daughters?' asked George, inspecting the ham through his quizzing-glass before carving himself several slivers. 'Ain't there a tribe of them?'

'Five. One is still in the schoolroom, thankfully. The two eldest are officially out – soon to be on the shelf if you ask me, twenty-one or twenty-two at the least. The next two are twins, and I am convinced they take after their Aunt Lydia; I shouldn't be at all surprised to hear of either of them that she had run off with some unworthy fellow. Oh, yes, those young ladies are surely destined to throw their bonnets over the windmill. Only listen, George, the eldest girl, Letitia, has been made to look such a fool. Did you ever hear of Tom Busby?'

George Warren listened with rapt attention to the tale as he ate his breakfast, only breaking into his stepmother's stream of talk to call for more coffee and demand that the servant stoke up the fire a bit. 'Capital!' he cried when she had finished. 'Lord, I wonder how that will strike Darcy, him being so damned stiff and proud. She'll never get a good husband now, not once she's been made a laughing-stock.'

'Captain Allington has been assiduous in his attentions, he's after her fifty thousand pounds, naturally, but he won't get it, let his hussar's whiskers be ever so handsome. He's going to be elbowed out by the Reverend Mr Valpy, that is what will happen there.'

'Valpy? Never heard of him. Well, if she marries a clergyman, it'll serve her right. Fifty thousand pounds, eh? A tidy fortune. What about the rest of them?'

'They each have fifty thousand pounds, and very likely more, for Darcy is grown so rich there's no bearing it, the hateful man.'

There had been a time in her salad days when Lady Warren had striven hard to engage the affections of Mr Darcy, and she had been mortified when he married a nobody in the shape of Elizabeth Bennet. She had never forgiven Mr and Mrs Darcy this affront, and George knew perfectly well the animosity that she felt towards them.

'Heigh ho,' he said. 'Shall I have a tilt at one of the sisters? Fifty thou ain't to be sneezed at.'

'No, you shall not,' said Lady Warren instantly. 'For Letitia, as I told you, is going to marry this Valpy; besides, my dear friend Lucy Ancaster will be bringing her daughter out next year – eighty thousand pounds, no less. The girl has always had a soft spot for you, ever since you knocked her off her pony and abused her so.'

George frowned at the effort of remembering the Ancasters' daughter. 'I have it, brown little thing, all teeth and eyes. Lord, is she ready for her come out? Eighty thousand you say? Well, well, that might be worth waiting for.'

'Let me tell you the cream of the jest about the Darcy girls. The next sister, Camilla, is a sharp, witty young woman, who would be guaranteed to make any man's life a misery. She has just jilted Sir Sidney Leigh, all in the most scandalous manner, the whole town is in an uproar over it. She made no secret of her preference, eyes fixed on him at balls, simpering and smiling whenever he looked her way, appalling behaviour, so ill-bred.'

'Hold on, Caro,' said George. He wiped his mouth and sat back in his chair with a sigh of satisfaction. 'Sir Sidney is a terrific swell, but he has some funny habits. He don't like women much, not to put it plainer.'

Out in the world, Lady Warren took care to keep a genteel curb on her tongue, aware of the new decorum of language that had fallen on society. But in private, and among her intimates, she was accustomed to express herself in the more forthright terms of the previous century. 'The man's a sodomite, which no one dared say, even if they suspected it, and one has to admit that he was discreet about his perverted amours. It's all come out now, and of course that is why Maria Harper left him at the altar, all those years ago; the Lord knows how she found out, she's such a fool of a woman, but she did. No, Sir Sidney don't like women, it turns out, but he needs an heir, just the same, and he wouldn't be the first of his kind to make a marriage of convenience. It gives that type of man some cover of respectability, you know, for there is nothing people hate more than a sodomite.'

'He'd better go to Italy. Plenty of pretty boys in that country, and they ain't so particular over there.'

'That is exactly what he has done,' his stepmother said triumphantly. 'Packed up and gone, couldn't stand the scandal, reputation ruined. Of course, it would not have come out, whatever they may say about a footman laying evidence against him, if Miss Camilla Darcy hadn't fancied him so wildly and made such an exhibition of herself – a betrothal and family party, Sir Sidney's sister up from the country, everything as it should be, and then pouff! All off, and London ringing with the talk of it.'

'I like Leigh,' said George, picking at a molar with an ivory toothpick. 'We belong to several of the same clubs. Very knowledgeable man, he's put one or two good things my way – *objets d'art*, you know, he's a notable connoisseur. It don't seem right that some provincial miss should have him run out of town.'

'One cannot approve of sodomy,' said Lady Warren. Her moral sense might not bear close scrutiny, but there she was quite definite. 'Everyone must be disgusted by such beastliness.'

'Oh, in your position I suppose it is so, but when one is a man of the world, one can take the larger view. Attitudes abroad are different, as I told you. In any case, some of these men are very cultured fellows, like Leigh, in fact, and can be entertaining company. One or two of my friends from school – but I shan't go into that,' he said, recollecting himself. 'It's all absurd, this talk of hanging them and so forth. You can't do that kind of thing to a gentleman, not these days, it ain't civilised. So one of the Darcy girls is responsible for his disgrace, is she? I don't like that, it don't seem right at all.'

'She has hardly come well out of the affair herself, which is no more than she deserves. Mud sticks, as the saying is, and she was a great deal too forward in showing her affections, and doesn't she look silly now, when it is obvious to everyone that he didn't care tuppence for her; it was the footmen he fancied.'

'Even so, the opprobrium will rest mostly on him. Miss Camilla Darcy is well-connected, rich – is she pretty?'

Lady Warren shrugged. 'If you like those kind of looks. I

don't admire her myself, and she is not the equal of the three other sisters. The youngest one is no kind of a beauty at all, but she is a mere girl, so it doesn't signify.'

'Well, Caro,' he said, rising from the table. 'I rather think we might have some fun with this Camilla. Would that please you? I dare say you'd like to see her father's haughty nose put out of joint for once.'

'I would indeed,' said Lady Warren with great enthusiasm. 'But do be careful, George. I wouldn't for the world have you fall in love with her.'

'Fall in love? What do you take me for? No, no, there will be no danger of that, none at all. I shall simply set out to hit her where she is most at risk – her reputation, ma'am. You know better than anyone the power of rumour and gossip, and what excellent sport to bring about her ruin without her having a notion of what's afoot.' He rubbed his hands together. 'I came back to England at a very good time, I see. What fun we shall have. I shall need your assistance, Caro.'

Lady Warren, her heart as cold as her stepson's, her eyes full of malice, smiled as he bent his elegantly tousled head to kiss her cheek.

'Arrange for me to meet this piece of nature, if you will.'

'Nothing could be easier,' said Lady Warren instantly. 'Lydia Pollexfen, who is their aunt, gives a rout, and they are invited and will feel obliged to attend, even though there is little love lost between Lydia and the Darcys, I can tell you.'

'Ah, Pollexfen, Prinny's friend.'

'Yes, and Lydia Pollexfen is very fast, and it will do those girls no good to be seen much in her company, aunt or no aunt. I believe the eldest two see little of her, but the twins are much taken with her circle. They are headstrong, foolish girls, with heads full of frivolity and romantic notions. However, on this occasion I know that you may be sure of seeing Camilla Darcy among her guests, she told me it would be so.'

'Then arrange an invitation for me. We shall begin our little game directly, and don't I wish she may enjoy it.'

He gave his stepmother a graceful wave of his hand and sauntered out of the door.

SEVENTEEN

Fell, excellent butler though he was, was outmanoeuvred and outnumbered. Mrs Pollexfen and Mrs Gardiner arrived, from opposite directions, on the doorstep of the house in Aubrey Square at the same moment, their carriages jostling for space in front of the house. They were more than a match for any quantity of butlers of whatever experience and stateliness. Moreover, they had right on their side: neither of them was some mere caller to be denied; they were both family.

Sophie, a pouting, bored expression on her pretty face, tripped into the house after her mother and cousin.

Camilla had run upstairs on returning from her visit to Mrs Rowan to restore some order to her hair, blown about on her rapid walk back, and to cool the high colour from her cheeks. She hurried down to the drawing-room when she heard the voices.

Letitia was already in the drawing-room, her embroidery frame laid down on a small table, her silks in a box at her feet. Camilla noticed the marbled cover of a book peeping out from under a cushion – she was not much surprised to find that her sister had been reading a lurid novel rather than setting stitches or perusing a more solemn tome. Letty was clearly eager to present a serious appearance to the callers – had she been expecting a visitor?

Camilla did not particularly want to see her Aunt Lydia, whom she mistrusted. Anyone, though, was better than odious Mr Valpy with his insinuating ways and his open hints about Pemberley. He was, she was quite sure, fishing for an invitation to Derbyshire, one that might well be forthcoming if he were to persuade Letty to do what she said she longed for: to shun London life and return to the country with her sisters.

Camilla could imagine nothing more tiresome than being cooped up at Pemberley with Valpy, Letty at her most sententious, and two – no, three – sulking sisters; Alethea would most likely have to be dragged kicking and screaming into any coach intended to take her away from Signor Silvestrini's lessons. With some cause, for it was remarkable how her singing had improved, and her playing upon the pianoforte, too. Not to mention that she seemed to have taken up the flute – she had wondered where had the instrument come from, but Griffy's closed face when questioned on the matter had precluded further enquiries.

Aunt Lydia and Mrs Gardiner, old enemies, were exchanging civilities.

'So this is little Sophie,' cried Lydia, all smiles. 'Why, child, how pretty you've grown, I should hardly have known you! I declare it is an age since I last saw you, and here you are quite grown up and with a very eligible *parti* to your credit, you are to be felicitated. Of course, the match has its drawbacks, for Wytton is eccentric to his bones. All that family are eccentrics, have you met his mother? No? She is abroad? Well, that is all of a piece, she jaunters about all over the place just as though she did not have a perfectly delightful home, for Wytton would never turn his mother out of the abbey. Of course, there is the Dower House, but it is dreadfully ancient, I believe, so I am sure he means her to make her home with him – whenever she happens to be in England, that is, and indeed she cannot keep on with her travels for ever, for she is by no means a young woman. But you will not mind having her there, Sophie. I dare say you will be glad of the company, for your husband will certainly not intend to stay at the abbey, or even spend much time in London. He has itchy feet as the saying is, which is perhaps a change from most other men, who have itches quite elsewhere in their anatomy, and so he will constantly be abroad, visiting all those horrid places like Egypt and Greece; however, they are dangerous, that is one thing to be said for them, and so you may not have to be a deserted and lonely wife for long –

widows do have much the best of it, I assure you, once the appointed period of grief is over and done with.'

Sophie was, for once, utterly at a loss as to how to reply to this flow of talk. Mrs Gardiner, well used to Lydia's ways, merely gave her a quelling look and said that the young couple would only spend part of the year at the abbey.

'You *may* change Wytton, Sophie,' said Lydia, ignoring Mrs Gardiner's interjection. 'It is amazing what being married can do to a man, I have often remarked upon it. But if I were you, I would make the most of my London season. Have you been to the assemblies at Almack's, and danced the night away at all the most fashionable balls?'

Camilla suspected that her aunt knew perfectly well that no Almack's vouchers had been forthcoming for Sophie, and had guessed that Sophie minded this very much. Mrs Gardiner had too much sense to fret about whether the patronesses of Almack's approved of her or not, but she must feel for her daughter's disappointment, and sensible or not, no one would relish having their nose rubbed in this act of social exclusion – least of all by Mrs Pollexfen.

Letitia provided a diversion by beginning a plaintive complaint against the excesses and worldliness of London and the season, causing her Aunt Lydia to roll her eyes upwards in disbelief and shrug her elegant, bony shoulders.

'That may do all very well for when you are in your dotage, Letty, my dear,' she said, interrupting her without apology. 'However, it is a great deal of nonsense for a young woman of your age and position to condemn what you hardly know. Take care; such sentiments will make you seem sour, and that, with the Busby affair so fresh in people's minds, will never do.'

Camilla had to admire her Aunt Lydia, who had the knack of striking at her prey with the precision of a marksman. Camilla should feel sorry for her sister, she knew, but she couldn't help an inward smile at Letty's discomfiture. Letty's naturally serious outlook on life had turned – under Mr Valpy's unhelpful influence – into daily preaching and more sanctimoniousness than any rational creature could be expected to bear.

Sophie, flushed and unhappy, rose and walked across to the

window, where she studied the street below with intense and spurious interest. Her shoulders drooped, and it was only at the entrance of the twins that her spirits seemed to revive a little. Georgina came in through the door as though making an entrance on to the stage at Drury Lane, and Belle drifted after her in her usual floating way. They pulled Sophie to a sofa, and the three of them sat with arms wrapped round each other, heads close, whispering in voices not audible to any of the others.

Mrs Gardiner frowned at this want of manners, but she wisely chose not to rebuke Sophie – much to Camilla's relief, as, judging by the tension in Sophie's body, any criticism might provoke a flood of tears, or even hysterics.

It was odd, for Sophie had always been one of the robust kind, not given to emotional displays and fanciful turns; Camilla would have said that under all the exquisite prettiness there was a clear-headed, practical person. Lately, though, her young cousin's nerves had seemed balanced on a knife edge and, going by the anxious looks Mrs Gardiner was directing at her daughter, she wasn't the only one to form such an opinion.

Lydia was now telling Mrs Gardiner about the ravishing silks new come over from France, and on this safe and interesting ground, the two women conversed in temporary harmony. Letty listened with keen attention, Camilla noticed, although her sister was pretending to be absorbed in her own thoughts to show she had a mind above such fripperies. A little more of silks and clothes and a little less of sackcloth, and Letty would be much happier; how she wished they could get her out of her doleful ways.

She had had such hopes of Captain Allington, so willing to squire Letty to the park and on riding expeditions, and always on hand to request a dance when the opportunity offered. One had to remember, though, that it was the gallant Captain who had taken Letty to Mr Valpy's church in the first place, and Camilla could have pulled the whiskers off his handsome face with fury at his having done them all such a disservice. He was less attentive to Letty now. Belle seemed to have claimed him for one of her many victims, which left Letty even more at the mercy of the Reverend Valpy.

Camilla's mind drifted, still casting its own private cloud of unhappiness. It was like an aching tooth, a pain that might at times be acute, at others no more than a dull reminder of its power to hurt. If that was what love was about, then she was done with it. Aunt Lydia had the right of it, you did well to choose a husband that you liked, to be sure, but for whom you would never feel any more intense passion. That way, whatever he did, you would not mind, and you would not be taking any more hostages to fortune the way she so foolishly had by allowing herself to fall in love with Sir Sidney.

Her heart gave a jolt, as at that very moment she heard her aunt speak his name. Lydia flashed her a look – not at all a kind one – and continued in a somewhat louder voice to talk to Mrs Gardiner about the scandal that still had the polite world entranced.

'Have you not heard? He fled to Italy, as you must know. He left everything behind, and the household is all at sixes and sevens not knowing if he will return or if dust covers and boxes to be sent on are the order of the day. The knocker is off the front door, and there is not a single footman remaining in the house.' She leant towards Mrs Gardiner for emphasis, nodding her head. 'They say Mrs Delamere has dismissed every single man but the butler, who is too old to have been up to any mischief. Even the bootboy has gone, and only the female staff are left.'

Camilla gripped the back of a nearby chair. Never mind Sophie and her fragile nerves, how could she herself manage to maintain an appearance of indifference before the sharp-eyed Lydia, who was keenly searching her face for any signs of weakness to report back to her interested friends?

So much for family feeling!

Mrs Gardiner came to Camilla's rescue. 'I expect they will let the house,' she said in a dismissive voice. 'Now, Lydia, it is most interesting what you were telling me about shawls. Are they genuine cashmere? For there are many on sale of greatly inferior quality – although they pass them off as cashmere, they are no such thing.'

The moment passed, several deep breaths did their work,

and, although pale, Camilla was able to give a perfectly collected answer on being appealed to by Georgina and Belle about the respective merits of white as against sprigged muslin for summer dresses.

If only one's mind would leave one in peace, to think of nothing more than silks and shawls and ribbons for one's shoes. She wanted none of the regrets and anguish and futile going over the sterile ground of a relationship that had turned out to be so different from what she had once imagined. She forced herself to answer a query about how many feathers one might becomingly wear on one's head. Bother feathers, bother hats, bother everything.

Lydia was rising to her feet, fussing about her to collect her parasol, her reticule, to adjust the hang of her dress. 'So it is all quite settled, you will bring the girls on Thursday to my rout, and your Sophie, too, of course. So many pretty creatures, all at once, I do not know where my dearest Pollexfen will look in the face of so much youth and beauty, he will be in raptures.'

The instant that the drawing-room door had closed behind Mrs Pollexfen, Camilla and Letitia burst into exclamations of vexation and dismay about the invitation that Mrs Gardiner had accepted on their behalf.

'For I do not wish at all to go,' Camilla protested. 'It was understood between ourselves and Mr Fitzwilliam that we should not go about in society while Fanny was away.'

'Why, as to that, it is only a matter of a chaperon, and I am quite as well able to chaperon you on this occasion as Fanny, better indeed, for I am related to Lydia Pollexfen, and she is not.'

Letitia was eager to have her say. 'A period of quiet and reflection, dear Mrs Gardiner, that is what we were promised while Fanny is away, a pause in the round of dissipation and idle pleasures to allow ourselves time to think about how our lives should best be spent – in duty, and humility and service to others.'

The words were pure Valpy. Humility, indeed! There was nothing humble about Letty, no, nor about Mr Valpy, however much he bowed and scraped and pretended to be one of the meek destined to inherit the earth. Camilla acknowledged the clergyman's desire for a great inheritance, but was sure he intended it to be in the shape of a certain number of thousands of pounds and provided by Miss Darcy rather than by divine beneficence. Unless he considered that Letty had fallen into his hands at the direction of the supreme being; yes, he might even be capable of such sophism and be convinced that he deserved a rich and well-born wife as a sign of his favour in the sight of the Lord.

Letty was still prating, and Camilla silenced her with an impatient gesture. 'Do be quiet, it is hardly our immortal souls that are at risk here. For myself, I am sure I shall find it as intolerable and boring an evening as you will, it is of the others that I am thinking.'

'Oh, no, you shan't prevent us from going,' cried Georgina. 'You need not look in our direction! I can see it in your face, you think that you and Letty shall go, if anyone has to, and that we shall stay at home like children. We shan't, that's all. We love visiting my Aunt Lydia's house, she knows the most delightful people and everyone is always very gay.'

'And just how much time have you spent there?' said Letitia, rounding on them. 'Is this the reason for your long sorties to Bond Street? From which you return empty-handed as often as not, I have noticed.'

So Letty wasn't quite so bound up in her good works as not to have her eyes open. Of course, that was what the twins had been up to, while Letty had been off attending to her societies for the prevention of this and that, and she herself had been going about London like a lovestruck dairymaid, ignoring what was under her nose.

Pray God Alethea had not likewise been up to any secretive expeditions, although at least in her case Miss Griffin was on hand, more than able to repress any tendency to go beyond what was permissible.

'My dears,' said Mrs Gardiner, drawing Letitia down beside her. 'Do not upset yourselves. I know your sentiments, Letty, and I sympathise with your desire not to go about in society just at present, Camilla, but indeed it will not do. Fanny is bound up in her daughter's well-being, as is only proper, and that is why she has not considered the consequences of your withdrawing from company at the height of the season. People will talk; people are already talking. Not to go to Lydia's rout, which will be a very smart affair, when you are known to be her nieces, would give rise to even more gossip and speculation.'

'One should have a mind above gossip and speculation,' said Letitia.

'One may, but the rest of the world doesn't,' said Mrs Gardiner, sharply for her. 'Now, you will please allow me to advise you in this matter. The twins have often been seen at Lydia's house, and it has been wrong of them to go and in such an underhand manner; however, if all of you, and myself and Sophie are there, it will give the lie to some of the wilder stories that are about town. I move enough in the world to hear what is being said, and I have not brought up a family of girls without learning how to counter foolish chatter and gossip, which springs up at the slightest opportunity, as well you know; it is the same everywhere, London or Derbyshire. I have no doubt that your dear mother and father are discovering that Constantinople is a perfect hotbed of scandal. It is the way of the world.'

There was no gainsaying this. The twins smiled and sparkled at the promise of a delightful party, Letitia's face took on a brooding, sullen look, and Camilla resigned herself to the inevitable, although she was not in the mood to make the prospect of any kind of party seem agreeable, least of all this one.

'And am I to go, Mama?' asked Sophie. 'I should so like to if Belle and Georgina are to be there.'

'Indeed, yes, you shall go with us, as I told Lydia,' said Mrs Gardiner. 'For she is to send an invitation to Mr Wytton, indeed, has probably already done so, and I am sure he will accept, so you need have no qualms.'

How odd, Camilla thought, noticing a petulant, disagreeable look flit across Sophie's face. One would imagine she would rather he were not to be there. She dismissed the notion; what nonsense, you had only to look at them to see how passionately they felt about each other.

★

'I think Sophie is a little frightened by Wytton,' said Mrs Rowan, as she and Camilla walked together the next morning. They had both their sketchbooks with them, having agreed to meet and sketch some of the Greek items from the Towneley Collection, presently housed in the British Museum. Mrs Rowan, who had considerable skill with her brushes, planned to paint some scenes on the walls of her morning room and had decided on the pastoral as a theme. Nothing could be more pastoral than classical nymphs, did not Camilla agree?

Camilla's mind was on a present-day nymph. 'Why, have you seen them together recently?' she asked, as they threaded their way across the building site that would in time form part of Regent Street under Nash's ambitious scheme of London improvement. They reached the other side of a muddy road without mishap and brushed down their pelisses before setting off for the ungenteel squares of Bloomsbury. 'I was not aware that you were particularly acquainted with my cousin Sophie.'

'I am not, but I have often seen Mr Wytton in Sophie's company.'

'He seems sincerely attached.'

'Besotted,' said Mrs Rowan. 'We take a left turning here, I think you will find. Wytton is a man with an ardent nature, and his feelings for Sophie are strong. I think she would prefer a milder man, one more within her powers to control and subdue.'

'I am sure she is very much in love with him.'

'I think she fell in love with his handsome face and romantic appearance. All this travelling and cosmopolitan address gives a man great charm, especially when combined with a good income and a fine abbey and those dark looks. He is an attractive man; she was attracted, she felt flattered and liked him well enough – many a marriage has been founded on much less.'

'Oh, but this is dreadful,' Camilla said, distressed by her friend's cynicism. 'What a bleak picture you paint. How can their future together be happy if it is based on passion on one part and mere fancy and fortune on the other?'

'I do not think they will be happy at all. I think they will be wretched together, and it saddens me, for I know Wytton well, have known him all my life, and he deserves better. He fell for Sophie on the rebound, as the saying is, after that unfortunate liaison with Mrs Beecham.'

'Mrs Beecham!' Camilla had heard murmurs and whispers of an old relationship; she had not known the lady in question had been Mrs Beecham.

'Why, yes. It is all history, now, of course. I may tell you privately that she has the morals of an alley cat. She got Wytton thoroughly into her clutches, but she is rarely content to have but one man at her beck and call. Wytton would not stand for her sharing her favours, and so openly. There were some violent scenes, one gathers, at their parting; Mrs Beecham is not used to being thrown over in quite that fashion.'

'Is there not a Mr Beecham?'

'Indeed there is, but he prefers to rusticate, and is indifferent to the behaviour of his wife. He has found his own consolation in the country, so people say.'

'And so, Wytton fell in love with Sophie, I can see how a man might well do that. From one extreme to the other, it could be said. Well, I hope that, after all, they will be happy. Such a deep attachment must be a good foundation for any marriage.'

'Sophie will bore him quickly enough; within a twelvemonth Wytton will be wondering why he ever fell in love with her, and as for Sophie, once she is grown used to her abbey, she will realise that they have little in common.'

Camilla was silent for a while, lost in thought. It grieved her to think of Sophie – and indeed, Wytton – trapped in a loveless marriage. It would arouse no concern outside the couple's immediate family, it was hardly an unusual story, but it worried her. Then she remembered the glow in Wytton's eyes when they rested on her cousin. Mrs Rowan was mistaken in supposing such feeling would quickly vanish. 'Sophie has no wickedness in her, she is as good a girl as you will find any-where. She will strive to make him happy.'

'No amount of striving will give her a spirit of adventure, she is not the sort. Whereas with him, love of adventure and exploration of new places and new ideas lie deep in his make-up. And it is impossible for her to be any kind of a match for him in intellect or understanding. If you mean she will pander to his wishes and foibles, that in itself is enough to ruin any man, or any marriage.'

'Oh, you are quite wrong, you know you are. Neither Wytton nor any other man looks for intellect and understanding in a wife. Prettiness and an amiable temper are the qualities a man seeks in a wife, and those Sophie has.'

'You sound bitter, Camilla, I don't like to hear you saying such things with that tone in your voice. And, forgive me, but is Sophie so perfectly amiable as you make out? I have some idea that she has a sharp tongue and a lively temper when she is not striving to be on her best behaviour.'

Camilla recalled the tantrums of Sophie's youth. 'She did have a wilful streak, but all that is behind her now.'

Mrs Rowan said nothing more, for they had come to Montagu House and she had to hunt in her reticule to find their tickets of admittance. They went upstairs and into the room where the treasures brought back from Greece and Turkey by the late Charles Towneley were on display.

'I intend to copy the great vase,' Mrs Rowan said, opening the stool she had brought with her and settling herself down before the giant Roman urn that had been discovered in a thousand pieces and carefully reassembled for the benefit of admiring Londoners.

Camilla began to wish she had not come. Mrs Rowan quickly became absorbed in her work; for her part, she was restless and had no desire to sketch any of the antique objects set about the room in a dusty display of past glories. For a few moments she amused herself by imagining the finer pieces cleaned up and set out in one of the great rooms at Pemberley, but as an occupation it soon palled. She wandered over to one of the windows, and leaned over the table to look out into the square. The trees were bright with new foliage, children ran about the central garden, a squirrel flitted across a path and ran up a tree.

Then she saw a familiar face. 'It is Mr Roper,' she said over her shoulder to Mrs Rowan. 'I wonder what business he has in this part of London. I am sure it is not to visit the Museum, it is not his kind of place at all.'

To her great surprise, he crossed towards Montagu House and then disappeared from her view, only to reappear a few minutes later, an apologetic smile on his face, at the entrance to the room.

'Why, Mr Roper, whatever are you doing here?'

He grinned at her. 'It is not my idea of a lively place, I can tell you. Those stuffed giraffes doing guard duty on the stairs, however did they come by such a pair of horrors? The fellow below didn't want to let me in, either, said I had to have a ticket of admittance or some such thing. There's no point to that, I told him, you'd have to pay to get me through the doors in the ordinary way, let alone me going to the trouble of obtaining a ticket. However, I told him I had an urgent message for you ladies, and so he obligingly let me in – after I'd greased his palm, need I say. What a dreary collection,' he added, looking around the exhibits. 'You'll cast yourself into a gloom if you stay here long, and on such a fine day.'

He wandered over to look at her friend's drawing. 'My word, you do the thing most prettily, Mrs Rowan, you do indeed.'

'So do you have a message for us?' she asked.

He swung round to face her, pausing to blink at a winged creature – a dog, perhaps? – with a smug-looking human face. 'Whoever would wish to look at such things? I cannot think what Towneley was about, bringing all this back to London at such vast expense. Have we no sculptors here? Is not Wedgwood good enough for any Englishman?'

'It is classical, Mr Roper,' said Mrs Rowan, amused. 'Historical, you know.'

Roper eyed a rather rampant satyr with an air of discontent. 'I don't see it myself, but then I don't set up for a connoisseur, of course. Now, as to the message, Miss Camilla. Well, it is not precisely a message, but a piece of news I think should be told you. Miss Belle and Miss Georgina are aware of it, for your aunt has told them, but I've a notion it won't have reached you or Miss Darcy.'

Camilla fought a sense of rising exasperation. 'Yes, very well, Mr Roper, but what do my aunt and sisters know?'

'Oh, did I not say? Tom Busby is in London, and is invited to Mrs Pollexfen's rout. You are all going, are you not?'

'Mr Busby!' She was dismayed. 'Oh, no! Why could he not stay away? Lord, will he be accompanied by his wife, or is she left in Belgium?'

'She has come to England with him. They are presently with his family, and they will post up to London shortly.'

'And the twins know about this?'

Mr Roper gazed intently at a frieze depicting a group of spirited nymphs engaged in a dance. He did not meet her eye.

She sighed. 'You do not have to tell me. They know, but do not intend to tell Letitia, that is it, is it not? They no doubt think it will be amusing if Letty comes face to face with Tom Busby in front of three or four hundred of the greatest gossips and scandalmongers in the country.'

'They do not mean to do any harm,' said Mr Roper quickly. 'They are very young and merely think it fun. They do not quite understand.'

'If they are old enough to behave as they do, they are old enough to know what is funning and what is spite,' she said.

'Spite?' Roper was horrified. 'No, really, Miss Camilla, they are the sweetest-natured girls, you must not say such things about them.'

'I only say what is true. Allow me to be much better acquainted with my sisters than you, Mr Roper.' She saw Mrs Rowan's shocked expression, wished the words unsaid even as they fell from her lips. She forced a smile. 'Do not take me so seriously, Mr Roper. I am sure you are right, it is only their youth and inexperience that leads them astray.'

She wished this were the case, knowing that the twins most likely saw an unexpected encounter with Mr and Mrs Busby as a splendid payback for Letty's bossy ways and attempts to restrict their outings and her often expressed desire to pack them off back home.

'I am grateful for your telling me this news, Mr Roper. I shall tell Letitia at once, she must be prepared for such an encounter. It was bound to happen, I suppose.'

A more private meeting would be so much better. Were they still at Pemberley, then in the natural course of things the families would meet, and it might all pass off with no more than a few moments of embarrassment for Tom and Letitia.

'You didn't mind my mentioning it to you?'

'Not at all. Indeed, I am very grateful to you.'

He gave a relieved smile. 'I am so glad. One mostly knows pretty well how to go on, you see, only nothing of this sort has ever cropped up before and so I wondered what was the correct thing to do.'

'You followed the dictates of kindness, Mr Roper,' said Mrs Rowan, who had been listening to the conversation with intense interest, even while she worked on the drawing of the vase. 'To do so can't ever be wrong; that is something to re-member, by the way, as you get older and acquire more know-ledge of the wickedness of the world.'

The young man flushed. 'Just as you say, Mrs Rowan.' He backed towards the doorway, and hovered there for a moment or two, unsure of how to take his leave.

'We shall see you at the rout, Mr Roper?' she asked.

'Oh, yes, to be sure, most certainly. You are all to go, is that not so? Except for Miss Alethea, of course. She informed me – for she happened to be passing through the hall when I called, indeed it is to her that I owe my information as to your whereabouts – that wild horses wouldn't drag her to such an affair, all people and heat and noise. I suppose she will think differently when it is her come-out.'

'I hope so,' Camilla said doubtfully.

EIGHTEEN

Francis Pollexfen took Camilla by surprise. For some reason, she had been expecting to meet a buck, a beau, and had pictured to herself a corpulent, fashionable figure with florid face and swelling calves. Nothing could have been more different from her imagined uncle than this small, wiry individual in a well-cut dark velvet coat and frothy necktie, who extended a hand and bid her welcome. His face was full of wrinkles and crinkles that made his expression difficult to read. His glinting eyes, of a very dark blue shade, were a different matter. They were full of shrewd intelligence and also, if she were not mistaken, contained a gleam of amused malevolence.

His manners were well bred, his polite smile growing in warmth as he looked her up and down, an act that made her feel distinctly uncomfortable, as though she were standing there in her shift. 'We meet at last, niece, for I may call you so, may I not?' His voice had a husky quality that might charm some; it alarmed her.

Letitia won a more directly approving smile, her beauty often having that affect on older men. And when it came to Belle and Georgina, Pollexfen's gaze had little of the avuncular and much of the amorous about it.

The twins were quite at their ease in the glittering throng. They had complained of arriving so early, so provincial, so dowdy, they said, to be early for a rout, yet the lemon yellow rooms were already full to bursting and Camilla could not imagine them fitting another soul.

Mrs Gardiner soon put her right. 'That is the reason we came early, for there will be three times this number before the evening is out.'

Camilla stared, shook her head in disbelief. Why anyone should choose to spend their time in such civil discomfort was a mystery to her.

'Oh, you are so dull,' said Belle in her languid way. 'You have no notion of fashionable life; the crush and the squeeze are all part of the enjoyment.'

'Yours, maybe,' she retorted. 'Not mine. I prefer not to have my gown crumpled and my shoes trodden on, and I like to breathe my air fresh.'

The smell of hot humanity and the mingled odours of scents and perfumes worn by both men and women were over-powering. She knew that her nose would adjust to it in due course, but for now she found it unpleasant. And underlying these familiar smells she was aware of another, tantalising muskiness – the smell of intrigue and arousal. This was not one of the genteel gatherings that she was used to. For a start, there were few of the young debutantes here. These men and women were older, much older in some cases, and their faces and bodies and clothes bore a maturity and sophistication that made her feel uneasy and gauche.

She had encountered roués enough in London, and in Derbyshire for that matter, for not the most closely chaperoned and gently nurtured of girls could be unaware of the tendency of friends' brothers, uncles, fathers and even grandfathers to slip an arm around a slim waist, or touch and squeeze under the table at dinner, or press up against a pleasing young form in a tight corner.

This was different. So many men who had a rakish and even dissipated air; so many women with bold, roving eyes; so many undercurrents beneath the polite words and trivial gossip. There were sidelong glances, the fluttering of a fan, the tilt of a shoulder, the brushing of a masculine thigh, the direct look of an eye magnified by a quizzing-glass, a man's hand lying on a plump and naked arm. The heat was intense, and she, who had never been in the least prone to the vapours, began to wonder if she might actually be going to faint.

She pulled herself together, accepted a glass of lemonade from a passing footman, and found herself being addressed by Francis Pollexfen once more. Beside him stood a dark, almost swarthy man, elegantly dressed, with the physique of a sportsman and the face of a corsair, down to the curling lip and the enigmatic eyes.

'May I have the honour to present George Warren to you, Miss Camilla? He is a connection of yours, you will find.'

Warren bowed, Pollexfen slipped away into his throng of guests, leaving them looking at each other.

'You are Lord Warren's son.'

He bowed again. 'I am. And Lady Warren, who is my stepmother, is Charles Bingley's sister. He is married to your aunt, your mother's sister, is that not so?'

This man must be in his late twenties. She had been puzzled for a moment, for she could not see how Lady Warren could have a son of his age. A stepson, well, that explained it.

A large, fair, full-complexioned man in a coat that stretched with alarming closeness of fit across his well-fleshed belly and shoulders rolled over to join them. He nodded to Warren, but his bulbous eyes were fastened on her for a few disagreeable seconds. Then his interest faded. He said some words in a surprisingly high voice to Warren about his travels and went on his way.

Camilla was startled by this rudeness, and found that Warren was looking at her with some amusement. 'Do you know who that was?'

'I have not the least idea.'

'Ah, you are not an admirer of our royal family and their brood of dukes, then? I honour you for it.'

'Dukes? Good heavens, was that one of the royal dukes?'

'Do not seem so astonished, I assure you, it is bad form to seem astonished in the sight of royalty. You must pretend you are accustomed to rubbing shoulders with them and think nothing of it.'

'I don't think I should care to rub shoulders with him. Is he acquainted with my aunt?'

'Certainly he is acquainted with your aunt. Pollexfen is as

thick as thieves with Prinny, you know, and quite at home in those court circles. Here you see the cream of that part of society. It is a different set of people from your normal social round, I dare say.'

She looked around her; the room was fuller than before, as Mrs Gardiner had predicted, and still there was hardly a face that she recognised. 'I find I know few people here tonight.'

He smiled at her. His smile held little humour or warmth. 'Which is fortunate for me, since you won't be carried off by a bevy of your friends and admirers. I am sure you have many admirers.'

She wasn't sure she cared for this line of conversation, but her attention was diverted by seeing the royal duke standing beside Letty, his eyes feasting on her bosom. Letty's colour was high, and Camilla knew perfectly well that her sister was longing to edge away from the duke, but was hardly in a position to do so. Now he was laying a large hand on her arm, and guiding her towards a sofa, whose occupants rose like birds at the approach of royalty. He ignored them, placed the broad royal posterior in its straining breeches on the gold damask cover of the couch and patted the space beside him for Letty to sit.

'Oh dear,' she whispered to Warren. 'I fear my sister is in some distress.'

'Oh, he will attempt nothing in so public a place, he will merely ogle in that disagreeable way he has, and make her feel uncomfortable. Look how the colour flies to her cheeks!'

She didn't quite like the tone of cold mockery with which he spoke, but she was too concerned for Letty to wonder at it. No doubt her sister was having a wretched evening, waiting for her first sight of Tom Busby – of whom there had not been the least sign – and now to be hemmed in by a fat, lascivious duke! It would confirm all her worst prejudices of the wickedness of the world. Unfortunately, she thought, although the prince would pass, the moral reflections inspired by his bulky presence would linger far longer.

'Come, this is an occasion for enjoyment. Downcast faces and gloomy looks are never allowed at Mrs Pollexfen's parties. Take care, you will attract attention if you show your feelings so clearly in your face. Smile at me, if you please, and laugh; that is better.'

His look was quizzical, his assurance complete, and she did smile, more at the truth of his words about this brittle world they both inhabited than from any real feelings of amusement. He was right. The well-born and the successful kept a smile on their faces and never, ever let anyone for a moment suspect that all was not well.

A rival snatched a lover from under your nose? You smiled and joked, and shrugged it off. Your husband was unfaithful, a child ill? Keep your anger and fears to yourself, that was a reality that had no place in the crowded public rooms of the polite world.

The price paid if you forgot to smile and look pleased was high. Ostracism: you would be cast into the outer darkness of social exclusion, as firmly as though you had moved from the boundaries of fashionable London to take up residence in Wimpole Street or Kensington.

Her smile faded, and rescue came in the nick of time, and from an unexpected quarter. A touch on her elbow, and she looked round to see Wytton standing beside her. He gave Warren the briefest of nods and received a slight, chilly bow in return.

He addressed her. 'Your aunt desires to speak with you. May I escort you to her?' Without waiting for her reply, he hooked his arm, she laid her hand on it and they plunged into the seething mass of velvet, silk, satin and broadcloth. His arm was firm, his back straight, his manner determined, and his countenance, she noticed, while perfectly amiable, had a toughness about it that communicated itself to those through whom he was clearing a path.

I suppose, she thought inconsequentially, that this is nothing after grappling with bandits in Albania or the hostile inhabitants of Egypt. She told him so, and he looked astonished, before replying with a smile.

'Oh, no, they are not half so dangerous as this crowd, I assure you. There, you know exactly who your enemy is; here, they all hide their ill will and hatred.'

It was her turn to be amused. 'So whose company is preferable?'

'Oh, the foreigners every time. They don't dress half so oddly, for one thing. Look at that turban over there!'

She looked, saw Lady Warren's head topped by a magnificent blue turban fringed with gold, and had to cough to hide her laugh – Lady Warren was looking in their direction with shrewd, narrowed eyes.

They had reached Mrs Gardiner, and she managed to edge to her side. 'You wished to speak to me, ma'am?'

'We have been here long enough,' she said, a tight smile pinned to her lips, her fan waving fast and furious before her face. 'Do you think you and Letty could extract the twins? Mr Wytton, Sophie is over there.'

'Miss Camilla and I will together make an out-and-out assault on our targets and haul them back to their duties,' said Wytton. 'Albanian bandits will be nothing to it,' he added, casting a wicked look at Camilla. 'Now, who shall we roll up first?'

He didn't seem a whit perturbed that Sophie was tucked in a corner flirting with a tall, good-looking young man with brown, curly hair, who was looking down at her with evident admiration.

Wytton followed the line of her gaze. 'That is only Gadsby. We shall leave them to enjoy themselves while we extricate your younger sisters, a much harder task, I fear.'

Camilla stood on tiptoe, trying in vain to spot either of the twins. Then a stout man in dark blue moved aside and she caught sight of Belle, standing close to a young man of somewhat foppish appearance. He was popping titbits of food into her open mouth, and between mouthfuls she was consumed by soft giggles.

'I wonder what she has been drinking,' murmured Wytton. 'The punch, I am afraid.'

'It is not the effect of alcohol,' she said. 'It is just her way.'

'Is it indeed?'

'You might add, how unfortunate,' she said bitterly.

'I would not be so impolite. I have a young sister who is something of a minx when let out of sight. There is nothing unusual in such behaviour.'

'Would your sister ever be allowed inside this house, let alone out of her mother or chaperon's sight?'

'Ah, there you have me,' he admitted. 'I doubt it.'

'My family do not show up well on this occasion,' she went on, determined to lash herself. 'My aunt is our hostess, and I am quite sure my parents would not wish us to be acquainted with most of her guests.'

'Not even royalty?' he said, quizzing her. They had come to a momentary standstill before a group of five or six men talking about a racehorse in loud voices.

'Most certainly not.'

'Do you count George Warren among the members of your family?'

His voice was carefully neutral, and it occurred to her that he did not like Mr Warren. 'He is no relation, merely a connection through an aunt's marriage.' She paused. 'Do you know him well?'

'We were at school together, we belong to the same club.' He began to say more, stopped, and then decided to go on. 'Take care, Miss Camilla. I have never known George do anything that was not to his own immediate advantage, and he has a destructive streak to him. Destructive to others, not to himself.'

Before she could reply, he had elbowed his way through the group of men, and she had to move swiftly to stay with him. How surprising, what an extraordinary thing to say! And why should he be concerned that she might fall foul of George Warren, what was it to him? Her relationship with Sophie? Perhaps, like many men, he preferred his bride's family to be as beyond reproach as the bride herself. Did Wytton suppose her to be at the mercy of any gentleman who looked in her direction? She coloured at the thought, trod on a fat admiral's toes, smiled in apology and squeezed past. That was the price she had to pay for her attachment to and disattachment from Sir Sidney being so generally known.

Belle was inclined to be truculent, but when she looked towards Mrs Gardiner, who had by now gathered up Sophie, she decided not to resist. She made a pretty farewell to her companion, who held her hand too long and said he would do himself the honour of calling upon her.

'Day dealt with; now for Night,' said Wytton.

So he knew their nicknames.

'Please stay close to us, Miss Belle,' he went on, 'or you may be trampled underfoot.'

Camilla's head was beginning to throb. The noise was rising to a deafening pitch, loud conversations, footmen at the door calling out the names of new arrivals in ringing tones, voices in the hall below shouting for carriages, the chink of glasses, the clatter of a tray being dropped. She longed to clap her hands over her ears, or, better still, to be out of there.

She gave Wytton's arm a little tug. 'Who is that man? Do you know who is with Georgina?'

'It is Joshua Mordaunt.'

She eyed the tall, rangy man with his high-arched brows, pale gold hair and fine, thin mouth. Her heart sank. Although a good fifteen years older than Georgina, he had just the kind of looks her sister admired. So dark herself, she was always drawn to fair men, and he had an air of authority about him that Georgina would always respond to.

'He is married, before you ask,' Wytton said. 'He has a wife in the country, and he enjoys himself in town. He is a cousin of mine, as it happens.'

How many of these people here tonight were related to one another or connected through those ties of blood and kinship that bound society together in tribal unity?

Most of them, and those who weren't, the men who had climbed from the middle classes through industry, enterprise, brains or sharp dealing, would sooner or later make those same connections through their own marriages or those of their children.

Georgina opened her violet eyes wide and fixed them on Wytton. 'Are you Mrs Gardiner's errand boy?'

'Indeed I am, and happy to be so,' he replied promptly.

'I do not want to leave. We have only just arrived.'

'An hour and a half to my certain knowledge, Miss Georgina. I think Miss Darcy in particular wishes to go home.'

That was a false move, she thought, Georgina would care nothing for Letty's well-being.

'What, has she bumped into Tom? Oh, famous, is he here? I have not seen him.'

'Tom is not here,' Camilla said crossly. 'You had better come, for if you don't, Mrs Gardiner is bound to mention it to Mr Fitzwilliam when he returns tomorrow, and there will be an end to any parties. Pemberley will be your next destination, you may be sure.'

'Oh, as to that, I am not afraid of being sent back to Pemberley. My cousin cannot force us to go. And as for now, there is no need for me to go, no, nor Belle. My Aunt Lydia can send us home in her carriage when the party is over.'

Wytton bowed to Mordaunt. 'Must beg permission to relieve you of your charming companion, Joshua,' he said, and with a vice-like grip on Georgina's arm, he swept her away before she could do more than utter a squeak of protest.

'Let me go! What do you think you are doing? You are hurting me! You have no right to lay a finger on me—'

'Be quiet,' Camilla said. 'Do you want to make a scene? Do you think you will be asked anywhere again if you do so?'

This threat worked as nothing else had done, and tight-lipped, with her chin set at a defiant angle, Georgina allowed herself to be pushed through the thick knots of people at the entrance to the room and all down the stairs. Breathless and rumpled, the whole party finally emerged into the night air and stood by the steps to wait for the carriages, their faces illuminated by the unsteady flames of the torches held aloft by the linkboys, the chasing shadows hiding whatever feelings of temper or pleasure might be found on their faces.

It fell to Camilla to visit the Gardiners the next morning to wait upon Mrs Gardiner and thank her for taking them to the rout. Letty said she preferred to wait in, she had a slight headache from the night before, and besides, it would not be right if neither of them were at home to greet the Fitzwilliams upon their return from Southend. Belle and Georgina had slept late, were not yet dressed, and were full of yawns and complaints at the suggestion that they might accompany her.

'No, for although Sophie is good enough company, Mrs Gardiner is bound to preach at us, which is such a bore. You go, you do not mind being bored.'

'I do not find the Gardiners in the least boring, and if you are going to yawn and throw yourselves on to chairs and sofas all morning in that unbridled way, I agree that it would be better for you to do so here, where nobody has to look at you.'

Belle only yawned even more widely, and wilted prettily until the maid came in with their chocolate. At that, she became much more alert, for she was passionately fond of chocolate.

It was a wet, windy day, the sort of day that made summer a distant dream. To her younger sisters' horror, Camilla donned a pelisse, ignoring all their cries of how unfashionable she was, and did she not know that no one with any pretensions to style would be seen out in a pelisse at this time of year? She did not choose to arrive at the Gardiners' house looking like a damp rag, however, and so set off well clad against the inclement weather.

She found Mrs Gardiner reclining on a sofa.

'Such a to-do, my dear,' she said, greeting Camilla with affection and gesturing for her to take a seat. 'Pray forgive me if I do not rise. I tripped on the bottom stair as I came down this morning and caught my foot in my gown. I have given my ankle a dreadful wrench.'

Camilla expressed her concern and was assured that there were no broken bones in the case. 'Dr Molloy tells me that it will heal in a few days. I am to rest it for now, though, I must keep it up. So I am especially glad to see you, for I have a favour to beg of you.'

'I am happy to be of any use at all,' she said at once, wondering what her aunt might need doing that could not be undertaken by her bevy of servants.

'If Fanny can spare you, for I know she returns today, I should like you to accompany Sophie on a drive out this afternoon. Mr Wytton is to call for her, it is a matter of looking over some jewellery of his mother's that is being reset for her.'

'Does she need anyone to accompany her?' Camilla was surprised. There was nothing improper or incorrect in a girl being driven out in an open carriage by the man to whom she was engaged. His groom would be there, and she could always take her maid.

Mrs Gardiner sighed, and rang the bell. 'I know you like to drink coffee, so I will order a pot to be made. Sophie is in her room just now, so I may speak freely. The fact is that with my being laid up, if you do not go with her, she will refuse to go, and I think Mr Wytton will not be pleased.'

'Refuse to go!'

Mrs Gardiner looked troubled. 'I do not know why it is so, for my other daughters were always delighted to drive out with their young men. It is almost as though Sophie fears to be alone with him, not that she is in the least danger from him in any way, he is far too much the gentleman to attempt anything indecorous.'

'Would that be likely?' Camilla said, surprised. 'In so public a situation, it would hardly be possible for him to behave in such a way, even if he wished to do so, which I am sure he would not.'

'I think it is rather his conversation, his quick way of speaking and the way his mind leaps from subject to subject that makes Sophie uneasy,' said Mrs Gardiner. 'Then he makes some witty remark or other, and indeed, he is often very funny, only Sophie seems not always to understand him. She has a straight-forward way of thinking, and it seems that the vigour and speed of his thoughts and speech alarms her. She will grow used to his ways in time.'

Camilla listened with growing amazement. Could Mrs Gardiner really be talking about the glowing young girl she had seen flirting last night, the composed, demure creature who sat basking in the evident admiration and love shown by Wytton?

Mrs Gardiner fidgeted with the lace trim on her sleeve. 'The thing is, and I know I can be frank with you, Camilla, that Mr

Wytton is a passionate man, and Sophie, well, Sophie is very young and very young women often find that side of a man's attachment threatening. It is only natural.'

Camilla thought of the twins, and said nothing.

'I sometimes wonder if he is not too passionate in his liking for her, whether such strong feelings may burn themselves out. I have mentioned this to Mr Gardiner, but he pooh-poohs the idea. Besides, he says that everything is agreed and settled, all the papers drawn up, there is nothing to be done but for the nuptial knot to be tied. Oh, Camilla, I wish the wedding might be brought forward. Sophie is not a sensible, clever girl like you, and she may work herself up into goodness knows what state of mind about Wytton if we are not careful.'

Camilla set herself to soothe Mrs Gardiner's fears, although she felt she had no right to offer comfort or advice; what did she know of such matters? Sophie was no doubt a little nervy, that was all. Girls were apt to be nervy in the weeks leading up to their weddings. It was only to be expected. It was best not to make an issue of it, to go along with her desire for constant chaperonage. 'If Mr Wytton finds it odd, well, he will have all the time in the world alone with her come the summer.'

'I am so glad I mentioned it to you,' said Mrs Gardiner, whose face was looking a good deal less worried. 'You are much of an age with Sophie, and are more likely to understand her than I am.'

And when Camilla protested that this was not true, she shook her head and went on. 'Young people have changed. They have all kinds of romantic notions, which we never gave a thought to when I was a girl. They want to love and be loved, and every other consideration must give way to that.'

'In which case, Sophie will do very well, for I am sure she loves Wytton, and you only have to see them together to know how deeply he is in love with her.'

Mrs Gardiner held out her hand to give Camilla's hand a squeeze of gratitude. 'You are such a good girl, Camilla. I cannot say how much I want you to make such an attachment, and I know you will, only you are not going to be easy to please. Just like your mother.'

'I don't seem wise in my choices,' Camilla said ruefully. 'Unlike my mother.'

'Oh, but your mother went through her own vicissitudes before she became engaged to Darcy, I do assure you. She would not like me to tell you of it, but it was so, you may take my word for it. Some young ladies meet a man and from there it is all plain sailing, but this is not the usual way it happens. Girls nowadays tumble in and out of love before settling their fancy on a particular man. You have plenty of time, I know your parents are in no hurry to see any of you married, however much the twins may moan about old maids and being on the shelf. The world has its share of intelligent, attractive, agreeable, good men, Camilla, and I am quite certain that you will meet just the man for you.'

Camilla had no such certainty, and indeed foresaw a life of lonely spinsterhood ahead of her. But she smiled, and asked if Mrs Gardiner would take another cup of coffee.

Mrs Gardiner's mind was running on eligible men. 'I saw you chatting to George Warren last night. He is a clever man, and handsome with it. He will have the title, too, when his father dies. It is only a barony, but there is no denying that a title can have its attractions. However, he has a reputation for wildness. There are rumours of certain doings abroad, in Italy you know, where it is easy for a young man to be led astray.'

'He is not such a young man,' Camilla said dryly. 'Nor does he appear to me likely to be hoodwinked by anyone.'

'You are right. He is what Mr Gardiner calls a tough customer. Now, you must not repeat that, but Mr Gardiner is a good judge of character. He would not have succeeded as he has if he were not.'

'I have no designs on Mr Warren, and I am sure he has none on me.'

'Not amorous ones, perhaps, but take care. There is little goodwill in that family towards yours.'

Camilla raised her eyebrows in surprise. 'Now, that is odd! I met George Warren for the first time last night, and Mr Wytton also warned me to be on my guard with him. Little goodwill towards my family? Why should that be?'

'I suppose I should not tell you, it is all gossip from long ago, but you may as well hear it. You know that Lady Warren is George's stepmother, not his natural mother?'

'Yes.'

'His late mother was Eudora Paxborough. I never liked her. She was a hard-hearted woman with a nasty tongue. All her servants were afraid of her, and I think Hartley, her husband, Lord Warren as he is now, was too. So why he chose another cold creature like Caroline Bingley, no one could understand; however, she did her duty by his son, and if she can be said to have affection for anyone, it is for George.'

'That is to her credit.'

'Oh, it is, and I may say that George adores her, and is protective of her. That is just my point. Caroline had wanted to marry your father, you see – not that she was ever in love with him, I am sure of that. It was his position and fortune that attracted her as much as his person and character. He never looked at her, especially not once he had got to know your mother, and she took the whole business badly. She is quite capable of doing you an ill turn, Camilla. I do not believe she has forgotten and forgiven, and that is why I say you should be on your guard with her.'

'I have met her only once at my cousin's house, when the Warrens dined, and again last night. It is a slight acquaintance.'

Mrs Gardiner seemed relieved, and her thoughts returned to Sophie. 'So you are sure you do not mind driving out with her this afternoon?'

'No, indeed. Only I must return home to change, I am not dressed for driving. When does he call for her?'

As Camilla turned into Aubrey Square, she saw that her return had coincided with the arrival of her cousins from Southend. All was hubbub and uproar. The carriages with their steaming horses were drawn up before the door, servants ran about, a barking Pug threatening to trip them up as he frisked between their legs. Charlotte clamoured for Letty to listen to her cough and the baby howled. Fanny was uttering pleased cries of greeting to the Darcy sisters, as she disentangled herself from a shawl that had got caught up in the door of the carriage.

Dawson bade her keep still while she deftly unthreaded the fringe. 'There, my lady. Now, be so good as to hand me that package. No, Miss Charlotte, I can't attend to you at this moment, so quieten down, do, you make my ears ring.'

Fitzwilliam was surveying the front of his house, as though to reassure himself it was still standing, and then ushered everyone indoors. He wanted to go to his room and change before he hurried off to his club to make sure the Government hadn't fallen in his absence and to catch up on all the news and gossip.

The party flowed into the house and up the stairs, everyone talking at once – the delights of the seaside, the pleasantness of their lodgings, the agreeable company to be met with at Southend, the benefits to Charlotte, the brilliance of the baby in producing another tooth, the delightfulness of being home again.

Tea was called for and brought, while Fanny sank back into a sofa with a satisfied sigh. 'To be sure, it is very nice to be at the seaside, and our journey could not have been easier or more comfortable; however, it is best to be at home. Tell me, what have you been doing? Have you been very dull? I was so shocked when Fitzwilliam told me you were not to go out in society while I was away. I felt I should not have left you.'

The twins looked as though they quite agreed with Fanny, but Camilla and Letty were quick to reassure her and say they had not been dull at all, and that her trip away had been more than necessary, only look how well Charlotte was, quite recovered.

'Yes, she is, except for a little cough, and that is less troublesome every day. Dr Molloy will call round later today, I am sure, and he will be pleased to see her coming on so well. He will know just the thing to prescribe for her cough.'

'We did attend one party,' Camilla said, judging it best that

Fanny should be told right away, before her husband heard about it at the club. 'Mrs Gardiner took us, with Sophie, to my Aunt Lydia's rout. She felt our absence would excite comment.'

'She did very right, and I must thank her for it,' cried Fanny. 'Lord, I forgot all about it. In the normal way, I should not dream of taking you to such a party, for we do not move in that set, and I would not consider the company suitable for people of your age, but Lydia Pollexfen being your aunt makes all the difference. Was it a dreadful crush? Her parties always are, you know. Did you enjoy it?'

The twins launched into a rapturous account of the fashionable company, the crowded rooms, the excitement of a royal duke being present.

Fanny frowned. 'Was he, though? He is not at all the thing, however royal he may be. What of you, Camilla? And Letty?'

'It was horrid,' said Letitia. 'Such a squeeze, and nearly everyone there was a stranger, and the room so hot, and people pressing one so close!'

Camilla knew that her cousin didn't want to hear of any of them having a less than enjoyable time, so she said that she had met and chatted with some interesting people, and had taken great pleasure in observing the fashions. That distracted Fanny, who immediately demanded detailed descriptions of gowns and trimmings and how hair was being worn.

The sound of the knocker, voices below. Fanny looked attentive. 'I wonder who that may be? We shall admit no visitors today, of course. I am in no mood for callers, and indeed need to take off my clothes at once, so crumpled and rumpled as I am after the journey.'

Fanny in fact looked perfectly neat and untousled, but before she could say so, the door opened and to their great surprise, Mr Gardiner was admitted, holding a letter in his hand, a worried expression on his face. Fitzwilliam was hard on his heels.

He greeted Fanny politely, and then without preamble waved the letter at the sisters. 'Here is an express come from Mr Darcy. I had to come round at once.'

'From Papa!' Camilla exclaimed.

Letitia had gone pale. 'Tell us at once, I beg you. I know that some terrible misfortune has befallen them, an accident, an illness; oh, pray, do not keep us in suspense, let us hear the worst.'

NINETEEN

'It is indeed a letter from your father, a most disturbing letter.'

Like other important merchants and bankers working in the city of London, Mr Gardiner needed and maintained excellent lines of communication with those countries overseas where he did business. Now that the war was over, it was possible for him to send and receive information far more swiftly than via any of the normal couriers or mails.

He had sent correspondence to Mr and Mrs Darcy on their journey east; it would be more of a problem once they reached Constantinople, but his contacts with Vienna were excellent and he had forwarded the letter that Letitia had given him a little while ago without a second thought.

The reply had come addressed not to Darcy's eldest daughter, but to Mr Gardiner, with a request that he share its contents with Fitzwilliam at the first opportunity and send him an answer at his earliest convenience. That was what had brought him hurrying from his office, and in the middle of a working day – an unheard of circumstance that had set all his underlings and clerks to whispering and wondering what had happened.

'Letty, whatever did you write?' asked Camilla, when Mr Gardiner had been seated and offered refreshment and recovered his equanimity.

Letitia was defiant. 'I told him the truth, how London does not suit us.' Cries of protest from Belle and Georgina; she put her nose in the air and, ignoring the interruption, continued, her voice high and discontented. 'I said in how dissipated and purposeless way our time is spent, with our days and nights given over to parties and clothes and extravagance of every kind; how the twins have to be almost dragged to church on Sundays, how Alethea pays no attention to any study but that of music, and how unsuitable the songs she is learning with this Italian master are, and how wrong it is that she learns from a foreigner, a most ungenteel person. And I told him that Belle and Georgina go everywhere, as though they are out, which they are not, and think of nothing but beaux and flirting and fashions. I wrote, too, that the whole sad business with Sir Sidney, of which I am sure he has been appraised, would never have arisen but for the circumstance of our lives being given over to such worldly and frivolous activities.'

She finished this litany of sins with an air of great satisfaction. 'I do not in the least regret having sent the letter, for it is right that Papa and Mama should know how things are. I said that we ought to return to Pemberley without further delay, for although Fanny and Mr Fitzwilliam have shown us every kindness, it is an imposition upon them to have to cope with the twins and Alethea in particular, and that all of us would benefit extremely from a spring and summer spent among familiar surroundings, following our customary pursuits.'

Georgina could not contain herself. 'Customary pursuits! Yes, sitting at our needlework for hours on end, going for a dull walk in the dull park and then, perhaps, once in a while, when the moon is full, visiting one or other of our dull neighbours. You may choose to wither into crabbed spinsterhood in such a fashion, but you shall not force me and Belle to share such a horrid existence with you. I shan't go back to Derbyshire, whatever you may say, or whatever Papa says, for you have not told him the truth. You have made up a heap of wicked stories, just because you are so determined to get your own way.'

'Georgina! Control yourself, if you please, this is no time to be enacting scenes.' Mr Fitzwilliam's voice was sharp as he looked up from the letter he had been perusing with a frown on his face. 'It seems from what he writes here that Darcy has indeed heard some rumours about Sir Sidney, and he asks me to furnish him with details if I consider it necessary; otherwise he is disinclined to waste any time on what is no doubt mere gossip. I think I must inform him of exactly what happened.'

'I will write to him,' Camilla said, keeping her voice as calm as she could. Why had she not told her parents about it at once, in her next letter to them after that dreadful day? She had decided not to, judging that it could be mentioned when they met again, when it would be so far in the past as to seem of no importance – and what was the point of writing about what had not, in the end, come to anything? It would only distress them to hear of her being involved in any way in a scandal. She had deceived herself. She knew perfectly well that they were bound to hear of it, and probably in a way least flattering to herself. 'It is for me to explain.'

'No, for you will hedge and fudge and pretend it was all nothing,' said Letitia. 'I shall write and give him the details.'

Camilla's temper rose. 'You shall not. It is nothing to do with you. Why cannot you be content with your own affairs? Why do you have to meddle in everyone else's? Why did you not restrict yourself to writing about your good works, and ask if you might go back to Pemberley by yourself? Not that you would go alone, no, I feel sure you would invite Mr Valpy to offer spiritual guidance!'

'Please do not quarrel,' begged Fanny. 'It is of no use arguing about who should have written what, for Letty did write, and the letter was sent, and arrived all too quickly. Would that you had sent it by the slowest route possible, Mr Gardiner, that it might have lain about in Vienna until they returned from their mission to the Turks! How angry Darcy will be when he comes back! I pray I might not be in Town when that happens; I would not face him for the world if he is in one of his moods, Lord, how cold and frightening he can be when he is displeased; it makes me feel faint just to think of it.'

They all fell silent, each of them aware that Fanny had spoken more than the truth. None of them could think of Darcy at his most formidable without a qualm; even Letitia, full of self-righteousness, looked a trifle alarmed.

She was in general a great favourite with her cousin Fitzwilliam, who approved of her serious ways and her practical piety, but he was far from pleased with her at the moment. 'It is a great pity that you did not consult me before you composed such a letter,' he said irritably. 'Or at least you might have mentioned to Fanny what you intended; she would have advised you on what best to say. You should not have taken matters into your own hands in this forceful way.'

Letitia wasn't used to being rebuked in quite that tone, and her face took on a disagreeable expression. 'It was my duty.'

'Oh, hang duty,' said Mr Gardiner. 'If we all did our duty, we should end up in a pretty pickle.'

'Which is just where we are,' said Fanny.

'I think we need to discover the truth of this matter,' said Mr Gardiner. 'I have not discussed the contents of the letter with Mrs Gardiner, I have not had time to do so, for I came directly here upon opening it. But I feel sure she would have mentioned it to me if the town were abuzz with gossip and unfavourable talk about you girls, as Mr Darcy says it is. Can it indeed be so?'

'Oh, yes,' said Letitia eagerly. 'You may take my word for it; although it pains me to say it, it is unfortunately so.'

Trust Letty to jump in again, before anyone else had time to collect their thoughts. Pained her to say it, indeed; she was loving every moment of this, savouring what she felt to be her triumph. Camilla had never been less in sympathy with her sister, and goodness knew, she was often at loggerheads with her over what Letty took to be her laxness in taking a strong line on moral matters. Moral matters, naturally, being what Letty chose to approve or disapprove of.

Alethea, who had heard the commotion and didn't want to miss a drama, had come running down the stairs, and now she bounced into the room. 'Why, what is going on? Has Pug run wild and bitten Dawson? Oh, Mr Gardiner, I am sorry, I did not see you.' She dropped a curtsy.

Camilla was amused by the look on Mr Gardiner's face. He hadn't seen Alethea since she was a girl, hurtling about the house and dropping out of trees. This tall, dark young woman, eyes gleaming with mischief, was a stranger to him.

'Alethea? Dear me, can it really be you? How you have grown! I have a letter from your father, that is why I am here. He has written because he fears that all is not well with you and your sisters' visit to London.'

'I am perfectly happy to be in London. May I read the letter?' Without waiting for his permission, she tweaked the letter from his hand and read it, her brows drawn as she turned the page.

'You have no business to be reading that letter,' said Letitia. 'It is nothing to do with you.'

'Yes, it is, for I see that you have written to him saying all manner of untruthful and unkind things about me; Letty, how dared you tell him such fibs? And to write so harshly of Signor Silvestrini — it is too much. What do you know about him or my lessons? Besides, you should not have gone bearing tales about Sir Sidney to Papa and Mama, that is Camilla's business. It is always the same, you are forever poking your nose where it does not belong.'

'Alethea!' Mr Fitzwilliam was thunderstruck by this outburst. 'A schoolroom chit speaking out in front of her elders and betters as though you have a right to an opinion, what are you thinking of?'

Alethea stared at him. 'If Letitia has been writing lies to my parents, of course I have a right to protest.'

'Alethea, it would be best if you went back upstairs to Mrs Griffin and your books,' said Fanny, alarmed at the turn the conversation was taking.

'It is most unfair. If Letty has her way, we shall all find ourselves back at Pemberley. No music, no singing for me, no beaux or flirting for the twins, and no one for Camilla to talk to. Let her go, and take that dreadful Valpy with her, only she needs to take care, for he is the kind of man who pats and squeezes and is not safe to be in a room with.'

Alethea had gone too far. Mr Fitzwilliam was looking even more angry, Fanny was sitting back in the sofa and covering her eyes with a hand, Mr Gardiner was eyeing Alethea as though she were some exotic and unfamiliar object that had been placed on his desk in a shipment newly arrived from the East.

'Upstairs, Alethea, this instant,' Camilla said, propelling her hastily to the door. 'No, not another word, you have said quite enough. You may rely on me to take your part in any discussion there is to be about our stay in London. Just be off with you.'

Alethea was outside and the door closed on her before Mr Fitzwilliam could catch his breath or Letitia control her indignation. Mr Gardiner was shaking his head. 'My word, what a stir she will cause when she comes out. Good Lord, Darcy to the life, and what eyes! She'll knock all your beauties for ninepence; they'll be nothing to her.'

Fanny looked pleased, glad to think of her young cousin taking the polite world by storm, unlikely though it seemed to her that she would do any such thing.

'Sharp tongues and mannish ways don't make for a beauty, and they don't catch husbands, neither,' said Mr Fitzwilliam, still simmering at being baulked of his prey. 'She is ungovernable, quite unfit to be loosed on any polite society.'

Mr Gardiner was more tolerant. 'She is young. I admire a girl with a bit of fire to her nature, and so do many men, let me tell you.'

'You see, I am quite right,' said Letitia. 'Only look how badly she behaves. It is London that has done this. London will be the ruin of all of us.'

'Now as to ruin,' said Mr Gardiner, 'that is another matter, and one that concerns me more than any other, and it worries Darcy, too, that Letitia has written of you girls not conforming as you should to the requirements of the London *ton*, of becoming the object of gossip, of turning those whose good opinion is essential against you.'

Camilla could not contain herself; she had to refute Letty's accusations. Honesty compelled her to admit that there was a grain of truth in them, but no more, and certainly not enough to be sending alarming missives to their father. To be sure, the twins were turning out rather wild, but then their youth and beauty and fortunes would probably bring them through. Her own attachment to Sir Sidney had caused tongues to wag, but the lesser scandal had been succeeded by the greater one of his exposure and flight.

'Letty is as likely as any of us to raise eyebrows among the highest sticklers,' she said. 'For although you may meet Mr Valpy at some of the grandest houses, since he is a fashionable preacher, his attentions to Letty will not have gone unnoticed, and will meet with general disapproval.' There, that should silence her sister for a few minutes at least.

Mr Gardiner seemed to ignore her outburst. 'Lady Fanny, are they in such bad odour as Letty supposes?'

Fanny roused herself. 'They are no such thing. It is all a great piece of nonsense. They have vouchers to Almack's, they all behave prettily, do not give themselves airs, and, what is of great importance, they have fifty thousand pounds each, enough to impress any of the hostesses and attract any eligible bachelor who has a mind to matrimony. They do not dress outlandish, nor engage in any frolics, or steal away from the dance floor to secret assignations. As to flirting and men, why, that is natural when you are young and pretty and at a dance or a party. Pray, what should girls do?'

'Modest behaviour—' her husband began.

'A fig for modest behaviour! Were they to sit in the corner with the dowagers and chaperons and never look at a man or stand up for a waltz, then that would be cause for concern, for such girls may be considered to be as good as gold, but I have noticed that they never find husbands – whatever you say, Fitzwilliam, and in matters such as these you must allow me to know what I am talking of.'

'Bravo,' said Mr Gardiner. 'No, be quiet, Letty, I think we have heard enough of what you have to say. You have made your opinion clear, but you must be guided in this by others who know more of the world than you do. Your parents arranged for you to spend some months in London, and circumstances do not justify your going against their wishes, and neither Mr Fitzwilliam nor I shall permit you to do so. If you choose to live a little out of society, and not to go about as much as your sisters, you may do so, provided that,' he raised a finger to quell her, 'provided that Fanny does not consider it will give rise to any talk, to any whispers that you may still be pining for Tom Busby.'

Fanny was nodding her approval. 'Write to Mr Darcy at once, Mr Gardiner, assuring him that Letty's natural dis-appointment has led her to take a harsh and extreme view of the life the girls are living here in London. He may be perfectly at ease, knowing that you and Mrs Gardiner, as well as Fitz-william and myself are taking the greatest care of his daughters' happiness and reputations.'

Sackree, who had lingered on the landing outside the drawing-room, a pile of Camilla's underclothes fresh from the laundry-maid in her arms, listened with keen attention, as did John the footman. They had flattened themselves against the wall when Alethea came out, but she had barely given them a glance, being too keen, as Sackree remarked, to get upstairs and tell Miss Griffin what had happened.

'All eyes and ears, Miss Alethea is. She had the right of it, what she said about that Valpy in there. Right free and easy with his hands, he is. He had Figgins pressed up against the wall, him and his nasty black coat and slimy ways.'

'Bet he didn't get far with that Figgins. Like a cat, she is.'

'He did not. She don't spend all that time hanging round the stables without learning a trick or two, and who's to blame her? A woman's got to look after herself in this wicked world, for nobody else isn't going to do it for her.'

'That's true enough. I've seen him giving Miss Alethea the eye and all. You'd think he'd have more sense if he's after the eldest one.'

'Miss Darcy to you.'

'Still, she's got that governess to watch out for her, tells her everything, doesn't she?'

'I reckon as how it all gets put down on paper by Miss Griffin; scribble, scribble she goes, all day long.'

'Going to wrap it all up and hand it to your master soon as he's back from foreign parts, I dare say, and never a good word to say for anyone by the look of her.'

Sackree got on well with Miss Griffin. 'I've known worse, and she won't be passing on secrets, she's not the type. It's a journal she's keeping up there, recording it all for posterity.'

'What all?'

'Life.'

John snorted. 'What's an old spinster stick like her know about life? Now, if it was you, Sackree—' he said with a leer.

'You keep your sauce to yourself. Ssh, now, Miss Letitia's finished her complaining, let's see what the others have to say.'

'I'll miss you if you has to go back to Derbyshire.'

'I'll not be going back to Derbyshire except as according to the original arrangements. Miss Camilla won't stand for it. There now, Lady Fanny's putting them right. Mind you, she's wrong about assignations. Assignation is those twins' middle name, and that's the truth of it!'

TWENTY

Camilla was pleased to see Mr Layard standing beside Mr Wytton on the street outside Mr Gardiner's house. His face broke into a welcoming smile as she descended from the carriage.

Hearing that she was driving out with Sophie that afternoon, Mr Gardiner had insisted on taking her. 'Then I can give this letter from your father to Mrs Gardiner. I am sure she will agree with Fanny, but I should not like to reply without her advice.'

Sophie came down the steps of the house, charmingly dressed in a fine Indian muslin. She greeted her father prettily, and smiled at Camilla, Wytton and Layard.

Their destination was a jeweller's off Maddox Street. Camilla would have walked there, it being only a short distance away, but Sophie was not at all a keen walker and much preferred the open carriage, where she could see and be seen. Besides, she confided to Camilla as Mr Wytton handed them in, her light satin shoes were not made for walking, and the dusty streets did dirty one's dress so. She settled herself on the seat and held up a lace parasol to protect her exquisite complexion from the sun's rays that had broken through the cloud. She gestured to Camilla to sit beside her; Layard took his place opposite, next to Wytton, and the carriage moved off.

'Egypt is very hot, is it not?' Camilla asked Wytton, her mind on sun and complexions.

He looked at her in some surprise. 'Extremely so, and for most of the year. Very dry and dusty, also. It is not so bad, though, for one travels everywhere by boat, on the Nile. The river breezes provide some relief from the heat.'

'I have seen drawings of those vessels, I think, with curved sails.'

'Yes. The prevailing wind blows one south and on the return journey, one relies on the current. The Nile flows from south to north, did you know that? It is most unusual for a river; but then, the Nile is altogether extraordinary. Only consider the incredible variety of creatures to be found in its waters and upon its banks.'

Mr Layard leant forward. 'Tell me, Miss Camilla, would you care to be introduced to a crocodile?'

'I believe I have met several these past few weeks in London.'

Wytton laughed. It occurred to her that she had not heard him laugh out like that before. He had a pleasant, resonant voice, and his laugh matched it. 'I think you might find the Nile sort a sad disappointment in comparison,' he said.

Sophie's face had taken on a discontented look. 'If you are to go on about Egypt, Camilla, I shall wish you had never come. It is so dreadfully boring.'

Wytton's smile faded, and he said no more.

'How I envy you the opportunities you will have for foreign travel,' she said to Sophie. 'Why, when you are married, you will see all kinds of places that most of us can only dream of. Not only Egypt, but Greece, and Turkey.'

'Your parents are in Turkey. Might you not have accompanied them if you are so eager to travel?' said Mr Layard.

'Oh, I should have liked it above all things,' she said. 'It was not thought suitable, however, and Mama and Papa wished me to spend some time in London.'

'Perhaps you would have found life under the Ottomans less restrictive than London society,' said Wytton.

'How can you say such a monstrous thing?' said Sophie. 'It is quite horrid in that part of the world, all harems and odalisques. The men are not at all respectable, and wear red hats all day long. Papa has been, and he told us all about it, tales that would make your eyes start out of your head, Camilla. You would not like it there at all, take my word for it.'

'Have you never been abroad?' Wytton asked Camilla. 'Not even to France?'

'Not even to France? Why, I have hardly been out of Derbyshire before this. We have led very quiet lives.'

'You may say that, but Pemberley is my idea of heaven,' said Sophie. 'It is the finest house I ever saw, so spacious, and so many fine furnishings and hangings. It is done up with great elegance and taste. Everyone says what a fine house it is. I am quite envied for having relations who live there.'

Yet Sophie would have her abbey soon enough; how odd to hear such yearning in her cousin's voice. And why should she suddenly think of Pemberley with such enthusiasm?

'If I lived at Pemberley, I should stay there always,' Sophie went on. 'I should never want to leave. Everyone is so happy there. How sad you will be, Camilla, when you come to marry and have to leave it. How shall you bear it?'

'I like Pemberley well enough, but it is still only a house, Sophie. People make one happy, not houses.'

Sophie pulled at the tassel on her parasol handle. 'I do not think so. Houses are more to be trusted than people.'

Wytton was not looking in their direction, but had his head turned round to give instructions to the coachman.

'I am sure Mr Wytton would rather be on the box than sitting here with us females,' Sophie said. 'He is never happy to sit and be driven by others, just as he fidgets in the drawing-room and strides up and down in a ballroom. He is a restless person who must always be doing something.'

'Now, that is not true. I have seen Mr Wytton sit beside you in the most amiable manner. Why do you abuse him so?'

Wytton brought this conversation to an end by announcing that they had come as close to the jeweller's shop as was possible, it being situated within a tiny cul-de-sac. It was just as well; Camilla didn't care to talk about Wytton in this way with Sophie, as though her future husband were elsewhere, or deaf, if not actually halfwitted.

The purpose of their outing was for Wytton to show Sophie the necklace that his mother was bestowing upon her as a wedding present, and to allow her to choose a clasp for it.

Sophie stared down at the garnets set in intricate webs of warm gold.

'How beautiful,' said Camilla, breaking the silence that lasted too long. She sensed that her cousin's lack of response was due to quite other feelings than appreciation of the necklace's beauty. 'It must be very old, I think.'

'Exquisite,' murmured Mr Layard, his cherubic countenance quite solemn.

Wytton never took his eyes from Sophie's face. 'It is Italian and was made by a Florentine master of the Renaissance period. It was given to an ancestor of my mother's as part of her wedding dowry, and it is the custom in our family for it to be passed on to the eldest son's bride. My mother wore it on her wedding day.'

The hint was obvious, and Sophie's mouth became decidedly peevish. 'Well, I shall not wear it on mine, for it will not do with my dress. You should have shown it to me earlier, and then perhaps the whole piece could have been reset in a more modern style. It is too late to change anything now. I cannot possibly wear it.'

Wytton frowned, and the jeweller, an old man with a serene and distinguished face, gave a slight cough. 'It would be wrong to attempt to reset such an heirloom.'

Camilla could see that Sophie was about to say something unforgivable, and she plunged in, exclaiming over the fine filigree and asking the old man how such intricate work was achieved.

She listened with only half her attention to his courteous explanations. Whatever had come over Sophie? Apart from mislaying her usual good manners, she seemed unhappy about the whole business. Her mother had spoken of nerves, was this kind of behaviour normal for her? It was so unlike the Sophie she had known. Could an engagement change a girl so much? It was apprehension, no doubt, fear of the unknown, a reluctance to shed her girlhood, and assume the role and duties of a married woman.

Whatever it was, no young woman should look this miserable only a few weeks before her wedding day, and in the presence of her lover, too.

Sophie had wandered over to look at some diamond bracelets that lay nestled in dark blue velvet. 'These are pretty. See, how modern and stylish. Old jewels are quite out of fashion, you know, Wytton. I would much prefer to have a diamond necklace.'

These last words were spoken so low that she wasn't sure if Wytton had heard them. If he had, he made no reply, but continued his consultation with the jeweller.

How could Sophie prefer one of the diamond necklaces to that exquisite garnet and wrought gold one?

'These diamonds are charming,' Camilla said to her cousin, 'but the necklace you are to have will make everyone stare – it is so beautiful and unusual. Anyone may have diamonds; an heirloom is an ornament of quite a different kind.'

For a moment there was a gleam of pleasure in Sophie's eyes, then it dimmed. 'Do you think so? I do not think Mr Wytton's necklace is at all in my style, it will never suit me.'

Mrs Gardiner's ankle was slow to heal, and Sophie was quick to call on her cousin again to accompany her when she went out with Mr Wytton.

As often as not on these occasions, they were joined by Mr Layard, as though Wytton, too, felt the need of a companion when he was with Sophie. This puzzled Camilla. If such uneasiness in the company of one's betrothed might be under-standable in the case of a seventeen-year-old girl, the same reasons could hardly apply to a man of eight-and-twenty. He had lived in the world, as the saying went, and bashfulness could not account for his behaviour.

Nor did she believe for a moment that Wytton didn't trust himself alone with the delectable Sophie. He was a man of strong feelings, that was obvious; yet, unless her judgement was at fault, and it was true that she wasn't too confident in her judgement of men just now, a man of his years, upbringing and temperament was unlikely to be so overwhelmed by passion as to forget himself and go too far with an inexperienced girl – and one, furthermore, who was destined to be his wife.

There was no explaining it. Camilla could only show herself

willing to help Mrs Gardiner by going about with Sophie and Wytton, and amuse herself by observing the strange couple and trying to come to some sensible conclusions about the true state of affairs between them.

Mrs Gardiner felt the awkwardness of her position. 'I would not persuade you to be with Sophie if it makes you uncomfortable.'

Camilla did not wish to seem a disappointed woman. 'It is nothing. It would be a different matter if I were obliged to spend time in Sir Sidney Leigh's company.'

There, the name was out; the first time it had passed her lips since that dreadful day. And she prided herself that her voice sounded calm. 'I cannot shut myself away so that I never have to see an engaged or newly married couple. I shall in due course become accustomed to the notion of matrimony.'

'Your own, I do hope,' cried Mrs Gardiner.

'Oh, well, as to that, there are not so many agreeable men in the world, but if I look around, I may find a man who prefers women to men.'

'Pray, do not make such remarks! It is all very well when you are with me, within the family, but out in the world you must mind your tongue. It is essential that you appear innocent, that you know nothing of that side of men.'

'How can I pretend that, when everyone knows why I fell out with Sir Sidney?'

'It is amazing what you may pretend. Nothing can do you more harm in society than an outspoken tongue on such matters. You must listen to what I have to say upon this subject, Camilla, if you are not to find yourself languishing on the fringes of the polite world, excluded from the best circles. Ostracised and derided, no less!'

Camilla couldn't help laughing at this dramatic picture. 'I do not think it will come to that.'

'Not your name nor your fortune, nor your youth and good looks will save you if you acquire a reputation for speaking your mind on subjects about which an unmarried girl is supposed to know nothing. And, as to everyone knowing why you quarrelled with Sir Sidney, you may be sure that the Fitzwilliams have taken care to maintain that you broke off with Sir Sidney at their instigation.'

'That is nonsense. Mr Fitzwilliam was furious with me. Votes lost, family made a laughing-stock, jilts cast into the wilderness – I had it all.'

'That was before Sir Sidney decamped to Italy. Now Mr Fitzwilliam tells a different tale.'

'Does he? Then I despise him for it, even more than I did for his caring more about votes than for my making a disastrous marriage.'

Mrs Gardiner raised her hands, warding off these rebellious ideas. 'My dearest girl, not so high, if you please. You are too vehement, you show too much of what you feel. Always a good face on everything, remember, and, at your age and in your situation, the face must also always be an innocent one.'

'Ignorant, you mean.'

'I do, and do not despise my advice. It is well meant, and I do know what I am talking about. It is true that in the very highest circles – in the top ranks of the aristocracy, among your Hollands and Spencers – young girls are allowed an astonishing amount of freedom in what they they say and think and even do, but, thankfully, you do not come from quite that level of society.'

Camilla saw that Mrs Gardiner was genuinely upset by her attitude, so she apologised, said that her tongue had run away with her, and indeed, she was careful about what she said when with any other than her intimates.

'Oh, my dear, do not imagine for a moment that your intimates are to be trusted.'

'I suppose not,' she said with the trace of a smile. 'I am coming to the conclusion that it is better to trust no one at all.'

'Now, that is not the case if you are thinking of men, as I know you are. Not all men turn out to be such sly, unnatural wretches.'

There was another reason for Camilla not objecting to being Sophie's companion, for if it hurt to be surrounded by the wedding preparations at the Gardiners' house, it was even more painful to be in company of her sisters in Aubrey Square.

Letty wasn't the problem. She was at her most disagreeable, it was true, still prosing about the frivolity of London life, still rebuking and criticising her younger sisters, but she was so involved with an ever-increasing number of societies and organisations and with Mr Valpy that Camilla saw little of her, and was able to keep on reasonably good terms with her. And it had to be said to Letty's credit that she was a dutiful guest, quite prepared to attend such parties and dances and functions as Fanny accepted on her behalf, and turning herself out like the beauty she was. Her aloofness brought her a number of new admirers, none of whom interested her at all. Unless a man were very caught up in the Evangelical movement, she felt he must be a flibbertigibbet or a moral simpleton.

The trouble lay, as so often, with the twins. Completely given over to the distractions and amusements of the London season, they filled the house with their talk and thoughts of love, of beaux, of this man as compared to that man. Freely expressed admiration, likes and dislikes, yearnings for some particular man, envy of other girls who had taken some favourite's fancy all rang through Fanny's elegant rooms.

'Fanny, I shall die, did you not notice that Mr Walmsley only danced one dance with me last night, and that a polka? And he stood up with that odious Amelia Fanshawe twice, and took her into supper. What can he find to admire in her, with her long face and feet?'

'Belle has no reason to complain, for Sir Joshua Mordaunt never so much as glanced my way, let alone asked me to dance.'

Fanny was shocked. 'My dear Georgina, he was there with his wife. You must not be making eyes at married men, it will not do.'

'He does not behave like a married man, at least not when his wife – and she is so odd, did you not think so? – is buried away in the country where she belongs. Why cannot she take herself back there, what business has she in London? Or, as she is French, let her go to France for a good long visit.'

'Pray do not let Mr Fitzwilliam hear you run on so,

Georgina. I know you are only funning, but he will not be amused at all by such sentiments, let me tell you.'

'Lucky Georgina, not to have Barleigh Barcombe dogging her steps. He sat and stared at me for quite half an hour at the Farquahar's drum. I longed to cross my eyes or stick out my tongue. No, Fanny, I did not do so, for Harry Salterton was there, the handsomest man in the world, and I would not for anything have him see me looking less than my best.'

'It is no use your setting your cap at Salterton.' Georgina had no compassion where her sister was concerned. 'For I had it from Rampton that he is to marry Sally Hawkshead.'

'What, that ugly little creature? What a waste of a man. Why ever should he wish to marry her? You must be mistaken.'

'Sally is a charming girl,' said Fanny. 'She will inherit everything from her uncle, who is very rich, and has lands that march alongside the Salterton estate. It is a good match for both of them.'

Belle was unrepentant. '*Tant mieux* if the children inherit her looks and his sense, is all I can say.'

The door knocker was never still. Billets-doux, posies, invitations and callers were constantly flowing through the house. Fanny loved it, despite a lurking feeling that the twins should not be encouraged in their already intense emotional lives. However, this bustle and frivolity was what she had expected when she had invited the girls to stay during their parents' sojourn abroad and she was delighted with the life and excitement that Belle and Georgina generated. True, they were not formally out, but you could hardly keep two such girls shut away. They were so admired, wherever they went, and they cast the older beauties quite in the shade.

It might have been different if Letty and Camilla had been more obliging as far as romantic adventures were concerned. They were a sad disappointment, however. Fanny had been thrilled by Camilla's attachment to Sir Sidney and distressed by its unfortunate outcome. Of course she felt for Camilla, only she could see that it would be a long while before she re-entered the ring, as Mr Fitzwilliam unkindly put it.

★

Mr Fitzwilliam pulled the covers irritably over to his side of the bed one night after he had joined Fanny in her bedchamber.

'It is no good, Fanny. Camilla is as obstinate a girl as ever I met, and she is not the kind of young woman to attract the men so easily. They are scared of her.'

Fanny rescued the last six inches of the sheet, all that was left to her. 'What nonsense. Why, when she is in looks, with those sparkling, expressive eyes, her grace of movement and her lively countenance, she is as attractive as any girl in London.'

'I dare say, only she is not in looks these days, is she? She's moping, that's what. If she does not give over thinking of might-have-beens and settle down to finding herself some other man to fancy, she will end up an old maid.'

'Not Camilla! Not with her spirit, and her fortune!'

'Her fortune is not to be sniffed at, I grant you, only men think she is bookish. I have warned you about that, Fanny; there is nothing turns a man off quicker than a whiff of learning about a young woman. Let her follow the twins' lead. They are as pretty a pair as you could wish to see.'

'They are flirts,' said Fanny crossly.

'And so they may be, with their looks and charm. Of course they flirt, but they mean no harm by it. The men flock to be with them, it is only natural that they should make the most of their opportunities. They are giddy girls, but they will settle down soon enough. Mark my words, they will both make excellent matches, while Letty settles down with that underbred clergyman of hers – a sad state of affairs, but I wash my hands of her, she will not listen to a word of advice. I have no patience with her these days, and to write to Darcy as she did! And as for Camilla, she will dwindle into an aunt and end her days running round after her brother's family at Pemberley, I am sure of it. If he will have her there, which may be open to doubt, unless she puts some honey on that tongue of hers.'

'You make her sound shrewish and spiteful and viperish, and she is none of those things.'

'She has a look about her as though she could see right through you. I do not like it, and I do not suppose any other man does, either. Or woman if it comes to that. Now, pray be quiet, Fanny, you are keeping me from my sleep.'

He stretched out a hand to seize the rest of the sheet, and it came to rest on his wife's silk shift. He rested it there for a moment, then slid his fingers upwards to the pretty breasts that so stirred his senses, and forgot all about sleep, the Darcy sisters, suitors and everything else besides.

TWENTY-ONE

Lady Warren was yawning her way through a humid, stuffy afternoon. Last night had seen her at a *levée*, two receptions and a ball, and even she, with more than her fair share of energy and stamina, was beginning to feel fagged from the relentless strain and demands of the London season.

Her stepson's firm steps outside the door caused her face to brighten. 'Come in, George, I am dull today, so I am delighted to see you. What news? You weren't at the Christchurch ball last night, I had thought to see you there.'

'No, I didn't feel like polite company, so I went slumming it round a few taverns.'

Lady Warren never had the least wish to criticise her step-son for the darker side of his social life, which he took no trouble to conceal from her. She took a vicarious pleasure from it, in fact, aware that, if she had been born a man, her own tastes would as likely as not have driven her to frequent those same low haunts.

'We ended up at Amy Wilson's.'

'One of the *demi-monde*?'

'Oh, a high flyer, quite above my touch, she is in Argyle's keeping. Her sister is the real dasher, though; Harriette – you've heard me speak of her before. What eyes! Wellington is one of her protectors, they say, although I fancy he visits her privately. I've never seen him in company with her.'

'Well, I am glad you had a good evening. I won't ask if you met Miss Camilla Darcy during your round, for she doesn't move in those circles.'

They both laughed heartily at the delightful if unlikely notion of one of the Miss Darcys coming upon the town and sinking into social oblivion among the frail sisterhood.

An unlikely scenario, although, as Lady Warren observed, it was a fate that had nearly overcome Lydia Pollexfen, when she was a mere Miss Bennet. 'For she ran away with Wickham you know, and lived with him before they were married. They never would have been married at all if Darcy hadn't gone seeking them out in his interfering way. So unnecessary. If only he'd left well alone, Wickham would have taken off with some heiress, and Lydia would have had no option but to seek another protector.'

'Really?' said George, who liked even old scandals if he knew the parties involved. 'That would have stymied the sisters' chances in the marriage market. Not even your good-hearted brother would have married into a family with such a disgrace hanging over them.'

'Oh, he is such a fool I dare say it might have made no difference. I do wonder about Darcy, though, for he has always been so proud.'

'In which case there would be no pert and forward Miss Camilla for me to take down a peg or two, and I should miss my fun.'

'You have met her, of course. Are you not charmed by her?'

'She is not my type. I observe her closely, see what she is about, and shortly I shall move in for the kill. I promise you, Caro, within a very little time, you will see her aristocratic name dragged in the dust. How will Darcy take that news when it reaches him in Constantinople? I'd like to think of him taking his pleasures there among the women who are truly a delight, but I suppose he is too strict in his ideas. A boring fidelity hangs about that family.'

'Who is it from?' asked Belle. 'Georgina, Fanny, look, Camilla has a note!'

'From an admirer?' asked Georgina. 'What a surprise.'

'You may read it, since you are so curious,' Camilla said, tossing it to Belle.

'Oh, Lord, it is only from Sophie. I would not forever be

demanding your company if I were her. Why does she not ask us to go with her for a change?'

'Mrs Gardiner would not consider you suitable escorts,' said Fanny.

'Why should she need an escort?' Belle shook her head in disbelief. 'Catch me asking for an escort if I were driving out with a beau! Camilla may like playing gooseberry; however, I think it is strange.'

'And why does she want to call on Mrs Rowan?' said Georgina. 'She is the oddest female, and everyone knows she is Mr Portal's mistress. I'm surprised Mrs Gardiner finds her respectable enough for Sophie to visit, she is such a stick in the mud about that kind of thing.'

Fanny was quick to suppress this kind of talk. 'Nonsense, Mrs Rowan is perfectly respectable, and you must not speak of her being anyone's mistress, such a suggestion is wholly improper.'

The twins shrugged, exchanged scornful glances, and then, with the note only being from Sophie, and there being no man in the case, they lost interest.

'If Mrs Gardiner wishes you to go, perhaps you should,' said Fanny. 'Only I do wonder at it. Are you sure you do not mind?'

'Not at all.'

She did not say so, but Camilla, too, found it odd that Sophie should want to attend one of Mrs Rowan's gatherings. They were not at all the kind of affair to appeal to Sophie, and she was sure she would find the company a sad bore.

Mrs Gardiner was not bothered, nor, apparently, surprised by Sophie's request. 'For Mr Wytton is often there, is he not? It is only natural that Sophie should like to spend time with him among his closest acquaintances. I don't doubt that is the sort of company at which he is most at his ease, for although he is an excellent dancer, and appears to advantage at any dress function, there is no denying that he is a clever man and enjoys more stimulating companions than are generally to be met with at ballrooms and routs and so forth.'

Aloud, Camilla could agree that Mr Wytton clearly enjoyed the hours he passed at Mrs Rowan's house; privately, she could think of nothing more boring for Sophie than the discussion of books, art, politics and travel that were the order of the day among Mrs Rowan's visitors.

Wytton was surprised to see Sophie come into the room with Camilla. Surprised, and not altogether pleased. He realised, with a sense of self-mockery, that he regarded Mrs Rowan's rooms as part of his masculine world, the part of his life Sophie could not share. Which was absurd, for women were always present at Mrs Rowan's gatherings, and he tolerated them well; even Miss Camilla Darcy, whose presence had at first bothered him. He had not thought her a blue-stocking, he had told himself, she would find herself shockingly out of place, she would be uncomfortable – but at least she would not come again. Only she had, and seemed to hold her own very well. He had to admit that she had a knack of talking in the most lively way to Mrs Rowan's male guests without a hint of coquetry in her manner.

Not that he hadn't noticed that she earned herself many glances of approval, and warmer looks, even, among the men who came to discuss and amuse and be amused. There was no flirtatiousness, however, on her side. And that didn't stem from a naturally serious disposition, he had several times seen her flirting with evident pleasure and enthusiasm at parties and dances. Sophie had commented on her cousin's behaviour more than once, and in no very favourable terms. Wytton laughed at her disapproval, saying he was sure that Camilla was casting out no lures for a husband, and that she had no desire to snatch away a beau from under a friend's nose, as so many young ladies were inclined to do.

He felt uneasy at Sophie's presence. Whereas he had no doubt of Camilla's ability to fit in well with the company, he felt that Sophie would be at a loss, and would show up badly. Unless, of course, she chose to converse with that dolt Allington – God alone knew what he was doing there.

If Camilla had wondered at Sophie's wishing to attend, she was even more astonished to discover Captain Allington among those present when they entered Mrs Rowan's sumptuous and crowded rooms. What in the world could have brought him here, of all places! No one could dislike the Captain, but not even his dearest friend could deny that his intellects were moderate, and this kind of company was not the sort where he would show to best advantage. Still, Camilla was always pleased to see him, and put out her hand to him with one of her warmest smiles.

He greeted her with enthusiasm, and said how happy he was to see her. 'I have come to pick Mr Portal's brains,' he explained. 'For my regiment is likely to be posted to India, and he is a great expert on the subcontinent.'

'To India! How I envy you such an opportunity. Are you not delighted by the prospect?'

He hesitated. 'As a soldier, in times like these, with Napoleon vanquished and no possibility of another European war, I should be glad to be posted to where we may see some action.'

'Only you are not?'

'In truth, Miss Camilla, I am not cut out for a soldier. It is my chosen profession, and as a younger son with no fewer than four brothers older than me and two sisters to be provided for, I must have a profession, I have to earn my bread. I had little choice: it was the Church or the army. I am not clever enough for the law.'

Camilla thought of his dutiful attendance at the Reverend Valpy's service. Any man who could endure to listen to Valpy preaching for more than five minutes must have a strong religious bent. 'Would you not have preferred to go into the Church?'

'Two of my brothers are in holy orders. Livings are hard to find, and such family influence as we have has been directed to securing their future in the Church. Another brother is in the navy, but I should like that no more than the army, less, in fact, for I have to confess I suffer most dreadfully from seasickness.'

'Come, come!' said Mr Portal. 'That's no obstacle to a career upon the seas. Nelson was always seasick for the first few days at sea.'

'Oh, I know, but in my case it is not merely a matter of a few days. I travelled out to the West Indies, and was sick for the whole journey, and all the way back.'

'Then the prospect of a voyage out to India must be off-putting, I do see that,' Camilla said. 'However, it is not a lifetime, only one journey. I recommend you consult Dr Molloy. He will have many friends among naval surgeons, and they should surely know one or two excellent remedies for the seasickness. With favourable winds, you will soon be secure upon dry land once more and only think of how much there will be to see and do! The people, the customs, the different landscapes, the abundance of animal and plant life, all of it quite strange to you.'

Portal laughed. 'Why, Miss Camilla, it is a thousand pities you were not born a man. What an adventurous life you might have had.'

'It is not just as you imagine it, though,' Allington said. He looked gloomily at her face, alive with traveller's zeal. 'Life in cantonments, a soldier's life, is not the same as that of the free-spirited tourist. India may have all to offer that you say, but I doubt if any soldier will get to see much of it.'

'Tell me, if you do not feel you are intended by nature to be a soldier, what occupation might suit you better?'

He had no doubts about that. 'A farmer. I should have liked above all things to be a farmer. My family comes from a farming country, and I can think of no better way for a man to spend his days than working the land. I should breed horses, too, if I had the opportunity.'

'You are in fashion there,' said Mrs Rowan. Her voice was sympathetic. 'So many of our great landowners now choose to live and work on their estates.'

'Great landowners, yes,' said Allington. 'Only not poor fellows like me, without an acre to our names.'

No one there could disagree with him, and no doubt many of them felt for his predicament. However, it was the way of the world: younger sons had to fend for themselves, and land was there to be passed down from eldest son to eldest son, not to be parcelled out.

Camilla knew of several others in the same case, younger sons of neighbours in Derbyshire. Perhaps it was, after all, preferable to be a woman than an impoverished younger son – at least, to be a woman with a good portion, when the right marriage might open all kind of unexpected doors to a new life. Although, more often than not, the landowner's daughter married another landowner, the bishop's daughter would marry a parson, an aristocratic girl would remove from her father's great house to her husband's similar one, and where was the change there?

Some did move from one milieu to another. There was Sophie, for instance. The daughter of a rich, successful merchant, even of such a gentlemanlike one as Mr Gardiner, would nearly always make a match outside that world. As Sophie had done. Her father's wealth and her fortune – combined with more than usual prettiness on her part – had given her the entrée into the world where birth and family counted for more than ability.

She knew she could hardly understand the social unease that pushed a Sophie out of her circle and into another. She and her sisters had the name, the connections, the great family behind them, and her cousin didn't. So it was easy enough for her to dismiss all that as not being of vital importance. But it mattered to Sophie's parents that their grandchildren would belong as of right and birth to a higher social order than theirs. The Gardiners were modern in their outlook, they would never have forced Sophie into an unwanted match solely on grounds of social advancement, but Wytton was perfect for both daughter and parents.

Wytton was fortunate enough to be an eldest son. Allington would inherit next to nothing. Yet he had youth and energy enough to make his way in the world, and the freedom and opportunity to do so if he wished. He was, in her opinion, better off than young ladies who had no choice of occupation. Marriage or spinsterhood were their lot.

That was not something to dwell upon, so she put the depressing thoughts from her and turned her attention instead to Sophie. She had been cornered by Piers Forsyte, a poet with a long angular frame, a lugubrious expression and an unstoppable flow of words. Captain Allington was standing close by her, and she was sending him such a look of appeal that Camilla almost laughed out loud. There was a rescue mission for the gallant soldier. Anyone who could deflect Mr Forsyte in midstream was a brave man indeed.

'Ah, you see, the Captain has cut Mr Forsyte out,' said Mrs Rowan, her eyes full of amusement. 'He has great address, if not many brains. What a nice young man he is, what a pity he has to go to India, where very likely he will succumb to some deadly fever.'

Sophie stiffened, and her smile of thanks to Captain Allington died away. For a moment she looked quite forlorn, but then she smiled again, thanked Mr Forsyte for enlightening her about the low value she should place on the works of Mr Wordsworth and presented a polite and neutral countenance to Captain Allington. He looked rather startled at the change that had come over her, ventured a light-hearted remark, which was met with a stony look, and retreated.

'Pagoda, do go over and talk to Miss Gardiner,' Mrs Rowan said. 'Before someone else takes the chance of boring her to death as poor Forsyte was in danger of doing.'

'She don't want to talk to a man of my age,' said Mr Portal. However, he rose dutifully and went over to Sophie.

'Now, you see, I shall cut out all the eager young fellows and claim you for myself. Won't they be envious, to see me sitting here beside you? Am I not a lucky dog to have the company of the prettiest girl in the room?'

'What a flirt he is,' said Mrs Rowan, her eyes resting on Pagoda Portal's wide back with great affection. 'Now, Camilla, how are things with you? You look rather pale; I know you will not mind my mentioning it. You take plenty of exercise, I am sure, with your habit of walking everywhere, so it is nothing physical that ails you. Perhaps the closeness of the weather and the dirt of London is depressing your spirits? It can be so un-pleasant when it is hot and there has been no rain.'

'Oh, my spirits are not depressed at all,' she lied. 'How could one be depressed in London where there is always so much to see and do?'

'You are worn out with dancing then, that must be it.'

Camilla's laugh was quite genuine. 'Oh, no, you are quite wrong; I am never tired from dancing.'

'Do you go to the Mershams' ball? It will be the high point of the season. When they give a ball – which they only do every three or four years – it is always the most brilliant occasion.'

'Yes, indeed, we are all looking forward to it. Belle and Georgina have received invitations as well; they are wild with delight about it.'

'They will adorn any ballroom, they are so beautiful. What a shame your mother is not here to see their success. I am sure it would make her very happy.'

It was kindly meant, but it made Camilla wince. It was a mercy her mother was not here; she would not be at all pleased to see the twins' headlong pursuit of pleasure and dalliance. And it was an even greater mercy that her father wasn't here, although if he had been, the twins would never have been permitted the social whirl they had thrown themselves into with such zest and she herself might be enjoying her season in London rather more.

'They will marry soon, and settle down,' said Mrs Rowan, giving Camilla a shrewd look. 'Do all your sisters cause you concern? Is that why you are looking so serious?'

'I have come to the conclusion that London is a dangerous place – for young, single women in particular.'

'A dash of danger adds spice to life. Would you care to have them lead safe, dull lives instead of following their natural inclinations?'

'Natural inclinations invariably lead to trouble. The twins will be branded incorrigible flirts and will find themselves cold-shouldered by the very men that would suit them best – if they were looking for husbands, which they should not be, not when they are only seventeen. And as for Letty and her societies and moralising, I don't know what has got into her; she has always had a tendency that way, but not like this. It is all the fault of that toadish Mr Valpy.'

'Such behaviour is seldom anyone else's fault. I expect your sister wanted a refuge from a world in which she found herself at a disadvantage. Her good sense will reassert itself, though, and the scales will drop from her eyes as far as that particular clergyman is concerned. Sooner rather than later, one hopes, since you clearly find her taste for the man alarming. As well you may; he is an odious man.'

Mrs Rowan paused, greeted a new arrival, and beckoned to a servant to bring Camilla some refreshment. 'And how is your musical younger sister? At least you need not have any worries on her behalf.'

Camilla did not share her friend's confidence on that score. 'She has a look of extreme, self-conscious innocence about her these days. Butter wouldn't melt in her mouth. I feel sure she is up to some mischief.'

'She has a good governess. Whatever it is, it cannot be anything serious, or anything that has to do with the outside world. The schoolroom is a blessing.'

'While it lasts.'

And provided that the governess in question did not devote so much of her time and attention to her literary efforts that she did not notice what her charge was up to. Camilla was almost sure that Alethea was doing something she ought not.

She pulled herself up. She was becoming as bad as Letty, with her endless fears and frets about people's health and safety. If this was what living in London did to her, then Letty was right, and she had better decamp for Pemberley as fast as the carriage would take her.

Only not until after the Mershams' ball.

Mrs Beecham's private life was one long scandal. Whether or not this gave her extra expertise in sniffing out the scandalous aspects of other people's lives, as some of her victims claimed, the fact remained that her insatiable curiosity and lively tongue made her feared by most of the fashionable world.

She liked the sense of power this gave her, and therefore went to great pains to see to it that no illicit assignations, no exchanges of words or shots, no lovers in the cupboard or extreme losses at the gaming tables went unremarked. She had a circle of like-minded friends, and delighted in knowing all that went on in the drawing-rooms – and bedrooms, whenever that was possible – of London society.

From the moment she first set eyes on the Darcy sisters, she was on the alert. Four fine-looking, rich girls, new to London, parents abroad – they must put at least one foot wrong, and there was a fair chance of wholesale flouting of the rigid rules of society as applied to young, unmarried women. Especially when two of them were far too young to be out – whatever was Fanny Fitzwilliam thinking of? Those twins combined memorable beauty with a voluptuous air that Mrs Beecham instantly recognised as being certain to lead them astray. No dutiful matches from this pair, oh, no, that was most unlikely.

She had bided her time, relishing the Busby story, licking her lips over the Leigh fiasco, but waiting until the hour was ripe for a mass scything down of any social aspirations or marital expectations they might misguidedly have formed. That they were cousins of that Gardiner chit, who had nothing to recommend her but her fortune, would have been enough to arouse her ire – yet there was more. Darcy, with that absurd haughtiness and pride of his, had once snubbed her with no pretence of civility. Mrs Beecham never forgot or forgave a snub. It would be a pleasure of a rare kind to cast down no fewer than four of his wretched daughters.

How unhappy he and that upstart Mrs Darcy would be when the news reached them in whatever outlandish part of the world they had so foolishly taken themselves off to! How annoyed that fool Wytton would be, to have connected himself with the Darcy family.

Mrs Beecham greeted George Warren with sharp-eyed warmth. She liked him for himself, for his handsome looks and rakish ways, but she valued him most of all for the vicious gossip he so often brought to lay at her pretty feet.

He had a rare liking for a pretty foot, and had recently given her more than a dozen pairs of shoes he had purchased on his travels abroad.

'I know your foot by heart,' he had told her, 'so they will all be a perfect fit, and I wish to see you wearing every single pair, a new one for every time I visit you.'

Which was why, upon hearing his characteristic knock at her front door, she had hurried into her dressing-room to remove from their wrapping of silver paper a pair of exquisite black velvet slippers with tiny glass heels. She slipped them on to her feet and went back to the salon, ready to greet him. Without the shoes to stimulate him, he was not half the man he was when his eyes fell on a prettily shod foot, and she was a woman who greatly appreciated ardour in a lover.

Even gossip could wait while more intimate matters were to be discussed and enjoyed, and it was with an air of great well-being and satisfaction that Mrs Beecham, smoothing down the front of her silk dress, finally asked him to relate the latest news.

'Rumour says that Rampton is thinking of making an offer for Belle Darcy, there are bets being laid in the clubs.'

'Do you think it likely?'

He considered this for a moment. 'Rumour does not take account of her father's likely views on such a proposal. No, no, it's my belief it would take an elopement or a rape to make any such marriage possible.'

Mrs Beecham's eyes lit up. 'Would Rampton take such an extreme course? I know he is in desperate straits, but even so. He is not a brave man, and it might well come to pistols at dawn, do you not think so?'

George shrugged. 'I doubt it. Who is to come flying to defend the girl's honour? Mr Gardiner, the merchant?'

They laughed.

'Or I believe there is a grandfather, a gouty fellow I dare say, no chance of his running to town in his Bath chair to take up the cudgels on his granddaughter's behalf.'

'There is Fitzwilliam, the girl is in his care, and he is one of the finest shots in London.'

'Fitzwilliam will do nothing. He has spoken out more than once on the folly of duelling, and has no wish to appear a greater fool than he is. No, the obstacle to any such action lies within Rampton himself. His manners are too nice for him to embark on such a course, however much he needs to get his hands on a handsome fortune. Besides, even fifty thousand isn't enough to tow him out of the River Tick, if what I hear is true.'

'A pity,' said Mrs Beecham with a profound sigh. 'And there is the other twin pining for Mordaunt, who will do no more than flirt with her. He is far too knowing a man to allow himself to be caught up in an imbroglio of such a kind.'

'Mordaunt is a man who plays his cards close to his chest. I don't suppose his servants—?'

'Clams, every last one of them. Neither bribery nor threats can wring a word out of them. It is too bad; I make no real progress with the Darcy sisters. I had such hopes of Busby coming to London, and then your dear mother dropped some hints, and I had thought that you might lead Miss Camilla a pretty dance and give her a taste of her own medicine – however, she does not take to you, it seems.'

She went across to the mirror and regarded her own, more successful self with considerable complacency. Miss Camilla might possess a pair of large and lustrous eyes, and an equally lustrous bosom, but she could not see the virtue and attractiveness of a man such as George Warren. What a simpleton the girl must be.

'She is not to my taste,' said George Warren laconically. 'No, I have other plans for her. Have you not heard how much time she is spending in Wytton's company? Where he and his affianced go, there goes Miss Camilla Darcy – now why is that? It is noticeable that he appreciates her conversation and that pert way of hers that some call wit. Is she trying to entice him away from her cousin?'

Mrs Beecham considered this enchanting scenario, then shook her head. 'It is too late for anything to cause a rupture there. The settlements are signed, the wedding day arranged and whereas she may jilt her lover, as she did so heartlessly to poor Sir Sidney, she knows that there is no way that Wytton can withdraw from his engagement to that insipid little Sophie Gardiner, however much Camilla Darcy may scheme for it. And take it from me, she knows this as well as anyone, and no doubt has far too much of the Darcy pride to be caught in that trap.'

'She made one mistake with Sir Sidney, why may she not make another one with Wytton?'

Mrs Beecham's eyes had narrowed. 'The chit is unlikely to be in love again so soon, she is full of wounded pride, take my word for it, and is no doubt pining over Sir Sidney, which is a good joke. What a fool she is; well, she will learn soon enough what life is about.'

'I dare say you are right,' said Warren. 'It is a pity. For any such scandal would leave Wytton high and dry, and you would relish that, would you not?'

'I care nothing for Wytton. He was a bore from the beginning.' Mrs Beecham said with a shrug. She turned over Warren's suggestion in her mind. 'Wait. It occurs to me that, while we may be aware of this, others may not. I believe you are right, and that a great deal of harm may be done to her character and to the bride-to-be's peace of mind and indeed to Wytton's reputation if it were to become generally known that she is set on stealing his affections away from her cousin.'

'Capital,' said Warren, pleased. 'I am glad you approve of my scheme. I thought it was an excellent one as soon as the idea popped into my head. Mind you, it will not be so easy. Wytton is generally liked, despite his droll tongue; we should have to employ a good deal of cunning to make a likely story out of it.'

Mrs Beecham's mind was running on ahead. 'Yes, it is a perfect opportunity to blacken Miss Camilla's name still further. She has been branded a blue-stocking, you know, and that is doing her no good at all. She should not go to Mrs Rowan's quite so often.'

'That will all be in our favour. She is not a blue-stocking at all, we can now say with authority; she only goes because Wytton is there. She attends on Mrs Rowan for the oldest of reasons, and the rest is mere excuse. I will be believed when I say this, for I was the one who brought into the open her distressing habit of discussing all kinds of unsuitable subjects with Pagoda and his set. Now I can say that was all a hum, and that it is nothing but a cover for her meetings with Wytton.'

'Perhaps it is so.'

'No, she truly is that worst of prodigies, a woman with a smattering of learning who pronounces upon all manner of topics about which she knows little and understands less.

Wytton is undoubtedly merely one of her audience, bored witless by her prattle, I shouldn't be surprised. However, we do not need to say that. Those who attend upon Mrs Rowan will think it beneath them to refute any rumours they may hear. They are philosophical types, who have minds above such mundane matters.'

TWENTY-TWO

Had Camilla actually seen what she thought she had, up in the gallery? No, it was impossible, she was imagining it, it was a trick of the light, nothing more.

If only the music would stop, and this wretched quadrille come to an end. How hot it was, how glaring the lights and colours of the ballroom. The music was too loud, it thrummed in her head, a tiresome, relentless tune. Why had she ever agreed to dance with this man, what an oaf he was, why did he keep wanting to make conversation when the dance brought them together, couldn't he see that she was not attending to a word he said?

At last the dance was over. The unfortunate man thankfully offered her his arm, ready to escort her back to a seat beside Fanny. She excused herself, almost tearing herself away from him in her haste.

It was a fancy, nothing more, yet she must be sure.

She moved as quickly as she could without attracting attention. But before she could leave the ballroom, the throng of people gathered at the doorway fell back to make way for a small group of new arrivals.

Rooted to the spot, Camilla looked, looked again. Oh, no, it couldn't be!

It was. Where was Letty? Nothing mattered now but finding and warning her sister.

She was too late. At that moment, Letty, dancing with grace and beauty, turned to come back into the dance and found herself face to face with Tom Busby.

And not just Tom Busby, who stood there, beaming with

delight at seeing his old friend, but his wife as well. Petite, dark – oh, why did she have to be dark? – a slighter, more kittenish version of Letty herself – with wide eyes and a soft, wilful mouth. An enchanting creature.

Letty took one look, faltered, lost her place in the dance and stood still, the colour fleeing from her face as she stared first at Tom and then at the woman standing beside him. He stepped forward to greet her, took his wife's hand to lead her forward, and then paused, stunned, as Letty, her eyes a blank, turned round, cutting the pair of them dead, and with unsure, unsteady feet, resumed her place in the dance.

It had lasted no more than a minute. Letty had done well to recover herself so swiftly, but those few moments were enough, the damage was done. She had exposed her feelings, mortification and temper to the whole company; those who had seen the confrontation gave an immediate account of it to those who had missed it, and in seconds the story was flying round the entire assembly.

Fanny was appalled. She knew, better than anyone, what a disastrous encounter it had been. So public! Letty's reaction so quick, so marked. 'How could that man be such a heartless fool?' she said to Camilla. 'He must have addled his wits, however much he seems to have recovered from his accident.'

'Tom never had the least sense, or sensibility,' Camilla said. 'I have no patience with him, no, nor with Letty neither.'

When the dance finished, Letty, her colour still high and a wretched look in her eyes, had come back to where Fanny and Camilla were sitting to ask Fanny to take her home.

'No,' said Camilla, before Fanny could say a word. 'There can be no question of that. You must stay, you smile, you must carry it off by behaving exactly as though nothing had happened. The more you are seen to mind, the more tongues will wag.'

Camilla had ruthlessly sent her sister back into the next dance in the kind and capable company of Barleigh Barcombe. He had been engaged to dance with Camilla, but his understanding was excellent, and it had needed no more than an exchange of glances and a few words before he led Letty away.

'It is better for her to keep moving and think about the dance,' Camilla said to Fanny. 'And, frankly, I do not think I can bear to hear another word about Tom Busby.'

'It is unfortunate that his wife is so pretty.'

'Yes. Letty would more readily have forgiven a plain wife. What business has a Belgian to look like that? I thought they all favoured Anne of Cleves, and here is this exquisite creature come among us.'

Fanny hesitated. 'Tell me, do you think Tom's loss of memory was genuine? For people have been saying, you know, that it was no more than a ruse to slide out of his engagement with Letty.'

Camilla had also heard this suggestion, pure malice in her opinion. 'No, I believe it happened as he said. Tom was forever getting himself into scrapes, but he never lied to get himself out of trouble. He has never been a deceitful person.'

Mr Valpy approached, smooth and sleek and neat, his eyes veiling the curiosity he undoubtedly felt. He sketched a bow. 'Not dancing, Miss Camilla? May I have the honour?'

'Thank you, but I am not dancing at present.'

He raised his eyebrows, pouted a smile, and went off on springy feet.

'Clergymen should be banned from the ballroom,' said Camilla crossly. 'They have no business in such a place.'

Fanny was watching Letty and Barcombe. 'Barleigh Barcombe is an exception, only see how good a dancer he is. He looks quite at his ease at a ball or in the dance. He is a worldly clergyman, to be sure. Of excellent family, that is what makes the difference. He knows how to conduct himself.'

'Not when in Belle's company. He gazes at her like any moonstruck booby.'

'Camilla, you are peevish tonight. Do not dwell on what Letty did; you must not look cross, you know, it will set people talking again. They will say that you, too, are upset by Tom Busby appearing with his wife, and that will only make matters worse. Besides, that fierce look will frighten all the men away.'

'Let them be frightened.'

Camilla recollected herself. Fanny was only trying to make

261

light of what had deeply distressed her, for Letty's reaction to seeing Tom Busby had been more than enough to set all her cousin's social nerves on edge. No one knew better than Fanny what a censorious world would make of Letty's display of emotion. She had no right to add to her cousin's woes; unfortunate Fanny, who had started the season with such light-hearted and happy anticipation of delightful times.

There was nothing to be gained by dwelling on what had happened. Tom and Letty were, after all, stale news, the excitement and talk would die down soon enough, there could be nothing more to say on the subject. And there was little she could do to mend matters, other than to put on a cheerful face and appear in good spirits, unconcerned by her sister's gaffe.

She would not dance with Valpy, no, but the evening was young, many hours must pass before they could leave the ball without causing comment, much as she might long to be anywhere but here, so she had best set her mind to dancing and talking and laughing and pretending to revel in the magnificence of the occasion just as though nothing had happened.

First, she must go up to the gallery. A quick glance upwards showed her nothing to cause her concern, she had imagined it, of course she had. Still, her mind would not be at rest until she had seen for herself that her fears were unfounded. She excused herself to Fanny, and slipped round the edge of the ballroom and out of the door nearest to the gallery where the musicians were playing.

A man stepped forward in front of her, she damned him mentally, moved to one side to pass out of his way.

It was Wytton, and he wasn't going to be sidestepped. 'Are you in some distress? Is something wrong?' he asked. 'May I be of any assistance?'

'It is nothing. I thought I saw someone – it is of no importance.'

'Your face betrays you, it is clearly of the greatest importance.'

She hesitated.

'You may trust me.'

His voice was slightly bored, which she found reassuring. He was showing no awkward curiosity, nothing beyond courtesy and politeness. Yet she might be mistaken in what she thought she had seen, and if so, she would be furious with herself for revealing her suspicions to him – and for believing, even for a moment, that her sister could have done anything so *outré*, so unpardonable.

What, though, if it were her sister she had seen? In that case, how could she deal with her on her own? Without assistance, she would only draw everyone's attention and bring about the very scandal she wished to avoid. There was Fanny, but how much better if Fanny knew nothing of what was going on. Once she knew, Fitzwilliam would know, she would be certain to tell him, she told him everything. She shut her eyes at the horror of the thought; of the shocked faces, the scenes, the accusations and condemnations that would ensue.

Had she any right to involve Wytton in what was essentially a family affair? Oh, if only Mrs Gardiner were present. Bother her ankle, bother her not being able to accompany Sophie to the ball. Because she had chosen not to go, Mr Gardiner, also, had stayed at home – with no great reluctance, she supposed. He would have been the very man in such a crisis; why were people never there when you needed them?

Wytton would soon be part of the family. If he were to be outraged by her sister's behaviour, well, then, he could cut himself off from any connection with the Darcys. Sophie was not on such close terms with her cousins as to make daily or regular contact necessary or likely. A greater consideration was that it would put at risk her own friendship with him, a friendship she now realised, it would pain her to relinquish. She could not, however, set that against her sister's pre-dicament. In any event, if her sister's appalling exploit became public, Wytton would learn of it along with everyone else, and if he chose to shun her acquaintance because of it, she could do nothing to prevent him.

'Very well,' she said.

They were standing at the side of the room now, with a clear view of the gallery where the musicians were situated. She raised her eyes, as though she were merely looking around the glittering company, then swept her gaze upwards to the gallery.

It was just as she had feared.

She met her sister's amused eyes for the briefest moment; then the slim, dark-haired figure took a pace backwards into the shadows.

Wytton was looking curiously up into the group of musicians. 'Do you see someone you know up there?'

'That dark youth, standing back from the others.'

'With a flute in his hand?'

'Yes.'

'What of him?'

'That is my sister Alethea.'

Wytton's reaction was as swift as it was surprising. He gave a shout of laughter and then moved at great speed towards one of the doors further along from them.

She followed him, a wavering, social smile pinned to her face, hoping they were not as conspicuous as she felt they must be. 'What—?' she began.

'Your sister sees that we have recognised her. She will try to slip away. To do so, she must come down the stairs to the side of the gallery. They are this way.'

They were just in time, for as they reached the foot of a spiral staircase, Alethea came flying down. Wytton put out an arm to block her way. She stopped, apparently quite calm, and looked at them with dancing eyes.

'The devil, you spotted me, and now you've caught me.'

'Alethea!'

'Hush,' said Wytton. 'Keep your voices low! Do you want the whole room to hear?'

Camilla looked Alethea up and down. Her sister was dressed in black breeches and stockings, with a serviceable if worn velvet jacket and a slightly tatty lace jabot round her throat. Just like the other musicians, and so like a boyish young man that she was amazed.

Wytton was laughing again. 'No, I shan't let go, or you'll be off. You've been discovered, so give in with a good grace, and be glad it is your sister and I who are here and not Lord or Lady

Mersham. Do you have any notion what trouble those musicians would be in if your disguise were discovered?'

Alethea gave him a startled look. 'It never occurred to me.'

'Many things seem not to have occurred to you,' said Wytton. 'The question is, what are we going to do with you?'

'I shall slip away, no one will notice. I can take a hackney, or walk, and go back to Aubrey Square.'

Camilla gave a cry of dismay. Even she, with her propensity to shun convention and take herself about town on foot and on her own, would never dream of venturing out alone after dark, let alone taking a hackney carriage. 'In London? At night? Alethea, have you taken leave of your wits?'

'It is not yet quite dark.'

'And that makes it all right?'

'No one will know I am not a young man and I am not alone, Figgins is here.'

Camilla looked round the small lobby. 'Is she wearing men's clothes, too? Apart from a cloak of invisibility?'

'I mean she is here, in the house. Dressed as a man, yes.'

'Can you find her?' Wytton asked.

Alethea nodded.

'Then do so. Discreetly, if you please.'

'And I warn you, Alethea,' Camilla said in a ferocious whisper, 'that if you do not do exactly as we say, I shall write to Papa even before the night is out.'

Alethea looked alarmed for the first time. 'You wouldn't!'

'I would. I may have to in any case, if we do not somehow manage to get you out of this scrape without it becoming the talk of the town. You silly goose, whatever made you think you could get away with such a mad scheme?'

'I have until now,' she retorted, and vanished through the door that led to the servants' quarters.

Wytton and Camilla stared after her.

She could feel her heart thumping. Until now? What in heaven's name had Alethea been up to? Could Griffy be so remiss as to have allowed other escapades?

'An astonishing girl, your sister,' said Wytton, and she caught the note of admiration in his voice.

She turned on him. 'This was the stupidest prank to play, as you must be aware. She is not astonishing, just foolish and naive.'

'She does not seem naive to me. And she plays the flute very well. I was not aware she played that instrument.'

That was why she had been practising and playing the flute with such dedication since they came to London. What company had she been keeping? How long had she been sneaking out of the house in men's clothing? How had she got away with it without being noticed?

All these questions tumbled through her mind, together with an unreasoning rage against Miss Griffin. A rage she knew was unjustified. They should not have depended so entirely on Miss Griffin's ability to control the vagaries of a sixteen-year-old, who was as self-willed as she was cunning. Alethea was a law unto herself, and always had been. It had made life less complicated for her family to consider her still a schoolroom miss; they should have known better.

Alethea was in some ways, she had to admit, much older than the twins, and far more resourceful, even if she had no more sense than the flighty pair. Like the twins, she had outgrown the schoolroom; unlike them, her desire to venture into the wider world was private, had been carried out in the utmost secrecy, and was not, thank God, driven by interest in the male sex but rather by a spirit of adventure.

Wytton, meanwhile, was turning his mind to practicalities.

'As long as her maid is with her, I can take her home.' He raised his hand to silence her protests. 'Do not make a fuss about it, it is a short enough journey, and I shall go and return within half an hour. No one will even notice my absence. The only problem is how she may get into the house in Aubrey Square undetected.'

'In exactly the same way she came out and has returned on her previous excursions, I dare say.' Her voice was pure acid, and it won an appreciative smile from Wytton.

'My word, you are angry indeed. I would not be in your sister's shoes for anything. I am surprised she risked incurring your wrath.'

'Would not you be angry if one of your sisters had behaved in such a way?'

'I am afraid my sisters, although dear girls, are dull by comparison with the Darcys.'

'You are being deliberately obtuse.'

'Not at all. Merely truthful. I thought you were impatient of convention. Would you rather I uttered a few insincere and platitudinous phrases of disapproval?'

'It would be more appropriate.'

He looked her straight in the eye.

She could not hold her gaze steady, and so took a different tack. 'And I should not be here alone with you, that is enough to set all the gossips' tongues wagging.'

'Let them wag. Oh, very well, if it worries you, return to the ballroom; we have not been gone above a few minutes, and I doubt if we were observed. Our disappearance coincided with the arrival of Prinny, in case you did not notice it. How unlike our fat prince to be of use to anyone, but on this occasion he provided an admirable diversion.'

'Are you making that up?'

'Would I do such a thing? Of course not. Go back in, and you will see him resplendent in all too many dazzling orders holding court among his cronies and hangers-on.'

She couldn't suppress a laugh, although it came out as a muffled snort.

'Go,' he said. 'You may safely leave your sister to me.'

Doubts assailed her. Should she let Alethea go with him, at night, in his carriage? Fanny would be horrified if she knew.

'I assure you, she will be perfectly safe with me. In that get up, her sister hardly knew her; no one will give her a second look, and as for the proprieties, I am not in the habit of forcing my advances on very young ladies travelling in my carriage.'

'Don't be absurd. It is only—'

He touched her hand, the merest brush, but it gave her disproportionate comfort.

'Leave it to me, all will be well. Back into the ballroom with you. Listen, the musicians are striking up for a waltz. I cannot believe you have not a partner for this dance awaiting you.'

'Oh, my goodness, I am promised to Mr Roper. He will be hunting everywhere for me.'

'Then let him find you where he expects to, among the guests and not in here with me and a dubious musician.'

Camilla waited for a moment beside the door, opening it the merest crack. No one was looking her way, there were nothing but silk and satin and velvet backs in front of her; in a trice, she was through, darting forward into the throng of people waiting to take their places for the dance.

To think how she had looked forward to this evening! How happy she and her sisters, even Letty, had been as they dressed for the ball! The twins were all in white this evening, their dresses made in satin and gauze and cut low across the bosom with wide, puffed sleeves. They wore pearls; Letty, very fine in yellow silk, wore a diamond necklace that had belonged to their grandmother, the icy stones suiting her style of beauty.

Camilla preferred darker shades, as dark as was permissible for a debutante, and she had chosen green for her ball dress, worn with a silver underskirt and, round her throat, a delicate chain interwoven with peridots. She looked, Alethea had said approvingly, like a river nymph.

'A naiad,' Miss Griffin said, as she inspected the four girls in their ball finery.

'Don't you wish you were coming?' Georgina said to Alethea.

'Not at all,' Alethea had said, with a swift, secret smile.

A smile that Camilla now understood perfectly. As she twirled round the floor with Mr Roper, her mind only half on his ecstatic admiration of Mrs Rowan's dancing, gown and looks, Camilla wondered what else her sisters might do to make the evening, awaited with such excitement and pleasurable anticipation, even more disagreeable.

As always, once she was on her feet and dancing, she felt better. There was Letty dancing again with Mr Barcombe, how kind he was. She gave him full marks for not letting his eyes roam around the room in search of Belle.

That was just as well, for where was Belle? Her own eyes might roam as they could, but she could not see either of the twins. When the dance ended, she would find them to tell them of what had happened to Letty, if they were somehow unaware of it, and warn them to be on their best behaviour, as sharp eyes would be on the watch for any more slips by the Darcy girls.

Would the twins care? Would it come as news to them? Surely they would already have heard about Tom Busby, and Letty's reaction; no doubt they would think it all a capital joke.

Nonetheless, she would look for them and try to make them understand that this was not a time for them to make sport of Letty.

It proved to be no easy task.

'I don't see Belle, or Georgina,' she said to Fanny, who was engaged in an animated conversation with Pagoda Portal.

Fanny looked up at her. 'Are not they dancing? They cannot lack for partners, they were besieged by men begging for a dance the instant they set foot over the threshold.'

'They have probably gone outside. The night is hot and, there are seats in the garden,' said Mr Portal.

'Yes, and do not be alarmed, my dear,' said Fanny. 'It is all perfectly seemly, the garden here is quite open, there are no dark shrubberies or shaded walks where couples might slip away. You should not be so ready to suspect your sisters of mischief.'

Fanny underestimated the twins' ingenuity in finding places to slip away to. If the garden were indeed open, with no shady corners and sheltering shrubs, then Belle in particular might well be tucked away behind some curtains or in a deserted corner of library or morning room.

She left Fanny and Pagoda Portal, and went further afield, looking into rooms where the doors stood open, first finding herself in a handsome morning room, where a little group of people stared her out of countenance before resuming their talk, and then into the library, a fine room with crimson silk brocade visible on the walls between the floor-to-ceiling shelves of books. There were voices coming from an alcove at the far end of the room, and she advanced hopefully towards them, treading carefully on the slippery Chinese rugs scattered across the floor – did Lord Mersham intend his guests to slide about as though on the ice?

Disappointment. As she drew near the alcove, she found that the voices belonged not to a twin and her companion, but to a tall man with greying hair and heavy-lidded eyes who was talking with her Aunt Lydia. He was telling her what sounded like a scurrilous anecdote while she sat back in a winged chair, listening to him with evident amusement. The man gave Camilla a cool, appraising, calculating stare; the kind of look she had come to dislike so much. She didn't wait for an introduction, but addressed her aunt.

'I am looking for Belle, have you seen her?'

The man answered. 'Miss Belle Darcy, the beautiful fair twin, the one they call Day? She was here some minutes ago, with Rampton.'

'Thank you, sir. Which way did they go?'

'Now, my dearest niece,' Lydia broke in, 'you are not to be following them. When a young couple slip away together on a sultry summer's night at a ball, it is a great piece of folly to try to find them. It is evident what they are up to; let discretion be your watchword. In such a crush, she will not be missed for a half-hour or so.'

'Except by her devoted sister. I assume you are her sister,' said the man.

Camilla could not avoid the introduction, did not take in his name, smiled mechanically at him.

'Have you no partner with whom to sit out the dance, Miss Camilla? A thousand pities! What a waste of a delightful evening for so charming a young lady to be chasing a sister about the place. If you should be about to enquire after your other sister – Miss Night, shall I call her? – I saw her pass by a while ago on Sir Joshua Mordaunt's arm.'

Camilla caught the contempt in his voice, flushed and, murmuring her apologies, went quickly out of the library. So Belle was with Rampton. Well, he might forget himself under the intoxication of being alone with a lovely creature like Belle, but she doubted it. Rampton had an eye to Belle's fortune, and that meant he would take care how he behaved at a ball with her family present. In any case, Belle must look out for herself; short of keeping her locked up, there was little her family could do about her flirtatious and reckless ways.

As for Georgina, could she really have been so lost to all sense of propriety as to slip away from the ballroom with Sir Joshua Mordaunt?

The present Lord Mersham, inheriting a vast fortune and the title upon the death of his uncle had, some years before, set about modernising Mersham House. A man of individual, not to say eccentric tastes, he had determined on top-to-bottom refurbishment in the classical style, his designs part gleaned from his visits to Italy, part taken from Palladio's works.

It was said that there had been columns in the kitchens and wall paintings in the Roman taste even in the housekeeper's room, until the staff had risen in revolt, the pillars had been placed elsewhere and several coats of whitewash applied to the servants' quarters over the bright figures of naked nymphs disporting themselves, which had caused such giggles among the younger members of staff and such dismay to the older and staider servants.

One result of all this was that, to the stranger, all the rooms, anterooms and small chambers seemed alike, with one triumph of marble floors and columns leading to another. In short, Camilla was soon lost, knowing that she had ventured away from the public rooms and was in a part of the house where she had no business to be.

She came at last to a circular hallway, with an elegant staircase rising in a flourish to the floor above, and several curved doors, each a classical perfection of architrave and fluting, all of them closed. She stopped, quite disoriented by now, and with no idea of the way back to the ballroom.

As she was about to turn and attempt to retrace her steps, one of the doors opened and a short, plumpish man in a rollicking good humour came bouncing through, accompanied by a bored-looking woman in a feathered purple toque. The woman was unknown to her, but she had noticed the startling headdress earlier in the evening. These must surely be fellow guests rather than family.

The man had evidently drunk rather more than was good for him, and was insistent that the supper room was this way, that the Mershams always laid out supper in the Venus Salon, you couldn't mistake it, not with that splendid statue perched in the centre of a huge marble table, and see, here was the very door, here in front of them, unless his memory was altogether at fault.

A footman in gorgeous livery and powdered wig stepped forward, but before he could explain that supper was being served in another room tonight, the man had flung open the door. He took a lurching step forward, then stopped so abruptly as to send the woman behind him staggering back.

With a sense of foreboding, Camilla started towards the open door, and the three of them gazed into the room, where a couple in some state of disorder were revealed in a close and amorous embrace.

TWENTY-THREE

'Curse you,' cried the man, as he and the woman sprang apart. 'The fiend take you for a set of prying busybodies.'

A few fierce strides, the plump man received a direct thrust from a formidable fist that sent him reeling from the room, and the door was slammed in his face.

'Well!' he said, when he had recovered his breath. 'Did you ever see such a thing? Sir Joshua Mordaunt, as I live.'

'Disgraceful behaviour, monstrous. And at a ball!' The woman's gleeful voice belied the disapproval of her words.

Camilla's swift glance into the room had told her all she would rather not have known. That second or two was quite enough for her – as for the others – to take in the identity of the woman in Sir Joshua's arms. It was Georgina, her violet eyes huge, her face soft, her whole being concentrated upon her male companion.

She retreated, coming to rest behind a pillar. She stood there, eyes closed, trying to shut out the images of her sister and that man – in vain, they seemed to have been etched on her mind. Sir Joshua, a married man. And Georgina in his arms, in full view of a woman who was so clearly a scandalmonger. Dear God, it was as though her sisters had deliberately set out to disgrace themselves this evening in a bout of midsummer madness.

She should go back, knock on the door, demand that Georgina come out. Yes, and arouse the interest and curiosity of everyone in the ballroom. Besides, she had distinctly heard the key turn in the lock after the door had been slammed shut in that drunken man's face.

What a fool Sir Joshua was. Why had he not locked the door in the first place?

She caught herself up; the wrong was in what he and Georgina had been doing, not in the discovery.

No, there was no purpose to be served in deceiving herself. It was hard to admit that one – or even two of her younger sisters might have so little sense of morality that they would engage in intrigues of so ardent a nature. She would have thought that an instinct for self-preservation would be stronger than their passions.

It was evidently not so, at least, not in Georgina's case. Camilla and Letty and her cousins had been at fault, for taking the easy way with an impossible pair, for not packing them off home to Pemberley at the first sign of trouble.

She felt sick with apprehension. It would not take that woman long to find out who the woman with Sir Joshua was, if she had not instantly known, and then Georgina would be left without a shred of reputation. There could be no salvation in marriage; Sir Joshua already had a wife. Loathsome man, to seduce a young, innocent girl, a stranger to the way of the world.

Seduce? She was using words and sentiments straight from a Minerva novel. She could not say whether it was a question of seduction, and if it were, there was no telling who was the seducer and who the seduced. She was in no position to cast stones at her errant sister. If Sir Sidney Leigh had been other than he was, if he had responded in any way to her, if he had felt half the attraction she had for him, and they had been alone together, then what might the consequences have been for her? What then would caution and self-control have counted for?

She found she did not care to examine herself on this point. She knew now what she had not known only a few short weeks before: that virtue was not so easily preserved and morality, sense and reason were but slender defenders against the on-slaught of passion and tenderness, let alone love. That was what your mother and governess and respectable women never told you when they spoke of reputations and good names, of ruin and of fallen women.

All these thoughts flitted through her mind in seconds, and

revelatory as they might be, they were of no help to her immediate predicament. She took another step backwards, hoping to slip away before the man and woman noticed her, and found herself gripped in a pair of strong arms.

She was about to let out a shriek, but was forestalled by a man's voice speaking low and close to her ear.

'Be quiet,' said Wytton. 'Do not say a word. Go back to the ballroom. The door under the stairway will take you there. Leave this to me.'

He released her, and gave her a push, and in a state of disbelief and disquiet, she went through the door he had indicated and, following the sound of music and people, found her way back to the ballroom.

The crowd on the dance floor and the people standing and sitting and talking round the edge of the room were a blur of colour and movement, the candlelight a cloud of flickering flames, the air was stuffy, fetid, full of the smells of hot wax and bodies. Nothing was in focus, nothing was clear or made any sense. What had Wytton seen? What was he proposing to do? Would he storm into the room, challenge Mordaunt to a duel, drag Georgina out and cast her to the society wolves?

What absurd fancies, there was no reason to believe he would do any of those things. Leave this to me, he had said. Leave what to him? Oh, why did he not come back, to explain himself?

Wytton went into the ballroom by a different entrance. He saw Camilla at once, standing apart with an air of aloofness, which he knew to be no such thing, but merely a mask for her anxiety and distress. He moved easily through the knots of people to reach her before she had noticed his entry to the room. She turned, and a little exclamation escaped her as he came to stand beside her.

She must look as though she were enjoying the ball, and had not a care in the world. 'Smile, look animated,' he said in a low voice. He offered his hand to take her into the dance and said in a more normal tone, 'I was promised to Sophie, but I missed my turn, I was not back in time.'

'Oh, but she will be waiting for you,' she said, drawing away from him.

'No, she is over there, dancing with Allington. I expect he saw that her partner had let her down and stepped in, which is very civil of him.'

'You do not mind?'

'Mind? No, I do not mind.' His eyes drifted back to Sophie. Now, she looked animated indeed, and so pretty, with her laugh breaking out and her eyes sparkling with her pleasure in the dance.

'Is Ala—' Camilla began, and then stopped.

'Wiser not to name names,' he agreed. Not with so many eager ears on all sides.

'Is she safely home?' she asked, her voice urgent.

'She is.'

'Without her absence being noticed?'

His hand tightened on hers. She looked up at him, alarmed, until she saw that his face was alight with laughter. She let out a small sigh of relief.

'Not exactly,' he said. 'There was a maid waiting up – your maid, I believe.'

'Sackree.'

'Yes. She seemed to have some inkling of what the young lady had been up to, and took control of her and Figgins in a truly terrifying way. Can she be trusted?'

'I believe so. I hope so.'

There was a pause as the dance separated them, and it was a few minutes before she was beside him once more, and able to ask the question he could see burning on her lips. 'Just now, what did you—?'

'Do not speak of it.'

'That man and the woman in the headdress, they will be running round with their tale at this very minute.'

'They will not. Rory Happiston is already half-cut, and I have settled him in a seat with a bottle of wine; he will soon be under the table and remember nothing of what has happened, except as some dream of inebriation.'

'The woman in the toque was not drunk, however.'

'No, but she will say nothing. She is a distant connection of my mother's; she will keep her mouth shut because Georgina will be my cousin, and her sense of family is stronger, fortunately, than her love of gossip.'

He didn't mention that he had also threatened her with his mother's fury, of which she had had some experience; he had no doubt that she would – regretfully, it was true – forebear from mentioning the luscious scene she had witnessed.

This had been well done, but other forces were at work, and less restrained tongues had been busy on the subject of the Darcy sisters. George Warren's serpent rumours spread their venomous way around the company, hissed from eager mouths to attentive ears.

People turned to stare at Camilla as she left the floor with Wytton.

'May I fetch you a glass of wine, or of lemonade?' he asked politely.

'Lemonade, if you please.' He left her side, and she looked about her for Fanny. Tiresome people, why were they looking at her in this way, and then turning to whisper to their neighbours? Was this the consequence of Letty's behaviour?

Camilla caught sight of Sophie. She had a disconsolate air as she stood beside Captain Allington. She was not speaking to him, but looking down at the floor, seemingly only interested in the rosettes on her satin slippers. There was none of the happiness or radiance of a bride-to-be about her – as more than one sour dowager remarked within her hearing. Oh dear, Sophie must have thought that Wytton had stood her up. Where was the man? He must go directly to Sophie and explain.

The voices around Camilla became suddenly audible.

'Poor child! It is not as though she had been sold to the highest bidder, it was a love match between her and Mr Wytton.'

'Her own cousin, did you ever hear such a shocking thing?'

One of Sophie's dear friends opened her mouth in an O of surprise before narrowing her eyes and giving her opinion in a low voice to another close friend. 'Well, that should pull Sophie

Gardiner down a peg or two, I never did like her, spiteful little thing as she is, and queening it over everyone with her fortune and splendid match.'

'That family are determined to cause one scandal after another. Did you hear what happened earlier this evening? No? Well, I shall tell you. I did not think there was anyone here who had not heard—'

'And the one they call Day. I have never seen such a determined flirt! First one man and then another; a heart as fickle as a cat's.'

'Of course, there was probably more to that attachment between Miss Darcy and Busby than meets the eye. It may have been a boy and girl affair—'

'My dear, they were engaged, positively engaged.'

'And he saw no other way of escaping from a disastrous marriage than the route he took. He could not jilt her, whatever she had done, so he made other plans.'

'Rather extreme, is it not, to spend so much time in Belgium of all places, simply to get away from a girl? Easier to end the engagement, I think.'

'You are a foreigner, Count, you do not understand how impossible it is for a gentleman to withdraw from an engagement.'

'It is so in my country, but here in England everything seems to be possible.'

'Not that. That would cause a really big scandal.'

'And this is not a big scandal, these oh-so-depraved sisters of such great fortune and beauty?'

His companion laughed. 'No, no, my dear Count. This is altogether a delightful tumbling down of a proud family name, but no more. This is improper and shocking behaviour. To end an engagement would be far worse, it would be extremely bad *ton*.'

Camilla wanted to clap her hands over her ears, but there was nothing to be done except to smile and appear unconscious of the malicious talk and glances all around her. She wished they had not felt the need to drag Sophie into it. She was not a Darcy, the scandal need not touch her.

Soon, supper would be over, the night would no longer be young; soon, they could go home without their departure attracting any comment. Soon, this dreadful evening would come to an end.

Camilla looked about her for the man who was to take her into supper. He was nowhere to be seen.

She was a little taken aback, but not especially perturbed. No doubt he would hurry up to her shortly, full of apologies. She saw Fanny, a bright spot in either cheek, sitting very upright on a chair set against the wall, and went over to her. As she went past, two or three women turned powdered shoulders to her, a man raised his glass, looked her up and down, and then made a murmured comment to his neighbour. Two debutantes tittered behind their fans and were silenced by their mamas.

She reached Fanny, and took the seat beside her. 'Fanny, what's amiss? You do not look well, may I fetch you a glass of water?'

Fanny's eyes were glittering with unshed tears. 'Smile, for God's sake, smile. Do not ask me what is amiss, but behave as though nothing were the matter.'

Suiting her actions to her words, Fanny bestowed a dazzling smile on an acquaintance going past, and, laying a trembling hand on Camilla's arm, babbled on about fashions and the music and the news from Paris, all with a brilliant smile and over-bright eyes.

'I seem to have mislaid my partner for supper,' Camilla said, unable to think of anything else to say. 'I suppose he will appear in due course.'

'Smile,' hissed Fanny. 'He will not come.'

Camilla was beginning to feel more annoyed than perplexed by this strange behaviour of those around her, including Fanny.

'Then I shall go to the supper room on my own.'

Before Fanny could prevent her, Camilla rose from her seat and moved away. She walked with resolute steps across a ball-room that seemed empty and hushed; she had the sensation of being watched by dozens of pairs of eyes. Undaunted, she reached the doors, and turned round to flash a quick glance at the expectant faces all about her.

A plain girl sidled up to her, a fellow debutante, what was she called? Selina something, not a girl she had ever found interesting or amusing company.

'Never mind them,' she said, taking Camilla's arm. 'I shall come into supper with you.'

So Selina had no partner. Well, she was plain, and had a malicious tongue to go with her very ordinary looks and blotchy skin.

'I do not believe a word that they say,' Selina went on. 'I have told everyone who asks me that you are devoted to your cousin Sophie and of course you would not dream of casting your eyes in Mr Wytton's direction. I mean, apart from anything, Sophie has ninety thousand pounds. My mama said the same. "What man of sense," she said, "would exchange ninety thousand pounds and a pretty face for a mere fifty thousand and only a moderate degree of beauty?" Not that I don't think you pretty also, but dear Sophie is so very pretty, is she not? It is all lies and scandalmongering, that is what I have told everyone, for Mr Wytton is far too much of a gentleman to break Sophie's heart; why he would not do such a thing – and certainly not at a cost of forty thousand pounds. It is not such an inconsiderable sum that a man could be throwing it away any day of the week as if it did not matter. That is what my mama says, too.'

Camilla tried to disengage herself from Selina's tight grip on her arm. 'Excuse me, but I am not going into supper yet.'

'No, for you were engaged to go down with Snipe Woodhead, only he is nowhere to be seen, and I heard him say that he did not care to be seen with a girl who would behave in such a manner and try to cut out her own cousin, and one who had been a friend since childhood. If I might have spoken to him, which I could not, of course, I would have said to him that he entirely misjudged you, that close as you are to the Gardiners, you would never serve them such an ill turn as to take Wytton away from Sophie.'

Now, finally, Camilla did manage to draw away from Selina. Her eyes were too bright, she knew, and her heart was thumping so that everyone must hear its wild beats.

'I do not know what you are talking about. Excuse me, I see someone who—' She fled, almost falling into the arms of a disturbed-looking Barleigh Barcombe who was standing at the head of the stairs.

'Mr Barcombe, do you know – have you seen any of my sisters?'

His face softened as he saw her distress. 'I do not know where Miss Darcy may be. Miss Georgina is with your aunt, and Miss Belle—' He paused, his mouth tight. 'She is in a little chamber off the ballroom, surrounded as usual by numerous advisers. When I left, she was informing her attendants that the last man in the world she could love, let alone marry, would be a clergyman. Clergymen are stuffy, unfashionable, tedious men, always preaching morality and criticising women.'

Even in her agitated state, Camilla was touched by the pain in his voice. 'Pray, Mr Barcombe, do not take Belle's words too much to heart. She is young and thoughtless and means little by these kinds of dramatic outbursts and proclamations.'

'You are very kind, but I believe she meant what she said. It is not the first time she has attacked me as a man of the cloth. I did hope that it was my profession rather than my person that offended her so, but tonight I see that any warmer feelings have only been on my side. I am nothing but a black-coated bore in her eyes.'

Camilla took his hand and pressed it. 'I am so sorry. She would never have done for you, you must believe me when I say so. She is not good enough for you.'

'You are a rationalist, Miss Camilla, and I admire you for it. But reason cannot dictate to our hearts, however much we wish that it could.'

They stood for a moment, hands clasped, and then she gently detached herself. 'You should not be with me, Mr Barcombe; you will not wish to be seen in my company.'

He raised an eyebrow. 'Why not, pray? Is my rejection by your sister any reason why we should not be friends?'

'Oh, friends. I do not think that I or my sisters have a friend left in the world.'

Except for Wytton, whose actions this evening had gone far

beyond what could be expected of any friend, and whose name she had now, through no fault of hers or his, dragged in the mud.

Mr Barcombe gave an elegant bow. 'I trust I shall always have the honour to be numbered among your friends.'

'My dear sir, have you not heard what they are saying about me? And you yourself have seen the – misfortune is the kindest word I can think of – that has befallen all of my sisters this evening? It has been a disastrous time for us, and no one mindful of their place in society will want to do anything but be away from our presence as soon as may be.'

'I seldom believe what I hear in the way of rumours, although I understand your alarm. I have never subscribed to that weak nostrum of sticks and stones. As a clergyman, I have to hold by the power of the word, and that goes for the word of foolish men and women as well as the word of God. Now, I see your cousin Fitzwilliam approaching, a most terrible and war-like aspect to his brow. I only trust he is not going to call me out for accosting you.'

For the first time in what seemed an age, this wrung a laugh from her; a laugh quickly suppressed as her cousin began without preamble: 'Where, may I ask, is Letty? For she left the ballroom some while ago, and now Valpy is nowhere to be seen, and Fanny is all of a flutter as to where they may be.'

'Lost, I dare say,' said Barcombe at once. 'Mersham's house is a labyrinth, you know. Let us see if we can find her. And do not worry about Valpy, he is too cautious and wary a man to commit any solecism on such an occasion and in such a place as this.'

Camilla would never forget that nightmare traipse through those same marbled rooms, with her cousin ruthlessly opening and closing doors and drawing aside sheltering curtains, reveal-ing any number of couples engaged in more or less innocent conversation or dalliance. Mr Fitzwilliam's face was red with rage. 'In my day, we never behaved in such a way at a ball. I never saw such improper behaviour in my life before.'

'He must have had Cupid's blindfold on in his dancing days,' Barcombe whispered to her. 'From what I know and hear, people were a great deal more reckless of the proprieties formerly than young men and women are today.'

'That is all very well, but surely he does not expect to find my sister closeted away with Mr Valpy? It would not be at all the thing, and no one is more mindful of what is and is not proper than Letty.'

Whatever Mr Fitzwilliam had expected, what met their eyes as they entered Lord Mersham's splendid orangery was Letty, cowering in the corner of a wrought iron bench and distractedly flapping her hands to shoo away Valpy. He was advancing upon her on his knees, his hands clasped together in supplication, the light of synthetic adoration shining from his eyes.

'Ha!' cried Mr Fitzwilliam, darting forward. Barcombe was there before him, grasping Valpy by the back of his collar and wrenching him to his feet.

The clergyman gave a squawk of protest. 'Unhand me, sir, how dare you treat a fellow gentleman of the cloth in this unmannerly fashion?'

Camilla turned on him. 'How dare a gentleman of the cloth behave in such an unmannerly fashion?' she cried, as she went to the aid of her half-fainting sister. 'Letty, it is all right, we are here. You must pull yourself together.'

'Oh, Camilla, you have no idea, such a dreadful thing, how could he ever have thought—' Her voice dissolved into an inelegant sob of distress. 'He is so bold, to behave in such a way. To me!'

'It is exactly what anyone might have known would happen with all the encouragement you have been giving the wretch.'

'I? Encouragement? Camilla, how could you say such a thing?'

'All those good works, all that time with pamphlets and causes, could you not see what the man was up to? Now, for heaven's sake, Letty, do not have hysterics. You are not to start sobbing and wailing, we have all brought enough harm upon ourselves tonight without your attracting any more attention.' She beckoned to her cousin, who was hustling the unfortunate and incoherent Valpy to the doors that led from the orangery to the garden. 'Please, order the carriages. I will stay with Letty.'

'If you will permit,' Mr Barcombe said, stepping forward, 'I will accompany your sister to where she may wait for her carriage. Does she have a shawl, a cloak of any kind? Do you collect her things, and pass the word to Mrs Fitzwilliam to come with the others as soon as may be. It is early, but guests are already leaving, your departure will not be remarked upon.'

No, it would be expected, the Darcy girls slinking away in disgrace, she thought, as she sped away to find Fanny, hoping against hope that Georgina and Belle and Sophie would all be, for a miracle, where they should be, in the dance or in the supper room, so that they might all slip away with the least possible fuss.

It was not to be. Although her other sisters were indeed in the ballroom, Sophie had felt it incumbent upon herself, as Fanny gathered her little party together, to reproach Belle for being an outrageous flirt.

'Everyone saw, everyone noticed you up to your tricks with all those men. And Captain Allington, too, could you not leave him alone?'

'If Captain Allington chooses to show me some gallantry, what is it to you, cousin?'

Sophie flushed. 'It is improper and unbecoming.'

'When I want lessons in propriety from you, miss, I'll ask for them.'

Their voices were raised, heads turned to see what was going on. Was there to be no end to the evening's misery?

They made their way to the entrance hall, where they waited for the carriages like so many figures upon a stage. The details were etched in Camilla's mind with the utmost clarity: the blue feathers on Fanny's head, the sparkle of Letty's spangled shawl, the delicate silk rosettes on the flounce of Belle's ball dress, Sophie's ringlets lying against her white skin, the sheen on Mr Barcombe's reddish hair, the set of Wytton's coat across his shoulders.

Wytton.

Wytton, who was watching her cousin Sophie, not saying a

word, not moving a muscle, just watching his betrothed with a thoughtful look on his face.

Camilla stared at him, her mouth dry, her whole being transfixed as a terrible realisation came to her. This was not, could not be happening. Dear God, no.

Then the tableau broke up, the carriages were announced, all was bustle and urgent movement, she was up the steps, the door was shut behind her, the coachman clicked to his horse to come up, there, the wheels were in motion, they were rattling away, jolting over the cobbles.

Camilla sank back into the seat, shutting her eyes, oblivious to her squabbling sisters, mindful only of Wytton, of what he might have seen in her eyes. Guilt swept over her.

She had given no cause for the rumours that had circulated so freely in the ballroom, she had made no set at Wytton, had never had the slightest intention of attempting to steal his affections from Sophie, of cutting her cousin out. Until this evening, she had thought of him only as Sophie's betrothed, as someone sharp-witted, often sharp-tongued and frequently amusing. Not as a man whom she might have any connection with or feelings for beyond those of the family tie.

Fool that she was.

Why had she not realised what was happening, and withdrawn before any harm was done? Innocence might be its own reward, but when it bordered on naivety, if not stupidity, it was unforgivable. What damage might not have been done to those that she loved and owed duty and affection to?

She knew now that what she had felt for Sir Sidney had been mere attraction in comparison to this. Her feelings for Wytton had grown, unnoticed, into an intensity of quite another kind.

She had prided herself on having coped with being in love, and having got over the frenzy. She had deceived herself into thinking she was innoculated against any further onslaughts from Eros or Cupid, and in her folly, she had fallen into the oldest and deepest trap of all.

It was a bitter pill to swallow, to have to acknowledge that she was in love with a man forbidden to her by the rules of the world in which she lived. Wytton was in love with her cousin. He was going to marry Sophie.

She thought she had suffered over Sir Sidney? Good God, she would have that pain back twice over, and it would still not touch what she felt now.

'Home at last,' said Fanny in a bright, unnatural voice. 'Letty, Camilla, I wish to speak to you as soon as you are risen in the morning.'

Two days after the ball, and the first pale yellow and turquoise signs of dawn were tinting the sky as the chaise turned into Aubrey Square and drew up on the south side. The clip-clop of four sets of hooves echoed for a moment around the square, then died away. The only sounds to be heard were the clink of the horses' bits as they moved their heads up and down, snuffing the early scents of the morning, and, from the garden in the centre of the square, the tentative calls and chirrups of the birds nesting in the trees.

The black-painted carriage was shrouded in anonymity. Its lamps were not lit, and a cloth had been hung over the panels of the doors, obscuring the coats of arms emblazoned beneath. Inside, a man sat alone, relaxed but watchful, drawn back into a corner and barely visible from the street. The coachman was still and silent on the box, rubbing his fingers up and down the handle of his long whip.

From the house on the other side of the square came the wail of a fretful baby. A light shimmered in a window on the top floor. The cries turned to whimpers, then ceased.

Silence fell once more over the square. A door opened, a figure slipped through, closed it, ran down the steps and across to the waiting carriage. The man was out and down on to the road, holding open the carriage door. A bandbox and an ill-tied bundle were tossed inside, the figure climbed nimbly in, the steps were folded up by the man who jumped in after her, the coachman gathered up his reins and flicked the whip lightly across the horses' backs, the chaise started to move.

★

'Stand to your arms!'

The stentorian bellow awoke Camilla with a start. At the same moment she became aware of someone shaking her shoulders.

'Wake up, miss, do! Here is your sister gone, stolen away in the night, and the master in such a state and everything in an uproar. You must wake up, you are wanted directly downstairs.'

Camilla opened her eyes, fuzzy with the sleep that had taken so long to come to her, focused them on Sackree's urgent, worried face, and blinked.

'Sackree? What is this? What was that shout?'

'It's Mr Fitzwilliam, miss, like he was back in the army, summoning us all to our duties, making us jump about with a yes, sir, no, sir. Here is your wrap, you have no time to dress, or he will be up here, threatening you with a court martial, I shouldn't be surprised.'

'But Sackree, who – which of my sisters – what has happened? A kidnapping? An abduction?'

'Oh, miss, I couldn't say, she's gone, that's all. Best get yourself up as quick as ever you can.'

With that Sackree was gone, leaving Camilla to tumble out of bed, searching with her feet for slippers, reaching out for the wrap her maid had left across the bed.

It was early, although well past dawn. The noises in the square were not those of full daytime; only the first of the street sellers, the cheery whistle of the road sweeper and the plodding hooves of a horse drawing a wagon broke into the stillness of a summer morning.

At this time, within the house, normally only a few servants would be up and about, but today the whole household was astir. As Camilla ran down the two flights of stairs to the drawing-room – no doubt about where her cousin was, his voice was still booming out in a most military fashion – she was glad to catch a whiff of coffee in the air. Fanny began her day with a cup of chocolate, but Fitzwilliam preferred hot, strong coffee, a taste that Camilla shared, especially on such a morning as this, when it seemed she would need to have her wits about her.

Letty, looking extravagantly pretty in a pink silk wrap, rose as she entered the room, and cast herself into her arms. 'Oh, Camilla, what a disaster! Now all is truly lost, whatever is to become of us?'

That answered one question; whichever of her sisters had gone missing, it was not Letty. Not that she had supposed it would be. She removed herself from her sister's clutches. 'Alethea, where is Alethea?'

TWENTY-FOUR

'Alethea is still abed,' said Fanny, looking at Camilla with some surprise. 'She is young and needs her sleep. We have not woken her, she will be unable to help us.'

Thank God! It had been Camilla's first, her most immediate fear: that Alethea had run away. So it was one of the twins who was gone. Well, she should have guessed it would be Belle or Georgina, desperate not to be forced back to the schoolroom and the rural delights of Pemberley.

'We can get no sense out of Belle,' said Fanny. 'She is in her room, in floods of tears. She says she knows nothing about Georgina's disappearance, has no idea in the world where she may be.'

'Pray, Fanny, sit down,' she said. 'Here is your chocolate; drink it, and it will restore you. Tell me what has happened, how did you learn that Georgina had gone?'

Fanny subsided into a sofa, raising a hand to silence her husband. All the authority had drained from him, and he looked tired and worried.

'It was Dawson who came to tell us,' she began. 'Baby is teething again, had been crying in the night, and the nursery maid was attending to him when she heard a carriage come into the square. She had a brief look at it from the window, but without taking much notice, supposing it to be a late-night reveller or an overnight traveller arriving home – it was a chaise, you see. Then she heard the staircase creak, you know how it does, and a few minutes later the front door opened and closed.'

Fanny sipped at her chocolate, then, one hand toying with

the lace on her pretty peignoir, went on with her story. 'The silly girl took fright, thinking of burglars and convinced everyone was going to be murdered in their beds. She let out a squeal, but no one heard except Dawson, who went to see what was amiss, comforted the girl, and sensibly thought to check on Charlotte and then looked in to see the twins, their room being the nearest. Belle was fast asleep, but Georgina's bed was empty, and there were drawers and cupboards open and things strewn all about the room, just as though she had packed in a hurry, as indeed she must have done.'

Camilla let out a long breath. 'She has not been abducted, then, she has gone of her own accord. Was there no note, no message for us?'

'She has gone with a man,' said Mr Fitzwilliam with certainty. 'The waiting chaise, the departure at that hour, the packing, all this indicates an elopement. She left no word of where she has gone, or who she is with.'

Camilla was beyond being shocked by what Georgina had done; there was nothing that the sisters might do that could surprise her.

'It was a mistake to take such drastic measures,' said Fanny, sinking her face into a delicate handkerchief and giving way to the tears she had been struggling to hold back.

The scene in the library flashed visibly before Camilla's eyes: the morning after the ball, with Mr Fitzwilliam pronouncing the sentence of banishment to Derbyshire on all the sisters. And while arrangements were being made, he laid down that Belle and Georgina must remain within doors, receive no callers, and have all their fine new clothes packed away.

'The twins felt the restrictions on them so very keenly,' Fanny was saying. 'Oh, where can she be? She is ruined, she will have not a shred of reputation left, and as for the rest of you—'

'I thought we were already social outcasts, quite beyond the pale.'

'Camilla, do not say so. Time would have softened people's memory. In time, you and the others could have resumed your place in society. A good marriage, you know, would set all to rights, and when your parents are back— However, the case is different now. Tell me, do you know of any man to whom Georgina is particularly attached?'

As soon as he reasonably could, Mr Fitzwilliam hurried round to Sir Joshua's elegant mansion in Sackville Street. There he was greeted by an aloof and uninterested butler, who informed him in frosty tones that his master was not at home.

'Of course he is not at home, not at this hour of the day. However, I must see him upon the most urgent business.'

'When I say Sir Joshua is not at home, I do not mean he is not receiving visitors, I mean that he is not presently in residence.'

'He has gone away?' Mr Fitzwilliam's voice was eager. 'When did he go? Where has he gone?'

'I am not at liberty to disclose details of Sir Joshua's where-abouts. If you care to leave a message—'

'Damn it, you oaf, this is important. How long is he to be away?'

'It is not for me to say.'

Try as he might, Mr Fitzwilliam could gain no more from the stolid figure, and, cursing in a manner most unusual for him, he turned away to go back to Aubrey Square, in the hope that his womenfolk might have got some sense out of Belle. Thumb-screws and hot coals from a brazier might not be out of order; who would have thought a pack of girls could bring so much trouble down on a man? One thing was certain, Charlotte would be allowed none of her cousins' freedom of thought or behaviour as she grew up. Could you still send girls to convents? Until they were eighteen perhaps, or better still, twenty-five or so.

Once Mr Fitzwilliam was out of the way, on what both Fanny and Camilla suspected would be a fruitless errand, the two of them set to work. They felt sure that the twins' maid knew more than she had let on.

Fanny rang for Dawson. 'Dawson, what news have you gleaned from the other servants? Do any of them know anything useful?'

'Sackree is this very minute shaking that wretch so hard that it will be no surprise if all her teeth rattle about in her head,' said Dawson approvingly. 'She's bound to know more than she's saying. Figgins has popped over to the stable to talk to her father and to the stable lads, not something I approve of, hobnobbing with the riffraff out there, but she may learn something of use. One of the footmen knows a man in Sir Joshua Mordaunt's employ – seemingly the under-footman there comes from the same village as he does, so he has run to Sackville Street to see what he can find out.'

In the house in Albemarle Street, Sophie and her mother were taking a late breakfast.

Sophie toyed with a piece of toast, crumbling it in her fingers, brushing the pieces on to the cloth. A glass of milk, still full, stood beside her plate.

Mrs Gardiner was brisk as she drank her tea and looked over the morning's correspondence; she did not want to show the anxiety she felt about her daughter. 'Eat, my dear. It will be a busy day, with the dressmaker this morning to fit your wedding dress, and this afternoon, you know, we are to drive out to Hampton Court.'

'No, we aren't.'

'Aren't what?'

Sophie pushed her plate away, like a child. 'We aren't going to Hampton Court. I don't want to go to Hampton Court, and I don't want to see Wytton. Not today.'

'Such a beautiful day, and the grounds there are always so pleasant to wander in.'

'I don't want to have a fitting for my wedding dress, either. I've already been to Madame Lucie three times. That's enough.'

'A wedding dress must fit perfectly.'

'What does it matter? I shall only wear it for a few hours.'

'That's not true, of course you will wear your wedding dress several times more, when you dine out as a bride. It is expected of you.'

Sophie shrugged, and got up from her seat. 'Silly old tabbies and fusspots. Why should they care how I am dressed? Why should I care for their opinion?'

Mrs Gardiner's attention was diverted as she heard voices in the hall and Sophie made for the door, eager to slip away. Before she reached it, however, it opened, and her father came in, a frown on his face and a letter in his hand.

'Are you not at work this morning?' asked Mrs Gardiner, surprised to see him at this unaccustomed hour.

'I have come directly from there. I have received a letter with the most disturbing news. I must go to Aubrey Square, but I wished you to see it first.'

'Another missive from Mr Darcy, I suppose,' said Sophie. 'I hope you have written to him and told him what a dreadful creature that Belle is.'

'Belle?' said Mrs Gardiner sounded surprised. 'You mean Camilla?'

'They are all the same. There is nothing to choose between them when it comes to men.'

'Listen, I beg of you,' said Mr Gardiner. 'This is not from Darcy, it is from Fitzwilliam, and so ill-written that I can hardly make sense of it.'

'I do not think he can have anything to say that I wish to read,' said Mrs Gardiner. 'Unless something has befallen poor Fanny.'

'No, no, this is nothing to do with Fanny. Read it, read it.'

'Tell me what has happened, Papa.' said Sophie, now very curious. 'Surely my cousins cannot be in further trouble.'

'Very dire trouble, for Georgina has eloped – run away – gone off at dawn in a chaise and four.'

'No!' Sophie clapped her hands to her cheeks. 'She has run off with Sir Joshua, that's what she has done. The slut!'

'Sophie!' cried Mrs Gardiner, looking up from the brief letter. 'You are not to say such a thing.'

'It is the truth. They are all sluts, all of them except for Alethea, and I dare say she will be just the same when she is let out of the schoolroom.'

Mrs Gardiner and her husband exchanged glances. 'You will go round at once, of course,' she said. 'Do you have any idea of their destination?' She quickly scanned the rest of the letter. 'No, I see you do not. Sir Joshua has left London, that is in itself suspicious.'

'Yes, but we are no further forward if we cannot discover when he left and what his destination was. If his servants will not say, I do not know how we can find out.'

'Someone in Fanny's house will know. Never did a girl run away without some member of the household being in her confidence. Her sister, a maid—' She rose quickly from the table. 'Sophie, ring the bell for Jenkins. I shall want the carriage in ten minutes.'

'The fitting is not for an hour.'

'We shall have to forget the fitting for today.'

'So where are you going?'

'To Aubrey Square, of course.'

'Aubrey Square! But why? Yesterday you were going to have nothing more to do with the Darcys.'

'They are family, and they are in grave trouble. The rest is bad enough, but this will reflect on us all, and will, if Georgina is not apprehended, bring Darcy posthaste back to England. He left his daughters in our care as well as in the Fitzwilliams'; Mr Gardiner is named joint guardian of them, you know, while Darcy and Elizabeth are abroad, and a poor show we have made of our duty, between us all. I have been too wrapped up in your wedding. I have left Fanny to cope alone, and with young children of her own, how could she ever take proper care of five headstrong girls?'

As she was speaking, she walked into the library. She sat down at Mr Gardiner's desk, quickly wrote a few lines, sealed the note and handed it to Jenkins.

'Have this taken round to Mr Wytton's house, Jenkins, at once. If he is not at home, the footman is to enquire where he may be found and take the note to him wherever he is.'

'Why are you writing to Mr Wytton, Mama? Does he have to be told everything that happens to the Darcys? Is he so interested?'

'It is to beg him to excuse us from our drive to Hampton Court.'

Sophie's face brightened, at least she had got out of the excursion without yet another argument with her mother.

★

Camilla watched the two women on the sofa, so alike in many ways, so sure of their roles as wives and mothers and protectors of the status quo.

'Well, my dear Mrs Gardiner,' Fanny was saying, 'we know more than we did when Mr Fitzwilliam sent round to Mr Gardiner.'

The twins' maid had, in the end, broken down and confessed that she had known that Miss Georgina was planning to run away, although she didn't know where to, or whether or not she was running off with a man.

'A likely story,' Sackree had said, unimpressed. 'Miss Georgina wouldn't go off in a chaise of her own accord, not at that ungodly hour, without there was some man making the arrangements.'

'Tell us who she's with, you snivelling little piece,' said Dawson, giving the maid another vigorous shake. 'You shan't keep your place here, if I have anything to do with it, or if you do, you'll regret it. We've no time for a dishonest servant. But, if you was to tell the truth for once in your life, who knows? You might be given a character of some kind.'

The sniffs stopped for a moment and the maid's slightly protuberant eyes looked resentfully out from behind a rather grubby apron held up to mop her flowing tears.

'I don't need no character. I'm going home to my auntie, to help on the farm, they'll be glad enough to have me, and when my mistress comes back, she'll take me on again.'

'Your mistress come back!' Dawson's voice was full of scorn. 'Fat chance of that, and what kind of a household might she be setting up, pray, seventeen years old and gone off with a married man?'

'How do you know he's married?'

Sackree edged Dawson aside and put her face only inches from the maid's tearstained one. 'Because she's run off with Sir Joshua Mordaunt, that's how we know, and he has a wife alive and living in Hampshire.'

'Then it's not him as she's gone with, for she said as how she was going to be wed.'

'Not to him, she isn't.'

'Maybe she can marry him abroad. They can do anything there, they are all heathens and Papists.' Then she gave a great wail and buried her face in her apron, inconsolable and beyond any further questioning.

Sackree let her go with a dismissive shove. 'There, Miss Camilla, I don't think you'll get any more out of her, although if you don't mind my speaking frank, Miss Belle knows a deal more than she's letting on.'

And Sackree and Dawson could hardly set about her the way they had done with her maid, although Camilla almost wished they might. It was Alethea, sauntering into the room in her unconcerned way who gave them the information they wanted. 'Georgina will be in France,' she said offhandedly. 'With Sir Joshua Mordaunt. He has a house in Paris and another somewhere in the country. They will have gone there.'

How did Alethea know this?

'I keep my eyes and ears open, and Georgina is such a fool, she thinks I don't understand what she and Belle are talking about. I don't know why you are all making such a fuss. Let her stay away. Without her, Belle may turn into a sensible human being.'

Alethea was dismissed to the top floor; Camilla had no intention of letting either Mr Fitzwilliam or Mr Gardiner hear her most unconventional and unladylike views on her sister's elopement. Did the wretched girl have no principles?

'Surely he must be aware that her family will make every effort to trace her, to bring her back?' Fanny said. 'She is not some unprotected miss, and even if her brothers are still in short clothes and her father abroad, there are others who would not let the matter rest.'

'He will surely not linger in Paris,' said Mr Gardiner, 'and he does not need to with a country house at his disposal. However, he takes only French servants with him, and no one here seems to know where this house is.'

Camilla's opinion of Mr Gardiner was going up by leaps and bounds. He was showing himself to be active and decisive in a way that Mr Fitzwilliam, military man though he might have been, was not. Within minutes of hearing of the possibility of the chaise going to France he had sent men from his office to London Bridge and out along the first part of the Dover road to glean what news they could of a black chaise and four passing by in the early hours of the morning.

Mr Fitzwilliam was deep in conversation with Mr Gardiner. 'It is better that I should go,' Mr Gardiner was saying. 'I have contacts in many parts of Paris, both commercial and private. I have only a smattering of the language, it is true, but that is easily remedied with the help of a trustworthy interpreter. If Fanny is in agreement, I propose that Camilla should accompany me; she speaks good French, I believe, and one of Georgina's sisters should be with her when we bring her back to England.'

France! Paris! She could not believe her ears. 'I? Go to Paris with you? Oh, sir, do you mean it?'

Fanny was horrified. 'Oh, no, it is quite out of the question. It is such a long way, you will be travelling so fast, and then there is the sea journey. It cannot be considered, not for a young and gently nurtured girl.'

Mr Fitzwilliam, Camilla could tell, did not at all take to the notion of her accompanying Mr Gardiner to Paris. Tracing runaways, bringing unfortunate fallen women to their senses and returning them to the bosom of their reproving family was man's work.

'I am not so poor-spirited as that, I hope,' Camilla said. 'Mr Gardiner is right, and since Belle cannot possibly go, it has to be myself or Letty.'

They all knew there was no choice. Letty was so full of the inhalations from her flask of smelling salts that Fanny was beginning to fear for her wits; nobody had the least expectation of her rising from her couch of woe to set forth across the Channel to rescue her sister. 'Camilla must not go,' she intoned from her sofa; her eyes tightly shut. 'For she will very likely fall into worse trouble of her own, she will speak to strangers, and she will be murdered, seduced or entrapped by some Frenchman, I know it.'

Mrs Gardiner cast her eyes heavenwards, and prudently

removed the cut-glass vinaigrette from Letitia's grasp. 'Camilla is well able to look after herself. She will be all the time with Mr Gardiner and will be perfectly safe.'

'Camilla might be able to encourage Georgina to see the error of her ways and persuade her to return,' Fanny said, but her voice lacked conviction. Young ladies who ran away with married men at dawn were not likely to respond to encouragement or persuasion to return to a former life.

Camilla could not but agree with her, it was a vain hope. When had Georgina ever taken any notice of any advice she or Letty had to give? She was not going to express such an opinion, now, though; not while there was even the slightest prospect of a happy outcome.

For Georgina must be aware of how serious her position was. Ruin was an easy word to use, but a terrible state to have to endure. Though if you were in the habit of living only for the present, and had a child's carefree certainty that tomorrow would look after itself, perhaps it wouldn't seem so terrible. And were she to be genuinely attached to Sir Joshua, if there were more than passion involved, and she were actually in love with him, then, to a romantic like Georgina, the world might seem well lost for the sake of love. It would be shocking, to be sure, but comprehensible.

Mr Fitzwilliam was still fuming. 'Encourage! Persuade! What language is this? She must be found and brought back, willing or unwilling.'

'No, no, Fitzwilliam, that sort of an approach will never do,' said Mr Gardiner. 'Take my word for it, young ladies cannot be told what to do or made to come here or go there. Your children are still in the nursery. You will understand the situation better when Charlotte is of an age to have a mind of her own.'

'No daughter of mine shall ever have a mind of her own, I shall see to that.'

Mrs Gardiner raised her eyebrows and gave Fanny a look of wonder.

'This is not about Charlotte,' said Fanny. 'It is about Georgina.'

'It is indeed,' said Mrs Gardiner, 'and if Camilla is willing to go, I fancy it may answer very well. Mr Gardiner has experience in these matters, you know, this is not the first runaway he has had to deal with.'

'It is the first in my family,' said Mr Fitzwilliam.

'No, that is not true,' said Fanny. 'For do not I recall hearing that your cousin Georgiana, when she was very young, only sixteen or so, nearly eloped with a most unsuitable man? And was only prevented by Darcy discovering in the nick of time what was afoot?'

'She did not actually run off with anyone, whatever may have been planned. Like a good girl she confessed all to Darcy, and whatever you may say about him, he took his duties as her brother most seriously. He put a stop to it at once. It was all hushed up, and is quite forgotten by now.'

'Then there was my Aunt Lydia, was there not?' Camilla said brightly.

Mrs Gardiner closed her eyes. 'I do not care to remember that time.'

'Well, then, let us take heart from the family history, for if they make a habit of running away, it has, so far, ended happily,' said Fanny. 'Georgiana never did elope, and Lydia was married within a few weeks, and preserved her good name. I do not see why something of the same kind cannot be managed for Georgina.'

'Dash it all, Fanny, don't you understand? How can she marry Sir Joshua? She isn't a Muslim, you know.'

'No, but perhaps it can all be hushed up. No one will be in the least surprised not to see the girls out and about. Mr Fitzwilliam can tell all his cronies at the club that the twins are indisposed, are keeping within doors. Everyone will assume they are in disgrace; they will not suppose that one of them has gone running off to Paris. As to Mr Gardiner going abroad, it is the best plan, for he is often away on business, and no one will think anything of it. If Mr Fitzwilliam went, it might arouse comment, with an election so close, but he will be here, just as though nothing had happened.'

You had to admire Fanny and Mrs Gardiner, no one could be

more practical. Once the decision to pursue the runaway to Paris was made, they wasted not a moment in blaming or wringing their hands or going off into fits and faints. There was not much show of morality, either, only a fierce desire to salvage what they could of Georgina's tarnished reputation, and keep up a united family front.

And an even stronger if unexpressed wish to put everything right before word got to Darcy of what his daughter had done.

Camilla and Mr Gardiner could not leave that day, for papers had to be obtained – not, in itself, a difficult matter since Mr Gardiner had many contacts in Government departments, but one that took a little time.

'We are twenty-four hours or so behind them,' said Mr Fitzwilliam with a frown, as they took tea in Aubrey Square that evening.

'It is not so very much,' said Fanny.

More than enough for ravishing and ruination was the unspoken thought of all of them. Camilla was philosophical as to that. They must assume that Sir Joshua would have bedded Georgina by now, and from what she had seen, it was more than likely that he had done so long before any flight from London were proposed. This opinion, however, she kept to herself.

Why the couple had decided on so dramatic a scenario, she could not imagine. Georgina had no doubt slipped a note out to her lover telling of incarceration and soon-to-be exile, and if he were to be leaving London and making a stay in France, it might well suit him to take a pretty young woman with him. It seemed strange to her, but what did she know of Sir Joshua?

Very little, beyond noticing that his evening clothes fitted him uncommonly well, and that, judging by the set of his mouth, he would not be a good person to cross. Not a man for flamboyant gestures, she would have said; night-time flits did not look to be quite his style. However, the dawn flight would undoubtedly have appealed to her sister's extravagantly romantic notions of how journeys should begin.

Mr Gardiner, not at all a romantic, said that the hour had certainly been chosen to catch the tide at Dover.

Everyone was up to see them off, despite the earliness of the hour.

Letitia, dark smudges under her eyes, looked hagged and forlorn, and begged Mr Gardiner not to fight Sir Joshua.

'Fight him? I should think not indeed. I am hardly of an age to meet my man at dawn. Besides, he is reckoned a capital shot.'

'The Duke of Wellington is no longer young, and he fought a duel a little while ago. Men are forever fighting one another, especially in France, from what one hears.'

'Men are fools. There is no worse way to settle a dispute, and go hang with your gentleman's code of honour. All of that should have died out with the old century. There is no place for such fustian goings-on in the modern world.'

Camilla could not help looking at Mr Fitzwilliam, any references to modernity usually being accounted by him as evidence of Whiggery, but on this occasion he restrained himself to a mild snort of agreement. She did not suppose he actually wanted Mr Gardiner shot in a duel, however much all that was redolent of Old England. She had no fears on that score, Mr Gardiner was a man of great good sense who would use his tongue, his wealth and his influence to persuade Sir Joshua to give up his prize.

Reason, not passion, would win the day in France.

France! She still could not believe that in a few hours she would be setting foot on foreign land, travelling across that wicked country, England's enemy for so many years, a country surely still marked with the blood of the guillotine, and its capital, Paris, full of such revolutionaries as might have survived the revolution itself and the years of the Corsican monster. Although at Mrs Rowan's house, she had heard men speak approvingly of Napoleon Bonaparte, of his laws and reforms, of his modern approach to government.

She longed, too, to see French fashions, not in fashion plates in *La Belle Assemblée* and on the few Englishwomen who had the taste and means to wear such clothes, but worn by every fashionable woman. It amused her that Letty, recovering momentarily from her decline, had asked her to obtain one of the enchanting new Leghorn hats they had seen pictures of.

'This is not a shopping expedition,' said Fitzwilliam.

'I dare say there may be a few spare hours in which to visit the shops,' was Mr Gardiner's more conciliatory response.

TWENTY-FIVE

The moment the packet drew away from the harbour in Dover, Camilla felt as though all her worries and concerns for her sister, for her own future, for all their futures, had been swept away into the sea.

It was an extraordinary and inexplicable sensation, for nothing had changed, but the lightening of her spirits did much to make the crossing to Calais, the night in a crowded noisy inn, and another day on the road more like an entrancing dream than an ordeal.

They had fair weather for the crossing, with a favourable breeze speeding them on their way. Sackree, who succumbed swiftly to a severe bout of seasickness, stayed below in the cabin Mr Gardiner had obtained for them, but Camilla had stayed for most of the time on deck, rejoicing in the sounds of the ship and the sea, the crack and flap of the great canvas sails, the hissing of the rigging, the shouts and whistles and stamping feet of the sailors and the rush of foaming water streaming along the boat's sides.

She spotted a man-of-war on the horizon, a fine sight under a magnificent set of sails, its pennant streaming out behind it. Another big ship was, Mr Gardiner told her after one expert glance, an East India merchantman. They passed a fleet of fishing boats, whose men shouted unintelligible remarks into the spray as the packet sent the little vessels tossing to and fro in its wake. Then the thin line in the distance grew larger, took on shape and definition, became a country, with houses and landmarks visible on the shore.

France.

The language spoken on the quay and at the inn was not quite the French she and her sisters had learned from Mademoiselle Leclair, but after a while her ear became accustomed to the sounds and she was able to make herself understood and to understand the particulars of the menu, which were sung out to them with great rapidity.

At first Sackree refused to touch the food that was put in front of her.

'It will make you feel much more the thing,' Mr Gardiner assured her.

'I will begin to wish I had not brought you,' was Camilla's own, tougher, inducement to her maid to eat. After a few mouthfuls, Sackree announced she did feel much better for the food, however peculiar it was.

The weather was fine the next day, the sky blue with puffs of cloud, the sun burning through a morning haze as they set off from the inn. Camilla was surprised to see how like northern France was to England as far as landscape went, although the towns and villages they passed through were vastly different, and the road, as Mr Gardiner observed more than once, was uncommonly ill kept up.

She was fascinated by the clothes of the villagers and the townspeople, by the bustling markets with their extravagant displays of cheese and fruit and vegetables and most of all by a group of nuns hurrying down a street in their wide white hats and dark habits.

'Why, I thought the revolution and Napoleon had quite done away with all the convents and nuns,' she said, forbearing to add that according to Mademoiselle Leclair, every nun in France had been ravished and hacked to pieces several times over.

'They do a great deal of charitable work, visiting the sick and nursing and so forth,' said Mr Gardiner, fanning his face with his hat. 'When we reach Paris, Camilla, we shall put up at the Deux Signes. It is a respectable inn, where they are used to English visitors, and it is in what passes for a quiet street there.'

As their carriage made its slow way through the narrow

streets of Paris, Camilla could barely contain her surprise. 'It is so dirty,' she cried. 'And the smell!'

'You will become accustomed to it,' said Mr Gardiner. 'See how many cafés there are. Now that is what you will not see in London.'

She tried to believe him with regard to the smell, and indeed, as every few yards brought new sights and sounds, she soon ceased to notice the all-pervasive odour. They drove along one of the boulevards, and she exclaimed at the handsomeness of the houses, each set in its own gardens. 'And the trees, only look at the trees bordering the road. They must be a century old at least.'

She tried to ignore the earthen road, with its cracked and imperfect pavement and a dirty gutter in the middle carrying all manner of filth towards the river. They passed into the oldest part of the city, and while the pointed roofs and domes and tiny windows on high buildings might be picturesque, she found the glimpses she had of alleys and dark and narrow streets presented a squalid appearance.

She was relieved to find that their destination was in a pleasanter area of the city, and while far removed from the elegance and style of the fashionable part of London, was tolerable enough as to light and air. They rumbled through the porte-cochère of the Auberge des Deux Signes and into a large courtyard laid with flagstones. A plump woman with red cheeks and a voluminous apron came hurrying out of a door to greet Mr Gardiner as an old friend.

The inn was old-fashioned and labyrinthine. Sackree sniffed her disapproval, as they were led along winding corridors and up and down flights of stairs.

'What if the inn catches on fire, that's what I'd like to know? I wouldn't trust a Frenchie with a candle. And I don't care to think about what's going to be in those mattresses, bugs the size of weasels, I shouldn't be surprised. Damp, too, you may be sure, and rooms not properly aired. I've heard about foreign ways, never washing the rooms down, find yourself sharing the sheets with the Lord knows who.'

'Stop muttering, do,' said Camilla. 'It is a delightful place, and since it stretches a long way back from the road, we may be spared the noise of the streets.'

They were; the woman leading them into as handsome and quiet a set of rooms as could be imagined. There was a good-sized private sitting-room, with windows opening on to a small balcony. Stepping out on to it, Camilla found that it overlooked a little garden, with a tree in its centre and a tiny rectangle marked out around it with low box hedges.

'Why, it is charming!'

The garden, it transpired, was for their use; a flight of steps led down to it. There were two bedchambers, each with a minute room off it for a servant. She had to hide a smile as Sackree inspected her quarters with gloomy relish. 'Wouldn't put a dog in here in England. Smells, too.'

'You may sleep on a truckle bed in my chamber.' With no window, the small room was indeed hot and airless and she did not want Sackree to suffer a sleepless night.

'We shall have a meal brought up here,' said Mr Gardiner. 'You will not wish to eat downstairs in the restaurant. It is no place for a young lady.'

It would be much more interesting in the restaurant, and as a stranger, an English stranger, in the city, no one would know her to approve or disapprove of her presence there. However, it was a hot and sultry evening, and Camilla had a lurking headache, no doubt brought on by being rattled to her bones on the bumpy ride from Calais. It would be better to refresh her toilette and dine in comfort here, before the open window with its slight promise of freshness.

There was a knock on the door, and a chambermaid entered with a jug of hot water. Hard on her heels came a slender man with improbably black hair and a quick, knowing air. He bowed obsequiously to Mr Gardiner, regarded Camilla with a keen interest as he made an even deeper bow in her direction, and then informed Mr Gardiner in reasonable enough English, that a gentleman had called enquiring for him.

'Send him up,' Mr Gardiner said, and the man made a grimace of a smile and bowed himself out of the room.

'That is M. Goujon, the proprietor. Come to give us the

once over. He is not used to my being here with a female companion; he is a nosy fellow, but he likes to keep his house respectable. However, it is a comfortable place to stay and they know me, and will look after us well. Paris is not quite the same as London, my dear, and it is best not to enquire too closely into some of their habits and customs, which are different from ours.'

'Who is this gentleman he is sending up?'

'It will be Perrault, who looks after my affairs in Paris. I sent a messenger on ahead of us, to announce our imminent arrival to him, and to request that he make what discreet enquiries he might about Sir Joshua's whereabouts. He must have been brisk about the business, for I did not look to see him before the morrow.'

Another knock on the door, a loud 'Enter,' from Mr Gardiner, and Mr Wytton walked into the room.

TWENTY-SIX

It was a visit to Layard, two days earlier, that had brought Wytton to Paris. Layard was back in London after a visit to Leicestershire; he was sitting back in his favourite chair wearing a brocade dressing-gown and with his feet propped up on a footstool, when Wytton was shown in.

Layard looked his visitor up and down.

'You look pale and positively unwell, my dear Wytton. Come, help yourself to coffee, ham, a beefsteak. Ring the bell and Green will bring you fresh toast.' He waved a hand towards the food.

Wytton remarked that his table resembled the plains of Egypt after the plague of locusts had been through, accepted the offer of coffee, said that he was not hungry and began to prowl about the room.

'The devil take you, Wytton, can't you be still? You're as nervy as a cat, what have you been up to while I've been away? How was the Mershams' ball? Was it as smart an affair as it usually is? I am sorry I had to miss it. Did you enjoy it?'

'I did not.'

'Ah, is Sophie giving you trouble?' His voice was casual, but his eyes were alert. It wasn't Sophie giving his friend trouble, in his opinion; rather that Wytton's own feelings were playing merry hell with him. What had the girl been up to? Playing off her tricks, bored with the no-man's-land of the time leading up to a wedding? These longish engagements were always a mistake. For an eager young couple, it was too long to wait for the natural end of their passion; for a pair marrying for prudent

308

rather than romantic reasons it was long enough for them to realise how ill-suited they were.

For a man as impatient and as much in love as Wytton, it had been a trying time.

'Not long now. The wedding is fixed for June, ain't it? Then off to hotter climes for your honeymoon, that'll be a relief.'

'Damn it, Layard, do stop going on about my wedding.'

'Sophie being difficult?'

Wytton kicked at the fender, earning a reproachful look from a tabby cat perched on its leather top. It rose, arched its back and stalked towards Layard.

'No, no, shoo, go away, do,' said Layard. 'No, don't kick the cat, for God's sake. It belongs to my landlady and she dotes on it. Amiable enough creature, but it makes me sneeze.'

'I have no intention of kicking the cat,' said Wytton, picking it up and setting it back in its place. He smoothed its ruffled fur and tickled it under the chin.

'Women are like cats,' observed Layard. 'I don't mean they make you sneeze, though some of them do with the scents and perfumes they drench themselves in; I mean you never know when they'll turn round and fly out at you. Sophie been doing a bit of scratching, has she?'

'If I am in an ill mood, then Sophie is not to blame. It is not her fault. She has done nothing.'

There was a long pause, while Wytton gazed into the empty grate and Layard watched him. He couldn't remember ever seeing him so blue-devilled. If it wasn't Sophie, then what? Or who?

'I thought I'd call round to Aubrey Square this morning,' he said.

Wytton's head shot up. 'Aubrey Square? Why?'

'Don't snap my head off, old fellow. To call on the Miss Darcys. To join the queue, I should say, Fitzwilliam's door knocker practically comes off in your hand with all the use it's getting while he has those girls staying.'

Wytton's short laugh held no humour. 'You won't find yourself jostling among the crowds today.'

'Are they all out on an expedition?' He sat up. 'Has something happened? Out with it.'

Wytton's face was grim. 'I suppose I may as well tell you, for if I do not, you will hear a highly coloured version at the club. Rumours are flying all over London about the Darcy sisters.'

'Rumours in London? You astonish me. Still, I'm sorry to hear it. Ring for some more coffee, and tell me about it.'

Wytton gave the bell-pull beside the fireplace a savage tug.

'Now, sit down like a good fellow and compose yourself. You may think you're dashed romantic with your hair all tossed about and with that pallid and drawn countenance, but it don't impress me, you know. I think you look a regular mess, and fretting up and down isn't going to help.'

Wytton said something terse and rude under his breath; then his face relaxed into a smile.

'No, no,' said Layard. 'You can't wind me up, Alexander, you know you can't. I've known you too long and we've been through too much together for you to get under my skin. Calm down and tell me more.'

Wytton sighed, sinking back into the saggy armchair he had chosen. 'First of all Busby turned up, behaved like a crashing fool, upset Letitia.'

'Ah, the oldest one? Full of sanctimonious views, spends too much time with that ill-bred clergyman, can't remember his name.'

'Valpy. Yes, he was all over her, actually proposed. She didn't like that at all, and being at the ball, that set all the witches' backs up.' He rubbed his eyes. 'God, was that damned ball only two nights ago? It seems a lifetime.'

'What happened there to put you in such a mood?'

'Oh, that was only the beginning. Belle was there, and in high spirits.'

'Flirting with anything in breeches and setting all the turbans twitching, was she? Irresistible when she's like that, only I shouldn't care to be hitched to her.'

'If she carries on as she is doing, there is not a man of reputation in London who will think of her as a wife. Much can be forgiven to one so young and pretty, and God knows, I am not one to set up as a moralist, but you cannot tease and arouse so many men without tripping up sooner or later.'

'She needs to be spanked and sent home to that beautiful house of theirs until she's learned some sense. That's what I'd do if she were my sister or daughter. Still, I can't see that any real or lasting harm can come from flirting.'

'She quarrelled, publicly, with Sophie. Or, to be accurate, Sophie accused her of being a heartless flirt. At the top of her voice, in front of Lady Sefton, Lady Jersey, Princess Esterhazy, the Countess Lieven and a good few others from that damned cliquey set.'

Layard winced.

'It was ill-behaved of her, and she could not have picked a worse time and place. I have no idea why she felt so provoked by her cousin's ways. Belle does not attempt to flirt with me, so why should Sophie be cross with her?'

Layard looked up. 'Spurned, are you?'

Wytton shrugged. 'I am not her type.'

'Belle may feel it would be wrong to flirt with her cousin's betrothed.'

'She may.' Wytton's voice was dry.

'So, two sisters and a cousin in some disgrace. Not enough to turn away the entire horde of admirers and fortune-seekers, I would have thought.'

'I saved the best for last.' He tilted his head back, shutting his eyes for a moment, then looking up at the ceiling, once white, now a yellowing pattern of smoke stains. 'George Warren and Mrs Beecham chose the occasion of the ball to spread the rumour that Miss Camilla Darcy has been trying to alienate my affections from her cousin Sophie and attract them to herself.'

Layard couldn't believe his ears. Camilla Darcy, of all people, how could anyone say such a thing? His hackles rose. 'George Warren is a regular commoner. Dear God, you'll have to call him out, Wytton. You've no choice.'

'I have no grounds. He has not accused me of allowing my attentions to drift from Sophie towards her cousin. The actions and the intent are all on her side. She is besotted by me, you see, so that honesty and family feeling and propriety and any kindness she has towards Sophie are set at nought.'

'What she must be going through! Every feeling must be offended, she of all people. You can't let it rest, Wytton. You have to prove there isn't a shred of truth in it.'

'Have I? Is that so easy?'

'You mean because the world will always believe the worst? That is true, however . . .' He paused, as an unpleasant thought occurred to him. 'Wytton, you don't think there is any truth in it, do you? You do not imagine that she's setting her cap at you, or any such thing? Why, I've spent as much time in her company as you have, and I'd as soon maintain she was making a dead set at me – which she most certainly ain't, more's the pity. If you want my opinion, I'd say she hasn't got over that shocking business with the sodomitical Leigh.'

'No. She isn't setting her cap at me. Or you, either, as you so rightly say.'

'Well, then. There you are. Out you go, pour scorn on it, accuse the scandalmongers of ill-informed tittle-tattle. Tell Warren he's a liar and an ass – and if he calls you out, then so much the better.'

Wytton was silent. Layard looked at him with deep concern. 'This has hit you hard, hasn't it? Is Sophie very distressed, as well she might be? Is that what's wrong?'

Wytton shook his head. When he spoke, it was in a tired, flat voice that Layard had never heard before.

'Camilla isn't setting her cap at me, far from it. The devil of it is that I've fallen in love with her.'

The silence stretched out into minutes. Layard heard the soft ticking of the clock on the shelf above the fireplace, the low purr from the cat, the creak of the stairs outside the door, the distant rumble of wheels on cobbles, the soft cooing of a pigeon perched on the windowsill. What could he say? His friend was in the worst bind imaginable, betrothed to a girl that he certainly had loved, or at least had been bewitched by, and now claiming to be in love with her cousin.

With a sense of revelation, he told himself it wasn't so strange, once one had got over the initial shock. Camilla Darcy might not be her cousin's equal in looks, Sophie was a monstrously pretty girl, but for intelligence and humour and vivacity, there was no comparison. Sophie would make any man a decorative and doubtless obliging and agreeable wife. Being married to Camilla would be to begin a lifetime's journey of love, liking and discovery. Would that she cared tuppence for him; any sign of affection and he'd marry her like a shot.

Oh, hell and damnation. She was the very woman to suit Wytton, he could see that now. Why had his friend fallen so hard for Sophie? It was all the fault of that wretched Beecham woman, curse the day that his friend had taken up with her. She might be as well-bred as any woman in the kingdom, but she was a whore, through and through. It was understandable that Sophie's youth and innocence would appeal after that attachment, but why had Wytton not seen that Sophie's looks and fun and high spirits were not a sound foundation for happiness, not for a complex, clever, difficult man like him? And there was absolutely nothing to be done about it. He had proposed, been accepted and everything was arranged. That was a contract there was no going back from.

'I did have one slight hope,' Wytton was saying. 'I felt that Sophie might prefer to withdraw from the engagement. I hoped she might release me. She does not wish to.'

'She is in love with you.'

'I do not believe so. She, like Belle, is very young, and I think that although she likes me well enough, her feelings have never matched mine. It was my vanity that made me think her as much in love with me as I was with her. It is of no consequence. I am in honour bound to marry her if she so wishes, and she does.'

'Meanwhile, everyone exclaims at the wickedness of Miss Camilla, and she is shunned where she was courted, cold-shouldered by those who admired her and scorned by the harpies who envied her for her position, her fortune and her looks.'

Layard was visibly shaken. 'I cannot believe it.'

'Even her cousin the Earl, who never sets foot in London, has let it be known from his country fastness that he is severely displeased by the scandal attaching to this member of his family.'

'Pompous fool.'

The coffee came. Layard told his man to be off and get his clothes ready. He drained his cup at a single go, and stood up. 'It makes me even more sure that I should call on the Darcy sisters. I shan't ask if you go with me, that would be out of the question.'

'I am due to drive Sophie and her mother out to Hampton Court today. An outing of pleasure.'

Green returned. He was a short, stocky man, who had to stand on tiptoe to help his master, himself not tall, into his close-fitting coat.

'If I may be so bold, sir,' he said as he flicked a cat hair from the shoulder of Layard's dark green coat, 'but I couldn't help hearing that you had the intention of calling later on in Aubrey Square. I doubt if the family are receiving any visitors at all today.'

'You must break yourself of this nasty eavesdropping habit, Green, or I shall have to let you go. Why are the ladies not at home?'

'Sir, the whole house is in a turmoil. I heard of it from Figgins as is maid to the youngest Miss Darcy. She came round on her father's behalf, him being head coachman to Mr Fitzwilliam and having promised your groom an ointment for your hack, that sore place by the withers as he suffers from.'

'Yes, yes, I know all about the sore place. Get on with it, what has this to do with anything?'

Wytton was watching the man intently. 'What has happened there, Green?'

'Why, one of the young ladies has run off. Eloped! In a chaise and four! At dawn! Right under their noses.'

'Which of the young ladies?' said Wytton.

'One of the young ladies as are twins, Figgins didn't say which, she was in that much of a hurry.' He gave his employer a sly look. 'Figgins says as how the man she's taken off with is an older man, not one of their young beaux. And he's married, so it won't be the Border that they're heading for.'

Wytton's voice was cold, but perfectly calm. 'Was a name given?'

'For the man? Figgins says they believe she's with Sir Joshua Mordaunt, no less, and that he's taken her to Paris. Mr Gardiner is setting off for France as soon as may be to find her and bring her back before she's ruined.'

'And you be off before you are kicked to kingdom come,' said Layard unfairly. He ejected his man from the room and slammed the door shut behind him. 'Wytton, if that's true, then those girls are truly ruined. Where are you going?'

Wytton was flying across the room to the door, sending his coffee cup tumbling to the floor in his haste. 'To France.'

'France?' Layard called after him as he clattered down the stairs. 'Whatever for? The twins are not anything to you – are they?'

Wytton stopped at the bottom of the flight of stairs and looked back up at his friend. 'Anything that rebounds on Camilla is to do with me. Sir Joshua is my mother's cousin; I have friends in Paris who may know where he can be found. Mr Gardiner does not move in that world; he may have difficulty in tracing the couple. I shall leave for Dover directly, and cross the Channel tonight. With luck, Haldane will be there, messing about with his yacht. He may take me to France.'

Camilla's heart was in her throat.

What was he doing here? In Paris, in this room? And looking at her, with his heart in his eyes. Wytton of all people; Wytton, whom she had thought she might never see again.

Mr Wytton did not at first notice Camilla, who had drawn back into the shadows. Then he saw her, and took two or three eager steps towards her, before he stopped himself.

'I beg your pardon,' he said, forgetting to make his bow to a startled Mr Gardiner and never taking his eyes from her face.

After a moment, he recollected himself and began to apologise to Mr Gardiner for calling on him so late in the day, and when he must be tired after a long journey.

Mr Gardiner was all amiability. He seemed not to have noticed the look that Mr Wytton had upon his face when he saw Camilla, although she knew that he had taken it all in; no one was shrewder than Mr Gardiner. 'Pray, be seated,' he said. 'A glass of wine?'

'Thank you, sir.' Wytton glanced at her, and at Sackree, who was hovering vengefully in the door to the bedchamber. 'I should like to speak freely,' he said.

TWENTY-SEVEN

'Sackree, you may go,' Camilla said. 'Close the door behind you, if you please.' She turned to the others. 'She will listen to everything that is said, you know, but she is discreet and trustworthy. She knows why we are here.'

'Which is, I suppose, to find your sister?'

Mr Gardiner pursed his lips. 'You had this from Sophie, I hope. I would not like to think that the tale is already all over London.'

'I do not believe it is generally known, but I fear that it will not remain a secret for long. Your family will not speak of it, but servants are not all to be trusted.'

'So why are you in Paris? You made no mention of any plan to travel abroad when last we spoke.' His eyes rested on his future son-in-law in an appraising way. 'You must have ridden hard.'

Camilla knew what was in his mind; he was wondering if Wytton were trying to escape from his marriage to Sophie by running away. As if he would. Did Mr Gardiner not know him better than that?

'My sole purpose in coming to France is to assist in your search. I do not know if you are acquainted with Sir Joshua?'

'We have met. I would not claim any great intimacy with him. He is seldom in London.'

Would that he had not chosen these particular weeks to grace the capital with his presence, Camilla thought bitterly.

'He spends his time in the country and in France, where he has property, and moves in the best circles.'

Mr Gardiner made an impatient gesture with his hand and his

words were scathing. 'His behaviour in this affair should preclude his taking a place in any but the lowest circles. Seducing a gentleman's daughter, a girl of seventeen, and taking her off to Paris with him, as though she were some Cyprian he had picked up at the opera – it is disgraceful, it is beyond belief. Is it also of no moment to him that Miss Georgina's father is a man of position, of wealth, of influence, with many great connections? Is he a fool, to risk the enmity of such a man?'

Wytton frowned. 'He cares little for what any man – or woman – thinks of him. He is possessed of a large fortune, and is in the habit of acting only to please himself. Do not misunderstand me, he is an amiable man, cultured, quite the connoisseur – a collector of fine things. He was a member of the society of Dilettanti at the time when that society of men—'

He was not allowed to finish his sentence. Camilla could not understand the look of anger and contempt that crossed Mr Gardiner's face.

'It is worse than I feared, then. Those men were – are – despicable. You will not contradict me when I assert that among the objects collected by those so-called connoisseurs,' he spat the word out, 'those Dilettanti, were beautiful women. I use the word object advisedly, for all the normal, civilised standards of proper behaviour between the sexes were set aside in the pursuit of perfection; perfection of form and sensual gratification – am I not right?'

Wytton tugged at his neckcloth. 'I have some association with the Dilettanti myself, sir, and I can assure you that whatever may have happened in the last century, it is now no more than a society that encourages scholarship and funds discoveries of the ancient world.'

'Away with your assurances. What you say of Sir Joshua fills me with dismay. It is terrible to think of an innocent young girl in his clutches. Has he no morals, no family to exert pressure on him to behave as a gentleman ought?'

'It is upon that point that I have come to speak to you,' said Wytton. 'He is – not a relation of mine, but a cousin by marriage. By his first marriage, I should say,' he added.

Mr Gardiner's face reddened alarmingly. 'First wife? Has he had another wife? The man is a veritable Bluebeard.'

'No, sir. He was married as a very young man, and his wife died in childbirth not a year later.'

'And his second wife? This unfortunate woman he has left languishing on his country estate in England while he comes to Paris to dally with Georgina Darcy? She is not dead, I believe.'

'There is nothing that can be said in his favour there,' said Wytton.

She felt cold; to hear Georgina's situation spelt out in this way made the stark horror of it seem much worse. How could her sister have done such a thing? How was it possible to ignore the wife, presumably of many years' standing, left behind in England?

'Does he have children from this second marriage?' she asked.

'No,' said Wytton.

Thank God that they were at least to be spared the shame and reproaches of wronged children.

'So what we have is a rich man with no finer feelings to be touched, who is not bound by the common ties of morality or convention, and who has one dead and one living wife, which should be enough for any man, only not for him. Very well, indeed.'

'Let Mr Wytton speak, sir,' Camilla said. 'There is no purpose to be gained by discussing Sir Joshua's many faults of character and deeds. Mr Wytton may be able to offer some help, some advice.'

He smiled at her, just for a second; a warm, intimate smile that was gone almost before she saw it. He turned back to Mr Gardiner.

'Lady Aldham, my aunt, is in Paris. I waited upon her the instant I arrived; she has lived here for many years, knows everyone, and is always well-informed about any English people who may be here as visitors or residents. She can give you an introduction to Sir Joshua, and smooth your path there, for however strong your need to see and talk to Sir Joshua, he may not choose to see you. His establishment is large, you might not even get through his gates if he is unwilling to speak to you.'

'Unwilling! I'll give him unwilling! He abducts a member of my family, commits a rape, let's not mince words, sir, on a seventeen-year-old girl of the highest breeding, and I am not to speak to him?'

Rape? No, Camilla doubted it, only she could hardly say so. Mr Gardiner's thoughts ran along respectable and narrow lines, in terms of innocence and experience, of morality and immorality, of seduction and deception and manipulation of one too young to know what she was at.

Mr Gardiner had not grown up with Georgina, had not lived at close quarters with her during these last hectic weeks in London. No, Georgina had left her home and her old life with zest and enthusiasm and not a single regret; she felt quite sure of that. She looked at the enraged Mr Gardiner. It was no good. Even if he could be brought to some better knowledge of Georgina, he would be still more shocked by her own awareness of what had probably passed between Georgina and her lover.

'Am I to take it,' Mr Gardiner said, 'that your aunt now knows of Georgina's flight? I cannot approve of what you have done. If I know anything of women, and aunts in particular, the whole of Paris will have learned our secret by tomorrow evening.'

Mr Wytton raised an eyebrow, not quite liking Mr Gardiner's tone. 'You need not be afraid of my laying the whole before her, she is not a gabmouth, and where family is concerned, she is scrupulously careful to guard her tongue. I have persuaded her to write a few lines of introduction to Sir Joshua on your behalf. Nothing is more likely to secure your admittance.'

'Very well, very well. There is nothing to be done about it, after all; words spoken cannot be recalled. If you have Sir Joshua's address, then I suggest we go immediately – do you have a carriage waiting?' He turned to Camilla. 'Eat your meal, my dear, and then go to bed. You need not wait up; it will be late when we return, and you must be sadly fagged by the journey.'

'I am not at all fagged, and even if I were, I should still come with you. Georgina is my sister, and it is my duty to see her as soon as I can – and it is not only from a sense of duty that I wish to see her. You cannot ask me to sit here alone, wondering what is being said and done.'

Mr Gardiner frowned. 'I think not.'

Camilla wasted no more breath arguing, but threw open her bedroom door, sending Sackree, who had her ear bent to the keyhole, flying. She took no notice of her maid's hasty excuses, but merely told her to find a light shawl. 'For it is so hot, I shall not need anything more,' she said to Mr Gardiner with a glitter in her eyes. 'No, sir, no more protests. I come with you, and that is that. Otherwise, I shall run after your carriage on my own two feet, and only think how that would make the French stare.'

Wytton was trying to repress a smile. 'I do have a carriage waiting, sir. It is not far, but it would not be safe to walk. Paris is an ill-lit city, there is no public lighting at all in the streets, and it is a dangerous place after dark, even if one is not alone.'

Sir Joshua's Paris residence was a fine, symmetrical *hôtel*, set back from the street and fronted by two large iron gates through which the formal patterns of a garden could be seen. It spoke of history, wealth and status. It was also closed to visitors.

When the carriage drew up by the gates, Wytton leapt down and called out to a dour gatekeeper, who was sitting outside his little cabin, smoking a pipe. No, it was not possible for them to be admitted. His orders were absolute. Very well, he would take the letter as Monsieur requested, or rather, hand it to a minion to be delivered within. Monsieur planned to wait? A shrug of the shoulders. That was his affair. The answer would be as he said.

They sat in the carriage, the flickering light of the great torches burning on the outside wall sending dancing shadows across their faces. Scents and sounds of the hot night air came to them from the less dignified streets along which they had come; food and ordure and smoke and fish and the faint, sour tang of the river. Voices coming from open windows, conversation, argument, snatches of music. More voices from the cafés and busy pavements, dogs barking, a child crying, a woman shrieking with laughter.

Every one of Camilla's senses was on edge, she heard and saw everything around her with the utmost clarity. She was intensely aware of Wytton's presence, and of the barely controlled tension in Mr Gardiner's body. The tired horses shifted their weight from one leg to another, the coachman gave an inaudible curse. Up in the inky sky, brilliant clusters of stars undimmed by the sliver of a new moon were but little obscured by the smoke coming from the hearths and fires of the city.

There was movement within the gates. Wytton leant out of the carriage, and had a brief, low conversation with the gatekeeper.

'It is no use,' he reported. 'Sir Joshua will not see us tonight. However, if we wait upon him tomorrow before noon, he will be at home.'

Mr Gardiner was not at all pleased, but there was little that he could do, and, not being a man to give way to irritation or temper, he accepted this philosophically enough, declared that they should return in the morning, and asked Wytton to direct the coachman to take them back to the Rue de la Fontaine.

Once there, he invited Wytton in to take a glass of wine with them.

Wytton hesitated, looked at Camilla, who was steadfastly not looking at him, and then bowed. 'Thank you, sir, I will join you for a few minutes only. It is late, and you will want to rest after your journey.'

'Not at all,' said Mr Gardiner, resting his hand on the younger man's shoulder in a kindly way. 'We owe you thanks for your good offices on our behalf. You have eased our way over seeing Sir Joshua, although I feel sure that once he was made aware of our being in Paris, he would hardly refuse a necessary meeting.'

'It astonishes me that he is here in Paris,' Camilla said, laying aside her shawl as she spoke, and flattening the fringes with her fingers. 'I should have expected him to have taken himself off to some remote part of rural France – a lonely cottage or a gloomy mansion. Do they have gloomy mansions here? If not, a grim old keep might do, or a ruined tower with a creaking door.'

'What fancies you do have. It comes of reading too many sensational novels, Camilla.' Mr Gardiner unstoppered the decanter and poured wine.

'Indeed, I have known more than one young woman left with permanently weakened wits from an excess of Minerva novels,' said Wytton, his face straight, and only a gleam of mischief in his eyes betraying him.

'Now, now, you cannot make a fool of me, young man. It does not matter what I say, it is just the same with Sophie, as you will discover soon enough; young ladies will do what they want, they do not care for sober advice and guidance.'

At the mention of Sophie's name, Camilla saw the light die out of Wytton's eyes. For a moment, she had forgotten Sophie, had forgotten how matters actually stood, had simply felt the ease with Wytton that made him so essential to her happiness – and made the impossibility of his continued acquaintance so unbearable. She had slipped into an intimacy with this man without being aware of it, that was what made it so cruel. The *coup de foudre* at the ball was no such thing in reality; it was instead the culmination of a closeness that had been growing on them day by day, unsought, unobserved – at least by her – and by the time she had recognised it for what it was, the closeness was so much part of her, that to tear herself away from it would be agony.

The chambermaid was at the door, bobbing a curtsy, addressing Mr Gardiner.

'A man called Perrault is downstairs to see you,' Wytton obligingly translated.

'Good, good. Camilla, get you to bed, we have a busy day ahead of us tomorrow.' He paused at the door, waiting for Wytton to finish his wine and go with him.

Wytton bowed to her and was gone.

TWENTY-EIGHT

Camilla stood quite still in the centre of the room, lost in her own thoughts, hardly hearing Sackree's muttered commentary on the French, late evening callers and gentlemen who didn't know when they should make themselves scarce.

A knock on the door, the latch was lifted, and Wytton was back. 'My hat,' he said hastily. 'I believe – ah, there it is.' He seized it from the table by the window, and as he headed back to the door, took her by the hand and pulled her with him.

Sackree's beady eye was upon them, she opened her mouth to protest, but they were gone, the door had shut behind them, the latch dropped.

Wytton released his hold on Camilla, and stood in the dim, narrow passage looking down at her with such a expression in his eyes that she was quite overwhelmed.

She heard voices coming from a great distance: Mr Gardiner, and a man who spoke English with a strong French accent; they belonged to a different world.

'I cannot part from you like this,' said Wytton, without preamble. 'Now that your sister is found I can be of no further use here, and Mr Gardiner will expect me to return to England – at any rate, he will not wish me to be in your company. He is a kind man, and although he is not as full of suspicions about me as his wife is, he has too much sense and care for the proprieties to wish me to remain with you.'

'If Mrs Gardiner suspects that your feelings for Sophie are not what they should be, how can she want Sophie to be married to you?'

The words were wrung from her, regretted the instant they

were spoken. She could not judge of the strength of his attachment to Sophie; she could be sure of her own heart, but not of his.

His eyes searched her face, he made as if to take her hand again, then dropped his own to his side. 'I fell in love with Sophie the moment I saw her. Such prettiness! Such a fine complexion, such entrancing ways. And an open, happy spirit! I adored her.'

Why was he saying this? She turned her head away, holding her hand up as though to ward off a blow.

'I was possessed. I longed to be near her; to hear her voice, to see her lovely face was scarcely enough. I was near enough out of my senses over her. She was very young, but I thought that was all to the good, she would soon accustom herself to my way of life, which is not what she would be used to, that she would share my pleasure in travel and discovery.'

His voice was controlled and bitter. Every word was a stab to Camilla, but still he went on.

'When I realised that she had no wish to see Rome, or tread the Argive plain, it made no difference. She would be waiting for me at the abbey, an object for my affections and desires.'

'Stop!' She could bear it no longer. 'Why are you saying this? Excuse me, but I must go back into our apartment, I have no wish—'

'Listen. You must listen to me.' His eyes were very dark, his gaze even more intense. 'I want there to be nothing less than the truth in our dealings. Like it or not, that is the way things were. I was enchanted by Sophie, yes, but like all enchantments, one day you wake to find the spell broken. And also,' he had to force these words out, it seemed, 'she was so different. So different to someone who—'

'It pains you. Please do not speak of it. I understand.'

'Do you?'

Camilla was no longer looking at him. 'Did that happen?' she asked in a voice striving to be normal. 'That the enchantment lost its power to hold you?'

He nodded. 'Yes. I still think Sophie is the prettiest creature imaginable – but the magic has flown. However, this being a rational world, and not one of fairies and make believe, we are bound together in such a way that I cannot in honour draw back. I do not think her feelings for me were ever so strong as mine for her, but we are betrothed with the full approval of her parents, already tied with legal knots – as you know, the wedding is but the blessing of the Church upon a commitment, an agreement made and confirmed long before a couple comes to the altar.'

'You should not be telling me this.' Anger was beginning to stir in her. 'What, to tell me how much you loved Sophie, that you no longer do so, but that you are to be married just the same. What chance of happiness is there for Sophie in such a match?'

'Every chance, for I shall make it my business to see that she has the happiness she is entitled to. She has made her choice, she could have released me in the light of what has happened. She might have been the butt of society's jokes for a few weeks had she done so, but none would blame her, and so pretty an heiress would not lack suitors for long. I would occur the opprobrium, not her.'

'Only she will not release you.'

'She will not.'

'Then I am sorry for both of you.' Camilla made a dart for the door, had her hand upon the latch. 'I hear Mr Gardiner calling you.'

'No, stay a moment longer. I cannot let you go without telling you – without giving some expression to my heart. I—'

Now she was furious. 'You can have nothing to say to me. Goodbye, Mr Wytton. It is not likely we shall meet again, at least not for a long time.'

He stepped in front of her, preventing her opening the door. 'Camilla, there may be another way, there is one small hope, and in that case, do not leave me without a word – without telling me that, if circumstances were different, you would allow me to declare my love in the proper form. Your sister—'

'Has followed the dictates of her heart, in selfish disregard for the hurt she does to others, to Sir Joshua's wife and family, to her own family, to the prospects and happiness of all her sisters.

Do not even hint that I could take such a course, for I would and could not.'

He flushed. 'Do not presume to read my thoughts. I had no intention of offering to run away with you, if that is what you think. I had rather wanted to say that my knowledge of how things were between your sister and Sir Joshua, and my silence upon the matter, should it come out, may cause Mr and Mrs Gardiner to consider that I am not a suitable husband for their daughter.'

'You are clutching at straws, Mr Wytton. You presume now to read *my* thoughts. You do not know how I feel about you, you cannot take my feelings for granted. You do not know me well enough to appreciate that I wish nothing but good to Sophie, and I would not have you separated from her by any tricks and schemes. I fear that you make light of her attachment to you, an attachment that may be a good deal stronger than you imagine.'

'I love you, not Sophie.'

'You have said enough. I bid you good night.'

Once safely within her chamber she stood in a daze, catching at her breath as though it hurt her to breathe. Her eyes were dry and bright, with no tears to shed, and she clenched her fists so tightly that they were numb.

'You were quite right, Miss Camilla,' said Sackree, placing a basin of water on the stand for her. 'I heard every word, and to think a gentleman should speak so! The sauce!'

'Oh, Sackree, how hard life is!'

'Harder for some than others, and there's hard and hard, miss, if I may say so. It's a crying shame, for he's as fine a gentleman as ever I saw, and a proper man, too, which the two things don't always go together, but he's promised to another, and that's that. You'll meet someone else, there are more fish in the sea, as the saying is, than ever came out of it.'

Camilla climbed drearily into the unfamiliar, lumpy-mattressed bed. 'But I am in love with him, Sackree. What am I do?'

'There's nothing you can do. You try to get some sleep, for

just at present you've got more urgent duties on hand with that Miss Georgina to be dealt with. You stick to that. Your sisters are more than enough to fill up anyone's worry-box, I tell you that for nothing.'

Mr Gardiner looked at Camilla with concern. 'My dear Camilla, you are not well. You are pale, your eyes are ringed with shadows. You slept ill, I can see, you cannot have been comfortable.'

She hastened to reassure him, a strange bed, the rigours of the journey, imagining one was still in a jolting carriage, concern for her sister, the heat of the night. 'Indeed, sir, I am quite well. Let us be off as soon as possible, I confess that I shall not be easy until I have seen Georgina, until this whole dreadful business is settled.'

This time, the gates were swung open, and a footman in morning livery ushered them through a magnificent hall and showed them into an elegant room overlooking a garden laid out with the geometrical precision that the French preferred; pretty in its way, but odd to Camilla's eyes. Formal portraits hung on the walls, the stiff-backed chairs were arranged with chill order around the edge of the room. This must be a public apartment, not one in regular use by the residents of the house.

It was a shock when Sir Joshua entered the room. Over these past days he had grown into Lucifer in her eyes, and she was prepared for a monster, for a beast with cloven hoofs, not for a mere mortal. Yet here was a human being, a man of excellent appearance and with an air of well-bred ease.

He was perfectly poised as he made his bows; indeed, he greeted her with some warmth, reminding her of their earlier acquaintance.

The audacity of him. No doubt Don Juans took all this kind of thing – irate relatives, distraught sisters and so forth – in their stride, and no doubt, if you were a man of a rakish disposition, then charm and lazy, attractive eyes and a finely moulded mouth were a decided help in the pursuit of innocent females – but even so!

Sir Joshua was ordering refreshments now, enquiring about their journey, for all the world as though this were no more than an ordinary visit, made out of politeness.

Mr Gardiner was growing visibly more annoyed. 'Sir, this is no mere morning call. I am astonished at your effrontery in refusing to see us last night, and now at your ease of manner, your lack of any sign of remorse or awareness of the wicked step you have taken.'

Sir Joshua's eyebrows rose. It was clear from his face that he felt that Mr Gardiner, however rich and distinguished in his milieu of commerce and banking he might be, had no right to speak to him in quite that way. 'I am not aware of any wickedness. The method of Georgina's departure from Aubrey Square was unconventional, I admit, but the need for speed was pressing. I had killed my man, you see – ah, did you not know? An affair of honour, a meeting by the river; perhaps the body has not yet been discovered.'

'You killed a man! In a duel! And then, since you had to fly the country, you calmly decided to take Georgina with you? Sir, this is beyond belief.'

'I could scarcely knock on the door and ask that ass Fitzwilliam to release her into my care. All that nonesense about her being sequestered for what her sisters had or had not done. A great deal of fuss about nothing, in my opinion.'

Camilla saw that Mr Gardiner was rendered speechless by these remarks, and she could hardly blame him. Was Sir Joshua mad? Drunk?

'Georgina will be here in a moment to wait upon you,' said Sir Joshua in his suave way. 'Why, here she is.'

The door burst open and there was Georgina, on wings as usual. She looked more beautiful than ever, although with a slightly heightened colour. She was no doubt feeling all the awkwardness of her situation.

This was not at all the case.

'My dearest Camilla, I would have been with you before, as soon as you were announced, but I am not completely well just now, and so I had to wait until I was quite sure I would not faint or some such thing, which Sir Joshua would not like, you know. Dear Mr Gardiner, how glad I am to see you. Are you in Paris for long?'

Mr Gardiner was going to suffer an apoplexy, Camilla was convinced of it. Normally the calmest of men, he was now in such a state that something must be done. She spoke sharply to Sir Joshua. 'A glass of brandy if you please, you must see that Mr Gardiner is in some distress.'

He busied himself with a decanter, and Camilla turned to her sister. 'Georgina, have you taken leave of your wits? You run off to Paris with a married man, and you prate on as though Mr Gardiner was come to chat about the weather. This is no social call, I do assure you. We have come here at great trouble and expense to find you and to take you home. Your absence has been covered up, but it cannot be kept a secret for much longer, and you seem to find it all a joke, an affair of no consequence. Only see how your and Sir Joshua's behaviour has affected Mr Gardiner, he is quite overcome.'

'You mistake the matter,' said Georgina blithely. 'I have no intention of returning to England, indeed, my present condition would render any such journey insupportable.'

'Present condition?' A horrid suspicion was growing in her mind. 'Georgina, you do not mean to say—'

'Oh, don't be missish. I'm breeding, that's all.'

At these casual words, Mr Gardiner gave a groan and sank on to the nearest chair, dropping his head into his hands.

'Georgina, how is this possible?'

'Come, sister, you are not such an innocent as that. You know very well how it is possible. You may wish me joy, for indeed, I am very happy, and so is my dear Sir Joshua.'

With which she laid her hand on Sir Joshua's arm, and gazed dotingly up at him.

Pregnant! Nothing had prepared her for this. This connection must have been going on far longer than anyone had suspected. It was no very improbable outcome of an illicit liaison, of course. Camilla was not so stupid as not to be aware of on what grounds, other than the teachings of the Church and the threat of the world's censure, young ladies were so carefully protected from the attentions of the opposite sex. The granting of the ultimate favour would always be disapproved of, but it happened, even in the best families, and a veil of respectability could be drawn over the unsanctified earlier relationship by means of a hasty wedding.

In this case, there could be no such happy outcome. With Georgina pregnant and Sir Joshua married, she would be doubly cast out from her world. The world would dub her a fallen woman, a creature of easy virtue – nay, why mince words? – a whore, and her sisters would certainly be involved in her ruin.

'Georgina,' she cried. 'What have you done?'

'Don't be so stuffy, it is not so bad. Now that I am Lady Mordaunt, no one will think anything of it, after all. And the baby is to be born here in Paris, and who except the most odious-minded old dowagers will be counting the weeks?'

'Georgina!' This time it came out as a shriek. 'You are run mad! You cannot become Lady Mordaunt, you know you cannot.'

'I can, and I have, for we were married three days ago, as soon as we came to Paris, for dear Sir Joshua had arranged everything, and the knot was tied not three hours after we arrived. Is he not the cleverest man?'

'Married! It is impossible!'

'And do not be imagining there was anything irreligious in the ceremony; you are not to be thinking that because this is France it was a papist wedding, that would be most improper. No, we had a Protestant clergyman who happens to be in Paris just now. Everything was just as it should be.'

'Just as it should be! Good God, Georgina, what are you saying. Do you not know that Sir Joshua has a wife living?'

TWENTY-NINE

It was dusk when the chaise reached Aubrey Square, the end of a brilliantly fine day, with the sky turning to pink and orange as the sun hung huge and red on the horizon.

Windows in the houses round the square were open to catch the least promise of a breeze, and the Fitzwilliam house was no exception. Camilla sighed as she heard Letty's carrying voice raised in some irritable protest.

Camilla had travelled abroad, had crossed into another existence and was now, with all that had happened in her brief time away, a different person from the girl who had left London on that dawn morning. Yet here nothing had changed and, as she mounted the steps to the front door, she felt she might never have been away, might only have been out minutes or hours, on a walk, paying a call, visiting the circulating library or the shops in Bond Street.

The minute she stepped inside the house, she knew she was quite wrong. What was going on? Doors were flung open, there was the sound of running feet, heads hung over the banister.

'Belle, is that you? Is it Belle?'

'Oh, no, it is only Camilla.'

'Camilla, thank God you are come back. Is Mr Gardiner with you?'

'Where is Georgina? Never say you did not find her?'

'Take care, Camilla, before you come in. Sister by sister, we are disappearing; I hardly expected to see you back.'

This last was from Alethea, who was leaning over at the top of the stairs. Miss Griffin, looking drawn and anxious, was standing on the next landing with Letty and Fanny. Servants hovered in the background and Pug was leaping down the stairs with happy grunts, eager to greet them.

'Why, whatever is going on?' Camilla said, much alarmed. 'Yes, Letty, here I am, safe and sound. Georgina is quite well, and she is not returning to London. Pug, do not bark so. Let me but remove my hat and I shall explain.'

As she reached the top of the first flight of stairs, Fanny rushed forward to clasp her in her arms.

Camilla could see traces of tears on her cousin's cheeks, and felt a renewed rush of anger at what anguish Georgina's thoughtlessness had caused. 'Fanny, do not take on so. Georgina's situation is different from what we had imagined. She is married, married to Sir Joshua.'

Fanny gave a faint scream. 'How can that be?'

'It is simple,' said Mr Gardiner, treading up the stairs behind her. Aware of the listening servants, he led the way into the drawing-room. 'It turns out that Sir Joshua, whose morals are a disgrace, was never married to his supposed wife in Hampshire; she is in fact married to another man, from whom she lives apart. There can be no question of a divorce since the lady in question is a Roman Catholic. In any case, her and Sir Joshua's liaison finished some while ago, so he coolly informed us. She stays on in his house merely as a matter of convenience, so there was no impediment to his marriage from that quarter, he said. Impudent fellow, if I were a dozen years younger, I'd have knocked him down.'

'So ruin does not after all stare us in the face,' said Camilla. 'There, Letty, is that not good news? Georgina married, and living in such style!' There was also the matter of the baby, of course, but one shock at a time was enough.

Letty was looking wretched. 'Alas, Camilla, it is of no avail! Disgrace, ruin, loss of reputation, nothing can save us now.'

'Oh, Letty, do stop it. There is surely no need to look and sound so miserable.'

'You say that only because you do not know.'

'Know what, for heaven's sake?'

'That Belle is gone. She too has eloped.'

For an incredulous moment, Camilla stared at Letty.

Conflicting emotions struggled within her, but in the end, her sense of humour got the better of her, and she had to laugh. She sat down on the sofa.

'Well, at least she cannot have eloped with Sir Joshua, at least the twins are not sharing him, even if they share a complete lack of morals.'

'Camilla! How can you be so unfeeling? How can you display such levity at a time like this? Be serious, I beg of you, for it is the worst news imaginable.'

'No, Letty, it is not. For Belle to be ill or dead, that would be the worst news. Now, pray tell me, with whom has she run away? Was she gone at dawn, just like Georgina? Where have they gone?'

'It is an elopement, a regular elopement,' said Fanny distractedly. 'They have gone to Scotland, if the letter she left is to be believed.'

Nothing that the twins said or did or wrote could be taken at face value, that was one thing all this had taught her. Belle's destination would depend on the nature of the man who had gone with her. 'Who? Who is the man?'

'She writes that she has run away with Captain Allington,' said Fanny. 'Can you believe it? We think that it is true, however, for I sent round to enquire, and he has not been seen for twenty-four hours. He is not in his lodgings, nor is his man there.'

'Have you questioned her maid? Dawson should have no trouble getting the truth out of her, not after last time.'

'She has taken her maid with her,' said Fanny.

'Where is Fitzwilliam?' said Mr Gardiner. He wiped his perspiring brow with a silk handkerchief; there were rather too many women around and he felt he could do with some masculine support.

'He is gone after them. He left the minute we heard of her flight. He has gone to Scotland, to Gretna Green, to stop them.'

'Gretna Green! How vulgar,' Camilla said. 'How commonplace of her.'

Since neither Fanny nor Letitia could refrain from interrupting each other, with Miss Griffin putting them right here and there and Alethea adding her own caustic comments, it was some time before the story was finally set forth in all its detail.

'It was our fault,' said Fanny unhappily. 'Belle was so vexed by being kept indoors, for you know that Mr Fitzwilliam insisted upon it, until she should be sent back to Pemberley. She threw a tantrum, claiming that it was monstrous unfair to keep her in, with Georgina and Camilla gone to France and Letty allowed to go about if she chose. She threatened to run away herself and said she could see why Georgina had done so. Of course, I took no notice, and made it clear that, especially in the light of her sister's disgraceful action we really had no alternative.'

Fanny paused, and sighed. 'And, pray, do not mention Darcy's name to me, for the mere thought of his rage makes me go into spasms. For what is he going to say when he learns that two of his daughters, whom he imagines still to be in the schoolroom, are married? Actually married, and in such dubious, not to say shocking, circumstances.'

Letitia had been pursuing her own train of thought. 'Georgina is not of age. Her marriage is not legal, it cannot be valid. It can be annulled.'

Camilla knew she would have to mention the fact that Georgina was going to have a baby. 'Georgina is increasing. She had much better stay married.'

'Georgina increasing! Camilla, no!' This was the last straw for Letitia, who was clearly about to sink into her usual refuge of hysterics.

'Oh, do be quiet,' said Camilla. 'No one has any time for you. If you want to whoop and wail, go and do it upstairs. Or, better still, have a good sniff of your smelling salts, if there are any remaining.'

'Mr Gardiner, will you not go after Mr Fitzwilliam?' said Letty, turning imploring eyes on him. 'He requested that you do so, should you be back in time. For they may have made efforts to cover their traces, in which case, another person on their trail will be invaluable.'

'From what I know of Captain Allington, any attempt he made to cover his traces would have quite the opposite effect,' said Mr Gardiner with some asperity. 'I am glad the war is over, for the prospect of such an officer having the lives and fates of his men, and of his fellow officers, in his hands is daunting indeed. No, I shall not go after them, and Mr Fitzwilliam would be well-advised to return to London. Let them be wed over the anvil if that is what they wish, they are as silly a pair as could be met with, and so I dare say they will deal well enough together.'

'Captain Allington has no money, no position, no title,' said Fanny. 'He has little to offer any woman, let alone Belle, used to the comforts of life as she is.'

'I have no opinion of titles,' said Mr Gardiner. 'A man must be judged on his worth, not on how some far from respectable ancestress sacrificed her virtue to the king. Captain Allington appears to be a thoroughly amiable young man, despite not being so very clever. He will make her a good and affectionate husband, I am sure of it, and fifty thousand pounds will provide an adequate income for any young couple.'

Fanny heaved a great sigh. 'I hope so, for it seems we have no choice but to accept him as her husband. Although let us hope that Mr Fitzwilliam may yet have caught up with them, he was not so far behind. He promised to send word to us this evening, Mr Gardiner. I should so value your advice on what he has to say; will you not stay and dine with us, if Mrs Gardiner can spare you a few more hours? She cannot have looked for such a swift return, we thought you would be away for many more days, hunting that unfortunate pair across France.'

'Now, my dear Lady Fanny, dry your eyes. Mrs Gardiner is well used to my being away on business, she will certainly not fret if I stay away a few hours longer. I shall send round to her, just to let her know that I am back.'

'I was on the point of writing to her to ask you to attend upon us the moment you returned, and telling her what has happened. I will say that you are at Aubrey Square and dining with us.'

Fanny rose with alacrity, went over to the writing table on which lay a pen and a half-written letter, dipped the pen in the standish, scribbled a few more lines in her looping hand and sealed the sheet with a wafer.

Mr Gardiner cleared his throat and coughed. 'Since you are ringing for a servant to take your letter, may I request a glass of lemonade for us, if you will, for I have a powerful thirst upon me after our journey.'

Fanny flew to the bell and tugged it. 'How remiss of me, what am I thinking of? Lemonade, or would you rather a glass of wine? Camilla, my love, you must be longing to wash your dust off and to change your clothes. Tell me, is Georgina truly married? How does she look? Is she happy? Did Sir Joshua look foolish when you and Mr Gardiner arrived? Such a situation for a man in his position to find himself in. He is vastly rich, you know. It is not such a bad match for Georgina after all. Do not you think your father will agree?'

'Papa will think that a man of one-and-forty had better have nothing to do with a seventeen-year-old girl.'

'Oh, as to that, age and youth, it is the way of the world, especially when there is money in the case.'

From outside in the square came the footsteps of the lamplighter, attending to his evening duty of lighting the gas lamps outside Aubrey House on the north side of the square. He was whistling through the gap made by the loss of two front teeth; he always whistled. As the flame grew from a flicker to a steady glow, the warm light touched the windows of the houses around the square, a gloss of gold against the darkness of the panes. The acrid burning smell drifted in through the windows along with the mingled sweet and unpleasant scents of a hot London evening.

His whistle faded into the distance, only for the returning peace of dusk to be broken by the sound of a carriage rattling at a dangerous pace into the square.

Everyone in Fanny's drawing-room flew to the windows, with the exception of Alethea. She was in the middle of a sonata and played calmly on, ignoring the excited chatter from the other side of the room.

'It must be Mr Fitzwilliam returned, oh, is Belle with him?'

'It may be a messenger.'

'Whoever it is, they are in a most dreadful hurry.'

'Is not that Mr Wytton's carriage?'

'Why, it is my Sophie!'

With these words, Mr Gardiner hurried out of the room. Camilla, lingering by the open window, saw Mr Wytton himself having a word with his groom before following Sophie into the house.

Camilla moved away from the window as Sophie came like a whirlwind into the drawing-room, her colour high, her hair loosened and tumbling about her shoulders, her eyes huge and full of rage. How pretty she was, how undeniably pretty. And there behind her was Wytton, from whom Camilla had so recently parted for the final time. To see him so soon was to open wounds that had not even begun to heal. Was she fated to meet him over and over again, so that she could never come to terms with her sense of desolation?

'Where is she?' cried Sophie. 'Where is Belle? I'll tear her eyes out, she shall not have him, no, indeed she shall not. She is a witch, a sly, scheming creature, a slut! Why can't she be content with all the other men she has under her spell?'

Alethea, delighted with the scene, played some trembling trills on the keys.

Mr Gardiner, who had come up the stairs at a rather slower pace, was staring at his daughter in amazement. 'Sophie, less drama if you please. What is this all about? Is your mother well?'

'Mama? What has she to do with it? She had a note, from Lady Fanny, and she showed it to me when I came home early from a party – I had the headache – she said that Belle had eloped. With Captain Allington!' Her voice rose alarmingly as she pronounced his name.

'Calm yourself, Sophie,' said Fanny, quite sharply for her. 'There is no need for you to shout it for the whole of London to hear. Belle has indeed run away, She is gone to Scotland, but Mr Fitzwilliam has gone after her, and we hope to have news of them soon.'

At last Camilla steeled herself to look at Wytton.

He stood quietly, watching Sophie; then, as Sophie took a few gulping breaths, obviously endeavouring to compose herself, he moved towards her, offering the comfort of his arms.

Alethea added her own comment, playing some bars that Camilla recognised as belonging to the lovers in Purcell's *Dido and Aeneas*. Camilla shot her a quelling glance just as Sophie sprang away from Wytton, turning her head and making a gesture with her hands to ward him off. Wytton stepped back, amazed.

What was the matter with Sophie? Why was she behaving in this odd fashion, so upset about Belle and openly spurning Wytton? Camilla had never seen her cousin so animated nor so distracted.

Sophie was crying now, but they were tears of despair that trickled down her cheeks, not the sobs of hysteria. 'She has tricked Captain Allington into going with her, for he feels nothing for her, I know he does not. Now he will have to marry her, and what is to become of me?'

Mr Gardiner was frowning. 'Sophie! Pull yourself together. What is Captain Allington to you?'

THIRTY

Sophie's knees crumpled, she gave a little moan, and sank to the floor. Mr Gardiner and Fanny ran forward to tend to her, with Letitia close behind, smelling salts at the ready.

'Oh, Lord, she has fainted clean away,' said Alethea in mock horror. 'What a bag of tricks she does have at her disposal.'

'Alethea, I don't want to hear another word from you,' said Camilla, exasperated with her younger sister.

'Ring the bell this instant,' Fanny cried. 'Where is Dawson? We must lift her up, oh, the poor child.'

'Alethea is right. Fainting is an excellent way to deflect unwelcome questions.' Wytton had crossed the room to attend to the bell-pull, and came to stand beside Camilla.

As she turned to him, she saw a look of caustic amusement in his eyes. 'Why, yes, it is indeed, for her father's concern will overcome any justifiable anger he may feel at her dramatic arrival,' she said.

'Her wholly unexpected arrival, I may say.' He went to join Mr Gardiner beside the recumbent figure. The smelling salts seemed to have had little effect, but Camilla would have sworn that her cousin was conscious, and had avoided inhaling the bitter fumes by holding her breath.

'Shall we lift her on to a sofa, sir?' said Wytton.

At that moment Dawson stalked into the room. She took one look at Sophie's motionless figure and made a sound of disapproval, but before she could take any further action, Pug had dashed into the room after her, keen to join in the fun. Seeing a body lying upon the carpet, he hurled himself upon it with snaps and snarls.

This onslaught roused Sophie to immediate life, and she twisted round to escape from Pug's attentions.

'Get off, Pug, you silly dog, do you think she is your dinner?' Camilla said, swooping down on the wriggling animal and picking him up. Pug gave an ecstatic snuffle and began to lick her face.

'He dearly loves excitement,' she told Wytton, tucking Pug under her arm.

'Then he must be pleased, for this is as entertaining as anything to be heard or seen at the playhouse or the opera.'

As if on cue, a footman opened the door, his own eyes popping out of his head with curiosity, and announced that Captain Allington had called, and was waiting below.

Sophie, her senses quite restored, gave a shriek, cried, 'He is here, he is with Belle,' and made to dash out of the room.

'Not so fast, miss,' said Mr Gardiner, putting out a strong arm to restrain his daughter. 'Is the Captain alone?' he asked the footman.

'Yes, sir.'

'Then desire him to step up.'

A clank of spurs upon the stairs, and the magnificent figure of Captain Allington stood in the doorway, in all the scarlet glory of his hussar uniform. Sophie wrenched herself free from her father's grasp and flew across the room to him. She stood before him for a long moment, looking up into his face, and then began to pummel his chest with her fists.

Wytton winced and shook his head.

'A mistake,' he said. 'Painful, with all those fastenings, very rough on the skin.'

Allington had seized Sophie's hands and was holding them clasped to his plated bosom. 'Sophie,' he was saying in what Camilla considered a very foolish tone. 'My dearest little Sophie, do not take on so.'

Mr Gardiner, in a state of complete bewilderment, strove to recover his wits. 'Captain Allington, I would be exceedingly grateful if you would explain yourself. Is Belle with you? Are you come from Scotland?'

A look of puzzlement spread over the Captain's face. 'Scotland? No, sir, I have just come off duty at headquarters.'

'Headquarters,' cried Sophie. 'Duty! Here in London?'

'Why, yes, where else should they be? The regiment has not yet left on its posting.'

This communication caused first radiant smiles and then a further burst of tears from Sophie.

Fanny took command. 'Sophie, Captain Allington, sit down, do. Captain, what brings you here? Have you seen Belle, is she not with you?'

'Has something happened to Miss Belle? When I came off duty, I returned to my lodgings and my landlady said that various persons had been enquiring for me. She mentioned your name, Lady Fanny, and so I thought I had better come round to Aubrey Square.' He looked around the room with a vaguely surprised air. 'I do not see her here.'

'No,' said Letitia, 'for she is in Scotland. We thought she was with you.'

This puzzled him still more. 'But I am not in Scotland.'

'In which case,' Camilla said, 'who is the man?'

'Never mind,' cried Sophie. 'What does it matter? She may have run off with half the regiment for all I care, as long as she is not with Allington.'

'Very affecting,' said Wytton dryly.

Sophie's face turned peevish. 'You may keep your sour remarks to yourself, Wytton, for I know you do not want to marry me.'

'I do not understand any of this,' said Mr Gardiner. 'Why should Belle say she has run away with Allington when she clearly has done no such thing? And you, Sophie, are behaving badly; please do not cling to the Captain like that. Whatever will Lady Fanny think?'

'I shall think what is as obvious as the nose on my face,' declared Fanny. 'Sophie is in love with the Captain, and I dare say has been so for some time.'

'In which case,' said Mr Gardiner, exploding, 'why have you led us all such a dance? Why did you accept Wytton's proposals? What the devil have you been about? Answer me, Sophie.'

Sophie's incoherent reply made little sense. Abbeys and fortunes and Greek remains and India and younger sons and horses all tumbled out in no particular order, until her father held his head and begged her to stop.

Wytton was laughing out loud now.

'Do you understand this?' Camilla asked him.

'Oh, yes, I believe I do.'

'Then for heaven's sake take pity on Mr Gardiner, and explain.'

'Don't say another word, Sophie,' he commanded, as she opened her mouth to pour out more disjointed sentences. 'Captain Allington, is your regiment to be posted to India?'

Allington nodded gloomily. 'Orders just through.'

A wail from Sophie, 'No, no, you must not go!'

'Sophie!' Mr Gardiner's voice was impatient. 'You seem not to understand. The army is Captain Allington's profession, and an army officer, as you well know, does his duty and goes wherever his superior officers choose to send him.'

'Papa, you are not even trying to understand. Allington does not wish to be a soldier, and he particularly does not wish to be a soldier in India, where it is hot and there are flies and insects of all kinds and snakes, and a long sea journey and fever and native women and—'

'She's off again,' said Wytton.

It took a glass of wine and several handkerchiefs before Sophie could be brought to a sensible account of her relationship with Allington.

'You see, Papa, I knew that you would never approve of him, for he is poor and has no prospects.'

'Whereas I,' observed Wytton to no one in particular, 'am rich and have excellent prospects.'

'Yes,' said Sophie with spirit. 'And you were in love with me, you need not try to deny it, for it was so.'

Wytton looked not a whit abashed. 'I was.'

'Only you are not now, so you need not pretend. You are in love with Camilla, and I suppose she will marry you, only I would advise her most strongly to think well what she is about, for she will either be left on her own in that horrid abbey or traipsing about abroad, having to put up with all the dirt and heat if she wishes to be at your side. Besides having to live with your abominable temper, and your moods, too, for you are always in a mood.'

'But Sophie,' said her father, 'why did you not tell us? Did you imagine that your mama and I would force you into a marriage with a man you no longer cared for, however great his fortune and position? Whatever have we done to deserve this? What have we said to make you think we cared for anything other than your happiness?'

'Younger sons are younger sons.'

'My dear, you have a fortune of your own, and I am, if I may say so, a rich man.'

'You mean you will let me marry Allington?' This was uttered in a piercing scream of delight.

'It is not so simple. Captain Allington will shortly be embarking for India. We cannot wish you to go to India, the climate will not suit you.'

'If we are married, he need not go! He can sell out, and we shall buy land and he can breed horses.'

'Breed horses!'

'Sir, it may seem—' began Allington.

'Young man, provided that you do not have another wife tucked away, or a mistress in your keeping, and as long as you are content to marry my daughter in an orderly way, in a church, in the presence of her family and friends, then you may have her with my goodwill, and breed horses, or dogs, or goats even.'

Wytton's eyes gleamed. 'A happy outcome.'

'For you as well, one may suppose,' said Mr Gardiner dryly.

'This is all very well,' said Fanny. 'But what of Belle? If she has not eloped with Captain Allington, then whom is she with?'

They were gathered in the hall while Mr Gardiner and Sophie waited for their carriage, and Captain Allington hovered about, still looking slightly foolish, but pleased, and giving Sophie an enraptured smile whenever their eyes met.

The talk was still of Belle, and under cover of more speculations about the outcome of her flight, and whom her companion might be, Wytton grasped Camilla's hand and drew her slightly away from the others.

'Is there nowhere we may be private for a few minutes at least?'

His voice was ardent, and there was a look in his eyes that made her blink. 'The morning room,' she said.

How odd that she should feel so shy now that she was alone with him. Where had the easy companionship gone? Why was she so ill at ease? Why did he seem a different man, almost a stranger, as he stood there in the firelight?

He held out his hands, and took hers. Then he drew closer. 'Look at me. I want to see your eyes.'

His voice shook slightly as he spoke, and the ardour and warmth she saw in his face when she looked up made her giddy. She was not in control of herself or her feelings, she had no awareness beyond his presence. They stood there in the shadowy room, motionless, until he lifted her hand, kissing the back of it, touching her fingers with his lips. Then, turning it over, he kissed her palm.

It was she who put up her arm to pull him to her, astonished by the intensity of the unfamiliar emotions flooding through her. He ran a finger down her cheek to her mouth, then kissed her, nothing tentative or gentle in his touch as his own passion was at last allowed some expression.

'Camilla!' came Mr Gardiner's voice, reproving, but with at least none of the outrage Mr Fitzwilliam would have shown in such a case. Wytton moved apart from her, self-possessed, still keeping hold of her hand.

'This is not the time nor the place for such a display of affection. Wytton, I shall take Sophie home in my carriage,' and I have called for yours.'

They all had to remain in suspense as to Belle's fate until the following morning. A disgruntled Mr Fitzwilliam had returned home in the early hours to awaken the household with his knocking.

He received Fanny's news that Captain Allington had not run

away with Belle with a philosophic shrug. 'It makes little difference. There is no sign of them, whoever she is with. No trace upon the road north; they have not gone to Scotland in my opinion.'

Fanny was wide awake now, and all her worries crowded in on her. 'Scotland would be bad enough, but if they have not gone there. Belle might have run off with anybody, a drawing master, a handsome footman even.'

'Do not you believe it,' said Mr Fitzwilliam, sitting in his dressing-gown in Fanny's bedchamber and drinking a glass of wine before he ate the food that she had thoughtfully provided for him. 'Belle is not such a frippery creature as all that, she knows the difference between a man of her world and one who is not; she has not been in the habit of wasting her attentions on footmen. No, no, she is with some other of her numerous admirers, some stupid fellow she has hoodwinked, who does not know what he is letting himself in for, and who most certainly has never encountered her father! I do not want to waste another moment's thought on any of these Darcy girls.'

'No, but you must listen for a moment. I have not told you the half of what has been going on in your absence, such an astonishing evening as we have had. Sophie Gardiner is to marry Captain Allington, what do you say to that?'

Mr Fitzwilliam was unmoved. 'The man's a blockhead. I am glad I never had him serving under me.' He rose and stretched. 'Wytton's the poorer by ninety thousand pounds then.'

'No,' said Fanny. 'Forty thousand pounds the poorer . . .'

Mr Fitzwilliam pulled a nightcap firmly on to his head – always a sign that he was not feeling in an amorous mood – and climbed into bed beside Fanny to gave her a chaste kiss before turning over and taking all the covers with him.

The family were at breakfast when Belle came home, cool and demure in a white muslin dress, lounging into the breakfast room as though she had slipped out for a walk instead of returning from such an indecorous flight.

'Breakfast, oh good, for I am quite famished, and dear

Charles would not stop, even though I did so want something to eat.'

Chairs were pushed back, cups tumbled over, Pug made a sortie to snatch a piece of toast that had been dropped on the carpet. Only Belle appeared perfectly calm.

'Charles?' said Camilla.

'He is downstairs with Mr Fitzwilliam. I dare say he will be up directly, for he must be as hungry as I am. We have come sixteen miles this morning, is that not a distance?'

'Sixteen miles? Belle, where have you been?' Camilla said. Her sister looked remarkably pleased with herself, and not at all contrite. Sixteen miles? Was it the lonely farmhouse again?

It was not. 'Charles took me to his house.'

'Charles?' Charles who? Camilla racked her brains. Who among Belle's admirers was called Charles?

'Charles Roper, silly, who else would it be?'

Roper! The sisters exchanged glances across the table.

'Cradle-snatching, I call it,' said Alethea. She reached for another piece of toast. 'He's only a baby.'

'He is not! He is twenty.'

'Oh, tra-la, a wise old man of twenty.'

'Alethea, we can do without your views,' said Fanny.

Charles Roper. Camilla would never have thought it, had never noticed him showing any particular affection towards Belle; indeed, he had seemed only to have eyes for Mrs Rowan.

Fanny's mind was on the detail. 'Where were you last night? Did you pass the night at Mr Roper's house? Where may that be?' And, sharply, 'Was his mother there?'

'Of course, and his father too, an amiable, kind man. They live in Surrey, near Box Hill, it is very pretty round about there. I should like to live in Surrey of all things. It is much prettier than Derbyshire.'

'And your maid was with you?' asked Letitia, still suspicious and sounding a little disappointed.

'Of course. I couldn't dress myself for dinner without her.'

'So why did you leave a note saying that you had run away to Scotland?'

'You found that, did you? Well, when I wrote it, I thought

347

that we were going to Gretna Green. It was what I wanted, and I was cross with dear Charles when I discovered he had tricked me, and that we were not eloping.'

'Why did you say you were with Allington?'

'That was a good joke, was it not? Did Sophie know I wrote that? How I laughed at the thought of her rage when she heard I had run off with her precious hussar. For she is not in love with Wytton at all, and I think her behaviour is just as bad as Georgina's, and she has been so rude to me, as though no one in the world must speak to Captain Allington. I might very well have run away with him, just to teach her a lesson, such a goody-goody as she is, if it were not that Charles is the only man for me.'

'Belle, how can you speak so?'

Belle's lovely face took on a mulish expression. 'You were not here, Camilla, you do not know how they have all been on at me, how I must mend my ways, how much better it was for me to be at Pemberley, how I should attend to my books and music and give my mind to rational pursuits, meaning anything but men and flirting.'

'And rightly so,' said Letitia. 'You have become a most outrageous flirt.'

'Oh, la, only an old maid like you would make such a fuss about that. It is not so dreadful after all, and I like flirting with men and having them make love to me.'

'Well, upon my word!'

'Hark at you, prosing away for all the world like an old dowager. Who are you to play Miss Prim with me, or with Georgina? Since you were so stupid as to fall for a man who wasn't in the least bit interested in you, you grudge the rest of us any contact with attractive men. It's all jealousy; you should take care not to let it show so much. Nothing is more ruinous to your looks, than that peevish, crabby expression you are wearing even now.'

There was so much truth as well as cruelty in this that Camilla and Fanny did not know how to look or what to say.

THIRTY-ONE

'Come away from that window, Camilla. You can be seen from the street, with the window open like that.'

Letty was being particularly tiresome and fretful this morning; Camilla felt sure it was because Mr Barcombe had not called for two days. How she wished that Letty was going to accompany the younger girls when they went back to Derbyshire next week, to spend the remaining summer months there.

Belle, to her rage and chagrin, was not to be allowed to stay in London, nor to enter into an engagement with her dearest Charles. Mr Roper's parents, while liking Belle for her charm and beauty as much as for her fortune, were of the opinion that it would be better if the young couple waited to marry until Charles came of age. By then Mr and Mrs Darcy should be back in England, Belle would be eighteen and it would be altogether more suitable.

Belle had not received this news gladly; Camilla still shuddered at the memory of the tantrums and scenes that had followed the decision that she was to return to Derbyshire for the present.

Tears, threats, hysterics were of no avail. Seeking safety in numbers, Mr Fitzwilliam and Mr Gardiner had written to Mr Bennet, laying the situation before him, and asking for his support. He was not overly delighted at the prospect of having a lovelorn Belle at Pemberley, but he knew his duty, and was in complete agreement about there being no engagement for Belle until her parents' return to England.

Miss Griffin was to go to Pemberley with them, of course, charged especially with the onerous task of keeping Belle out of mischief.

'I make no promises, but I will do my best. She may be more tractable with her sister away, and with her affection for Mr Roper to sustain her.'

Alethea had no such expectations. 'She will have forgotten Charles within a fortnight, and will be making eyes at the grooms and any neighbouring squires who chance to ride across our land.'

Camilla had politely but firmly resisted all attempts to make her return to Pemberley, and, rather to her surprise, Letty decided to remain in London as well.

'If we may stay with you, dearest Fanny, for a while longer, or, if it is not quite convenient, I believe that Mrs Gardiner would be willing to have us both.'

'What is this, Letty?' said Camilla, not hiding her disbelief. 'You were wild to go back to Pemberley not so long ago.'

The reasons Letty gave seemed vague. Chief among them, she said, with a flash of her old sanctimoniousness, was that Camilla had been invited by Mrs Rowan for a long visit, in the event of it not being possible for her to stay with any members of her family. Letty wholeheartedly disapproved of this proposal, and was supported by Fanny and her husband in her opposition to the plan. The mere suggestion of such a visit caused Mr Fitzwilliam to shut himself in his study for several indignant hours, muttering about nests of vipers and Radicals and making threats upon the character and well-being of Pagoda Portal.

'But you like Mr Portal,' Fanny said, when she coaxed him out with offers of cold meats and beer.

'That is all very well, but the fellow is not to be trusted when it comes to politics. A man is entitled to his views, I suppose, but he is not to be corrupting the minds and morals of innocent young women.'

'He would not dream of doing any such thing. And the matter does not arise, since I have begged Letty and Camilla to stay on with us.'

'I am not so sure— Oh, very well, if you wish it.'

'You make a great deal of nothing,' said Fanny buoyantly. 'It has not turned out so ill. Mr Wytton is the most agreeable man, once one is used to his eccentric ways. I shall be so happy to call him cousin when he and Camilla are married. Georgina is become a great lady in Paris, and if she produces an heir, she will rise even further in Sir Joshua's affections. Belle's match, if it comes to anything, is well enough, and I shall think it a blessing for her to be married and settled with her own nursery to occupy her. That will keep her out of mischief. Three husbands is not so bad, you will admit, and it will very likely be four before long. I am sure Letty will soon be engaged.'

'However, there are to be conditions,' Fitzwilliam said. 'I will have no carryings-on under my roof, and young men may call only at reasonable hours. And,' he added with a frown, 'It is to be hoped that Darcy is never made aware of how close his daughters came to ruin.'

Camilla stepped out on the narrow balcony, as a familiar figure turned the corner into the square. She leant over the wrought iron railing and waved.

'Camilla, stop that, how can you behave so?' cried Letty, getting up from the sofa and running across the room to catch at Camilla's gown and bring her inside.

'It is Wytton,' Camilla said. 'He is come to see our cousin, to ask Mr Fitzwilliam when we may be married.'

'Married, indeed. You always want to rush into things. How can there be any question of marriage until our parents are safe returned to England?'

'Letty, how can you say that? It may be a year, or more, before they are back. Oh, I so long to be married, to be with Wytton, and to go about just as I please, and to travel abroad.'

'Your trip to France has gone to your head, and as to going about just as you please, that is what is to be avoided at all costs. This is no doubt why our cousin is so set against your marriage at present. An engagement, even, is out of the question, with the scandal that still hangs about us.'

'Oh, I don't give that for scandal,' said Camilla, snapping her fingers in the air.

'Camilla, how can you be so vulgar?'

'Vulgar, who is vulgar?' asked Alethea, dancing into the

room. She still had on her straw bonnet from a visit to the park, and she tugged at its ribbons before pulling it off and tossing it on the sofa. 'Oh, it is so hot, and London is so boring, with Signor Silvestrini gone to Italy, and no concerts to be had.'

'Well, as to that, miss,' said Letty crossly, 'you will soon be at Pemberley, where you may sit in the shade of the trees and take your leisure.'

'Leisure? Oh, no, I have so much I want to do. I have put in an order for quantities of music that I want to study and play, and I shall write some songs. By the time the Signor is back, he will find me altogether a different kind of a musician.'

Letty drew in her breath, and Camilla gave Alethea a sharp look. 'Take care, I think you do very well as you are.'

Alethea shrugged. 'I know, I have to behave; as if I ever do otherwise.' This with a wicked look from under her eyelashes.

Camilla, with Wytton to lend moral support and wordly authority, had done her best to bring home to Alethea how careful she must be, how close to disaster she had come with her foolish prank at the ball. Even as she uttered her words of caution, Camilla had a suspicion that she knew only a part of Alethea's unsanctioned musical activities. Wytton, laughing at her, had advised her not to delve, but merely to extract promises as to future behaviour.

'The threat of bringing her lessons with the Italian master to an end should make her see reason,' he had said.

'I had not thought you to be so censorious,' Camilla had exclaimed. 'It would distress her beyond anything to lose her lessons.'

'Then let her behave with more circumspection. I am not talking of threats; I am talking of what the consequences will be if she runs wild again. I do not criticise her, but you may be sure Mr Fitzwilliam and your sister Letty long to put an end to musical excursions of whatever nature, and only need an excuse to do so. Alethea needs to learn how to get over rough ground lightly.'

'It is her slyness that alarms me.'

'She is not sly, rather single-minded and with too much energy and intelligence to enjoy a restricted schoolroom life.

She will be better when she comes out and has other things to occupy her mind.'

Camilla felt that as Wytton got to know Alethea better, he would quickly realise that the social whirl would hardly satisfy her sister's lively sense of adventure or her passion for music.

'Where she is going to find a husband to suit her, I cannot imagine.'

'Oh, time enough to worry about that. The firebrand of sixteen is often the meekest and most amiable of creatures by the time she is nineteen or twenty. It was so with my youngest sister, who is now most happily settled.'

'Would she have dressed up as a boy and gone out in public to play the flute?'

'Why, no, for she has no ear for music and has always been rather plump. One must say that Alethea looked well in breeches, she has the figure for them.'

Camilla cried shame on him, and their discussion had ended in a stolen kiss; stolen, since Mr Fitzwilliam was taking the greatest care to allow them little time alone together.

Camilla paced up and down the room, seeing in her imagination the study below. What would Wytton be saying? How would Mr Fitzwilliam reply?

Wytton came into the drawing-room. He greeted Letty and Alethea with civility and warmth, but his eyes rested on Camilla.

One look at his face told Camilla that he had not met with any success.

'It is not to be thought of,' he said angrily. 'Nothing, if you please, can be decided, no consent to an engagement given until your father returns. And we are to comport ourselves in such a way as will give no rise to any further talk or gossip.'

'Oh, that is unfair,' Camilla exclaimed.

'No, it is only right and proper,' said Letty.

'Letty,' said Camilla, turning on her sister. 'Do not interfere; this is nothing to do with you.'

'Damn it,' Wytton went on. 'Your sister Georgina takes off like a *demi-mondaine* and is allowed to live in married bliss, and here we are, quite prepared to do everything that is proper, and with no hope of being married for a year or so! You know how these diplomatic missions are prone to drag on far longer than was originally intended. I had meant to return to Egypt in the winter, when the weather is at its best, and I should have liked of all things for you to go with me, as my wife. Now there is no hope of it.'

Letty opened her mouth to say more, and Camilla, as annoyed as Wytton at Mr Fitzwilliam's intransigence, was about to say some sharp words, when Mr Barcombe was announced. Camilla could have laughed out loud as the shrewish look left Letty's face, and she looked eagerly towards the door, her face suffused with blushes, and a smile on her lips.

'Lucky fellow, she may marry him whenever she wishes. He does not have to wait for a father's consent,' said Wytton when he heard the news that Letty had accepted Barleigh Barcombe's proposal of marriage.

'Oh, but he does, for Letty says she will not dream of getting married before our parents are returned. She insists that Papa must be there to give her away, and Mr Barcombe agrees with her. He says he wants to be able to ask her father for her hand in the proper way, even if she is of age.'

Wytton's face darkened. 'Folly!'

'It is customary to have one's family present at a wedding.' Camilla did not sound entirely convinced, and indeed she found Letty's willingness to wait strange, and much at odds with her own desire to marry Wytton as soon as possible; the prospect of waiting for so long depressed her exceedingly.

'Why do you not write to Papa?' she said. 'He will only hear what Mr Fitzwilliam and Mr Gardiner choose to tell him, and they are prejudiced, as you know.'

Wytton wrestled with his conscience. 'For I agreed, in the end, with Mr Fitzwilliam, you know, that it was not to be thought of—' then he wrote to Mr Darcy in Constantinople, setting out his circumstances and declaring his love for Camilla in clear if impassioned tones.

Unbeknownst to either Wytton or Camilla, Fanny had also wrestled with her conscience, and – sympathising entirely with the lovers whatever Mr Fitzwilliam and Mr Gardiner might say about prudence, how a marriage would look in the eyes of the world; how waiting did no harm to a young couple – had written a long, private letter to Mrs Darcy, without her husband's knowledge or consent.

Mr Darcy, it turned out, remembered Wytton from their meeting some years before, and had retained a good impression of the clever, turbulent young man.

'How extraordinary,' said Mr Fitzwilliam one morning, as he lingered over the breakfast table. 'I would not have believed it possible. Fanny, pay attention, for here is a letter from Darcy in which he agrees that Camilla and Mr Wytton's marriage should take place directly. It seems he has written to Mr Wytton suggesting that he and Camilla travel to Constantinople as soon as they are wed, so that he and Lizzy may become properly acquainted with him. Did you ever hear of such a thing! What will people say?'

'What they always do, but Camilla and Mr Wytton will not mind it, and they are the only people who matter in this, you know that.'

'I know no such thing. Hasn't there been enough tittle-tattle? However, Darcy says that it is to be so, and I cannot argue with him when he is a thousand miles away.'

Fanny smiled to herself, pleased at the success of her efforts, and forbore from pointing out that Mr Fitzwilliam would most certainly not argue with Darcy however close at hand he should be. 'And given the alarums and excursions of the last few months, my love, Camilla's marriage to a man as respectable and rich as Mr Wytton must be a cause for general relief.'

Camilla's first view of Sillingford Abbey, country house of the Wytton family, should have taken her breath away.

Formerly home to an Augustinian order, the abbey held a high position against a backdrop of rolling, wooded hills. A river ran its lazy course along the valley, with one of its tributary streams diverted to feed the lake that lay to the side of the long front part of the house. Cattle cropped the rich grass of the meadows alongside the river, and sheep grazed under the trees of the orchards, which stretched almost to the river. It was a scene of rural harmony and prosperity.

Gentleman's seat it might now be, but everything about it, from the long, low lines of the stone building, to the tall windows and the heavy, arched wooden doors, proclaimed Sillingford's mediaeval and monastic origins. Wytton's father had prettified some of the more austere windows with elegantly pointed arches in the Strawberry Hill style, which had the effect of softening the rather stern lines of the original abbey, and in the late afternoon sunlight, with the windows reflecting the slanting rays and the shadows of the great trees making a pleasing patchwork across the lawns, it looked mellow and beautiful.

Camilla, however, had eyes and heart for nothing and no one but Wytton. He was sitting beside her in the open carriage, and as they turned through the park gates, she could sense the eagerness tensing in his body.

'That tree there, the big oak, that was a famous one to climb. I had a tree house in it until I fell out one day. They thought I had broke all my arms and legs, but it was no such thing, I was merely stunned.'

Camilla looked at the tree with no great satisfaction, thinking how nearly it had deprived her of Wytton. He was leaning forward now, and pointing to the east side of his house. 'Most of the cloisters remain, you know, you will catch a glimpse of them in a minute. How your Miss Griffin will like to wander about that part. There are cellars and all manner of vaulted chambers, the very thing for an author.'

The days before her wedding were a time of great happiness for Camilla as she explored every nook and cranny of the abbey in Wytton's company. There were kisses and embraces beneath the varied gazes of his ancestors in the portrait gallery, and happy hours spent walking hand in hand about the park.

The guests began to assemble for the ceremony, more than they had expected, but still a select gathering of family and friends. Layard, who was to be Wytton's groomsman, drove himself up from London and pleased everyone with his warm-hearted, good-humoured delight in his friend's match.

Aunt Lydia had been invited, for Camilla had felt that was only proper, but she had, rather to her niece's relief, declined the invitation. She was fixed in Brighton now, and Herefordshire was such a great distance away from Sussex. Mr and Mrs Wytton must be sure to call on them and enjoy the company at the seaside resort before they set off for foreign parts. She would, she added, think of her niece at the hour of the service, and cry just as much as if she were there.

The Gardiners arrived, on their own. Camilla had danced at Sophie's wedding only three weeks before, a smart London affair, but the Allingtons were presently touring in Scotland and could not attend. The Fitzwilliams came separately, Fanny coming on ahead to help with the bride's final preparations for the wedding, and bringing with her the bridal gown from London.

'And it is to be hoped that all the rest of your clothes will be ready in time, for the dressmakers are not used to be making such clothes at this time of year, when all their other customers are asking for velvets and heavy silks.'

Letty could not reconcile herself to Camilla and Wytton setting off on their travels.

'By sea!' she had exclaimed. 'There and back? To Constantinople and then to Egypt before returning to England, and at such a time of year? You cannot mean it, you could not be so foolhardy. The Bay of Biscay is a graveyard of ships, everyone says so. Even the sailors in our navy, you know, fear the Bay of Biscay for its storms and savage seas. Then there is the Mediterranean. I feel quite faint even to think of it. Pirates, there are Barbary pirates, apart from the weather; you are certain to be captured or shipwrecked.'

Wytton was amused by such extreme ideas. 'Our naval men go to and fro in all seasons, they think nothing of it.'

'It is their profession, they are obliged to go. It would be so much more sensible to remain in England until our dear parents return; even the thought of their journey fills me with alarm.'

'More sensible, perhaps,' said Camilla. 'But not half so interesting, you will admit.'

Letty would admit nothing. She could see no merit in visiting the Porte, as Wytton called Constantinople, nor the point of Egypt. Europe was bad enough, only think of poor Georgina languishing in Paris, so far from her family and friends.

'Languishing, indeed,' Camilla said to Wytton when they found themselves alone for a few minutes in the Great Hall. 'Why, she is as happy as can be.'

'Not as happy as you will be once we are married,' said Wytton with great affection.

Titus Manningtree, the grandest of Wytton's neighbours, came into the Hall just then, looking aloof and severe. He was a disappointed man, Wytton had told Camilla; he had fallen foul of the present administration and a hoped-for political career had come to nothing.

'I like Manningtree,' Wytton said. 'I am glad he is out of politics, for the life is not right for him. He is too independent-minded, it would never do. He will have to find some new interest, however; he is not a man to stay at home and be dull.'

Manningtree cheered up when Alethea sang to entertain the company, and indeed the warmth of his gaze when he looked at her sister caused Camilla some concern.

'You will have to get used to that,' Fanny told her. 'It is just as I said, she is growing into a beauty. Only wait, all the men will be wild for her.'

'A hugger-mugger affair, in my opinion.'

Lady Warren put down the newspaper, in which she had been reading the Announcements page. Her mouth was pursed and dissatisfied.

'A pretty poor show by the sound of it,' George agreed. He was lounging in a low chair opposite her, his highly polished boots up on the fender, his cravat loosened, quite at his ease.

'And at Sillingford, in the abbey chapel, not in Derbyshire, and without her father there to give her away. It gives a very off appearance, one feels.'

George flicked at a speck of dust that had had the temerity to settle on his gleaming Hessians. 'I wonder if Sophie Allington, as she is now, was a guest? That would make any bride uncomfortable, knowing the predecessor in her husband's affections was sitting in a pew at her wedding.'

'That is a most shocking match,' said Lady Warren. 'Allington may be a charmer, but he has not a penny of his own. You would think a man of Gardiner's wealth could buy his daughter a better husband than that.'

'He did, but the deal didn't come off, did it? He hadn't bargained with Miss Camilla's campaigns and stratagems.'

'Well, she has what she wanted, and much joy may it bring her. Her cousin's cast-off, a man of great volatility like Wytton. I shouldn't give a fig for that marriage turning out well. And Wytton's mama wasn't present, please take note of that. Neither of the couple's parents at the wedding; why, it's scandalous.'

'You can't blame Wytton's father for not being there, he's dead. Odd though, his mother not being present.'

'She is forever jaunting about Europe. She hardly ever comes to England these days. She cares nothing for her children, or she might have put a stop to this business. She is in Venice just now, I believe.'

'No, you're out there, Caroline,' said George, sitting up. This was something he could speak about with authority. 'No one is in Venice at this season, I assure you. It's devilish hot, the canals give off the most terrible stench and one is all too liable to catch some lethal fever. No, no if she's in Italy she'll be in the mountains.'

'Wherever she is, she was not at her son's wedding. I wonder what she will make of her new daughter-in-law when they do meet? I never cared for her as an unmarried young woman. I shudder to think what airs she will be giving herself now she is Mrs Wytton.'

None of her sisters or any of the women present could hold a candle to Camilla on her wedding day. Her whole being was focused on Wytton, and she admitted afterwards that the vicar could have been reciting lampoons for all she made of the words. But the serious way Wytton said his responses, and the look on his face when he turned to his bride brought tears to Fanny's eyes and a squeeze from Mr Fitzwilliam's hand in hers;

he, too, was taken back to his own wedding day and the joy he had felt at standing before the altar with Fanny beside him.

'They make a splendid couple,' he acknowledged, as the bride and groom came down the altar steps to walk the short distance through the small congregation and out of the ornate doors into the sunshine beyond.

'I never saw Camilla look more lovely,' said Fanny.

Her words were echoed hours later, by Wytton, after the feasting and dancing and merriment were over, when Sackree shooed the revellers away and at long last Camilla and Wytton were alone, alone in the huge bedchamber in which he and several generations of his forefathers had been born.

Shall I blow out the candle?' he asked, clasping her round the waist and kissing her loosened hair.

She wrapped her arms around him, rejoicing in the feel, the scent, the sound, the very being of him. 'Leave it be, what need do we have of darkness?'